Hanging Upside Down

ANTHONY OTERO

ACKNOWLEDGMENTS

I really want to thank everyone who helped make my dream of becoming a published author a reality. A big shout out and thank you to Monique Thompson for taking the time to edit this book. Thank you to Andre Cole for all the advice and guidance. Much love to Cassandra Falcon for always believing in me. I would be remiss not to thank my sister from another mister, Ynanna Djehuty. Your encouragement goes far beyond this publication.

A big thank you to all the test readers that took time out of their lives to give this book a read. I also want to thank the readers of my blog that have been following me on this journey.

I want to thank my family for their support even though I didn't have the courage to share this book with them until now. I need to give a special thank you to my father, in particular, for everything he has done to get me here.

Much love to my friends and fellow SU alumni who have supported me all the way. They're too many to name. I know the love is real, thank you.

Finally, I need to thank the love of my life, Zulay. This book would not have been possible without you. Thank you for supporting my dreams.

PROLOGUE

There are things that happen in life that define us. Sometimes these things last hours and sometimes they last for as little as a split second. My life has been defined by five seconds of motion. The spinning and tumbling of a wrecked machine only reminds me of how small and fragile my body and my life are. Only a thin strap separates me from life and the snapping of my neck. Yet, it is within those five seconds that I gain a clearer perspective on my life.

They say that a near death experience makes a person see a flash of their past, but that hasn't happened to me at all. I saw everything that just happened: the near head-on collision, the swerving of my out-of-control car, the tree we just hit, and my world spinning as the car rolled over onto its roof. As I sit in my car in utter silence, I close my eyes and wonder how I got here. I have no idea if the passengers in my car are alive or dead. I'm just hanging here, upside down, wondering what has become of my life. I can feel the blood rushing to my head and I wonder if the last few months of my life have been the absolute worst times I've ever had.

I know that I should be reflecting on the life that should

typically be flashing before my eyes right now, but all I'm thinking about is how selfish I've been. I say a prayer and thank God that I can feel all my limbs at the moment, but what about the poor girl sitting next to me? What could she be thinking about? Is she even thinking at all?

All I know is that right now my life is a complete mess. I'm not even done paying for this car and I've no idea what I'm going to do. I can't assess the damage from here so I guess I should unbuckle my seat belt and crawl out.

I just need to close my eyes for a few moments.

ONE

I waited for her. I purposely made sure that I got out of work early so that I can make it home in enough time to tidy up. I'm not entirely sure what's going to happen when she gets here, but the hope is that I'm getting laid. Over the last several months, our friendship has become very flirtatious. Pictures were exchanged, hot messages, and even videos. The only question on my mind is how far will this go?

I'm nervous, so sitting on the couch looking out the window doesn't help. I decide to play this word finder game on my phone while keeping one eye looking out of the window. I want to make sure I greet her at the door. This makes me think about what I told her on chat a few weeks ago. I mentioned—in a horny state of mind—that if she comes by I will answer the door naked and erect. This kind of thinking comes from a person with a great imagination, who has no regard for what's real. The reality is that I'm walking into a potentially dangerous situation. It's too quiet in here and I start to feel like a stalker. I keep myself busy by connecting my iPod to my stereo. I want to listen to A Tribe Called Quest.

Vera is a friend of my ex-wife. The jury is still out on how close they still are. It seems that when we separated, she choose to hang out with a slightly different crowd. They speak every so often, but not enough for either one of us to really care. I considered what it would look like if she ever found out that I was about to fuck her friend. Then I think about the endless fights and numerous amounts of boyfriends she has had and I realize that caring less is going to be quite easy.

The dangerous part is Vera's potential fiancé, Corey. They've been going out for years, but everyone knows he's a worthless piece of shit. This is a dude who is just not careful about whom he sleeps with. Any man knows that women have a "spidey sense". When that shit tingles in their medulla, they will stop at nothing to satisfy their quest for proving that feeling right. So, Corey getting caught with this busted white chick is no surprise to me. Vera had sensed this a long time ago, even before we started sending pictures to each other. I doubt he'll find out about this. I'm not all that worried even if he does find out because what is he really going to do? I know that Vera has vengeance in her heart even if she isn't saying it. I have no problem being a revenge fuck.

Corey and I were never really friends. We would hang out with them the way couples hang out at parties or go to the movies. The ladies had many things in common and would talk for hours. The guys would either watch sports or play video games. Quite honestly, I found him kind of awkward and as things started becoming sour with me and the wife, I felt that he became more guarded of Vera. I was never left alone in a room with her. She noticed it too and asked him about it. Was he worried that we would sneak away or was he being paranoid?

He had expressed to her in a private conservation that he didn't really trust me on account of my separation. I'm not sure how much he really knows about *my* situation. Of course all couples talk but I'm not sure what Vera has told him. She was in the unique position to hear both sides. Strangely enough, it was me she ended up speaking to the most over G-chat. Of course, he doesn't really know how much we speak.

I'm still sitting here trying to remember how this all began. I can't recall the first time I shared my lust for Vera. I've always thought she was quite hot. She has an ass that I could do so many things with. She's played hard to get for so long. She would mention to me how Raina would not appreciate it if she found out that I was hitting on her. I would point out that we are one phone call away from a divorce. I knew I wasn't getting back together with her, so that guilt trip wasn't working. The other thing was that Raina barely called her anymore. How much was that friendship really worth? Besides, I'm the one she ended up coming to when Corey was fucking up.

It also turns out that Vera isn't so innocent herself. She's been trying to do her own thing for a while. Unlike Corey, I don't find anything wrong with women being bi-curious. Ok, that has everything to do with me being more of a pervert than me repping a rainbow flag. His problem is that he doesn't eat her pussy or so she says. Of course, if another woman were to do that to her, he would only assume his days were numbered. I mean, this is just an opinion, but something is wrong with any guy who turns down a threesome. Corey must be very paranoid to think that Vera would leave him because of that.

So in the midst of telling me all these stories about the women she has been flirting with, she sends pictures of them to me and then it becomes a game. We began sending pictures of all the chicks we are either interested in or have been with. It was really simple at first. But all the while, I just wanted to see her naked.

It felt like it took months to finally get what I was striving for. Vera had indeed taken pictures of her shaved vagina and, according to her, she was sending them to women she was trying to woo. I felt she was lying and I told her so. The way I looked at it, after all these months of telling her how much I wanted my face between her legs, she finally decided to throw me just a small bone.

Of course it didn't help that I had been sending her naked pics of myself for weeks. Her Facebook page had so many pictures that I would randomly open one and take a snap shot of her face and my dick in the same photo. Granted, it probably wasn't in good taste, but neither is trying to sleep with the friend of your soon-to-be former wife.

This is how I got here. Listening to *Midnight Marauders* and waiting for a woman that I've been lusting after for quite some time. I can't remember how long it's been, though? A year? Maybe more? However long it was, my divorce went through in the time it took for her to finally come around.

I finally see a car pull up into the driveway. She is here. I wasn't sure what car she would be driving but it's a small car that looks like a Toyota. I turn off the music, and then open the front door as she gets out of her car.

"I thought you were going to answer the door naked," Vera said. She grabs her purse and closes her door. She's looking cute today, as expected. She has on a nice little brown leather jacket. It's September in Syracuse and you can never really know how cold it will get. Her short brown hair is exactly how it looks on her Facebook page and it falls right below her ears. Her bangs barely graze the rims of her round glasses.

"Well, I didn't want the neighbors to talk", I replied.

"Heaven forbid," Vera replies as she flashes a smile. We hug each other as friends would, though it does seem a bit awkward. Perhaps she's nervous. I'll have to play this by ear because I fear I may have overplayed my hand. Maybe she'll just tell me that we should chill. But then again, she did come over, so this cannot be a bad sign.

She sits down on the love seat across from me. I smile as I sit on the couch. We make small talk and I ask her how her day was going. Vera is a pediatric nurse at one of the hospitals around here. I feel my anticipation growing as she starts talking about her job and how she is glad she got out early today. I barely pay attention because I don't really give a shit about her day. I come to realize quickly that she has to be here for a reason, so I will need to take the lead on this. Vera stops in the middle of her sentence and smiles. I think the look on my face has given her a slight hint about what I'm thinking. "What is it? What's that face for?" she says coyly.

"I was thinking that after all this time, seeing each other in pictures in various states of undress, we're just sitting here having small talk when I really want to see the Brazilian you've been showing me for the last few months." I wanted to say something shocking even though it was true. There comes a point in a marriage when pubic hair stops being trimmed. Vera always seemed to take care of herself in this regard.

"You want to jump right into it, huh? No glass of water. You don't even take my coat," she laughs. I thought for a moment she was serious but she continues to smile as she takes off her jacket. I also fail to notice that she has on her work scrubs. They're a nice shade of purple that match her sneakers. I get up as she takes off her glasses. My first thought is to hang up her jacket but I decide to just kiss her. I knew that I caught her off guard but she welcomes my kiss.

"What was that for?" she says as we pull away.

"I wanted to test out your lips," I reply.

"*Eres malo*…you know that, right?"

"Me? But here you are in my arms, about to be naked...*que mala*, indeed."

For all the posturing we were doing, we seemed to be at an end point. The one thing I told her I want to do more than anything was to lick her pussy. I bragged about how good I was and talked so much shit about it that I knew she wanted it. I learned a long time ago that if you are ever worried about performance anxiety, going down on a woman was a good way to not only ease that pressure but to get her in a good place so even if you perform badly, she won't forget your tongue.

Vera sits back down and unlaces her shoes. She notices the bulge coming from my sweats. "I thought it would be a good idea to go commando today," I say cleverly. I bought a few breakaway sweats because they were easy to pull off when I went to the gym. Times like these have given them a better purpose.

"Really," Vera replies. "I had the same idea." My eyes widen. This is why our communications over chat are so filled with lust. Unlike Raina, she was very quick with the comebacks. I tear off my breakaways like an NBA player to reveal how hard I am and then off comes my shirt. She is still sitting there looking at me. "So am I the only one who is going to be naked in this scenario?"

"Not at all, I was hoping you would take off my pants." Vera lifts up her legs and I pull off her scrubs. She indeed has no panties on. I just stare at this sight. There were so many times in the last few months that I thought about what I would do at this very moment. I can't help but just enjoy the sight of her brown skin. I get on my knees and spread her legs apart.

"This is going to be fun," I say.

I dive right in headfirst...

TWO

I'm at work a few days later. This is one of those busy days where I get no work done because I'm in sessions all day and evening. I haven't heard much from Vera since our encounter. I still think about all of it. Her lips. Her ass. The way she tasted. I always joked that I felt that she would taste like cinnamon. It turns out that I was wrong–she tasted much better than that. We must have had, maybe, 90 minutes to have all the sex we had. It wasn't nearly enough time, but it left a memory.

I've been stuck at this conference for the third straight day. At least they're feeding us decently. I considered myself lucky to be able to host a conference instead of going to one, but the planning alone is a nightmare. I spent more than a year planning this regional conference for Latino Male Retention that spans across the northeast. There are representatives from at least 20 schools here, so I'm quite proud of the effort we put into this. However, I've been really tired over the last few days due to all the running around. I've been so busy that I had to park in the back of the building today. This is something that I rarely do, but I was running later than usual. Sure I'm risking getting a ticket, but at least I still got to work relatively on time.

This is the last day of the conference and I can only thank

God that it's over. It's a tremendous amount of work to make sure all the logistics are taken care of while trying to attend as many sessions as possible. Today was the day that I decided I was going to take things a little easier and just go a few panel discussions. I'm such a sucker for information on retention rates for Latino males in higher education. It's no secret that in many predominately white institutions these rates are extremely low due to academic performance and/or socioeconomic conditions. Latinas have a greater rate of success while the men just seem to fail at a greater number.

All this information is food for thought as I begin to eat at the conference dinner. We are in this huge room on the third floor of the student union. There are several tables spread across the room that features a unique fireplace in the center that just about separates the room into two sections. There is a small riser stage with a podium on the south side of the room in front of these large bay windows where you can see the majority of the campus. On a clear evening like this, with the sun about to set, the view is stunning.

I'm picking at what's left of my roasted chicken when I feel my phone vibrating in my jacket pocket. I'm wearing the grey suit today. It's more comfortable and allows me to carry all the necessities like keys, wallet, a shit load of business cards, and my iPhone. I almost welcome this call as I fumble for it in my pocket. Sitting in the same table is one of my colleagues, Marvin, and all he seems to do well is be short and monologue like a super villain. He's on the conference host team with me and as an elder statesman, I felt compelled to add him to this event. He was one of the first black staff members I met when I was hired back in 2003.

Marvin has been talking about how tiring it is to work for the university and all of the political crap that seems to happen. He was making some good points too about the lack of African-Americans and Latinos within student affairs. He's also an old school dude that doesn't understand terms like cisgender and transgender, so he is real good at talking circles around people when it comes to racism and oppression until you bring up homosexuality or gender identities within the community. Then he gets all biblical about the subject. This is why I cannot take this dude seriously, at all. Not to mention Marvin has a short man's complex. He's like barely five foot five and is probably mad about it.

"Shit," I whisper to myself as I look at the phone screen. I recognize those numbers even though I deleted the contact from my phone: the ex-wife. She rarely calls and when she does it's never good. I debated for a second on whether I should entertain her call since I can come up with a thousand reasons to not answer. For one, the program is about to start at any minute. But, I do need a reason for Marvin to stop talking to me, so I will just press my luck and answer.

I start to say hello but as soon as I put the phone to my ear I can barely get the word out when I hear her angry voice say, "You motherfucker!"

This can't be good. It takes me a few seconds to try and ascertain the situation. I'm at work and cannot react the way I normally would. I'm in a room full of people, including students, so however I respond to her needs to seem natural.

"How can I help you?" I say in a very customer service expert kind of way. I have no real idea why she would be calling me, outside of her possibly finding out about Vera. But shit, that was like two days ago! How can she possibly know I was balls deep in her friend by now? I will need to play it cool.

"Don't give me that bullshit. Did I not ask you to change the registration on the car? Why is it that I walked past your car and it still has my plates on them?" I almost forgot about this issue. There was a point in time in our marriage when I wanted to get a car but I needed someone to co-sign for it. The only way for this to successfully happen was to buy the car under her name. Since we got divorced, she asked me to change it last year, but the only problem was that the deed was lost somewhere. After she moved out of the house, I couldn't find it anywhere. Last year when the registration was due for both cars, it turned out that she was too broke to pay for own car. The sucker in me caved and I paid for both...yet they remained under her name. Now, she as a new job, a new man and a new life and she wants to bitch about this.

Very calmly, I reply, "I sent you a message about this two weeks ago. I could not get the license plate off because one of the bolts is rusted." That was no bullshit either. I did go to the DMV a few weeks ago with the sole purpose of putting an end to this registration debate. However, I was none too pleased by the fact that the back plates would not come off despite my best efforts. In the middle of my struggle, I decided to text her this fact from the parking lot of the DMV. This way she can never say I didn't tell her.

"That was weeks ago. You mean to tell me that you could not find the fucking time to get those fucking plates off? I asked you to do one fucking thing and you couldn't do it. You just don't give a fuck, huh? You don't give two shits that I want my name off anything associated with you." Raina was on a roll. I had to give it to her, she could go on and on without so much as a breath. I was getting annoyed, however. Calling me today, of all days, to bitch me out about something that's just not that deep is annoying and very much her style. At this point, all I can do is say, "Uh huh"

"I am giving you until tomorrow to change those plates or I will rip them off myself. I don't care if the police pull your black ass over. DO YOU UNDERSTSAND ME?"

"Yep," I say as I hang up the phone. My blood is boiling at

this point and it takes everything in me to remain calm. Everyone at the table seems to be completely oblivious to the conversation I just had, which is a good thing. Marvin, however, has worked with me for a few years and knows my expressions. He asks me if I'm ok and I just wave him off saying that it is not a big deal.

"It must be a woman thing," he says laughing. I give him one of those fake smiles as he continues, "Let me tell you, my wife won't leave me alone for shit. Always naggin' me about some bullshit, but you know what? She's the boss! I know your wife is a firecracker."

Please stop, are the only words I want to say right now. I drink the rest of my apple juice smiling. I almost wish he would spill something on that black suit of his. I get up and excuse myself from the table. I forget that there are still some people on this campus that think Raina and I are still married. I need to walk and think about all this. I'm trying to not let this anger fester and get the best of me but I need to set her crazy ass straight. I'm officially tired of being yelled at.

Rather than call her back, I text her:

Do me a huge favor, don't you ever fucking call me like that again. I am at work. My schedule is busy and I do not give two shits about your threats. I will get it done. PERIOD...and don't text me back because you will be ignored.

I felt so much better after doing that. This will show her that I'm just done with the craziness. We are not married any longer and I really don't need to go through shit like this anymore. Maybe I can sit back and enjoy the rest of the conference. This is the last day and I would really like to network with some of my colleagues from Columbia University. Then again, the more I think about the situation, the unhappier I get. Something just doesn't sit right with me. I replay the conversation in my head. *Why is it that I walked past your car and it sill has my plates on them?* Oh my God. She wouldn't try to take those plates off my car now would she? I totally did not think of the fact that she doesn't work too far from here.

I start to pace a little bit. What do I do about this? Do I check the car right now? What if she's down there with her man? Do I really want to fight that big ass dude? I don't even have my bat and I'm in my suit goddamn it. I have to do something though. She is probably jacking my plates right now and no one will stop her because she is a university employee. Fuck me.

Wait. This actually might be hilarious. The back plates are rusted shut! I decide to rush down to the security office where they monitor the parking lot cameras. The student union operations person on duty is a buddy of mine. "Homeboy, can we check the camera from the back of the building?" My buddy, Frank, and I go way back. We were college roommates for about a year. It just so happens that we also started working for the university around the same time, too. We still manage to hang out from time to time when things are not so hectic.

"Everything alright?" Frank replies. He turns his chair around to the LCD screen that live streams all the cameras around the building.

"Um…I may have a situation with my car. The Ex called."

Frank smiles "This should be good."

He scrolls though the camera feeds until he gets to the one in the loading dock that is aiming directly in the direction of my car. There is no movement. I feel a bit of relief.

"What did you think was going to happen?" Frank asks,

still looking at the screen.

"I just got into an argument with Rai. She's still on that shit about the car registration."

"Still? What's she so worried about?"

"I have no idea. I just thought she might try to take the plates off the car." I look away and start to head back to the conference. Maybe I still have time to catch the keynote speaker. "Thanks man, I need to get back to this conference dinner..."

"Yo... son... look at this shit!" Frank exclaims.

I turn back around and on the screen I can see Raina and her man standing at the rear of my car. "They must have just come from the front of the car because they just appeared out of nowhere," Frank says pointing out the fact that this camera is pretty much stationary. Since it does not move you can't see the front of my car.

We watch in awe as we see my ex on her knees with what appears to be a screwdriver trying to get my rear license plate off. The big guy is just watching. "Do you want me to do something? This is crazy. Why would she do something like this?" Frank asks.

"No. I want to see what happens. There is no way they're getting that back plate off," I reply as I pull up a chair.

We watch for a few minutes as she unsuccessfully tries to get the plate off. She catches a fit. The big guy soothes her and then takes her place behind the car. He is also unsuccessful. They begin to argue and then she begins to yank at the license plate.

"This is hilarious!" Frank laughs.

"Look at these two fucking idiots," I say, as we both laugh. They both leave appearing to be defeated. "I'm going down there to make sure there's no damage to the car."

"Mind if I tag along? I may have to log this incident."

"Sure. If the big guy is there, then he is all you."

"Nah, he's cool. I met him before."

"You met him before?"

"Yeah."

"When??"

"It was a few weeks ago. We had a double date."

"Well isn't that special." I roll my eyes as we leave the office. Despite all this being funny, chances are she took the front plate, which means I will have to find a way to get the rear plate off tomorrow. Frank and I joke about her yanking on the plate all the way to the loading dock. The sight is something we will not soon forget.

We get to my car. A blue Hyundai Elantra. I can see a slight upward bend on the license plate. I bend down to look at the screws as Frank inspects the front of the car. The screws are completely stripped. She must have been really digging for gold with that screwdriver. Shit, that's going to make this harder to take off.

"The front plate's gone," Frank reports. "They even took the screws," he chuckles.

"Just fucking great. All I need is to be pulled over as I go home tonight. What am I going to do?" In my mind, I can already see the cops pulling me over and having to explain this not-so-funny story. I suppose I can just use the back roads to get home. Perhaps I can avoid any type of attention. I remember when one of my front lights went out—it took the cops five minutes to pull my ass over for that.

"Why don't you take a pic of your back plate and print it out in the office?" says Frank.

"That's fucking genius! That should buy me some time until tomorrow. Now I know why they hired you all those years ago."

"Yeah, they love me so much they forget to pay me more."

I take the picture but before I walk back to the office, I decide to move my car somewhere else on campus. The last thing I need is for these two to come back with whatever and get this plate off. I will have to go to the DMV tomorrow and register the car in my name. I suppose with all that yelling she will finally get her way. Not much has changed there.

Walking back to my office makes me think about Vera. Is there a possibility that she found out? I'm not sure how possible that is. Raina would have definitely confronted me about that. I do wonder how she's doing. I haven't hit her up because I have been busy with this conference and I can't text her now. Besides, I'm sure Corey would be upset to see that I'm texting his woman at this time of night. I will have to hit her up tomorrow.

At this point I have missed the rest of the conference closing dinner. I'm not very happy about this because I was really counting on talking with this woman I met from Columbia. I haven't told anyone that I have been looking to move back to New York City. I'm just waiting for the right opportunity. In any case, I suppose I could just go to the bar with the rest of the contingent, but I need to upload this picture and print it. This was such a great idea. I'm actually mad I didn't think of it myself, but I suppose that's what friends are for.

I walk back up to the third floor of the student union and I was right, the dinner is over. People are clearing out as the catering staff starts cleaning up. I see a couple of people and they tell me that everyone is heading to the bar at the Sheraton across the street. I quickly head to my office on the lower level so I can use my printer. The picture is finally uploaded to my desktop and I press print. I decide to check my email. I'm quite sure I have over 300 emails since I haven't been at my desk. My iPhone has certainly given me an indication of all the emails I have been getting throughout the day. I just have been choosing to ignore it with all the conference activities.

I scroll through. Spam. Spam. Facebook notifications. Delete. Delete. Then I scroll down to an email from Vera from this morning. Hmm, she never sends me an email. There is no subject line, either. I open the message and it reads:

He knows.

THREE

Why did I not think of a drill? Brian came up with this idea of drilling a hole in the center of the bolt with a 1/8th drill bit and it worked like a charm. The back plate came off with ease. I consider Brian to be the all-purpose utility man. I suppose that's the life of a man that has a master's degree in theater production because every time I need something fixed, he's always there.

"Dude, I know that I'm your favorite white boy," he says.

"That's true. Maybe I should take you with me to the DMV. I'm quite sure I won't get pulled over with you in the car. In fact, I'm also pretty sure I'll get better service, too."

"I highly doubt that. Everyone is oppressed in the DMV," he chuckles as he puts his drill back in the toolbox he brought.

"You're such an idiot," I say as we laugh. Brian always makes me laugh. He tries very hard to understand the world I live in. Very few white people try to even care about such things. Him and I joke about race relations, but for the most part he seems to get it. Of course, just when I think he really understands, he puts on a Rush album and I remember just how white he is.

"So you mean to tell me Raina came and tried to take your plates?" he asks. I decided to return the scene of the crime in order to make it easier for Brian to run out with his toolbox.

I nod. "It was crazy."

"I'm so mad I missed that."

"Frank made a copy."

"What? No fucking way."

"Go ask him. I asked him to make one for me just in case. But, let me get out of here. Thanks again, man." We shake hands and he gestures to me a peace sign until he blurts out, "That's two you owe me, Junior." Ah, *Star Wars*. So many movies and so many quotable lines. I give him this look that is my universal sign of *"really?"* He laughs as I shake my head and get into the car. I shake my head because he's right, I do owe him two. It's not like he's really keeping count but I do recognize all that he's done for me.

My printed license plate is on my dashboard as I say a silent prayer that no one in law enforcement notices me today. What I really want to know is how Vera is doing. Her two-word email has me freaking out a bit. I returned the favor with a one word email simply asking–How?

It's times like these I try not to over think things, but that will be difficult. The question is, what is going to happen next? I need her to answer my email. I did text her (with no response) and I'm not even sure that texting her was a great idea. In any case, I do feel that I have a target on my back now. I suppose I should've at least been prepared for this, I just don't understand how he could've found out. Maybe she told him.

I never considered the possibility that she would just tell him. I feel like an idiot right now. Of course she would tell him. Vera's whole purpose of fucking me was to get her revenge on Corey. There would be no better way to get to him than by fucking me. Now he knows and it must be driving him crazy. I just know that I need to watch my back. Between Corey and that big dude the ex is dating, I seem to be a walking pariah. What else could happen?

I pull into the DMV for the second time in a month. I begin to wonder just how they're going to react when I give them one plate. Then again, I would not put it past my ex to have already given the other plate in. I wouldn't put it past her to already be inside. I will try not to think about this fact. She is the type to get up early and do shit. I'm more casual. I will get up at 10, masturbate, shit, and then shower. Before I know it is almost 1pm—typical guy shit really. I'm just glad I took the day off.

I look down at my phone as I walk into the building. It's 2:30 and I have 5 text messages. I get my ticket from the courtesy desk and I wait. I look around very casually. This place is not as packed as I thought it would be. I remember my days of going to the DMV on Tremont Ave in the Bronx. That place was a shit show. There is no sign of her. Maybe I can relax a little bit while I look at these text messages:

Brian Keegan: 2:26 pm Son! That video is so fucking funny. LMAO!

Judy Lee: 2:20 pm How can Raina do that? I thought she was a professional woman?

Zenia Ocasio: 2:17 pm Hey there.

Frank Pope: 2:15 pm There's another camera angle. U have to see this! Lol

Vera Morales: 2:14 pm Be on chat at 4. Don't text me.

Clearly, Frank is showing people in the office. I don't blame him. I would, too. While I should be concerned with Vera's message, it's Zenia's message that catches me by surprise. We haven't spoken in months. I'm not even sure that I'm ready to have a conversation with her, especially today. I will have to think about this.

Judy is, for lack of a better term, my work wife. Co-workers turned good friends; she's always on the look out for me. Although we've never dated, people think that we have or they think we are like brother and sister. She was always critical of Raina and her outbursts. They never cared for each other and Raina thinks I fucked her.

I'm not sure I'm going to be able to be on chat by 4pm. So I will have to log on with my phone, which is something that I really don't want to do. I can only type so fast with this thing. I guess I will have to make this work.

Before I fill out the paperwork they gave me when I walked in, I answer Judy back. It's a typical snarky response of "what do you expect?" I tell Frank that I will look at it when I get back in to the office. I decide not to text Zenia back yet. The last thing I want to do is make it seem that I'm so eager to speak to her. Our back and forth history suggests that I will cave to her eventually. I just need to keep up the appearance that I won't cave in, at least, not so quickly.

I need to fill out this paperwork.

It's 3:24 pm by the time my number is called. I have my completed paperwork, the deed that I had mailed to me, and my one license plate. The lady at the window just looks miserable. I can tell that she wants to be here less than I do. I give her everything. "I hope its ok that I only have one of these plates..." I say this thinking that I may have to explain my situation. She punches in something into the computer and she says very dryly, "No problem, sir. The other one was handed in this morning."

I wanted to do my best Fight Club impression by saying that *I am Jack's complete lack of surprise.* I ask her when the other plate was given in and her response was 11:10 am. Then she says, "She also canceled the registration of the car. I assume you're paying to get a new registration."

Interesting. I knew I was right. I just didn't think she would have gone so far as to cancel this shit. I'm lucky because I would have been so fucked had I been pulled over. I reluctantly paid the fee again with a huge feeling of resentment. I think she owes me some money since I paid for her current car to be registered. I can't think about this right now. I need to get to a computer by 4pm.

Without breaking too many laws, I manage to get home with 5 minutes to spare. I quickly get into my house and boot up the MacBook. She is not online yet. I stare at my phone. I got another text message from Zenia: *Do you not want to talk to me anymore?* This is killing me. Perhaps I need to come up with a lie as to why I cannot talk right now. What can I tell her?

Then the Vera's chat box comes up:

Vera: Hi

Me: Hola. How are you?

Vera: I'm ok, all things considered.

Me: What happened? How did he find out?

Vera: Remember how I caught him chatting with that

white bitch?

Me: Yeah…

Vera: Well, he did the same thing to me.

Now I remember. Vera was convinced that Corey was cheating on her but she just had no proof. So one day, when he was at work, she went through his computer to look for evidence. He was very good at cleaning up his tracks. So she installed a spy program on the hard drive that records everything being said and done. This is where she found all the evidence she needed to nail him. Pictures, chat history, and emails. It was almost like a full confession that he was sleeping with this other woman.

She could get away with doing this because they had two computers. One was the desktop that they kept out in the living room and the other was her personal laptop. So that only means…

Me: Wait. So he installed that program on your laptop.

Vera: Yes.

Me: What did he see? Did he see everything?

Vera: No, thank god. But he did see how we planned to see each other and he read your emails.

Me: Fuccccck.

I want to scream. This is what I get for taking things too far. I wrote an email to her the next day. Basically bragging how I was so glad I was able to fuck her all over my house. Wow dude. Good job. Now I really have a target on my back.

Me: I'm so sorry

Vera: No need to apologize. I had a part to play in this too... it wasn't just you ya know...

Me: I know. What are you gonna do now?

Vera: He still wants to marry me. He understands that he fucked up and this was my way of getting him back for all the dumb shit he has done. He's just upset that it's you.

Me: Why is he so upset that it's me?

Vera: He mentioned something about guy code. Maybe he thought you were friends.

Me: Clearly, I missed the memo

Vera: I think we need to chill. I know we're friends but I think after all these years I owe it Corey to try to make this work. He is a dick...I know...but I love him.

Me: That is completely understandable. I have my own shit to deal with.

Vera: What do you mean?

Me: Zenia hit me up today...

Vera: Wow. What timing huh?

Me: Tell me about it.

Vera: What're you gonna to do?

Me: I dunno.

Vera: I have a feeling things will work out. I told you one day she would hit you up.

Me: We'll see what happens.

Vera: Look I gotta go.

Me: Wait! Do you think Corey will do something?

Vera: I don't think so. He's mad but he promised to leave things alone. He says he's a changed man.

Me: Ok

Vera. Take care of yourself, Louis.

Me: Cya

Vera is offline. Messages you send will be delivered when Vera comes back online.

FOUR

What is there to say about Zenia? Different people would tell you different things about her. Raina will tell you she's a homewrecker. Judy would tell you that she changed my perspective. Frank would probably tell you she is the one. I would tell you that she is global warming. She's the one that completely altered the climate of my life and like the people on this planet, I'm not ready for her.

I'm not ready for her because my life is in shambles as much as I try not to admit it. We stopped talking months ago because our basic relationship or whatever you call it was just too much for either one of us to handle.

I can't help but think about all this as I drive to work. After my conversation with Vera yesterday, I did text Zenia to let her know that I did receive her message but I've been busy at work. While that's not entirely true, I need some time to think about what it is I want to say to her when we do talk. I told her I was going to call her when I got the chance.

When I get out of the car I can't help but look at my new license plates as I walk away. I shake my head knowing that this little incident may not be the last from the ex-wife. I also can't help but think about the fact that I have way too much woman drama in my life right now. How did things escalate so quickly? The answer to that is pretty simple. It's clear to me that I cannot seem to keep it in my pants and now everything seems to be coming back to haunt me.

My dad always told me, "what comes around goes around," and right now its coming around. Perhaps I should not have had sex with Vera. Perhaps I should not have cheated on my wife. Then again, perhaps I should have never gotten married in the first place. Unfortunately, hindsight is 20/20 and I cannot unmake the decisions that I have made.

Judy says her customary good morning. "There is someone waiting to see you." I pause for a minute. I don't recall scheduling a meeting this early. In fact, my phone didn't send me a reminder. I never schedule a meeting earlier than 10 o'clock. I look over and it's the big guy, Raina's boyfriend.

"How can I help you sir?" I've never officially met this guy. Sure, I've seen him around. We've been in the same room together, but we have never officially met. This type of situation, where the ex and I still hang in the same circles, was never awkward for me. I never cared enough for it to bother me, but our mutual friends thought it was awkward as hell.

"I would like to have a word with you" the big guy says. Perhaps I exaggerate when I call him big guy. He is indeed taller than me. If I had to guess, he was a guard for some high school or college basketball team. Of course that type of guess is only compounded by the fact that he has athletic gear on, a pair of grey sweatpants and a black Syracuse University hoodie. I try not to roll my eyes and I have this quote from *Mean Girls* in my head, "she doesn't even go here!" I have to thank Global Warming for making me watch that movie.

"Sure, I was going to get some coffee, care to join me?" I ask.

"No...Thanks. I don't drink coffee."

"Well that's too bad", I say as I open my office door. "Come in, have a seat." I take off my coat and place it on the back of my chair. I sit down at my desk and I noticed that he already sat down and closed the door. I turn on my desktop and look over to him. "What's up?"

He has this cold stare. Did I anger him? "I need you to be a man about your shit," he blurts out.

"Excuse me?" I reply.

"Is everything a joke to you? You think Wednesday night was funny?" His tone begins to rise slightly and I've no idea where he's going with this.

"You mean how both of you decide to take my plates like kids? Sounds a bit amusing. Is this why you are in my office, to complain about this?"

"Oh it's amusing? So posting that video on YouTube was your idea of a joke?" he glares at me.

"What are you talking about?" I say in disbelief. I have no idea what he's talking about. YouTube? What idiot did that? Would Frank have done such a thing?

"Don't bullshit me nigga. All I'm saying is you better take that shit down or you gonna find yourself in a situation that isn't so fucking funny!"

"Wait, you come into my office to threaten me when you have no proof that I'm the one who posted anything. Secondly, who the fuck do you think you are? You don't even know me."

"I don't need to know you. I've seen and heard all about you, so I'm going to make this real simple for you..." He gets up. "…You keep trying to play me and my girl, and one day someone around here is going to hear about how you love to fuck your students." He opens the door as he stares at me then leaves. I just sit there staring at the chair he was sitting in for a few seconds.

I log into my computer and wait for it to boot up. Judy walks in asking what that was all about. The big guy's voice was loud enough for people to hear, but not loud enough for people to hear the content. I explain what his issue is.

"Who would have put it on YouTube though?" Judy asked.

I really wish I knew. After getting a web browser open, I'm finally able to search for this video. It doesn't take me long to find. 705 page likes already! I'm expecting to see a screen name of someone I know, but I have no idea who this is. The screen name is jaded_mf2012. I click on the name and see other video of random stuff, mostly yoga. What? I sit back on my chair and look at Judy. "I don't know who the hell this is."

I turn the screen her way and she looks at it and she is dumbfounded as well. "I have no idea." It is indeed the footage that Frank and I saw that night, but there is no way that he would post this. In fact, I'm sure he would never upload any type of media on any site much less YouTube. He doesn't even know how. So the question is, how did this end up on here?

I ask Judy, "Who first showed you this video?"

"I didn't post the video", she says defensively

I roll my eyes. "Did I ask you that? How did you see the video?"

"Oh, well Frank showed it to me."

"Ok, but how? Did he come to your desk? Did you go to his?"

"No, he emailed it to us."

"He emailed it?" Now, I'm frustrated. Was I copied on that email? I check my outlook and scroll down. Shit, I have a lot of email. This may take awhile. "Did he email this to just the staff or other people than that?" I asked. I already know Judy doesn't know. I suppose I just asked the question in hopes that she would tell me it was just her and Brian.

"I don't know." Judy says.

"Of course you don't." I smile so that she's not too offended by my sarcasm. I finally find the email and open it. He did email an attachment of the video to a group of people. Some of the emails are people I know and some that I do not. I begin to rub my temples.

"That doesn't look good," Judy says.

I look up at her. "This motherfucker emailed this to a bunch of people. It can be anybody. I need to talk to him. Do you know when he comes in today?"

She shakes her head. "So what are you going to do about Kevin?"

"Who's Kevin?"

"Um...the Black guy that was just here, Raina's boyfriend?" Judy was astonished that I didn't know his name.

"His name is Kevin? Shit, how am I supposed to know? Wait...how do you know?" I smile.

"Well, we were talking before you walked in. He seemed nice." She looks very innocent at this point.

"Seemed nice? What you're really saying is that you think he's cute."

"What? No! I mean he is tall…"

I lower my voice so no one else hears "You want to see that man naked don't you?"

"Why would you say that? Me? I'm a good girl!" She's not looking so innocent now.

"Please, I call bullshit. A Black man is always up your alley."

Judy seems faux shocked. "That is so racist!" She walks out and I start to laugh. She walks back in. "I will have you know that he has very big hands…" and walks out. I start to roar with laughter.

Judy and I always have a good laugh. She is the type of fun loving person that everyone should have in their office. When it comes to doing work, she is one of the best people. She's still the lowest person on the totem pole since she was hired less than four years ago, but she has proven to always have my back no matter what. I'm glad I hired her.

I didn't even get my coffee this morning. I can't help but watch the video again and laugh. I walk to Judy's desk. She is on the phone so I just wait until she gets off. "I'm going to get coffee, but to answer your question, I don't know what I'm going to do. I certainly don't like being threatened, particularly over something that I didn't do."

"Yes, I know but do you think he will start telling people

about you and Zenia?"

"So what if he does, the boss knows about her anyway. Not to mention the fact that she was a grad student who didn't even report to me...directly." I say defensively. Judy knows some of the story, just not all of it. In fact, very few people really know the entire store about Zenia and me. Most of it is just highly personal to me. The fact of the matter is I fell in love with her and it changed my world. Like I said, Global Warming.

FIVE

The rest of the morning was much better. I got a lot of work done and cleared some emails even though I could not shake the feeling of knowing that someone put that video out there. Frank is not in yet and I'm getting antsy. However, meetings have a way of distracting me from my real life and today I had back-to-back meetings leading into lunch. Not to mention lunch is always a shit storm of not knowing what to get with the limited amounts of choices in the student union and the limited amount of choices on Marshall Street. I settle for a Jimmy John's turkey sub, which is usually what I always eat anyway.

I bring my lunch back to the office and eat at my desk, which again, is something I always seem to do. I open my Gmail and hit compose. I need to write Zenia a long overdue email. Since our fallout months ago things were left on shaky ground. I honestly didn't think I would hear from her again. It has been about eleven weeks since we last spoke, not that I'm counting.

I type her email into the box when I hear a Facebook chat alert. I click the tab on my browser and its Corey. *What's up Asshole?* Damn it! Now I have to deal with this guy? Vera said he wasn't going to say anything to me, but I should've known better than that. To be honest, I kind of forgot about him. I will just assume that is a bad thing.

Louis Ortiz: What do you want?

Corey Smith: What I want is to kick your ass

Louis Ortiz: You know where I live.

Corey Smith: Don't tempt me nigga. I told Vera I wouldn't touch you but we need to talk.

Louis Ortiz: All right, so talk.

Corey Smith: You all smug. You think that shit is cool to be fuckin' my girl huh? Meanwhile you all smilin in my face and bein all in my house like we cool. I knew I shoulda never have trusted you from the jump. What the fuck you got to say for yourself, what if I decide to fuck your girl or ex, I bet you wouldna liked that shit at all.

Louis Ortiz: I don't have to explain anything to you and you're welcome to try with my ex, I'm not sure she would go for you, she is into big muscular black dudes now, not a scrawny light skinned Skeletor like yourself. I don't have a woman anyway.

Corey Smith: Oh, you a real fucking clown with your big teeth. Is that why you all up on Vera? You can't find yourself your own bitch?

Louis Ortiz: Are you really coming at me like this? Like you weren't fucking any white girl that came across your path?

Corey Smith: I know I fucked up. I know! That shit burns me that she had to fuck you to prove a point to me. Any nigga woulda been better than you.

Louis Ortiz: Any nigga? So you wouldn't have cared if any other nigga came on her face? So because I jizzed all over her lips and she liked it...YOU MAD?

I'm totally lying to him right now but I just want to rile him up.

Corey Smith: You MOTHERFUCKER.

Louis Ortiz: I'm just asking? You talking about any other nigga would be better than me like I stole her from you when in reality, you're about to get married.

Corey Smith. I swear to my mother the next time I see you I'm gonna knock you the fuck out.

Louis Ortiz: Please, I'm not afraid of you. You just mad because you know what it feels like for her to be with another man besides you and there's nothing you can do about it.

Corey Smith: Stop trying to analyze me, just cuz you work for some college don't make you that smart. I'm pissed because we used to chill together all the while you trying to get in to my girl's pants.

Louis Ortiz: So what do you want then? You want me to apologize? Fine, I'm sorry, shit just happened.

Corey Smith: I don't want your sorry ass apologies. I read that email. You "loved plugging every hole she has" How the fuck you gonna talk to her like that? I don't even talk to her like that.

Louis Ortiz: Maybe that's the problem. You too busy trying to hit off these white chicks when you have a fine ass Latina at home that wants to feel wanted. Maybe you should ask her if she liked being talked to like that.

A few minutes pass and he types nothing. I'm unsure what to do at this point. I know that I'm pushing his buttons, but I can't come across as someone who is going to be afraid of a fight. I know I got myself into this mess; maybe I can talk my way out of the worst part. Shit, I'm quite sure he hates me now and I am ok with that.

Then he finally decides to answer.

Corey Smith: I did ask her and she does like being talked to like that. I just never really thought about talking to my woman like that. Those white chicks I hit off, they didn't mean anything to me. I was having fun with them saying nasty shit and they loved it. But because of that, I couldn't respect them. Now Vera wants me to do this because of you, or maybe not because of you, but I have to live with the fact that she wanted your dick.

This is what I did not want from this conversation. I'm starting to pity him. While I don't really regret what I did, I do feel bad now that I have shattered his sense of being. However, I suppose I could argue that he's a better man for it. He recognized he was in the wrong now that he's in her shoes. Not that I should be in any position to do this. If Zenia had done this to me then I would've lost my mind. Although I have to admit that Raina has sort of done this to me too based on my own indiscretions.

There is silence again. Clearly this dude doesn't think I work.

Louis Ortiz: I understand, but I gotta go. I have work to do.

Corey Smith: I'm still not letting you off the hook on this nigga. Your still fucked up for what you did.

Louis Ortiz: *you're

Corey Smith: Smh

Louis Ortiz: Somehow, I think you can live with me being an asshole. Don't think about it too much on your wedding day.

I close out. I'm betting he'll leave a message trying to continue this conversation. I just felt like this wasn't going anywhere. I may just block him on Facebook too. I noticed that I have been unfriended by her and I would assume after today he will do the same. But clearly, I was wrong about him before. At this point, I have other things on my mind. I still haven't written this email to Zenia and I still haven't seen Frank today.

I take out my phone and start texting Zenia. *Hey there, I'm sorry I have been busy, but I really want to talk to you. There are just a lot of things that have been going on and I suppose I just haven't had a chance to really talk to you. Can I call you tonight?* I check for any typos then I press send. I take a big sigh. Maybe things will be all right between the two of us.

Then the phone vibrates in my hand. Frank is calling me. I answer, "What's up buddy? I've been looking for you." I can hear a lot of air on the other end. He is definitely outside somewhere.

"Yo. I need you to come get me. Lidia threw me out of the house," I'm in shock. I tell him I'm on my way, but if the last few days haven't been weird enough, now this.

Frank and Lidia have been together for a while. They got married a few years after I did. Frank made it seem like everything was cool between him and his wife so this comes as a surprise to me. Although, I suppose you can never tell what happens behind closed doors. I put on my jacket and tell Judy that I will be back.

"What is going on?" she asks. Judy is a nosey one. She always wants to know the scoop.

"I will tell you later," I reply.

"Come on...tell me," She smiles. She also has a "spidey sense" about this stuff.

"Later!" I say as I grab my keys and close the door.

I speed walk to the garage. I can hear my phone going off with text messages. I quickly check them as I get to the car.

Judy Lee: 1:47pm Damn! This better be good! lol

Lidia Pope: 1:45pm Hurry up and get this punk ass out of my house!

Zenia Ocasio: 1:44pm I would love that.

What the hell is going on over there? I know that she can be abrasive but I have never see her act this way toward Frank. Judy is right about one thing, this better be good.

Frank and Lidia live less than ten minutes away. So getting to his place was easy. When I pull up I see them outside arguing. Correction: He is just standing there and she is yelling at him. Its almost a funny sight to see this short Puerto Rican woman yelling at this big Black dude. I don't need to get out the car to hear her going in on him. I get out of the car and I look around to see if there's an audience. There are a few neighbors here and there. I open the back seat.

"...And that is another thing...you are one lazy ass son of a bitch. The least you can do is grow some fucking balls and tell that bitch ass boss of yours to start paying you more because you are not definitely not making it around here…" Lidia is letting him have it and she doesn't stop for a second when she notices me in the vicinity, in fact, I'm not even sure she is taking in breath right now.

"…So what you need to do is take your shit and go with your fucking friend here and get the fuck out of my face because you make me sick!" Frank has two bags in his hands, a duffle bag and a suitcase. He looks extremely frustrated as he heads away from her and towards the car.

"Hey guys….uh everything uh…alright?" I ask this stupid question because I have no clue what else to say. They both say NO at the same time. All I can manage is… "K".

I look at Lidia and ask, "How long am I keeping him? You know gas is expensive and I don't want to just drop him back tomorrow."

"You can keep that motherfucker for as long as you want. I don't give a fuck."

"Ok Lidia, nice talking to you," I say as I walk away.

By the time I get to the driver's side Frank is already in the passenger seat with his stuff in the back. I ask him if he's ok and he just nods and tells me to just get him the fuck out of here. Lidia just stares at us as we pull away. I'm still in a state of shock; I can only imagine how Frank is feeling. I'm almost afraid to ask him what is going on, but considering that he is about to be my roommate I don't think I have much of a choice.

Frank tells me about the problems they've been having financially. When she married him, she also married his debt and after years of what seemed like running in place, she began to resent the fact that they could not seem to get ahead of the bills. Much of this was due to the fact that Frank may come across as lazy and doesn't handle money quite so well. The other issue is that Frank loves to smoke weed. This is something that many people don't know about him. He can be a bit of a pothead and he's always been this way since his last girlfriend. I knew this and never really held it against him, but when he's always late for work or forgets shit, I know what it is.

For a time I thought he stopped and he admitted that he did stop, but according to him once the fighting got worse he just couldn't deal and started this habit all over again. He originally quit when she begged him to, but when she found a box of blunts he tried to hide underneath his Xbox 360 she had a fit and kicked him out.

"Maybe it will blow over," I said. I knew how much he loves her, but like most men, he made a poor decision. He has never cheated on her and I think he never will. But, I'm not so sure about Lidia. If there is one thing that I have learned from Raina and Vera is that if a woman wants to get you back badly enough, she will.

"I dunno son. We've had our fights before but this one seemed different," Frank said in a distant sort of way. Maybe he's also in disbelief of the whole situation. "I mean you know how Lidia can be. She can be loud and its not like she hasn't threatened to kick me out before...I guess I never thought she would actually do it." He said it very somberly as he looked out the window. The rest of the trip to my place didn't take more than five minutes but it was quiet the rest of the way.

I drive up to the house and I ask him if he needs help with his stuff. He declines as I open the front door for him. He heads up the stairs. Frank has been to my house several times so he knows where the guest room is. There is a full size bed in there and a dresser. Almost like it was meant for him.

I live in a colonial style house that was built sometime in the 1940's, a four-bedroom with one and a half bathrooms. It looks like something that we could've raised a family in. A nice big backyard and a decent-sized basement made purchasing this place that much easier. But then again it slowly became a money pit when things just started breaking all the time. It's funny that I spent most of my adult life complaining about renting an apartment and now I would love nothing more than to not have this responsibility.

"I'm going back to work, are you coming with me?" I ask from the bottom of the stairway.

"Yeah, give me like five minutes," he replies.

Five minutes is usually ten. I know how slow he can be. So I take this time to sit in the car and check email on my phone and then browse Instagram. All work and nothing too important that can't wait at least an hour. At this point, it looks like I'm going to need a drink this weekend. I know my cousin has been dying to go out, so I will have to hit him up. I text Judy to let her know I will be back within the next twenty minutes. At least Instagram provides me with a little bit of entertainment.

Frank comes down quicker than expected. I toss him the house keys and he locks the door. I start the car up again and I wait for him to come back in. I leave the car in park and I ask him "Did you post that video of Raina and Kevin on YouTube?"

He shakes his head. "No, why would you think that?" he asked.

"Kevin was waiting for me when I got in this morning. He

accused me of putting up the video."

"Are you serious? What the fuck, I could get in trouble if that video is out like that."

"Yes, I know that. I figured it wasn't you."

"Damn, who could it be?"

"Shit, Frank, I was hoping you would tell me…some person name jaded mf I think"

"Jaded underscore MF 2012?" he asked in disbelief

"Yes…that is it"

"That is Lidia's screen name."

What. The. Fuck.

SIX

I'm not sure this day is going to end. It's like 6:30 pm and I'm sitting in front of Lidia's because I have to convince her to take this video down. The only reason she even entertained me coming over to discuss this was because I was willing to take more of Frank's stuff back with me. That would only mean that this standoff between them is going to last longer than I thought.

I suggested to Frank that it would probably be easier for me to talk to her about this because she will not listen to him. Besides, this is my issue that I need to deal with. I'm just not sure what kind of mood she's going to be in. All I know is that I need to be home by nine so that I can call Zenia.

I walked up to the house and I noticed that the door was ajar. I knock slightly as I walk in. "Hello?" I walk into the house and I see a few small duffle bags by the stairs. It smells like pine cleaner and I hear Bachata coming from the other room. I close the door and step over the bags as I'm going into the living room.

"Helloooo," I say again. I then I finally hear her reply. "Come in! I'm in the kitchen!"

This place looks as clean as it smells. I look all around and everything seems to be in its right place. I almost trip on their cat as I walk into the kitchen. There I see Lidia on her knees scrubbing the oven. "Did I come at a bad time?" I ask. She gets up and says no. She walks over to the sink, where the water is running, to rinse off her yellow rubber gloves before she takes them off. "Sorry, I'm just about done with the oven here. After all this bullshit with your friend, I needed to just clean. Have a seat in the living room and we will talk in there."

I sit down on the couch and just relax. The grey cat jumps on my lap and I stroke its back. "Do you want something to drink?" she asks. "I will take a beer if you have it," I respond.

She walks out with a beer and a bottled water. "I hope you like light beer. This is all Frank drinks. The man will smoke all damn day and then drink light beer," she gripes as I take the beer.

"I'm good with this. It's like water, but I'm good," I respond.

"So why did you come here? Are you trying to give him back already?"

"Ha! No. I'm here because of something completely different."

"Oh really? Do tell," She seems intrigued.

"Well, there's an issue with something that you posted on YouTube."

"Ok, did Frank tell you I was posting some nasty things on there?" She jokes.

"No! Imagine that. But, it was a video of…"

45

ANTHONY OTERO

"Raina and her man trying to take your license plates," She interrupted. "Yeah, I posted it. I thought she was pretty fucked up to do something like that. I wanted blow up her spot a little."

"Really? Well it worked. Kevin came by this morning threatening me."

"No Shit?!?"

"Crazy right? Anyways, I'm asking you if you can take that video down for me. I don't need that kind of drama in my life right now."

"Done. Let me get my laptop." She puts her water down on the coffee table and heads back into the kitchen. This beer is so watery right now that I can barely stand it. I would give it to the cat but it's probably too smart to have any part of it. I suppose I don't have to worry about Frank drinking all the beer in my house. However, I'm worried about the fact that he might decide to smoke all the time now.

I'm not the type of person who condemns weed smoke. He's a grown man and can do what he likes, I just don't care for smoking in general. Ever since members of my family have gotten cancer because of all the cigarettes, I have been wary of that habit.

Lidia comes back with her laptop. Clearly this is the source of the Bachata music since it is still blasting. She sees my face and notices the music might be a bit loud. She mouths "sorry" and lowers it. She starts typing and asks "Do you not like Bachata?"

I smile and respond, "I wouldn't say all that. I just like my music at a normal decibel level."

"Sounds like you're an old man."

"I'm an old man now? Like you aren't thirty ni---"

"Don't do it to yourself or I will leave this video up!" She laughs. She continues to type then she shows her screen to me. "This is so you can see that I'm in the video manager area." She walks me through what she is doing. Lidia has a list of videos on her page. She selects the box next to the video titled *Check these idiots out* and then moves her mouse to the actions drop down menu. She clicks delete and a window pops up. *Are you sure you want to delete 1 video?*

Lidia looks over to me. "Yes, I'm sure you want to," I say. Then she clicks ok and the video is gone. "Thank you. What are all the other videos you have on there?" I was just curious to know because she seems to have a ton of stuff that I cannot make out at first glance.

"Oh, well you may not know that I'm a part time Yoga teacher. So, I do sessions online. It was a little something I started that seems to be catching on." She clicks on one of the videos where she is on a mat explaining some breathing techniques. "This one has over fifteen hundred views."

"Wow, that's pretty amazing," I say. My astonishment is real because I never really paid attention to what she does. I just figured she worked as administrative assistant at some office. "Seems like you're doing well."

"I'm starting to. The extra money comes in handy especially now that Frank is not here. I can handle the mortgage on my own." There it is. That is the response I was looking for. I wanted to know how serious this split was and my fears about it have been confirmed.

"That does not bode well for him," I say. "So is this just

the beginning of a real separation?"

She closes her laptop. "I don't know. I'm just very frustrated right now. Every time I feel that we take a step forward, we take two steps back. I don't ask for much. I just want to be able to pay our bills and have a good life. I want him to be successful but he's so complacent on where he is right now. All I ask of him is to be honest with me. I feel this is something he's just not willing to do. So I need a break, some time to be alone and think."

"So I guess there's a chance that you could get a divorce then?" I ask this with the thought that this could really be sad. I know how the thought of a failed marriage feels. It makes you question every life decision that led up to that point. I certainly don't wish this feeling on my friends, but nothing ever seems to last long enough these days.

"Divorce is a strong word. I don't think I want to go down the road that you and Raina went through. But, at the same time, we need to reevaluate our marriage. Right now, I just want to have fun with my girls." After a moment of silence she continues. "But you know what? That's enough about me. How are things with you? How are the ladies treating you?"

God, I hate that question. That has to be the universal question when someone is single. There must be a guide that says *you must ask this question of a single man*. What am I going to tell her? Well, before Vera the well was dry. Sure, there was this one woman I was messing with from time to time and she would give me head but the last time was months ago. So the women are not really treating me at all. How come no one asks me how am I treating women?

"You know, things are good. I can't really complain." It is amazing how I can lie my ass off. But, I won't mention all this stuff to her anyway.

"I bet they are good. I knew you were a ladies man." She smiles. "As a matter of fact, what really did happen between you and Raina? Because she told me a lot of shit about you." I'm sure she has. Here is another instance where I'm not sure if talking to her about this is a good idea. People tend to take sides in divorces and I know if her and Frank are done, well we both know who's side I'll be on. However, I always seem compelled to tell my side of the story.

"Well Raina will be biased to the whole situation, but to make a really long story short, I fell in love with another woman."

"Really? Just like that? Was this the student?" Clearly she has some information. Maybe not all of it, but enough of it to ask a question like that. It does make me wonder how many people Raina told about this. Her big bad boyfriend is going around making threats to me, but they are getting emptier by the day.

I roll my eyes, "Yes, she was a grad student. I met her one day during an event I was working and we were drawn to each other. The relationship started out strictly platonic, we were just friends. She would ask me about advice on life and career and eventually she ended up working in my office. Early on Raina had this inclination that perhaps something was going on under her nose, but there really wasn't."

I take the last swig of my beer and continue, "But then something changed. My attraction to her was very apparent. We began to get to know each other so well that our normal conversations became ones of flirtation. Then before you know it, one thing led to another. We couldn't get enough of each other. There were times where we would leave work for a few hours and head over to her place. Other times she would come by my office outside of her normal hours and we would go at with the door closed. I have never experienced that type of passion before."

Lidia seemed really interested. "So how did Raina find out? Did she walk in on you mid-stroke?"

"God no. I had to finally admit it to her. I mean it didn't help matters that she suspected something was going on. There was the night where she must have interrogated me for hours. It was about 3:30 in the morning on a workday when I just told her that I was indeed cheating on her. The rest is history."

I can tell that she was enjoying this story. Not in the sense that she was happy about the misery, but glad to be hearing gossip from the source. "Yes, it was indeed history. Boy, she hated that little girl. I am surprised there wasn't a fight."

"There almost was. Thank god Zenia wasn't trying to fight. In fact, I had both women mad at me. Zenia did not appreciate me being so forthcoming with this information just weeks before her graduation. It really upset her before she was set to finish her final papers. But once she graduated, she went back to New York City." I almost begin to reminisce. I do miss her and we had some really good times together.

"So that's it? You guys don't see each other anymore? I thought you were in love with her? Does she love you?" Lidia has a way of just asking questions in such a rapid pace. I almost feel like I'm being interviewed, but such is the case when you start a story which creates more questions than it gives answers.

"We had a falling out so we stopped speaking for a while. She has her own life to lead. The whole divorce just took too long. I never thought she was really going to wait through that. Even if she did, is she really going to do a long distance relationship with me?" I can feel myself making excuses. The fact is that it really does hurt me that we are not together.

Explaining it again just makes it more real.

Zenia is too smart to be a side chick. She wasn't trying to be second to anyone. During our affair she never pressured me to leave my wife, but when Raina found out about us, I needed to make a choice. I thought I was doing the right thing by trying to save my marriage, but that just turned out to be a mistake. In the end I lost both women and after years of drama, it seems that I'm still reeling from it all. I don't need to tell this to Lidia because it is just too much to go into and quite frankly, I'm not trying to show my pain to her.

Lidia replies, "Well, I'm pretty sure you've not heard the end of Zenia. I just have that feeling you'll see her again"

"You think so, huh?"

"A woman has a sense about these things." Here we go again with this intuition that women have. Unfortunately, that "spidey sense" that tingles is usually right.

I finally stand up because I need to end this conversation. "Well, this has been a lovely discussion but I have to go. Apparently, I have a roommate now so I need to straighten up. Thanks again for the beer and for taking care of that video."

"No problem. Thanks for coming by and taking the rest of his stuff." She gives me a hug, which feels good, but there is no need for me to linger.

"Are these the only bags?" I point to the three duffle bags by the staircase. She nods and I pick them up. They are heavier than they look. "Jesus, what the hell are in these?"

"That is all his shit I assume he will need, sneakers, DVDs, and games." I walk out the door and reply with a sarcastic "Thanks." I pack the car and I notice she's still in the doorway.

I wave before I get into the driver's seat. Then she says, "Check out those other videos of my Yoga class. If you know anyone who is interested please let me know. I would love to have more business."

SEVEN

The one thing about owning a home is the large amounts of work that always needs to be done. I wanted to get home in enough time to take care of a few things and then call Zenia. Of course, things never seem to go as planned. I wanted to get some laundry done because I just assume that Frank will have tons of clothes to wash this weekend. I discovered that the belt of the dryer snapped when I used it the other day. The wet clothes that were in the dyer just sat there for days and the smell was rank.

This of course led to me going out, once again, to get a dryer belt. I have never done this before, so I can thank God for Google. I'm in my basement installing the dryer belt with my laptop on the washing machine and a half eaten Quarter Pounder with fries next to it when my phone rings. I stand up and reach for my phone in my back pocket. It's Zenia. Damn, what time is it? It's 8:30 pm.

I answer the phone. "Hey there, I was just about to call you!" Which was partially true, I would have done it if it weren't for this damn dryer. "Hello Señor, I figured you were going to call me eventually, but I know how caught up you get with work." Her voice sounds so good to me right now. I missed her sexy voice and of course, how could I forget how about well she knows me.

I smile, "I wouldn't say I got caught up too much…"

"Uh huh."

"…But I was in the middle of fixing my dryer…"

"Oh, so I'm disturbing you?"

"…No! Not at all, I was confirming that I might have been caught up…"

"I see, I can always call back later, you know."

"Oh will you stop it?" I laugh. She is fucking with me as she normally does. This is a promising sign of us at least having a friendship. That last time we spoke she was very cold. Most of her statements were just short and matter of fact. I was certain that we would never speak again.

"How have you been?" She asks after a little chuckle.

"I've been good. Just working a lot and surviving."

At this point I don't know how to respond to this question. The truth of the matter is, I think about her every day. I have this belief that everything I've done over the last several months has been to distract me from the fact that I'm not with her.

"How are you doing?" I ask

"I am well. I left my old job and I just got a new one."

"That is wonderful. Where do you work now?"

She explains that she is now working for a new start up

technology firm where she gets to do what she does best, designing web sites. The last job she had was a miserable experience for her. Her boss sucked, her co-workers sucked and the whole experience was something she didn't want to live through again.

During our break, she managed to find a new job, which I did hear about, but I will keep that to myself. It isn't that I have been keeping tabs on her (although she does seem to tweet a lot), it's the fact that we share some of the same friends and they have little trouble telling me about her. For example, I knew that she was dating this guy named Peter for a few weeks. I never knew what he looked liked and I never cared, but I did feel the full weight of what her dating another man meant and it wasn't fun.

"So what has made you so busy these days? I was starting to think that you were ignoring me." I find it very hard to say no to her and lying is equally as hard. But I figure that if we really do have a viable friendship or relationship down the road, then certain things will have to go unsaid until later.

"Frank was kicked out his house and he now lives with me."

"What? What happened? Did he cheat on this wife? Wait, did she cheat on him? I need details." Zenia has always loved gossip. So the fact that she seemed excited is not surprising to me.

"No, nothing like that. Actually, its much less than that. She found his weed stash underneath his Xbox 360."

"That's it? That's whack," She asked in such disbelief.

"Yup, she told him that she had had enough of his shit. Apparently, he smokes too much."

"I see," She says. I can tell that she is being skeptical.

"What is it?" I say with a snicker.

"I think she just wants to fuck. No woman is going to just kick out her husband because he smokes too much fucking weed. That is ridiculous. Although, maybe he can't get it up anymore!"

"Wow...I don't think..."

"Please, if he smokes *that* much weed I'm betting he is completely useless. She just wants to fuck. I'm telling you, a woman has needs."

"Well she did tell me that she needed to have fun."

"She told you that? Wait. You spoke to her?" I can tell she is having fun with this now, although, I may need to change the subject soon.

"Um, I was there today picking up Frank's stuff and we had a conversation about it"

"Really? I wouldn't be a bit surprised if she wants you."

"Oh come on, that is Frank's wife. Please," I say this trying to dismiss this possibility. Zenia and I have had this conversation before. Her belief is that most women cannot be trusted. This is not to say that men can be trusted because history has proven that we cannot. According to her, men are weak. A fact that I hate to admit but I don't have much of a leg to stand on considering everything that has taken place. Somehow I refuse to believe that there is something about me that women find all that attractive, especially considering that before Vera it had been months since I had been with a woman.

"Well, I'm just giving you friendly advice that you need to be careful. The truth of it all is that you are not a bad guy. As much as you like to beat yourself up about things, you are a catch. Any woman would be able to see that. Even her." Her saying this is starting to make me think that perhaps we can be friends. I would be lying if I said I didn't want more, but at this point I will take what I can get.

"But, not you." I feel the need to say this. It was more of a statement rather than a question.

"I never said that. I just don't think we are good for each other."

This is what I was afraid of. Our hiatus from each other has brought her to this conclusion. I would have hoped that we would've been able to rekindle something, but I guess that its true what my boys have told me, *you never make the mistress your girlfriend.* I suppose that it was never meant to work. I can still hope for something but I doubt it will work.

I can't help but not say anything after her remark, which makes for a brief awkward silence until I say, "I think we have a difference of opinion on this but, I'm glad we're still friends." I smile because after all we have been through I can live with this for a while.

"Louis, I really didn't mean for this call to be awkward. I called because I miss you in my life. With all the things that have gone on with me going from one job to another, I ended up missing the one person that I used to talk to that never judged me for the random crazy shit that I say or do. When it comes down to it, you ended up being one of my closest friends and I really don't want to lose that."

I'm shocked at this point. I never expected that response. "I've missed you too. It was hard to deal with things once we stopped speaking. I felt like a void somewhere in my life. I thought that I would get over it, but I didn't."

We begin to reminisce about the past, how we met, and how it all went wrong. In the back of my head I keep thinking about that guy she was dating. After about an hour, we finally get around to speaking about him. This guy, Peter, was not her type. I knew that, but it felt good to hear her say that. They went on a few dates but she didn't care for him or his fraternity.

Actually her indifference about him makes me smile on several fronts. While this is not the first guy she has attempted to date during the time that she has known me, she keeps finding men that are just not right for her. It makes me think that perhaps she is sabotaging herself. It makes me think there is hope for us.

EIGHT

I never told anyone about the first time I kissed Zenia, but the thing about hanging with my cousin is that after about the fourth beer, we will tell any and all stories. The best part about tonight is that we are at this new club that has Latino Night on Fridays and with all the shit that has happened with me lately, I just need to get away and be with my people. Of course, Ruben wants to know the story so I just tell them from the best perspective I can remember:

I'm not sure of the exact moment I fell in love with her, but when she walked into my office with that smile, I fight to keep myself from melting in my chair. She wore this black jacket that was about waist length and accentuated her body so well. When she took it off only to reveal she had no bra on, I knew that she would be irresistible. I found her to be so very beautiful in every way and yet her sex appeal was something I could barely handle.

We had been flirting for far too long, so we both knew and felt how strong the attraction was. Text messages and chat conversations can only do so much to mask our intentions. Because of our busy schedules, I never had the chance to seduce her in the way I wanted. It didn't help that I never felt this way for anyone, which made me very apprehensive. She did tell me she would be stopping by and it was something I was thinking about all day with anticipation.

It was very apparent that she knew I wanted her and she was going to play this out to her advantage. Her breasts were the perfect size. Not too big and not too small and very nicely accentuated by a nipple ring on her left breast. Through her white shirt, it peeked out like the silhouette of ecstasy. In fact, her shirt read: KISS ME, I am LATINA. She smiled at me as she sat down on the chair across my desk. She had me speechless and she knew it.

"Hold on…" Ruben interrupts. He takes swig of his Corona then continues. "…I know I told you to give me details but really? Why are you telling the story like that?"

I give him a look that basically says *fuck you*. He laughs. "Can I finish the story please?" He nods.

I was scared. I was at work and I didn't want to get into trouble. She had been to my office dozens of times in the past and even though we maintained a certain level of professionalism, I knew this day would be different. I was nervous because I wasn't sure if I could contain myself any longer. I had hidden my feelings from her for such a long time and I was starting to not care anymore about who would know.

I never told her exactly how I felt about her. In fact, I tried my best to be oblivious to the possibility I could be in love with her. We both did our best to concentrate on the obvious lust that we had for each other. Any talk beyond that seemed to be ignored by both of us.

I wanted to make love to her on my desk. I imagined this moment in my mind before. I would get up and just grab her from her seat. I would savagely pull off that shirt of hers in between lustful kisses we shared and pull down those tight jeans only to see that she is also very much commando. I would grab her breasts and kiss her neck. I can smell her perfume and it was intoxicating. But then, I realized that I'm daydreaming and I need to do something!

"Jesus man. Get to the fucking good part already. Did she suck your dick in your office or what? Technically, that's what

I asked...I'm not even sure why you giving me this extra shit,"
Ruben says...interrupting, yet again.

"Wow. Somehow you are related to me. Let me finish
dude."

*I finally spoke in hopes that she didn't realize that I was
fanaticizing. I asked her how her day was and I tried to keep my eyes on
hers. She replied that she was having a great day but there was something
that she needed to do, something that would make her day complete. I
wasn't really sure what she was referring to, but then, with a seemingly
devilish smile, she asked me if there was something on my mind.*

*At this point, I can see her nipples practically coming out of her shirt.
Her shirt was thin enough that I can make out their brown round shape
as well as the slightly metallic color of her piercing. I knew that it was cold
in my office and if I ever needed evidence of that, it was staring right at me.
It became almost uncomfortable for me to sit straight. Perhaps she knew I
was thinking incredibly bad thoughts of her being naked in my office.
Then it could also be that I was starting right at her breasts.*

*She regained my attention by alerting me that her eyes were on her
face. Then she asked me if I liked her shirt. I blushingly apologized and
nodded. I told her that I had so much on my mind due to work related
issues. I really wasn't all that embarrassed but I wasn't trying to objectify
her either. I had to divert my eyes to the computer screen instead and
pretend to read e-mails. She happily tells me that she went to the gift shop
today. I watched her reach into her bag and pull out a smaller bag of
Hershey's Kisses.*

*She knew I had a sweet tooth. I can work hard all day and not pay
attention to some of the things I eat. But, at the end of the day, I always
loved to have a piece of chocolate to sooth the nerves. So there she was with
a whole bag of them. She opened the bag and asked me if I would like a
kiss. She smiled yet again, but this time she had her tongue ring between
her teeth. This was something that she did to drive me crazy. I can hear
the noise her ring made as she gently slid it across her teeth.*

"You fucking dog! She has a tongue ring? I didn't even know that. You know what they say about women with tongue rings right?" Ruben clearly loves to interrupt me.

"Enlighten me" I say. I already knew what they say. But I wanted to hear him say it.

"Two words. Orally. Fixated. You know what? I'm not even surprised. These chicks love niggas like you. You dark skinned, so they just assume you're black…"

"…Um I kinda am…" I try to interrupt him

"…And you've always, historically, found women that love to give you head. So I'm not surprised by this."

"Dude! This is my future wife we might be talking about! Can I continue?"

"Global Warming is now a potential future wife? Pffft Go right ahead."

Anyway, my heart started racing as I sat back in my chair and looked at her. I smiled nervously and nodded. She got up and closed my office door. The jeans she wore seemed so blue to me, as if she instantly brought the color out in anything she had on. She turned around and smiled at me again. I got a full view of her standing in from of me and I had to look her up and down. She had to know what her smile does to me because I bit my bottom lip. She has such a genuine smile that I have never encountered before. She can disarm me with one glance and a flash of those teeth.

She slowly walked around my desk and I asked her nervously what she was doing. She quietly hushed me with a gentle "shhh" and placed her finger across my lips. I begin to shake in nervousness. What if someone hears us? What if someone suspects what's going on behind this closed door? All thoughts, clearly irrational, but made all the sense in the world.

Perhaps I was not ready for this.

She sat at the edge of my desk and I can feel those dark brown eyes looking into my soul as she asked me if she makes me nervous. I chuckled and denied such a thing even though I can clearly see my hands shaking. She gently unwrapped the foil from the kiss and asked if I was sure that I wanted one. I said, "yes" ever so softly.

She held the unwrapped kiss in her fingers and she put it in her mouth. I felt a slight wave of relief. Perhaps she was playing a game and I didn't have to do something that I was so afraid to do. Maybe she will go back to that chair and I can admire her from a far like I should. Then she leaned over and our lips met.

Her lips were as soft as I had remembered during our ever so brief encounter. We had kissed before but it an awkward first kiss that required a do over. I was so anxious to kiss her the first time that when I leaned in, she wasn't expecting it. I felt rather embarrassed by it. But this time, this kiss was special. I closed my eyes and enjoyed her affection.

"I call bullshit!" Ruben exclaims

"What? Why?"

"Nigga, you told me that this was a story about your first kiss with her and now you just said that you kissed before. What the fuck is that about? Did you miss her lips the first time?"

"No! It was just awkward. I don't want to talk about it."

"Oh! Now you don't want to talk about it. You giving me all this other extra Romeo shit but you can't tell me how you missed her lips? Continue!"

I felt her body on mine as she was now sitting on my lap, on my chair. I can taste the chocolate that was in her mouth as she pushes half of the kiss with her tongue into my mouth. The sweet taste of chocolate with the gentle touch of her tongue against mine was enough to give me goose bumps up and down my arms.

She bites my lip as she pulls way and we both begin to chew on our shared pieces. I just stared at her admiring her beauty and her energy. A part of me cannot believe that she is actually sitting on my lap. I stroke her long black hair and I realize this is exactly what I wanted to happen. I also notice that I'm not shaking anymore.

She asks me if I would like another one. This time, I responded in a confident manner. This time we both lean toward each other. This time we both share a kiss that only lovers share. This time I'm in love and I cannot fight it.

"Dude, you are so fucking corny" Ruben says. We both laugh.

"What do you mean?" I ask as I take another swig of beer.

"You tell this story like you are a fucking artist and shit."

Ruben and I have known each other for years. We grew up together. We have seen our family fall apart and put itself back together. The two of us are like brothers. He is one of the few people that I can tell absolutely anything to.

"It's better than any story you can come up with," I say

"You wish. I get to the fucking point when I tell you shit. You tell this story like you planning on writing it or something."

"Well that's not really the point." The truth is I really did write this story down. I just never did anything with it. "Besides, when have you ever gotten to the point in telling me something?" I ask him.

"Are you serious? What about that story I told you about Nina?"

"Which one was Nina again?"

"Come on dude, that bad ass Indian girl with the bad ass body?"

"Nope. Doesn't ring a bell." I'm definitely fucking with him because I do remember Nina. This was a great looking woman that he never really dated but they had many nights of great sex that apparently he will never forget. Nina was also one of the reasons why him and Janice broke up, so it is hard to forget.

"You gotta be fucking with me right now." He is almost smiling

"Maybe your storytelling made her forgettable."

"Oh fuck you!" He laughs

We joke around and I begin to look for the waitress. I ask him if he's hungry and he just nods his head. Like a couple of dorks we got here early so we can get a table. Usually we just talk shit and drink most of the night. If we meet a woman, that's cool. If we don't, then we are perfectly fine with that too. Besides, Ruben is seeing this older chick and she rocks his world.

"Where is our waitress?" I say a bit frustrated. My eyes scan across the crowd and then I see this woman in a red dress with an amazing body. She is on the dance floor dancing salsa. I think this is one of Frankie Negron's new songs. The guy she's dancing with seems to be barely keeping up with her rhythm but I'm not entirely sure who is leading whom. I can't help but notice her red pumps, as her footwork is something to behold. Her long brown hair seems to also have a rhythm of its own.

"Ruben, check out this chick on the dance floor." He turns around and we are both looking at her. "Wow that woman has some crazy moves." Reuben says. The dance floor gets a bit more crowded and we lose sight of her.

"Oh, well. I need to make a phone call. Order me another Corona," Ruben says as he gets up.

"I'm gonna to head to the bar. I have no idea where our waitress is," I say. I head over the bar and I'm feeling pretty good. The bar area is packed. I almost have to fight my way to get through. Then by the time I get to where the bartender can see me, it becomes a game of trying to get his attention. I begin to get annoyed that a bar like this seems to always have two bartenders working on either side to handle what seems to be a shit load of people. I pull out my phone and tweet my frustration about overcrowded bars and understaffed bartenders.

Just as I'm about to get the bartender's attention, I feel a tap on my shoulder. I turn around and it is Lidia...in a stunning low cut red dress. "Hey there," I say as try no to look at her breasts. I'm really not that sure how big they are and it could possibly be the four beers that make them appear larger than what they really are.

She greets me with a "Heeeey!" as she hugs me. Lidia asks me what I'm doing at this club and I explain to her that Ruben and I decided to come here on a hunch. Apparently this is her new favorite place and she is with her friends. She saw me walk by the dance floor as I headed to the bar.

"I think you should dance with me," she says and before I can protest she is pulling me with both hands onto the dance floor. I tried to tell her that I really just want another beer and that Ruben would probably want one too, but the words get lost as Marc Anthony is blaring over the speakers. Lidia puts my right arm around her waist and grabs my left hand and just begins to lead this dance.

I try my best to keep up with her and the rhythm. This is where I realize those beers are not my friends. There is a combination of being inebriated and having a semi-full bladder that makes my movements less fluid than I would like them to be. My only saving grace is that I know this song, *Vivir Mi Vida*. I get away with a few twists here and a spin there. She is smiling and is having a blast seemingly showing me up. I try to ignore that her tits are just about hanging out of her dress. She's not wearing a bra.

I thank God when the song ends because my legs are aching and I really need to use the bathroom. She claps when the song is over and asks if I want to dance again. "No, I'm good. Thanks! I need to get back to Ruben anyways," I say just about out of breath. She invites me over to the table where her girls are sitting.

I get back to Ruben. He's sitting at the table smiling at me. He has his beer and he got me one too. "So, I leave you alone for 5 minutes and you are dancing with the woman in the red dress. Very nicely done," he says as he lefts up his bottle to toast me. I tap his beer bottle with mine and before I take a gulp I say. "We know her. That's Frank's wife."

Ruben almost breaks his neck as he turns around looking for her. "That's Lidia? Who the fuck knew she had a body like that?"

"Well, Frank did apparently," I reply.

"And yet he let that woman kick him out. That must have

been some good ass weed."

"She asked us to go join her and her friends."

"Did she? How do her friends look?"

"I dunno. I never met them. She does strike me as the type to have busted friends though. Besides, what do you care? Aren't you are seeing someone?"

"I am dating someone, nothing exclusive yet. It's been three dates. Anyways, I can look."

"Whatever man."

"So are we going to join them or what? It seems like you're thinking about this."

I was thinking about it. I doubt it's a good idea. The only reason Frank is not with us is because he had to work late. I suppose I could keep an eye on her for him. "Sure, we can go. But WE are only looking."

Ruben replies, "Sounds like a plan."

NINE

We make a quick stop to the men's room. I needed to break the seal in such a bad way. The men's room in this place is pretty dirty so I don't idle too long. I'm starting to feel the effects of my fifth beer. I suppose I should've grabbed something to eat before we got here, but I wasn't really hungry then. I wash my hands and I look at myself in the mirror. I want to ask myself if I really know what I'm doing.

I can't help but hear Zenia tell me that she doesn't think that she and I are right for each other. If she did truly mean that then why should I really care about I do? I'm a single man again! Besides, I'm sure one of Lidia's busted friends may not look so bad.

We leave the bathroom and then cross the dance floor to get to the area where they are. This huge black man dressed all in black, stands in front of a roped off area. Apparently she is in the VIP section. I look at Ruben and ask him just how in the world does she get this type of treatment? "Must be the dress," he replies. I don't even want to ask this man to let us in. His black shirt says STAFF on it and he just looks like the Black Hulk. What happens when he's not angry? Does he turn less black? I guess I said this out loud because Ruben is laughing hard.

Before I can say anything Lidia walks up behind him and says a few words while pointing at my cousin and me. "Please step in gentlemen." He says as he unhinges the red velvet rope from the pole. I can feel his gaze. I make the quick assumption that he is not finding me funny at all. "Thank you Ramsey," she says while giving him a smile. We walk into this area that is slightly raised above the rest of the club. There are couches in the area, most of which are full.

"So you get the royal treatment in this place, huh?" I ask as she leads us into a rounded off booth.

"The owner owes me a few favors, so me and the girls cashed in," she replies. The rounded booth consists of what seems to be two sectional couches with a raised round table in front of them. This would be a good place for drinks or possibly having dinner if you wanted to. Both couches have people sitting on them, yet there seems to be room for others. She slowly introduces us to her four girls, though none of their names I seem to remember. Some of them are cute so it may not be a total loss. I can simply ask for their names again and blame it on the music being loud for my lapse in memory.

Ruben sits at the other couch with three of Lidia's friends while I sit right in between her and one of her other friends. She insisted that I sit in the middle because she likes to get up to dance and doesn't want to keep pushing her way out of the seat. There are four of us sitting on this couch. The two people to my immediate left seem to be into their own thing. One of her friends apparently found this guy and they are too engrossed in their conversation to talk to me. In fact, the only time they seem to look up is when the waitress comes by.

I order my sixth beer while the waitress puts down Lidia's drink. I asked her what she's drinking and she tells me a vodka tonic water. She offers me some and I decline, I'm not a fan of tonic. I haven't been able to judge how drunk she is as of yet.

"So where's Frank?" she asks.

"I invited him, but he has to work."

"Of course he does, he always *has* to work." She takes a healthy sip from the straw. "I can't tell you how many times he would come home late from work. Mind you, I know that he was never cheating on me, but come on, no overtime pay?"

"Yeah well, such is the life of a salaried employee," I say as I look around this place. It's pretty dark in here. My eyes have adjusted and now I can really see what could make this place so successful. Fake candles in a glass as the centerpieces gives this a whole place a certain brothel kind of feel that I can't put my finger on.

"Didn't Raina notice when you came home late?"

"Well at first she did, but once she started working for the university she got a better idea of why I always worked so late."

"Really? So tell me why would your work week be more than 40 hours when that is all you are getting paid for?"

"That's really simple. Student Affairs is a 24-hour job and I've come to accept that. The lives of these kids don't stop when I'm out of the office." After my statement Lidia remains silent. I can almost see that she is trying to come up with a response, but she can't. Although, she might be just as trashed as I am, maybe worse.

"So tell me why are you still single? I can't believe that after what I've heard about you that it could possible for you to not have a woman. Do you think any of my friends are cute?"

That is way too much going on in one statement right now. I look around. "Your friends aren't bad looking, but the one over my shoulder over here seems to like this dude. And the three over there seem thoroughly entertained by my cousin." As I look over they all seem to be laughing and he is animated as always.

Lidia's friends are really not bad looking. Sometimes you hear about how women may hang out with other women who are not as attractive so they can get all the attention. This is really not the case. Of course, Lidia is the best looking out of all of them, but the three women that Ruben is hanging with are bangin'. If I had to guess, I would say three of these women are either Black or Latina. The one sitting next to me is white. Of course, there really is no way to tell. Latinas come in all colors, shapes, and sizes. It is those shapes and sizes that Ruben loves right now.

I look over to Lidia. "What have you heard about me?"

"Well, I probably shouldn't tell you this but I am rather curious. I heard you have a big dick." She says this so matter of fact that it throws me off guard.

"What? Who would tell you that?"

"Raina told me." At this point I'm shocked. I have no idea whether to believe her. Not to mention, this line of discussion is turning me on. It's not everyday that a woman tells me they've heard about or even discussed my penis.

"There is no way she would've told you that." The waitress comes by with my beer and I welcome it. One thing this conversation needs is more beer.

"How can you be so sure that she didn't? Women do talk you know. I mean, I think she was just jealous that you gave it to that young girl."

I am speechless. I truly do not know what to say and that is when I felt it, her hand on my crouch. I try to adjust myself. I look over to Ruben but he is not even paying attention to me. "What are you doing?" I ask. She gives me this devilish grin. "You never confirmed what I heard, so I figured I would see for myself and I must say she is definitely not lying about you."

"I'm pretty sure that Frank would not appreciate this."

"I agree, he probably wouldn't, but guess what? Frank hasn't fucked me in weeks and I don't appreciate that. Besides, it's not like I have my lips around it, unless you want that."

This is getting bad pretty fast. I feel her unzip my pants and insert her hand. I can feel my heart beating hard in my chest. There is this sensation that is surreal coming over my body that can only be described as the moment you recognize that what's happening is wrong, but you enjoy it anyway. I lean back because now she literally has me by the balls. I can feel myself pulsating in her hand as she slowly strokes me rhythmically up and down.

"So what are we going to do about this? You can't deny at this moment that your penis is enjoying my hand. I will do you a favor and do most of the talking right now. I know you're Frank's good friend and you would pretty much do anything for him. But, I need you to do something for me," She says this very slowly. I look around to see if anyone could possibly be watching any of this. Ruben is too busy flirting to even look in my general direction. Before I know it, he gets up with one of the ladies to go to the dance floor. The couple next to me is now making out.

She continues with a very consistent hand motion. "What I want you to do for me is to become my lover. We don't have to do it all the time. But, I have been very curious about you. I see you walking around thinking you are a big deal at work with your sweater vests and your suits. I bet all those college girls want to take off their panties for you."

I muster up enough willpower to respond, "I wouldn't go that far." At this point, all my willpower has gone into making sure I do not cum all over her hand. Although, I'm starting to think she wouldn't mind if that happened. "Are you enjoying this as much as I am right now?" she asks.

"I think you know that I am," I say. She stops her hand movement as her friend on my left gets up with the guy she is with. They get up and motion that they will be right back. "Well it looks like our friends at our table are gone but you are very lucky that I care about my reputation in this place, otherwise I may have to do something you're craving for." She's getting even bolder as she speaks because she pulls it out through my unzipped pants fly. Thank God the tablecloth is still covering much of what's happening here.

Her friends at the other table start talking to her about some guy that is texting one of them. They scream over the tables without getting up and all the while she maintains the same steady hand motion. Every so often she will stop and that will allow me to regain my composure and also take a drink from my beer. At one point she looks down at it and then looks at me. "I just wanted to see it because I have feeling we are going to know each other quite well." Lidia runs her fingers across the head, which makes her fingers wet with the pre-cum. She then removes her hand and subtly licks her finger. Lidia smiles and dips her finger into her vodka tonic and stirs.

"You're a fucking freak, you know that?" I say it almost accusingly, but more in an impressed way.

"Oh, this coming from a man that is letting his friend's

wife jerk him off at a club." Lidia can be very quick witted and I have no real answer for that.

"You're right." I start to put it away when she grabs it again.

"I'm not done with you." She begins to stroke me with her hand again. "I could just make you explode right here, right now but I'm not gonna to do that because then you would be of no use to me later. So, what's going to happen is that I'm gonna to take you home and ride this fabulous dick for as long as I want."

"Why would I let you do that?" I ask.

"Because I will let you cum wherever you want. Just name it. My tits, my ass, or my face." Once again she has shocked me. I just gaze at her as she puts my penis back inside my pants. The waitress comes over with two trays of shots and Ruben comes right behind her, "Shots for everyone!" All of her friends are now coming back into the VIP section. I try to zip up my pants without anyone noticing, but I catch Ruben looking at me with a smug look on his face. I raise my middle finger during the commotion.

We all take a shot of what I think is tequila and I chase it down with my Corona. I start really feeling the effects of the all the drinks. I tell her that I need to use the men's room. I walk past everyone and out of the VIP area. I smile at the Black Hulk as I walk by. I wonder if he would be mad if I called him Bulk? He might not like that. Right now, I'm not sure what's really happening now, my main focus it to make it to the bathroom without tripping or bumping into anyone. The amount of concentration just to do this is high. It also keeps me from thinking about what just happened at that table.

I finally make it across the club and through a sea of

people. The line for the urinals is minimal and once I finally release it takes everything in me not to moan. I've always wondered how much liquid a human body can hold in its bladder because for a time it seemed like I could not stop pissing. I zip up and stumble over to the sink and wash my hands.

"Yo! What was that all about? You got Lidia to blow you?!?"

I have no idea when Ruben walked in. I explained to him that she basically jerked me off at the table. When he asked me what I'm going to do I just simply replied that I didn't know. She did a good job of getting me going, but going home with her would mean crossing a line that I'm not sure I want to cross. On the other hand, Frank may never know. What she's promising is a steady amount of sex, which is hard to turn down at this point in my life.

"I don't know what to tell you man. I mean, I'm an asshole for sure and I've done my fair share of fucked up shit, but even this would be tough for me too. I can't. I wouldn't do it, but damn her body is just ..." This was Ruben's best attempt at advice. Fuck it. I straighten myself up, dry my hands, and in my best attempt at appearing to be to sober I say, "I'm just gonna go out there and tell her that I won't fuck her."

I walked past Ruben. He laughs and pats me on the back "Good luck with that."

I fight the sea of people again to finally get to the VIP area and I see Lidia with her friends. "You ready to go Papi?" she asks and I turn around to see Ruben hugging some of her friends. "I didn't pay my bill yet." I say.

"Don't worry about it. Once the manager knew you were with us, he took care of it." She puts her arm around mine and we proceed towards the exit.

"Look, I don't think this is a good idea. Frank and I are friends."

"Yes, I know you're friends and I can respect that very much. It makes it that much more endearing to be honest with you. But, let me tell you something." She pulls me in real close. "This will be the best pussy you will ever have. Just give me tonight. You can fill any hole you want. I promise I will make you forget all about Zenia."

The door opens and it's raining hard. Shit, none of us has an umbrella.

"Look, you stay here. I will get my car, it is not too far from here." I say. I look over to Ruben with a slight head gesture to come with me. I have no idea what time it is, but the line outside is still pretty full. There is a plethora of umbrellas everywhere.

"Don't you think you are a little drunk to be driving?" Lidia says.

I look at Ruben, "She has a good point," He says

"Well, how about we go flag a taxi?" I ask

"In Syracuse? How does that even work?" Ruben answers

"I'm sure we can get one! Come on. We'll be right back." Ruben and me begin to walk out in the rain.

"What happened to whole shit about you not fucking her?" Ruben asks with a smile

As we dodge people I quickly respond, "Shut it." We finally get to the corner and someone bumps into me hard. I almost lose my footing. I look up and it is Corey and he's smiling, "Hey Motherfucker." Before I can react I feel a blunt pain in my face and I fall to the ground.

It's raining a lot. I'm soaked and my face hurts. Was that Corey? Did he really just punch me in the face? I hear some commotion and I look up.

"Get up Motherfucker! You thought making fun of me was fucking funny huh? I told you I was gonna knock you on your ass!" Corey is yelling and I can see the crowd that was waiting on line to get into this club looking down at me. Some of the guys are laughing. Some of the women look concerned. I can see my cousin in the distance, but I think someone is holding him back.

"I said, get up!" He kicks me in the ribs. I try my best to hold in a yelp of pain. Now I'm gasping for air. The wind is knocked out of me for sure. I'm holding my side with one arm while trying to lift up myself up. My head is spinning from the alcohol and I feel like there is water everywhere. I may need to fight this dude and I've no clue how I'm going to do this.

I think I hear someone say to call the police. Another person asks what's going on. I can hear Ruben struggling and telling someone to let him go. "This asshole right here fucked my fiancé and I'm going to take it out on his ass," Corey yells. I crawl slowly through the puddles toward the nearest parked car. I try to use it as leverage to get up. Then I hear some girl say in a sarcastic tone, "It must take a big man to sucker punch a drunk guy." Other people chime in saying all kinds of things, in fact, there are some people telling Corey to kick my ass.

Corey grabs me with both hands and pulls me up and leans me against the car. He's looking me straight in my eyes. For a brief second I can see everyone in the rain. Two black dudes are holding my cousin back and it seems like the entire crowd is watching this from the barrier used for crowd control. "I don't see you laughing now? Is it funny?" He yells at me. I can feel his hot breath as I look away from him. I begin to struggle with him because he's holding me tight against the car. He punches me in the ribs while holding me up. I struggle to break free but the rain and the pain are not helping. He punches me again in the stomach. I do the only thing I can do. I head-butt him. Hard.

I feel a sharp pain in my forehead and I thought I heard a crack. Corey lets go of me to grab his face and I grab my forehead. I hear him screaming about his nose as I check for blood. I'm bleeding somewhere on my face. I can feel the pain from his punches. I'm finally stand up on my own and I look at Corey. I really do hope I broke his nose. I think about ending it right here but when I move I feel the pain in my ribs. His hands are still covering his face, so I kick him in the balls.

The crowd seems to just say "oooh" at the same time as Corey falls to his knees clutching his balls. His face is twisted with pain as I can see the rain mixed blood flowing from his nose. I stand over him and look around. The two guys let Ruben go and I can now see Lidia coming from behind them. "Let me tell you something Corey. Maybe if you're weren't such a fucking asshole sleeping with different white girls maybe, just fucking maybe, Vera wouldn't have felt the need to ride me the way she did."

Ruben and Lidia try to pull me away.

"I hope your fucking nose falls off, you fucking prick!" I begin to shout. The bouncers come out as the two guys who were holding Ruben back begin to pick up Corey from the ground.

"We need to get out of here. The owners have already called the police," Lidia says. Both of them help me limp away quickly from this scene. My car is a few blocks away. Luckily, Lidia was able to stash a small umbrella in her purse and it's coming in quite handy right now.

"Dude, you are bleeding a lot, are you ok? Do we need to take you to the hospital?" Ruben asks. I say no as I check my forehead. I can feel a nice little gash on my head where I banged into Corey's nose. Lidia reaches into her purse to give me some tissues to cover it. I press it against my forehead firmly.

"I'll be fine. What happened back there?" I ask Ruben

"I think those are his friends. When I saw that he just sucker punched you, I tried to run over but they grabbed me and said this was between you and him."

"I don't understand. How did he know I was here? I can hear the sirens in the distance.

"Sarah told him." Lidia responds

"Who the fuck is Sarah?" Both Ruben and I ask at the same time.

"She was the girl sitting next to us in the booth. She recognized you from a picture he sent her and she texted him that she was sitting right next to you."

I pull my car keys out of my pocket and give them to Ruben. "But I don't understand. How does she even know anything about me?"

"Sarah used to sleep with Corey."

Bingo. Now it all connects. She was woman that constantly had her back to me on the couch. I don't even remember what she looks like.

Ruben interjects, "Wait, so when did she tell you that she texted him?"

"She kinda bragged about it when you went to get the taxi. She knew he was waiting for you. By the time I got over there. You had head-butted him in the nose."

"This town is way too damn small," Ruben says as he opens the driver seat door and gets in the car.

Lidia stops me before we get in the car. "So, is it true that you fucked his woman?"

I nod. "Yeah, it's true." The car starts.

"I see. I guess you do have experience in fucking your friend's girlfriends."

"Corey was never my friend."

"Are you sure about that? I think you hurt his feelings."

"I'm quite sure."

"Did you debate fucking her half as much as you are debating about me?"

"I think we need to go."

I grab her umbrella and open the passenger side back door for her. I get in on the passenger side and slouch down in exhaustion. I barely have the strength to buckle my seat belt. I can see the lights from the police cars pulling up to the club. I close my eyes as Ruben pulls away.

I just feel...like...passing...out.

TEN

I hate the fact that I can't go into work but I've been sick for the past three days. It should come as no surprise that I caught a cold from being in a rain-soaked fight with Corey. I'm still wearing a Band-Aid in the middle of my forehead and my ribs are sore. Other than that, I guess I can consider myself lucky for not having a concussion.

After I passed out, Ruben took me to the Emergency Room. It turns out that I have minor scrapes and bruises, but no concussion. The doctors suggested that perhaps I shouldn't drink so much. Ruben convinced the nurses I simply fell. There was no sign of Corey there, so who knows what happened to him. I spent the last few days pretty much on the couch feeling like shit. Frank hasn't been much help other than being someone to talk to. I told him about what happened last Friday night but conveniently left out the fact that his wife gave me a hand job in the club.

Very few people know that I got into a fight a few days ago and I would like to keep it that way. In a weird way being sick has been a blessing so that I do not have to go outside looking the way I do. It looked even worse on Saturday because of the welt on my head where he punched me.

Amazingly I have had people to chat with online, particularly Zenia. I did tell her about my issues with Corey and my involvement with Vera. She didn't seem to be too bothered about my affair with Vera. She was more concerned about my general well being.

Lidia hit me up on Facebook a few times. Surprisingly, she kept our conversations relatively PG. She was there at the hospital with Ruben and me. She ended up not staying the entire time, but she was there. One of her friends was able to pick her up and take her home. For the most part Lidia was making sure I was ok. I'm sure somewhere in her mind she must think that she's not done with me.

I've had the last several days to reflect on everything. They say that everything happens for a reason and I think that this fight may have saved me from making an even bigger mistake by sleeping with Lidia. I'm pretty sure that if I had not bumped into Corey, I would've had sex with her. I guess the real question is what am I going to do now?

Currently there is nothing I can do right now other than to try and get over this cold. I've already seen Sportscenter for the third straight time and I'm unwilling to change the channel. Sleeping is not an option because I have done that too much as it is. So I do the only thing I can do at this point, go on Facebook. The first thing I do is to update my status: *at home sick :(*

I check my email and I noticed that I got some emails from my dad. Since he has been retired he has had nothing but time on this hands. He is a retired firefighter that has spent more than 30 years in action. He was one of the lucky men that were able to get out of towers at the World Trade Center before it came down. I've thanked God just about every day that he's still alive. Unfortunately he contracted a rare form of cancer that was treatable due to the clean-up efforts afterward.

My dad has been retired for about 11 years now and he has the ability to send emails whenever he wants and watch TV all the time thanks to his DVR. I open up one of the emails with the subject line "For you." The message says: *I just found these the other day. I scanned them. Enjoy. Love Papi.* There are 4 attachments. I open each one up and they are old pictures of when I was a child. The first picture is me and my older brother standing next to each other with FDNY sweaters on. Another one is a picture is Ruben and me in our old backyard pool. The third picture is of my dog, Rocky and me. The last one is a picture with my dad sitting with his feet in the pool and me standing next to him. He is holding me. This has always been my favorite picture of the two of us. I must have been around 4 or 5 years old.

I have always been close with my dad ever since the divorce several years ago. My parents had a messy break up that has affected me for most of my young adult life. It really came down to me making a choice between my mother and my father. New York State law allows a kid at the age of 16 to be able to choose custody. I could've gone six months with either parents and live a life of constant upheaval. But, instead, I chose a to live with my dad because I had a deep desire to be my own man.

I still would've became a man while living with my mother, but all the smothering and trying to keep me close made it hard for me to deal with life. When I was a teenager, my lack social status made the bullying in my life almost unbearable. I had no idea how to talk to girls, much less how to act in front of them. I was polite and I smiled but to talk to one? I could never do that.

This is not to say that I didn't love my mother. I think the divorce brought out a very unpleasant side of her. At the time I needed parents that were going to support me rather than destroy each other. Unfortunately for her, I felt that a powerful woman was suffocating my life as young man. Things were said over the years and we drifted apart. Every so often I will talk to my brother and he would update me on the family. I do know that at some point I will need to reconcile with her because she's not getting any younger. Also, I have come to learn that every relationship with a woman has been affected by the lack of a relationship with my mom.

I stare at these pictures thinking about my childhood. Life was so much easier back then. Girls were not apart of my life because I never thought they liked me. It was bad enough that the other boys picked on me in school, but when the girls made it seem that I was too dorky for them, I withdrew into comic books and video games. It was because my fear of girls that I decided to go an all boys high school in the Bronx. I felt like they would have been a distraction to me. I think that I just needed to not be reminded that I wasn't the ladies man that my dad wanted me to be. It wasn't until college that I got my first girlfriend, Isabel. My father was so proud of this moment. He responded with, "I'm just glad you didn't go fag on me."

Of course, once he met her he didn't care for her. Isabel was my first love and my first major heartbreak. It took me two years too many to get over her. When we broke up, I called him to tell him what happened. He could hear the pain in my voice. I remember the tone in his voice saying, "Son, it will be ok. I understand what you're going through. I've been there." It took everything that I had within me not to break down over the phone. It was at that moment that my father and I became as close as we are now.

I told myself that after Isabel, no one else would hurt me. No matter what happens or who I'm with, I will always get mine. Of course, fast forward fifteen years later and I'm in this situation. I suppose I never let go of that philosophy. My marriage didn't even last 8 years. For as long as I had been with

Raina, I felt like I was still looking for something. My constant flirting with women online was hurting my relationship. I would try to stop but it would only get worse. I never told her about the two women I ended up sleeping with. It wasn't until Zenia came into my life that she really saw that I was no longer interested in saving our marriage.

Raina always seemed to know there was something going on with Zenia. Her "spidey sense" was kicking into overdrive even when there was nothing going on. She had seen a glance that we shared during an event at the student union. I didn't pay much attention to it, but Raina thought Zenia was giving me the bedroom eyes. I played it off. A month later Zenia and I would get hot and heavy in her apartment.

I finally admitted that something had happened a year later. I only admitted to kissing her. That night that Raina interrogated at like 3:30 am, I felt like one of those suspects that police berate in order to get a confession. Raina cried all night when I told her about the kiss. I wasn't about to tell her that I was seeing Zenia three times a week. I wasn't going to admit to her that I was putting fake meetings in my outlook calendar in order for me to leave my office and go see her.

I'll give it to her, Raina tried to save what we had. Somehow, she felt it was a good idea for us to have an open relationship where we dated other people if we chose to. I think she felt my obsession with other women, particularly Zenia, was just a phase. By this time Zenia had moved back to the city. Sure, we would still have a rendezvous whenever we could, but it was Raina that really started to let loose. The big guy she is with now, Kevin (that is his name, right?) is boyfriend number four. I know deep inside that I'm an asshole for categorizing some of these dudes as her boyfriend but it's a way of keeping things in perspective or perhaps it's a way for me to punish myself.

I can't say that I blame her either. I've never judged any woman for the number of partners she's been with. We started out having rules of engagement, all of which were set by her. Neither of us could have encounters at the house. We were not to introduce our partners to family or friends. Protection had to be used at all times. One by one she slowly broke all these rules.

She had a pregnancy scare that turned out to be just that, a scare. The argument about that was epic, but I fought just hard enough to know that in some small way all of this was my fault. Then there was the time she introduced boyfriend number two to her dad. That was a great thing to see on Facebook and I was beside myself with the idea that she broke her own rule for the second time.

What really did it for me was the night I came home early from work from an event that had been cut short early. I saw a car in the drive way parked beside hers. At first, I was thinking that maybe Vera and Corey had come by, but something told me to park in front of my neighbor's house. I walked up slowly to the house and looked through the window. There they were naked on our old couch. Raina was bent over the side getting pounded by boyfriend number three. I watched for a few minutes then I left to catch a show at Adult World. I did mention this to her weeks later and the only response she had for me was, "Did you like what you saw?"

I hear the Facebook alerts kicking in. I look to see who is writing on my wall. A few co-workers post well wishes hoping that I feel better. Nothing to really think too much about, I'm starting to get hungry. I wonder if I have soup in the pantry. It's always funny how I never think about having soup in the house until I'm sick. The truth is I'm hardly ever sick so I never see the need for it. I think Frank eats soup, so there may be hope for me yet.

I manage to get up from the couch and walk over to the kitchen. I can still feel my sore ribs, damn that Corey! I open the pantry next to the fridge and begin my quest to find some soup. After about 2 minutes, I find nothing. This sucks, sore throat and no soup. I suppose that I could text Frank and ask him to pick up a can or two. I get back to the couch and I notice a few more messages. Judy posts on my wall that she hopes I feel better and my dad (yes, he's on Facebook too) posts, *Son, I hope you feel better.* I crack a little smile and remember that my dad has always raised me to be independent. I can survive this little cold of mine.

A chat message pops up. It's Lidia. Doesn't she work?

Lidia Muñoz-Pope: Hey Papi, how you feeling?

Louis Ortiz: Not well.

How did I get here again? Are we now at a point where she can just hit me up whenever? I have to give it up to this woman because she is quite persistent. I was hoping that I had dodged a bullet on Friday night.

Lidia Muñoz-Pope: I can't tell you how bad I still feel about Friday night.

Louis Ortiz: Bad? How?

Lidia Muñoz-Pope: About my friend, Sarah, calling that guy and you getting into a fight.

Louis Ortiz: It's really not your fault.

Lidia Muñoz-Pope: Now you're all sick. Is there anything I can do?

This has to be a loaded question. Is this where I say that I'm dying for some soup or does she take that as a sign that I want her to seduce me again? One thing that I remember the most about going over to Frank's was the fact that his wife can cook. There always seemed to be a plate of rice and beans waiting for me when I came by.

Louis Ortiz: I think I'll be ok. I have enough DayQuil to last me.

Lidia Muñoz-Pope: Are you sure? I made some *sancocho* last night. I have no problem dropping it by.

Here we go. Lets trap me with some food...and *sancocho* too? That is like making a soup and putting everything Puerto Rican in it and serving to me. She made it last night too? This must have been her intention all along. But this is an offer I can't refuse. This will be better than any can of soup that I can ask Frank to get from the store.

Louis Ortiz: Wow. You made *sancocho*? I don't want to get you sick though.

Lidia Muñoz-Pope: Get me sick? I will be ok. I'm just dropping off the soup not sucking you off.

She had to go there.

Louis Ortiz: SMH. What time are you coming by? I'm not sure if Frank's coming by for lunch.

Lidia Muñoz-Pope: What's he gonna do? Walk? Again, I'm just dropping off the soup. No worries.

Louis Ortiz: Well, I told him that he could borrow my car. So he can be here whenever.

Lidia Muñoz-Pope: I should be there in about an hour and a half. I put it in a nice big Tupperware.

I still don't trust her. I haven't been at full mental capacity since that night, but I should be able to fight her off if I had to. Besides, I'm sick so any sex appeal I have has got to be out of the window at this point. Of course the enormous amount of used tissues lying around won't help that cause either.

She signs off of chat and I wonder what I need to do next. At some point I need to clean this tissue mess up. It would be a decent thing to do when having visitors. She's going to have to deal with the t-shirt and pajama pants I have going on though. For shits and giggles, I decide to add another update on Facebook: *Of all the days not to have soup…but alas thanks to a friend, sancocho is on the way!*

All of a sudden I feel this need to just knock out, maybe I will nap for a minute. I close my laptop and drift off.

I dream of a better place that is serene, perhaps a place I have been to before. I can see a small dog running to me from a distance. It's my dog, Rocky, a Lhasa Apso. How I've missed him. He was one of the few living things in this world that has always loved me unconditionally and without regret. He leaps in to my arms happily as I rub his tan colored fur. I can smell his hot breathe as he licks my face and then nudges his head into my chest.

I blow in his face for fun and he barks. But, it doesn't sound like a regular bark. It sounds more like that of a familiar chime. Wait…is that my computer?

I open my eyes and I see a message from Frank.

Frank Pope: Yo! Is my wife coming over to give you soup??

Oh shit. This cannot be good. Best thing to do is just be honest.

Louis Ortiz: Yeah, she's dropping it off soon.

How did he know that she was coming over? Did she tell him? How long have I been out? I look at the time and I have only been asleep for twenty minutes.

Frank Pope: Fuck, dude I'm in trouble. I'm sorry, I know you're sick, but I need you to help me before she gets there.

Louis Ortiz: Sure dude. Did you leave some weed lying around?

Frank Pope: No. I need you to get rid of the girl in my room.

My jaw drops.

ELEVEN

Frank is the type of guy that never gets in trouble. Women know him as this teddy bear figure and guys know him as good dude that is cool with everyone. I suppose you can call him a gentle giant. No one expects anything out of the ordinary with him. Yet, his past with women suggests that he was always the friend. He was always so busy being the nice guy that he lost many women to men that were more aggressive. If the friend zone were a real place, he would be king. Personally, I think he smokes weed to dull some of the demons in his past, but I could be wrong about that.

That is why all of this comes as a complete shock to me. I've never seen Frank hit on a woman, much less hear him talk about how good looking one may be. Sure, he's had girlfriends in the past but I've never witnessed whatever magic he had going on with them. I have so many questions right now that I don't know whether to be proud of him or angry with him for putting me in this situation. In any case, I practically hack up a lung before I can respond.

Louis Ortiz: What? When did this happen?

Frank Pope: She's been there the whole weekend.

Louis Ortiz: The WHOLE Weekend? How did I miss this?

Frank Pope: Come on man, you're sick. I think today's the first day you left your room.

Louis Ortiz: Ok, you got me there. Who's the woman?

Frank Pope: Her name is Annette Tejada.

Louis Ortiz: Why does that name sound familiar to me? Is she a student? :-o

Frank Pope: Not at the university. She's Jessica's sorority sister.

Jessica is one of my best work-study students. She's in a Latina Sorority, which is why Annette's name sounds so familiar to me. But can it be the girl I'm thinking about? Frank pulled her? Word? Seriously? I cough again.

Louis Ortiz: Hold on, is this the girl with the curly brown hair?

Frank Pope: Yup. ☺

I stare at the screen and mouth, "What the fuck?" Annette is a very beautiful Afro Latina that has to be about 19 years old. She is one of those students that, as an administrator, you have to use your internal blinders for. I have done my best to train myself not to look at students a certain way. I use my peripherals if I have to.

Annette is a girl that I would've never that thought Frank could get. Shit, I'm not even sure that I would either. Anyone who knows her knows that she has an ass that Nicki Minaj would be proud of. I don't know her very well but she knows me as Jessica's supervisor. I've seen her several times either visiting Jessica or at events with her. Come to think of it, I've seen her in Frank's office before, but that would never be something that would alert me. We both have students who drop by our office hours all the time. Of course, Annette is different because she doesn't go to the university. She must go to the community college, or even worse, Lemoyne.

Louis Ortiz: Wow. I think I have a new respect for you. How do you expect me to get rid of her? Wait, before you answer that, doesn't she have class?

Frank Pope: She was supposed to leave with me in the morning but she wanted to sleep. Her next class is at 4:30.

Louis Ortiz: So what was she going to do when she finally woke up? Give me a heart attack?

Frank Pope: I was going to come get her during my lunch hour, but I can't do that now.

Louis Ortiz: So you just want me to knock on the door and tell her to get out? (I think that is kinda rude) Wait, does she sleep naked??? Maybe I will go upstairs! ☺

Frank Pope: I need you to calm that shit down. Just tell her to stay in the room until I get there, unless you want to tell Lidia that she is there to see you.

I hold my temples with my right hand and gently rub them with my thumb and middle finger. I think I'm getting a headache from all this. He clearly has no idea what I'm going through. If Lidia thinks Annette is fucking him then that will give her all the more reason to hop on me. Then again, if Lidia thinks Annette is fucking me then that will probably give her more of a reason to hop on me. Thanks Frank.

Louis Ortiz: You really think that Lidia is going to buy me being with Annette with how sick I am right now?

Frank Pope: You never know. She could've come by to take care of you. Besides, its not like you never had a woman come over just to give you head.

Louis Ortiz: Low Blow man. (no pun intended) Can't you text Annette about the situation?

Frank Pope: I did. I called her but her phone went straight to voicemail. I think her phone is off.

Louis Ortiz: Of course it is. Fine, I will take care of it.

Frank Pope: Thanks Bro!

This day is not looking good for me right now. I now have to drag my ass up these stairs to go wake this chick up. Again, I barley know her. She has only seen me in business style attire. Now she will see me all sick and in raggedy clothes.

I blow my nose a few times and then make my way up the stairs at a gingerly pace. I get to the top of the stairs and make a left to his room. The one thing about a four-bedroom colonial style house is that there isn't much of hallway. The rooms are adjacent to either side of the stairs. I get to the door and it's slightly ajar. I peer inside the room and I can see her on the bed laying with her back to me. Wonderful, she is bottomless so all I see is that nice brown ass that I've tried so hard not to look at.

I suppose this is not the time to be a pervert, especially since I have the urge to cough. I slowly close the door the rest of the way without making a sound. I then cough in my hands. After I gain composure, I knock on the door. I hear some rustling. Then I hear faintly, "Come in."

I open the door with enough room to just peak my head through, "Good Morning." I say with the best smile I could muster up. I try to do this without being awkward and I fail at it. She's looking at me with her eyes wide open. Perhaps she didn't expect it to be me since she is still bottomless. She quickly pulls up the covers over her and I look down.

"Frank has been trying to reach you. He thinks your phone is dead." I'm too sick to be embarrassed for her but I watch her reach over for her phone that is right next to her.

"Shit. It's dead. I'm sorry, do you have an iPhone charger?"

"Frank should have one," I look over the wall and see it. "It's right over there." I point to it then I continue. "Listen, I know that this may sound weird, but I'm having a visitor soon, I was hoping that you can just chill in here for a while." She looks at me and nods her head. I say thanks and I'm about to close the door when she says something.

"What if I get hungry or have to use the bathroom?"

Great, now I'm holding her captive? She does have a good point. "I would suggest that you do what you need to do now. There's cereal downstairs. I wish I could be a more gracious host but as you can tell, I'm really not feeling well." She nods and I close the door.

I walk back down the stairs and I can hear her rustling and walking around the room. I get back to my comfortable spot on the couch and pull up my laptop. I have six Facebook alerts. I check my last status and this is what I see.

Judy Lee: Funny how someone always seems to take care of you. lol

Lidia Muñoz-Pope: You will love the *sancocho!* Make sure you microwave it for about 4 minutes.

Brian Keegan: What is *sancocho?*

Lidia Muñoz-Pope: It is a Puerto Rican soup, Brian! lol

Judy Lee: I want some!

Zenia Ocasio: Well I'm glad someone is taking care of you.

I'm going to remind myself not to post shit like this on

Facebook anymore. Twitter is bad enough as it is and I use that sparingly but this is just a mess. I guess this is how Frank knew about the Lidia coming by. Although, I guess I could argue that had I not put this up, Frank might be in serious trouble right now.

I decide to write him a message: *I spoke to your girl. I think she's fine with hiding out. Her phone was dead but she should be charging it now. I would expect her to text you in a few minutes. Oh by the way, that is quite the landing strip that she has...* ☺

I giggle to myself after I hit send and I just start coughing. I wonder if Zenia's comment was for real or sarcastic. Sometimes she is hard to gauge in these situations. I know that we are friends, but considering our past there may be some lingering feelings of jealously. Of course, if you ask her, she never really cared for the word jealous. It implies too much, so maybe she is just overly concerned about the attention that Lidia might be giving me.

Annette comes down the stairs. I can hear her in the kitchen opening the cabinets and drawers. Then she opens the fridge. Frank hits me up:

Frank Pope: Really?

Louis Oritz: What?

Frank Pope: Landing strip?

I'm starting to laugh because I know how much of an asshole I'm being right now. I hear her go back up the stairs and into Frank's room.

Louis Ortiz: That's not my fault. I knocked and she told me to come in, maybe she thought I was you. lol

Frank Pope: Whatever. I got her text so we're in the clear. She says she has homework to finish.

Louis Ortiz: You know that sounds really creepy right?

Frank Pope: I didn't judge you when Zenia was in your office.

Louis Ortiz: No judgment here. I just didn't think you had it in her...oops I meant you. lol

Frank Pope: You got jokes. You must be feeling better.

Louis Ortiz: Not so much. I just need this soup. You will have to fill me in later on this girl upstairs.

Frank Pope: Of course.

I close my laptop because my head is pounding. I just want to close my eyes again, just to rest them. I hear a knock on the door and jump up. She's here already? I look at the clock on the cable box. Wow. It is 1:10 pm. I must have been out for about an hour. I walk to the door and open it. Lidia walks in. "Hey there, Papi. How you feeling?" She caresses my face with her hand. "Wow, you feel warm. Go lay back down."

She closes the door as I head back to the couch. She's wearing a long black raincoat with ankle strap black pumps.

"Did you want me to heat this up for you?" she asks. I tell her no, that I just want to go back to sleep. She puts the Tupperware down on the coffee table and sits in the love seat that Vera sat in a few weeks ago.

"Have you been laying there all weekend?" she asks. I see her looking around. I wonder if she is trying to assess how well Frank has been living.

"No, I spent most of the last few days in bed. This is the first day I decided to leave it." I say this as I begin to channel surf.

"Do you have a thermometer? You do feel very warm."

I point to the bathroom by the kitchen. She gets up and walks there as I look out the window. I'm wondering if its raining, I couldn't tell when she came in. The curtains block my view but it does seem to be overcast outside. She comes back in the room with the digital thermometer in hand. Lidia hands it to me and I put it in my mouth. This is probably not a bad idea considering that I did have a slight fever yesterday.

"I do have another little something that might make you feel better," she says as she opens her coat to reveal a see through nightie. I almost choke on the thermometer and I'm about to take it out when she says very authoritatively, "Leave it in there. You are sick. I just want to show you what you missed this weekend."

I cannot take my eyes off of her as she spins around slowly. "Do you like? I just bought this yesterday." She's practically naked. I managed to nod and grunt something that was supposed to be a yes. I'm not even sure why she has that on but it may be the shortest thing I have seen any woman wear in front of me. I'm not good at guessing bra sizes but I would venture a guess of a 34 C. Her areolas are very round and brown. She has a bellybutton ring and a Brazilian wax. She turns around again so I can see her ass. Is this what yoga does to a body? I need to ask Frank why in the world is he fucking this girl upstairs.

"I never get a real chance to feel sexy anymore. Dressing like this for Frank used to be fun but then we got married and things weren't so fun anymore. All my energy went to bills and other things that I really don't want to think about right now." Lidia is smiling. I can only imagine what's going through her head right now. I'm just amazed how I got two pussy shots in one day. Go figure, I guess that is my luck these days. I'm not fighting hard to contain my erection.

The thermometer beeps and I take it out of my mouth. Then I say, "How are you going to try to take my temperature while doing a striptease? Is this supposed to make my body cooler?"

She grabs it from me and looks at it. "100.3. I suppose I should leave you alone. I don't need you to die on me. But, I did want to give you something to remember." She looks down towards my pelvis. "It seems like I did get the reaction I was looking for."

She puts on her coat. "As much as I want to take advantage of you right now, I'm going to wait. I'm going to give you a week to get better. I'll call you to come over, we'll have dinner and then this body right here is all yours." I feel a little bit of a reprieve. I didn't want to get into this with her with Annette upstairs and Frank coming here at any minute.

Lidia gets to the door and then turns around. She looks upstairs and then looks at me. Did she hear something?

"By the way, how is Frank? Is he getting along fine without me?"

"Frank is fine. I will let him know you asked." I say with a smile

"He knows I'm here?"

"You did mention it on Facebook."

"Do you mind if I go into his room?"

"Yes, I do mind actually."

Good Lord, how do women do that? Is this her intuition nagging her to check the bedroom? Her "spidey sense" must be going bonkers right now.

"Why not? Does he have girl up there?" she asks with a smile.

"Ha, please, Frank is not capable of such a thing. I just think he should be afforded a certain amount of privacy. This is my house and I don't even go into his room."

She pauses for a moment. "I just want to see if he's still smoking weed"

"So, why don't you ask him?"

"Oh please, he will lie about it like he always does."

"Well then ask me."

"Is he still smoking weed?"

"As a matter of fact, he is not"

"I find that hard to believe."

"I see, so you really didn't come here to give me soup or to get me aroused. You're just trying to check up on your husband. Noted. Go on, go upstairs and make a fool of yourself." I really hope I'm not over playing my hand here but I really don't want Frank to get caught. Of course, they are separated so does it really count as cheating for him? Not that I should talk. "I think the real reason why you're not on your knees right now is because you're still concerned about him."

This stops her dead in her tracks. She gives me this look. "Really, look who now finally has the balls enough to say something? I was starting to think that you were gonna be a pussy about this whole thing in order to guard your friendship with 'poor little Frank'." She begins to walk toward me and unbuttons her coat. Clearly, I've overplayed my hand in the wrong direction.

Her coat hits the floor and she walks slowly to me. I move

up on the couch and she sits on my lap. "Are you sure this is what you want lover or are you just talking shit?" I say nothing as I rub my hands on her legs. Her skin is so cold to the touch that it feels exhilarating. Lidia shifts her pelvis on top of mine and we're beginning to dry hump. I grab her breasts and she releases a slow moan as I gently pinch her nipples.

She looks down at me and smiles, "This changes nothing. I still want to see his room."

"Are you suggesting I'm stalling? I thought you of all people would enjoy this." I say while still pinching both nipples. She whips her head back. Lidia pulls away now sitting on top of me. "For someone who is sick you certainly know what you're doing." She begins to pull down my pajama pants when we hear a car pull up. She stops as if frozen in the moment.

She asks me if that's him and I nod. She jumps off me and puts on her coat quickly and says, "Well played. This isn't over." I begin to laugh and then cough. I pull up my pants as his keys jingle in the doorway. Somehow it takes her less than a minute to fix her hair and adjust her coat to make it look like nothing happened at all. Frank walks in and sees me on the couch channel surfing and Lidia just standing there next to the Tupperware of sancocho on the table.

"Hello Frank," Lidia says in a cold voice.

"Hello Lidia," Frank responds. There is this awkward silence that I find so strangely familiar. It's like being trapped in the middle of a cold war. I've seen this type of awkwardness before when my parents were in the same room both during and after the divorce. Come to think of it, I've experienced this myself during the painful end of my marriage.

"How have you been?" he continues.

"I'm fine," Lidia says while mastering the art of giving zero fucks about what he may be thinking about right now. I'm amazed at the transformation of sexual tension to pure coldness. She turns to me and says, "Remember, four minutes in the microwave. I have a class to get ready for. I hope you feel better." She walks past Frank and walks out the door. Frank just follows her with his eyes as she walks by him. He closes the door and locks it. He leans his back on the door and waits for the sound her car pulling away before he moves.

"Did she say anything?" he asks me.

"No, but she wanted to go upstairs."

"You're kidding."

"Nope." I get up from the couch in an attempt to finally get what I want… soup!

"How did you stop her?"

"I told her that you deserve your privacy. Besides this is my house if I don't go in your room why should she?" I'm so going to burn in hell for that one. I grab the Tupperware and head to the kitchen. The only thought in my foggy head right now is how bad this could've turned out.

"She bought that?" Frank asked. He seems surprised that I managed to keep her from going to his room.

"Did she yell at you for having a girl in your room?"

I go into the kitchen, take the top off this Tupperware and finally put this thing in the microwave. I hear him go upstairs. Maybe, he can finally get landing strip girl out of here. I plug in four minutes and wait. As I go to grab a spoon, I hear the bed squeaking.

This man has got to be kidding me. Here I'm thinking that I'm going to enjoy this sancocho in peace and now I have to listen to him impale this little girl. She has a set of lungs on her too. How the hell did I sleep through this?

I'm trying not to be annoyed. But hearing her being loud with the bed squeaking violently is making me think how close I came to getting caught up today. The soup is finally ready and I take it back to the couch and finally dive in.

TWELVE

Judy considers me a mild-mannered freak that has no real male friends. I don't know how to take that but I've never thought there was anything wrong with being a freak. I would consider Ruben a real friend but I guess that may not count because we're related. However, I find it interesting that I have to think about whom I would consider a real friend, why would she not include Frank?

A few days have gone by and I'm feeling much better. I finally make it to work and I'm feeling pretty lucky that I don't have any visible bruises on my face. The number of emails in my inbox seems infinite, but it is all a welcome distraction from what's going on in my life. I haven't heard from Lidia in days but I know I haven't seen the last of her. Her sancocho was probably the best soup I've had in a long time and I'm truly grateful for that. I guess that means I owe her.

Frank is just a mess. He has gotten himself involved with this girl, Annette, and I'm truly sorry to have heard him bang the hell out of her...for three straight days now. I'm surprised she can even walk when she is done with him. But, I will give them both some credit, she still manages to go to class and she never stays overnight anymore. I try my best to not make it awkward when I see her on campus hanging out with her sorority sisters. She always manages a smile and a small wave. I can only imagine what's being said around her circle of friends.

I haven't spoken to Vera since she told me that Corey found out about us. From what I can tell on Facebook, the wedding is still on. I did break Corey's nose forcing him to wear one of those masks you see NBA players wear to protect their faces but its so big on him that he looks like a poor cosplay of a super villain In fact, I think I may just rename him flaco-Bane. I found all this out from Facebook too. People never seem to learn how to deal with their privacy settings. I suppose that makes me a stalker in a way. In any case, it seems like Sarah was trying to help Corey (aka flaco-Bane) get a little revenge that night but it didn't work out quite the way she wanted it to. Lidia is not entirely sure what she expected to happen.

I haven't spoken to Raina since the license plate incident. I'm sure her reputation on campus has taken a few hits since the YouTube video. People still ask me what could have made her so mad that she would resort to such extreme measures. I can't say for sure, although I know that I'm not an easy person to deal with at times. I do things at my own pace and time and she has always had an issue with that.

I also haven't heard from Kevin since he threatened me in my own office. I'm still trying to figure out how he knew about the video being posted when I didn't even know. Regardless, that is one less headache in my life at the moment. The video is down like he asked and if I never see him again I will be ok with that.

The one thing I would really like to do is focus on Zenia more. Even with all the drama and the sickness, we have managed to talk every single day. I'm getting into the habit of talking to her as much as we did when things were good between us. I haven't gotten around to asking her if she's seeing someone. I'm almost afraid to ask because I'm not sure I really want to know the answer. However, I have to get used to the possibility that she has moved on.

The good news is that her birthday is coming up in about a week and I've not yet decided if I should go down to New York City to see her. She has made it a tradition for her to have a birthday dinner with family and friends. This year, because her birthday falls on a Saturday, she is planning to have the dinner on Friday night and then go to a club on Saturday. She did this so she can pack all the fun into one weekend. I was thinking of heading down there for the club portion of the celebration.

She did act uncertain about whether I should go or if our friendship is even at that point yet where feelings would not get in the way. I get the feeling she's saying this to protect me from making a fool of myself, but I think I'll be ok. I don't plan on doing or saying anything that might jeopardize what we currently have going on. I haven't given her a definite yes or no. Maybe I will surprise her.

As for Ruben, he's supposed to be coming by the office

today. Because he works and travels as a consultant he feels the need to come by and use my office as a satellite base of operations, even if its just for an hour or two. Ruben travels to Syracuse so much that anyone would think he lives here when in reality he has a studio apartment in Spanish Harlem. He's still seeing this older chick, Gloria. They met a few months ago on one of those salsa cruises that people seem to rave about. I call it the Spanish Circle Line because the ride is about an hour or two and all people do is dance while the boat goes up and down the Hudson River.

I had the pleasure of seeing them meet. Ruben had convinced me to come down to the city in July so we can hang out. We've both never been on a salsa cruise before but when we heard that there were always cute looking women in attendance, we had to check it out. Anyway, after being there for like twenty minutes we run into Gloria. She was with a bunch of her friends that completely ignored me, but she had an eye for him. She was the one who introduced herself to him and they hit it off right away. I remember taking the train back to his apartment alone. Oh well. Only time will tell how serious this ends up being.

"Wow, that's quite the recap" Judy says. "Your life has certainly been a busy one." Judy is sitting my office listening to everything that has happened to me up to this point. She can keep a secret so I have no problem telling her what's going on. Today is not that busy so we have the luxury of eating lunch in my office. We ended up getting our food from the dining hall in the student union. I ordered what I normally get from there, a turkey wrap and chips. Judy got the huge slice of pizza that they serve. The conversation at this point, has led us back to my office where she sits across from me at this small little round table. Sometimes I meet with students in situations that call for a workspace. This table serves that purpose and it's great to just sit in my office and eat.

She is very excited for Ruben to come by the office. Judy has quite the crush on him. Most women that meet him tend to have a crush on him. He is a former small-time model that ended up getting some small parts in a couple of indie films and off Broadway plays. Unfortunately, he never really caught on anywhere, but he's still a member of the Screen Actors' Guild and has an IMDB page.

Judy is a third generation Korean American. Ruben and I have debated the legitimacy of her heritage. We are both convinced that somewhere down the line there had to be a black person in her ancestry because she has the ass of a black woman. She has often commented that Asian men and White men don't nearly seem to pay attention to her as much as Black and Latino men.

"You know I have some questions," Judy says. She always has questions. But, that is why I talk to her. She asks me the questions I really should be asking myself. It helps me move forward. "Shoot," I say.

"The first question is obvious to me, but are you really gonna fuck Lidia? Let me just say for the record, that she is batshit crazy. I can't believe that she would even do something like that to her husband."

I chuckle.

"Truth be told, I don't know what I'm gonna do. I feel like I have a conflict of two heads. On one hand, I know it is completely wrong and I shouldn't do it. But, on the other hand, she is so damn bold and says some of the nastiest things to me that are such a turn on. A part of me really wants to nail her so badly. It doesn't help that she's a yoga teacher and has an incredible body."

Judy shakes her head with a snarky grin. "That's why I call you Cock Kent."

My eyes open wide. "What?" I say shockingly as try to hold in my laughter. "Why would you call me that?"

Without batting an eye, she says this so matter of fact "Because you are the mild-mannered freak. You are completely professional at the workplace. Nobody can ever match the work you do and it would be a sad day if you ever leave here. But, holy shit, you have a whole other side of you that few people have ever seen."

She has a point and we do laugh about it. "OK...ok, let me stop. I do have another question and that is when is Ruben getting here?"

"Geez, aren't you a thirsty one. Next question," I say.

"Alright fine. Are you planning on telling Zenia any of this?"

"I don't know. I might."

"I don't think you should."

"Why not? We're friends."

"I think you may need to rethink that, she loves you."

"What? No she doesn't, at least, not any more. She told me she doesn't want to be with me so I highly doubt that she loves me."

"You know what I find funny? The fact that you talk about how you live in the grey, that nothing's ever black and white to you, as if the possibility of her loving you and not wanting to be with you can't be mutually exclusive."

There are very few times that she can stump me like this. This possibility has not been factored into my thought process. But, I'll have to dismiss this because I'm not sure that makes sense to me. I've always thought that if two people love each other then they need to be together. So if she doesn't want to be with me maybe it is because she doesn't love me.

"I get what you're saying, I really do, but we've been on this road for a long time. Things just feel different. I think she took a nice break from me. Maybe she got pounded by a few guys here and there and realized that I'm just another dude."

"That is ridiculous. I hate when you sound so negative, its really not you."

"Situations change people."

It forces me to think about how I got here. I'm not even talking about my marriage. I'm talking about Isabel, the woman who changed my life back in college. The one thing about growing up a nerd is that you don't know any better. I was one of those dudes that thought true love existed even if my parents never found it. I believed that if you catered to a woman and did everything she wanted that in the end, she would always love you. It became a lesson in futility.

We dated for two years in college. Isabel was the kind of woman that was so good looking that other guys would ask me, *how the hell did you pull that off?* It wasn't that she was too good for me; it was that other guys may have been too intimidated by her. She always came across as both shy and uninterested, at least that is how I saw her until one day I got up enough courage to ask her on date. I went into that situation fully thinking she was going to say no because I was used to that word.

We had a great first date and after that, everything seemed to fall right into place. This is not to say that the entire two-year run was paradise, but I thought things were going well for the first year and a half. What few people did not know was that we never had sex. She was a strict Catholic girl who wanted to wait until she got married (or at least engaged) before her first time. This didn't mean that other things were off the table but for the most part, her panties stayed on.

Everything changed when she went to visit her family in Colombia for two and a half weeks. I missed her so much that I would write letters to her so that she could read them when she came back. This was a time when cell phones didn't exist so we literally did not speak for that entire time. I waited for her at the airport with flowers but when I saw her get off that plane I knew there was something different about her. The hug that we shared lacked the warmth that it used to have. When we got back to her apartment, she promptly broke up with me telling me that *she didn't want a boyfriend anymore*. From that point on, I never realized that the woman I'd given my heart to could be so cruel.

So when I say that situations can change people, I know what I'm talking about. Isabel never told me exactly why she broke up with me but I was able to figure it out. Luckily, her friends felt incredibly bad for me and after months of anguish I was able to figure out that on her trip to Colombia she lost her virginity. First I was horrified thinking that maybe she had been raped. But that horror turned into a greater heartbreak when I found out that the guy she lost it to lived in Queens. It was a guy whom she had a crush on for years before me.

That is all I needed to hear. It changed the way I looked at women forever.

"Well I still think she cares enough about you to tell you that she misses you," Judy says.

"Fine, next question?" I ask.

"What are you going to do about Frank and his new girlfriend?"

"Not sure there's anything I can do. He's his own man. Although, I would like to talk to him at some point because this whole situation with him has surprised the shit out of me."

"Why would he cheat on his wife?"

I make a big sigh. "I'm not sure about the rules of a separation so I dunno if this constitutes as cheating."

"They are still married and he is hiding it from her. Obviously he thinks they are doing something wrong." She crumples up her paper plate and throws in into the trashcan.

"That was kinda forceful. Did I strike a nerve?"

I know that Judy's past relationships have been difficult for her. I remember one time she was crying in my office because she broke up with her last boyfriend. She would tell me that he was a nice guy but he just had a way of talking to her that made her feel small. She could never prove that he was cheating on her, but she just had this feeling he was.

"I'm upset because I don't understand why people cannot just call it what it is. You would think that people would try to work on what's left of their marriage instead of sleeping around."

I didn't expect this conversation to get this intense. "Judy, you don't know what happens behind closed doors. Who knows if they have some sort of arrangement that we are not aware of? I do find it strange that she wanted to go to his room…but then again, we can't assume what's going on in and around their marriage."

Her face softens. "You're right. You are the only one in this room who has been divorced." She smiles.

"Gee thanks."

There is a knock on the door and Judy gets up to answer it. She opens the door and it's Ruben. I know Judy didn't yelp or make a noise but I feel like she did. Ruben has his normal smug face. "Hey guys...what's going on?" He walks in and sits down on the seat across from my desk.

Before I can answer, Judy chimes in "Nothing much, how about yourself?" She sits down at the table again. I smile and shake my head as I witness these two carry on a flirtatious conversation. She asks about his weekend and he asks why is she still single. This is a song and dance I have witnessed all too often. I laugh when a joke is made but I really want to tell both of them to get a room.

I switch chairs and sit in front of my computer and see a chat message from Zenia. She wants to know if I finally made a decision on whether I am going to the party. I simply write back: *I will be there.*

THIRTEEN

I finally manage to relax even though I've been home for about an hour. Lately, the idea of relaxing hasn't happened often now that I have a roommate. I find myself either having to cook for the both of us or to clean up after him. I'm not the messiest person in the world and neither is he, but together we can accumulate a lot of dishes and garbage. There is also the fact that he has more visitors than I do. So, it helps us both to not live in filth on the off chance someone visits me.

No one is here which makes me feel good. I grab a Corona out of the fridge after I change my clothes. I think I will spend my free time playing my PS3. I won't be home alone for long so I would like to get a game in since I haven't done so in awhile. I have the game console in the living room because of the mounted HDTV. I grab a controller and turn it on. As soon as I sit down, I hear the keys in the door. Well that didn't take long.

I take a swig of my beer as Frank walks into the living room. He seems to be alone. He plops himself on the couch seemingly exhausted. "Long day?" I ask. I fiddle with the controller as I try to decide if I really want to get into a game right now.

"Yeah man. I had to smoke a bud in the car before I came in. You missed the fire alarm. It took us forever to locate the problem in the fire panel." He kicks off his shoes and explains that someone was cleaning out the ducts and the smoke set off the fire sensor. The problem was finding which sensor was tripped since all of them seemed to go off. Frank had to wait for the Fire Department to come and reset it. I'm glad I missed it. I left right before it happened.

I came home early today because I had a phone interview with Columbia University. All that networking I did a few weeks ago has seemed to pan out. I knew there was a position opening up in their Multicultural Office and I made sure I jumped all over it. It just so happened that the director of that office attended the conference we put together a few weeks ago. I did my best to make sure she knew that I had applied for the position. I think the interview went well, but it's hard to judge exactly how well I did. Phone interviews can go either way since you can never really see a person's reactions. A wrong answer or an ill-timed joke can be disastrous. I will just have to hurry up and wait.

Frank wasn't kidding about smoking in the car because I can smell it on him especially when he gets up to get some of the chips we have in the cupboard. I've always had to make sure we have something for him to munch on even though he hasn't been smoking all that much lately. He comes back to the living room with something on his mind.

"I was just thinking about something. You know what I've never seen? A homeless Asian."

"What?" I reply. "I'm sure there are homeless Asians somewhere in America."

"Are you sure about that? I have never seen one in Syracuse. Have you seen one?"

"No."

"What about in New York City?"

"I can't say that I have, but that doesn't mean they don't exist."

"Yeah but it says a lot that you haven't SEEN one. It should make you think."

"It makes me think that you're smoking some real potent shit."

"Don't you find that weird bro? Like anyone can be homeless except for Asians. You want to know why?"

'This should be stunning."

"Because they take care of themselves. Like they take care of each other. Why can't we all be that way?"

"Dude you are so hiiigh right now." I chuckle because I find this line of discussion amusing. He always tries to get all conscious when he's blunted.

"No, no. Fuck that, listen to me. You always talking about that socio-economic thing where Latino people and Black people need to come together because we're all the same and I get it now. These Asians be looking out for each other." There is a brief silence as if he wants me to really soak in what he just said.

"Where is your friend?" I ask because I really need to change the subject.

"Annette? She may be over later."

"Maybe you can get some rest." I say jokingly as I take another sip

Frank chuckles a little and lies back on the couch. "Yeah, I know." He closes his eyes while still eating his bag of chips. "This girl though, I can't get enough of her, you know? She has so much energy and I love it. I'm like 38 going on 19."

"So are you ever going to tell me what's going on?"

"What do you mean?" He says as he opens one eye to look at me.

I put the controller down. "What I mean by that is that none of this is like you. I would have never thought you were capable of this. I'm not judging you or anything, it's just that you've been living here like what? Two weeks? You haven't told me anything about what's going on here."

Frank takes a deep breath and then sits up. "What do you want to know?"

"Everything. What happened with you and Lidia? Is weed the real reason why your marriage is on the rocks right now?"

"I guess that's one way of looking at it, but it's more than that. I know that I obviously love to smoke but I was willing to give that up. In fact, I did give this shit up." Frank pauses for a moment as if he is reminiscing. "I never told any one about this but Lidia and I were trying to have kids for years but it just never happened. She was afraid that it was her and that maybe some of the past abortions she had effected her ability to have children. As it turns out, she is fine. The problem is me. I'm sterile."

The words just hang in the air during an almost endless awkward silence. I don't even know what to say. Frank eats some more chips as the weight of that news completely takes over the room. He continues, "It's amazing that no matter how much I try to forget shit, that day at the doctor's office is burned into my memory. He just sat there and told me I had a low sperm count."

"I'm so sorry man. Did you guys think about adoption?"

As soon as I asked this question, I just felt dumb.

"You know everyone thinks that adoption is a suitable alternative. Like that's going to make the feelings of inadequacy go away. Did you know that New York State requires you to take a six-week class for foster parenting even if you just want to adopt? Like 'just in case' you change your mind about adoption and go with having a foster child instead because the need is greater. You're given the 'tools' to understand what it is to be a parent under state law. The whole adoption thing felt like a sham to me because black and brown babies don't seem to be available, but they are totally willing to give you a troubled black kid from the ages of four to fifteen. My favorite part is how they have to send an inspector to your house to test for lead paint. Any little chips in the paint had to be cleaned up. Now you've seen my house, the entire thing needs to be chipped away. But what really got me is that lead paint is not a big deal when you have a baby, but since they 'unavailable' we had to starting chipping."

I can tell that this was something that was really bothering him. This is the first time I am hearing any of this so I just listen and not interrupt. He puts down the bag of chips and then shifts his weight on the couch before he continues.

"I tried my best to do what they wanted me to do. I started by striping away all the windows and it started to become a bigger job than I could handle. Then I realized I would not only have to scrape the paint in the front, but I may have to do the entire house. That means it would lead to the entire house being repainted. We don't have the money for that. So I gave up. I just started to smoke so I can just feel better. I thought it would help, but it didn't and it just made me smoke more."

Frank gets up and walks to the window. "Then we just started fighting all the time, you know? I think she knew I had quit on the whole idea of having a kid. Maybe she took it harder than me. Before you know it, I was this lazy bum who didn't get paid enough and never does anything around the house."

He turns around to me. "I own that. I know I gave up, but I just couldn't deal. Sex was a chore now. This is not to say that I don't love her but there is a failed expectation there. The more we tried to do it the more I felt like a failure. I really wanted to have kids. I wanted to have a son that looks just like me. Now I can't have that."

He sits back down on the couch and then grabs that bag. "She saw I was smoking too much. At that point, I didn't care, we were already at each other's throats. She wanted me to stop smoking and I lied when told her I would. I figure I could get away with smoking in the morning after she left for work. But, I dunno, two weeks later she found that stash under my Xbox."

It takes me a minute to grasp the entire story. Frank continues to attack those chips. "Wow, I had no idea this was going on with you. Everything seemed normal to me."

"That is because the weed calms me down."

"But now you're with Annette and that threw me for a loop. How did that shit happen?"

"Shit if this is going to be story time for me, let me at least get a beer." Frank gets up to go to the kitchen and then comes back with his can of watered down beer. "Ok, so I'm gonna keep it real with you. I've been flirting with Annette for a while. It was just harmless stuff until about a week ago. I saw her walking on campus alone as I was on my way out last Friday. She looked upset so I figured that I would cheer her up a little bit. She tells me that she having some issues with some guy she was seeing, then she had an argument with her roommate, and then she got into it with Jessica over some chapter business. She had no place to go so I offered her safe haven here."

I give him the kind of look that is equal to me saying "Really?"

"I swear to you, I wasn't trying to hit it...at first. I mean, the house was empty and she was hungry so my intent was to make her some food and send her on way. I really needed to smoke bad and she already knew that I do this, so we ended up smoking a blunt together and one thing lead to another."

"But every day though? You know you not that young right? I don't know who to feel bad for, you or the bed." I laugh.

"I still got moves though, I had to show her some math."

"Oh, is that what they are calling sex these days? 'Doing Homework?'" I finger quote that.

"Not all. I'm just showing her how many times 38 can go into 19."

He smiles and then laughs.

"Wow. You're just, wow. You crack yourself up now, huh?" I hold in my smile because I don't want to give him the satisfaction of laughing at his stupid joke, but then it just doesn't last.

"Dude, she has this friend named Paula that I may have to introduce you to. She is hot too. I think she can make you forget Zenia." Frank says this as he tries to get a little serious. It seems that him and Lidia both feel that I need to forget Zenia. At least they agree on something.

"Yeah?" I say feigning interest.

"Please, there is nothing and no one that will ever make you forget that woman. I just think that you might like Paula. But then again, it doesn't matter to me, I got that new math with Annette." He smiles.

"So I'm guessing you and Lidia are done then?"

"I dunno man. With Annette, I don't need to think about anything. She can ride my shit all day and I don't have to worry about getting her pregnant. There is no performance anxiety and no pressure. More importantly, there is no more nagging and complaining. Maybe I can get back to that with Lidia, but I'm not so sure about that."

"When was the last time you spoke to her?"

"When she dropped off your soup the other day."

"Are you serious? You two don't even talk?"

"Well, she did kick me out and if you remember, I wasn't putting up much of a fight. We just need time and space. Eventually one of us will break the silence."

"Wow. So you don't care what she's doing then? What if

she's out…you know, doing her thing?"

This is where I need to gauge his feelings on this whole thing. I'm still not going to tell him what Lidia has been trying to do with me, nor should we discuss how I've seen her naked. I'm going to hell, aren't I?

Frank sighs and then takes a huge gulp from his beer. "You know… I did think about that. I'm going to have to be ok with the possibility that she may fuck another dude. I feel like I'm pretty useless to her in that department right now. I just don't want to know about it, in case we get back together, I don't want to have that over our heads."

"That's a good point. I knew it was over with Raina when I found out she was out there."

"This is some real depressing shit you got me talking about. Are we gonna play a game or what?" Frank says as he gets up and walks toward the mantle where the other game controller is.

"NBA Live?" I ask as I open up the ottoman where all my games are.

"Yup, you know it." He replies. Frank and I have rarely gotten a chance to play any games since he moved in, which is peculiar because I used to go over to his place all the time just to play certain games. We are not gamers per se, but we grew up with video games being very prevalent in our lives.

I get up to put the game in and Frank asks, "So, what's going on with Zenia? Are you heading down to New York City next weekend?"

"I just decided today that I am." I sit down then continue, "Why? Are you looking to bless the rest of the house with Annette? You know cum stains are not easy to get out of the couch."

He laughs. "You are a funny guy, although that's not a bad idea. She did mention to me that she can squirt and since I don't want to sleep in any wet spots..."

"Stop it!"

"...Unless I can use your bed? It will be dry by the time you get back," Frank laughs.

"You're such an asshole. I barely have sex in there as it is, I would like you to keep all the sexual activity away from there."

"Nah, I'm joking, you're my boy. I wouldn't do that to you"

You know how there are times when someone says something and it just makes you feel so guilty? Well, Frank had to point out that we are boys and he would never do anything like that to me. I think I need to consider this. But first, I need to bust his ass in this game.

FOURTEEN

It's about a four hour drive to New York. I prefer taking Route 17 because traffic is always lighter than using I-81 going toward Pennsylvania. It also gives me a great opportunity for some alone time. I normally set up a playlist on my iPod of random songs that range from Hip-Hop to classical music, but this time to start my drive the *My Beautiful Dark Twisted Fantasy* album by Kanye West. Music relaxes me while giving me time to think.

I'm very excited to see Zenia. I think about how this whole thing started. We met six years ago while she was an undergraduate student. She was member of the Latino Students Association and I attended one of their forums called *The Origins of Quisqueya*. It was a brilliant discussion on the relationship between Haiti and the Dominican Republic. That was the forum where we first met when her boyfriend, at the time, introduced me. It was a brief encounter and from then on, I always seemed to run into her.

We really didn't start talking until a year later when she was a senior. She became the president of LSA and asked me to be on a panel discussion about Afro Latino Identity. This is a subject that is near and dear to my heart so I gladly accepted. Our mutual interest in Latino Heritage Month is what sparked a friendship especially since she had broken up with her boyfriend the summer prior. She would be a frequent visitor to my office, which was not all unusual since I had many students visit me. What Raina had an issue with was how often I communicated with her via text. I can honestly say that in the beginning the relationship was strictly platonic. There was nothing inappropriate being said or done, it was just a generic friendship that was forged upon mutual interests. She would date one or two guys on and off during this time.

It took me by surprise that she applied to be a Graduate Assistant for my office. The office of Student Programs consists of several smaller departments that revolve around the overall development of students outside of the classroom. My area is Diversity Engagement, which deals with the celebratory months, multicultural student organizations and mentoring. The other three areas are Events Management, Greek Life, and Student Activities. Each area is slotted to have one Graduate Assistant and it just so happened that the position that reported to me had been vacated due to graduation.

One of the most important things that I look for in a G.A. is the ability to do the job effectively. I also needed someone who could help with picking up the slack of meeting and advising undergraduate students. The reason why I hired Zenia was because of her experience as a former student leader and her general ability in computer programming and coding. I had a goal in mind that year which was to overhaul our entire website and have a multifunctional database that would match mentors with students. My previous G.A. had already started on the preliminary designs in terms of color scheme and layout but the project became too big for him to handle. The original thought was to hire a third party company or person to complete the design work, but when Zenia came onboard she expressed a desire to do it and apply it to her Masters Program in Computer Engineering.

Zenia graduated in May and because of the website being overhauled, I was able to get special consideration for her to start in July. I felt that we needed a two month head start before classes began in order to make sure we can launch the website by September and the interactive Mentoring component in January. This is when the both of us saw each other just about everyday. Our working relationship was intense and the schedule was ambitious. Raina took notice as to how increasingly busy I was especially over the summer since that time is normally a dead period. She was already convinced that something was going on.

It wasn't until after the launch of the website that Judy pointed out that Zenia had a crush on me. I admitted to her that I found Zenia to be attractive but I never thought anything would come of it. Then one night we were chatting casually online when we starting talking about our personal lives. We got on to the subject of past loves and sex. I found myself being very curious about her and her exploits. I never understood why she was presently single. Before you know it we were flirting with each other. We began to talk about everything.

The question that came up was: *Are you happy in your marriage?* As much as I wanted to say yes to this, it made me think about how much of a bad husband I already was. I had a constant problem with flirting with other women. I just couldn't get used to the fact that the moment I got married I became interesting to other women. I felt like I spent years being ignored by most women and all of sudden I was getting attention that I wasn't used to. Years later, I would discover that I was looking for something that my marriage wasn't providing me. But, answering that question, *are you happy in your marriage*, was something that I couldn't answer with certainty.

Why was I not happy? Was it because I was too young to get married when I did? Was it that I was just an asshole who loves women so much that I craved that extra attention? Perhaps it was the fact that I miss the attention I used to get from my mother. Maybe I was looking for something more unique and real. The problem with my faux happiness was that it was killing my marriage slowly and Zenia was shooting holes right through everything by just being the bright ray of light I may have been looking for. She had a Global Warming effect on me and I just chose to ignore it.

Our affair seemed to start with an awkward kiss. We were working late one day and she was sitting at my desk typing away. She called me over to show me some values within the mentoring database. I was looking over her shoulder and I could smell her perfume. It was an intoxicating smell that almost made me kiss her neck right then and there. As we talked, we both looked at each other and I went in for the kiss. Zenia was just about to say something as I kissed her and the whole situation seemed awkward.

I pulled away and her eyes were telling me that she was shocked. She gets up and begins to leave. "Where are you going?" I ask. She replies that she just has to go. I sit down on my chair thinking about how much of a fool I am. I can hear Raina's voice in my head: *it's only a matter of time before your online flirting becomes reality, ten cuidado.* I now wanted to fix this. I didn't want to lose her as a graduate assistant. All of our flirting gave me an indication that perhaps it might be ok, but I couldn't be so sure.

I went home feeling terribly guilty. Raina and I had a fight that night. I'm not sure who started it, maybe I gave an attitude about something or maybe she didn't like the fact that when she called my office Zenia picked up the line. At the end of the night I texted her:

I'm sorry. What I did was unacceptable.

She wasn't online either. Raina went to bed upset and I just stayed in the living room watching Sportscenter. My phone vibrates and it is Zenia.

I'm sorry I walked out. It just caught me off guard. There is something I need to do now and I was unsure about it until now. I will be in your office in the afternoon around 1pm. I already checked your calendar. You have no appointments.

I wanted to text her back, but I just knew that it might not be a good thing. I should've known better. Zenia was stressed about school and the viability of the project in general. Now I throw my dumb ass actions into the mix. I was mad at myself because she's one of the smartest women I know and the fact that I'm 10 years older than her and married made it worse. I wouldn't be surprised if she quit the next day.

I can laugh now about this because the next day was our "first kiss" that Ruben now loves to rib me about. As romanticized as that story was, the affair was very intense. The first time I snuck away from the office was during a campus wide event. Everyone was so focused during Family Weekend that they didn't notice that I took a two-hour lunch break. I strolled over to her off campus apartment and she greeted me at the door with nothing but a pink robe on. Her roommate was in class at the time and we took full advantage of the situation, twice. From that point on, we had two relationships with each other: professional and sexual.

Both sides of our relationship flourished. On the professional side, the Interactive Mentoring database was a complete success. We presented it to the entire Division of Student Affairs where we received tons of accolades. Both of us earned much respect for the work we did and she was able to gain credibility in her program. On the sexual side, we were like rabbits. We couldn't get enough of each other and any time we were alone, we had sex. There was a time when she wanted to push the envelope further and perform oral acts in semi-public places. I would respond by bending her over my desk any chance I could.

Our affair would last about a year before it ended. It didn't take me long to fall in love with her. The first time I blurted out those words made me want to take them back because I knew what it meant. I remember that day because I was listening to my Michael Jackson playlist when *Beat It* came on. I love this song because I remember the video and how awesome the choreography was. Zenia makes a comment that she wasn't even born yet when that song came on. Needless to say it ruined my flow and stupidly said, "You're so lucky I love you."

It made me want to put my face in my palms as soon as I said it. Zenia was surprised and we had this very awkward discussion on how could I possibly love her. She didn't return that sentiment until about a week later when she came to realize that she was in love with me too.

I tried to play it off, as if it was completely possible to be in love with two women at the same time. The reality was, I was only in love with one. It was obligation that kept me with the other. When I finally admitted to Raina that I had kissed Zenia, I was already way past the point of saving either relationship. Raina finally had all the information she needed to leave me. Of course, Zenia felt her wrath as she called her to curse her out. Zenia never liked Raina either. She felt that Raina nagged incessantly to get things from me. She thought that our marriage was a way for Raina to get a degree and thus use me to make herself a credentialed professional. Raina thought Zenia was a hoodrat that couldn't get a man on her own. She thought Zenia was using me to get higher position within the university.

Their mutual hate for each other almost allowed me a reprieve, but Raina filed for a legal separation when our open relationship experiment failed and Zenia left to New York City for good after her graduation. We barely remained friends after I told her that I owed it to Raina to try to save my marriage.

The fear of being alone fueled my sudden desire to remain married. That idea didn't last long because it appeared that both women moved on without me.

The year after all this blew up consisted of Raina moving out and dating while I had to fend for myself in a four bedroom house. Zenia started dating as well and although we maintained a certain level of contact, I could feel her slipping away from me. That's why I decided to just throw myself into my work. I forced myself to work longer hours in order to not have to think about anything. The pain of seeing pictures of Zenia and this one guy (I forget his name...I always seem to do that) on Facebook was hard to deal with and I felt then that I needed to just move on.

There was a period of time when I had a series of women come in and out of my life. They were there when I needed them. They filled a hole that was left from the catastrophic mistakes I made and in return I became a bit of a whore. That was the arrangement and they knew the deal. I made sure of that. The best thing I could have done was to be honest with them. It makes me laugh to think that after years of lying, the first time I'm honest with a woman it turns out to be with a jumpoff. It was Vera that helped me maintain some sort of sanity through most of those tough times and yet by the end of that year, I was finally divorced with a possible light at the end of this long, dark tunnel.

I remember when I told Zenia that the divorce was final. Her response was very simple. "You expect me to coming running to you now?" That wasn't exactly what I had in mind. I was hoping that perhaps I would get a real chance to start over. We did manage to see each other and go out here and there when I was in town. The sex was still great but there was something different about it, I just could not put my finger on it until I thought about the possibility she might be dating someone else.

I will never forget that day. We just got out of the movie theater at Union Square. I had taken her to see *Inception* and we were hungry. We decided to drop by one of the restaurants around East 18th Street. During our walk I noticed that she was texting someone and I asked her if everything was ok. "Yeah, I'm just answering some texts I got during the movie," Zenia responded. I always liked the fact that she took a trip to movies serious enough that she turned off her phone.

We go to a place that she has been to before and we sit down to eat. The waitress runs off to get water for us after she hands us the menus. Sometimes I find myself indecisive at restaurants I haven't been to before, so I am scouring the menu. "Do you have any idea what you want?" she asks.

I look up at her and I'm just admiring her beauty. I have always loved her jet-black hair and how it contrasted again her light brown skin. Zenia complains that her hair is too long but I have always found it to be perfect. "Not yet, what are you having?" I ask as I look back down at this menu. I hear her say softly, "Shit!" and before I can say something remotely clever about how appetizing that sounded, I see this guy approach our table. Zenia looks up at him as he comes over and hugs her and then kisses her on the lips.

Bang. I can feel a shockwave in my chest.

"What are you doing here?" She asks in complete shock.

The guy is dressed pretty trendy with a brown leather jacket and jeans with a black button down shirt. He looks Dominican to me, but I'm never really good at these things. His haircut looks like it was freshly done. It actually makes me wonder if he just walked here from the barbershop considering how thin his edges are, although his half beard proved that I might be wrong about that assumption. "You texted me saying you were here so I was in the area and I thought I would drop by."

Bang.

The waitress comes up to him, "Will you be joining them sir?"

Before either one of us can protest he says yes and she scurries away to grab a chair. Then he looks at me and asks her, "Who's this?"

"This is my friend, Louis." she replies.

Bang.

We shake hands and he says "I'm Avery, nice to meet you."

The waitress brings a chair over and he sits down. She asks him if he would like a menu and he tells her that he's not staying very long. Then he sits down between us. This has become an awkward situation. We're in a booth and he has his chair outside sitting in the walkway. I try to focus on the menu and not on their conversation or the fact that all the blood was rushing to my face. This is where I thank God for my darker complexion.

Unfortunately for Zenia, she is easier to read in this situation. I can tell that she is embarrassed, yet she manages to keep her composure. They discuss some work related things based on a question he asked as if I was not sitting here. I decided for her sake that I would be as polite as possible.

"Excuse me, Avery? But, we are kinda in the middle of a date."

He looks at me and then at her. She is wide-eyed. "Oh. I didn't realize that," he says as he gets up. I look at her and she is looking at him as she mouths, "I'm Sorry."

Bang.

Avery looks like he is about to walk away when he stops himself. "So, that means we're not really exclusive? I know we never discussed this very much, but you did leave some of your stuff at my apartment before you left this afternoon."

Bang.

I put my menu down. Zenia asks him if that was necessary. I remember thinking that I just need to remove myself from this situation.

"I think it is necessary. No offense to you my man, but I just wanted to know."

"Will you lower your voice? I don't recall saying shit about that chick that texts you all day," she replies.

I start to slide out of the booth. "I think I'm gonna bounce."

"...And you..." Zenia points at me and continues, "We? As in, you and I are not out on a date. WE ARE FRIENDS."

I stop and just look at her. He looks at her too. We look like two little boys that got scolded. I get up anyway and say, "It was nice to meet you Avery." I shake his hand and I look at Zenia. I do my best to not look at her with hurt in my eyes because deep down I know that in some cosmic sense, I deserve this. This is my karma.

"I'm not hungry anymore. Thank you for going to the movies with me." I turn around and walk out.

FIFTEEN

Every time I make this drive, I stop in Liberty, New York. It's a small town but it's roughly the halfway mark to me. This is usually the town where I rest for a few minutes and stretch my legs. I always stop by the McDonald's because it's cheap and the bathroom is clean. It's also a good way to get away from my thoughts.

I check my phone as I get out of the car and I noticed that I have some text messages. I do my best to not look at my phone when I drive. The New York State Police came to campus a few months back to talk about the dangers of texting and driving. After seeing their presentation I started thinking twice about using my phone at all while I drive.

Frank Pope: 10:36 am Let me know when you plan on coming back so I know when Annette can be here.

Zenia Ocasio: 10:55 am Call me when you get to your dad's.

Ruben Morales: 11:01 am Is Janice going to the party tonight?

Lidia Pope: 11:03 am Hey Papi I figured you would like this. {image attached}

This is the third picture that Lidia has sent me. She's completely naked. I can see why women get Brazilians. I can't help but admit that it's a fantastic look on her. I wonder how Frank would feel if I forwarded this message to him? I switch to Frank's message and I tell him that I plan to be back at the house by 6 pm tomorrow. I will have to answer Ruben later on when I find out the details on that. Janice is Zenia's sister and they have some history. It was my bright idea to fix those two up and it ended badly.

I call my dad to let him know that I'm making a brief pit stop. I decided to stay with him for the weekend since he recently informed me that he's selling the house I grew up in. He and my stepmother are moving to Florida to live out their days of retirement. They've gotten tired of the city life and the neighborhood isn't what it used to be. I grew up in the Clason Point section of the Bronx where things were pretty quiet as a kid. As I grew older and they developed the houses on Shore Haven, our neighborhood just seemed to get more and more crowded.

I think it will do me some good to stay in my old room for what could possibly be the last time. When I usually go down to the city, I either stay with a friend or just get a hotel. Luckily for me, I have some contacts in the hotel industry that provided me with corporate discounts. This time around, I think I'll need to savor the next few days, maybe there will be something in my room I can take with me before I leave.

After my bathroom run I order a cheeseburger, iced tea and small fries. I don't want to eat too much because I know my dad is cooking. As I wait, I just think about Zenia and Avery. I haven't thought about that incident in a long time. I thought that was going to be the thing that destroyed us but I'm so very glad that she didn't let me get very far after I walked out.

I had almost gotten to the corner when she reached me. I admit I heard her calling my name, but I just didn't want to deal with it. I suppose it was fate that the light had turned green and I couldn't cross the street. I turned around and saw her look of concern. She walks up to me and says:

"Sir, you ordered a cheeseburger and small fries?" I wake up from my daydream to this man holding a bag behind the counter. I grab my food and give him my thanks. I walk over to the vat of iced tea and fill up a supersized cup. I will need all the caffeine and sugar I can get to make the rest of this trip. I shake my head for thinking about this whole thing.

Avery was the first non-boyfriend that she had since she left the university. He was a real estate agent and they met when she and her roommate were looking for an apartment. I'm not entirely sure how the story went. But in my mind they fucked in every apartment he showed her. That kind of irrational thought is what continues to invade my brain when I know that she isn't like that. In any case, they dated for maybe a year or so with no real definition being placed upon them.

There was no change in Facebook status and no love messages written on her wall either.

It just so happened that this little incident was at the tail end of their relationship so every conversation was getting to be an issue for them. At first, she wanted more from him and was getting tired of all the nights of meeting at the club with friends, getting trashed and going back home to bang out the sexual tension. Zenia wanted something real and when she asked for it, he denied it to her. Reluctantly, she continued to see him but was giving less of a fuck about how things were going to turn out.

Of course by the end, Avery was feeling a certain level of coldness and began asking her to possibly take the next step in their relationship. She in turn, denied it to him. His little stunt at the restaurant was designed to cock block her.

I get to my car and start the ignition. I decide to just eat the burger and fries now because I didn't want to eat and drive. Before I pull away I think about what is was that Zenia said to me on that corner.

"Please, don't go. I'm sorry," she caressed my face with her hand. "I wish I could explain to you why I texted him because I'm not even sure why I did it. I won't lie to you and say that I wasn't with him last night because I was. But just know that whatever we are, friends or more than friends, this means more to me right now than anything I have with Avery." I could tell that her words came from a very tender place. When we hugged, I forgave her for the whole situation. Later she would tell me that she told him off in the restaurant.

Their fling would end weeks later when he posted on Facebook an official relationship status with another woman.

The rest of the drive down route 17 was uneventful. The roads are relatively clear in the late mornings, which is why I had to make sure that I was on the road by 9 am. I merge into route 87 and take that to the Bruckner Expressway. I enjoy taking this route and seeing the Bronx like this. I get off at White Plains Road and take the local route all the way to my dad's house.

He is right about one thing, this neighborhood is indeed more crowded now with all these cars. Thankfully, my dad has a house with a driveway, which means that no one can block him that is not a guest. So, I make sure to park my car in front of the house. I doubt I would even find parking on the block if it weren't for that. It is about 1:30 pm by the time I park and get out of the car. I look around at all the private houses that are connected with the different colored aluminum siding ranging from brown to blue.

The one thing that strikes me as weird is that there are no children playing outside. I used to do that all the time. In fact, I peer down the street and see someone sitting on their steps. That may be the woman I had a crush on when we were kids, Brenda. I smile as I open the back seat door to take out my bag. It makes think about all the times she used to tease me. She thought I was too nerdy looking to be seen with. My braces may have been a problem for her. Brenda grew up to be a very pretty woman, but while I went away to college she ended up getting pregnant by some rapper from a hip hop group called Apropos. I can't wait for her to be on the next season of *Hip-Hop Wives*.

I open the gate and notice the door is closed. As I walk up the stairs, the neighbor's door opens and out comes this older woman that I have known all my life. Gladys has been living next door for as long as I can remember. I remember my dad telling me that her husband, Henry died about a year ago. That makes me sad because they were such a happy couple. They had a little girl that lived with them named Marie that I used to see running around here when she was a kid. She is Gladys' niece. I haven't seen her in a long time.

"Hey Gladys! How are you?" I say as politely as I can.

"*¡Hola Louie! ¿Cómo estás?*" she says, totally surprised to see me. We meet halfway up the stairs and she gives me a hug and a kiss on the cheek despite the small fence separating us. It has been quite a few months since I've been here. She looks like she is about to put trash into her garbage can, so I will keep it brief.

"How is Marie doing?"

"She is doing well. Still no boyfriend, but doing well." Gladys is a short older woman with silver hair that kind of resembles Rita Moreno. She's totally rocking an Adidas sweatsuit and I can't blame her. She looks great for her age. I guess she may be working out.

"So you came to visit *tu papá*, huh?"

"Yeah, I don't come down here as much as I should. But you know, he said he would cook so I came down."

"*Yo entiendo.* That is how I get Marie to visit me. I just cook one of her favorite dishes and she comes by." She laughs, "Ok, let me take care of this. Good to see you."

I chuckle at her joke and we wave bye to each other.

I still have my old key but I have to fish around in my pocket for it. I finish walking up the stairs and open the screen door. Before I put my key in the door it opens up and I see my father. "Well look who it is?" he says. We hug and I ask him how he's doing.

He tells me he is doing well and then I'm hit with this incredible aroma. "What are you making? It smells great!" I say. I can also hear *El Gran Combo* playing from his CD player in the kitchen.

"I'm making beef stew. I haven't really started. All I did was brown the meat and add the *sofrito.*"

My father is one of the best cooks I know. There was nothing that he made that I didn't eat. While my mother seemed failed in the kitchen in comparison, my father was the one that the family counted on to make the big meals on the big holidays. Even after they were divorced, relatives from my mother's side of the family would comment on how good his cooking was.

My dad was very popular at the firehouse as well. It came to a point where no other firemen wanted to cook when he was on duty. His mastery of the culinary arts is something that almost led him to opening his own place. Time and money were not on his side and when he got cancer, he just decided to retire altogether. Fortunately for me, I learned how to cook from him. This does not mean that I cook as well as he does because he has a passion for it that I don't have. I just like to eat.

One thing that my dad has always told me is that if I want to get into a woman's pants, then I need to know how to cook. While that is not the be all and end all of all on his rules on women, this one thing is pretty damn important. He taught me that it shows a certain amount of independence because I won't need a woman to survive, which is true. My dad made sure that I knew how to do my laundry, iron my clothes and know how to clean. *No son of mine is going to need a woman to survive, if you can take care of yourself than you can take care of her.*

In any case, I love my dad's beef stew, which is not to be confused with traditional *carne guisada*. My dad is a Navy man and a proud American who's served this country. He did acknowledge his Puerto Rican side, but like most military men he believes that the stars and stripes are something that you bleed. During one of our numerous discussions about cultural identity, he told me that he no longer considers himself Puerto Rican. He was stationed at the Naval Base in Vieques for a few months and when he would talk to the civilians they would ask him where he was from. My dad would say with pride that he was Puerto Rican. Many of them would laugh at him at tell him that he was certainly not from *La Isla de Borinquen*, he must be from *Nueva York*, a *Nuyorican*.

To understand my father's complete animosity toward this is to understand that being a Latino in the Navy during the 50s and 60s is to see racism all around. While he had a love for country and uniform he still had trouble dealing with white people and black people. He was too light-skinned to hang out with African Americans during shore leaves and he certainly looked too Mexican to hang out with white people either. He never complained about life on the ships but when it came to his visits in the south, he might as well have taken a piss in the woods because he couldn't go into either of the segregated bathrooms.

This rejection from his own people was the last straw for him. *What good is it to call yourself Puerto Rican if the people of the island won't event claim you? No sir, I am an American.* It makes me wonder if this was part of the reason I was raised to learn English only. Of course, despite this fact, he does cook with a particular Latin flavor that is recognizable even if it's not a Puerto Rican dish. The truth of the matter is that he learned how to cook from his mother, *mi abuela*.

After some small talk about how my ride was, I go upstairs to my old room and he hurries to the kitchen to continue the cooking. I'm always amazed that he can take all day to cook and yet the results are totally worth it. I walk into my room I notice how immaculately clean it is. The bed is made neatly and there seems to be no dust anywhere. I put my bags down on the bed and look around. There are a couple of open boxes next to each other by the closet. These are probably some of the things he wants me look at. He told me a few days ago that he wanted me to give him the ok to either toss some of this stuff or tell him that I want to keep it.

I'm a bit curious about the boxes so I flip through some of

them. There are a few old 12-inch vinyl records that I want to keep. I may not have a record player anymore but I just can't throw away these old freestyle music classics. I see an old poster of the New York Mets from 1990 that I will toss out. I find a hardcover campaign book from Dungeon's & Dragons called *Ravenloft: Domains of Dread.* Wow, looking at this takes me back to high school. I thought I lost this book during my move to Syracuse. Right underneath that is a copy of one of my favorite graphic novels *Crisis on Infinite Earths.* This is a bound edition of all twelve comic books that came out in 1986. I forgot I had this. I have at least 15 comic boxes in my closet back home. I may have to fish them out.

Overall, the rest of this looks like junk that I should probably throw away but I feel compelled to keep. Then I come across a manila envelope that is filled with papers. There is nothing written on the front or back of it. I unlatch it and open the envelope to find that they are old love letters from Isabel. I'm completely shocked at this discovery. How did I not realize I still had these?

I take out the stack of letters that were written on loose leaf. They are in date order and as I pull them all out a pink piece of paper hits the floor. I remember the pink letter. It was the first letter she ever wrote to me. I put the stack down on the bed and pick it up. It's folded up nice but I can tell the paper is getting old. There is a reason that I don't want to open this or read any of the other letters. I decided a long time ago that Isabel never truly loved me and it was only after all the pain went away and my irrational dislike of women vanished that I realized this. Opening this letter would mean that I would entertain the idea that what we had with was real when I know it wasn't.

"Never again." I say to myself. I place the letters back in the envelope. I think I will burn these tonight. The thing is I know what these letters say. The pink one in particular has a line that I will never forget at the end, *I love you with every fiber of my being.* Well it took every fiber of my being just to get over her. I trusted no woman for years after our breakup to the point that I settled to marry Raina, and later on I could not even recognize how much in love I was with Zenia.

Never again. I think tonight I will tell Zenia that I'm still very much in love with her and that I never stopped loving her. When I'm done doing that, I will take these letters and exorcise my demons with fire.

SIXTEEN

I did manage to call Zenia and let her know I was still coming to her party. I can tell there is still a little bit of reluctance with her because I have never hung out with any of her friends before. Most of them will know me as an administrator from the university when they were students. It may be a little bit awkward for them to see me in this situation, but I have no worries since they are no longer students. She did warn me that there may be guys there that she has been intimate with so I need to prepare myself. I try not to think about this.

For Ruben's sake I do ask her if Janice will be there and as I suspected she will be. I'm not sure why he wanted to know since he will not be going with me. Zenia has some negative feelings toward him since he ended up breaking her sister's heart. I would encourage him to keep his distance for a while…a long while.

The rest of the day was spent talking to my dad as he cooked. I inquired as to where my stepmother was and he told me that she was visiting her mother this weekend. I wondered where she was because I knew that she was the person who cleaned up my old room. I can just tell. I remember when I lived here after college the days she cleaned would be marked by the *Pasillos* music playing in the stereo.

My father and stepmother have a unique relationship. They've been a couple since I was in high school and have managed to stick with each other through thick and thin. Ana is Ruben's mother, which tends to weird people out except for the fact that she is not related to my mother. So I guess you can say she was my aunt-in-law if there is even such a term.

My parents got divorced around the same time Ruben's parents did. My dad was always friends with her but at some point they started seeing each other and it has been that way ever since. There is long time resentment from my mother's side about this and they are convinced that these two committed adultery. My father denies this and while he is no saint, I have never known him to lie to me.

In any case, these events have led Ruben and I to be closer than any of the other cousins in my family have ever been. I suppose it makes sense in certain ways. We are practically brothers at this point. The both of us have seen drama from family that would make my current situation pale in comparison.

Over some beers, I fill my dad in on what my life has been like for the last few weeks. Without getting too descriptive I tell him about Vera and my eventual fight with Corey, which he wasn't happy with. My dad can be quite protective when it comes to family. I explain my issues with Lidia and Frank (which he seemed to completely amuse him).

"You mean to tell me that you haven't slept with her?" My dad can be quite direct in his questions.

"No...I haven't," I say thinking that I made that fact quite clear.

"Humph. You're better man than me, son. If I was your age and a woman who looks like that was on my ass, I would have screwed her 45 different ways. But, I'm glad you're not like me. I'm a dirty old man." He chuckles.

Then I tell him about the craziness with Raina and his joking manner disappears. I can't say for sure whether my dad always liked her but he definitely has strong opinions on her now. "What the fuck is wrong with her? You know, maybe she has a bug up her ass about you moving on. She really turned out to be disappointing to me. I thought she had more grace and class than that. I mean, really, over a license plate? What's the big deal?"

"I still haven't figured that out yet. I suppose I did make her wait too long."

"So what? Was the registration set to expire soon?"

"No, I renewed it last summer."

"*Que cabrona*, that is ridiculous. But, now you don't have to worry about that shit no more. Do you have any more financial ties to her?"

That's the question I didn't want to answer. "Yes, I do. Her name is still on the house and we have loans with both our names attached."

"Why? I thought you were going to take her name off the house?"

"There was no point. First off, the bank wants the divorce decree. So I have to fax that. Then they want both of us to fill out some forms. I'm not trying to go through any process that is going to make me ask her for cooperation."

My dad sighs in annoyance. "But that's what you're supposed to do when you get a divorce. There are always papers to sign. You do it now so that you don't have to deal with her 20 years later. You think it was easy when your mother and I went through it years ago? We had lawyers and got things done. It was a pain in the ass, but I don't have to deal with a fucking thing now."

"I understand that, but I find it hard to justify going through all that when after all is said and done, they still have her down as responsible for the house if I default. For that, I might as well just sell the house."

"Is that what you want to do?"

"I'm strongly considering it."

"Really? Where are you going to live?

"I may just find a job down here and move."

This is something that I had not expressed to anyone as of yet. I have been considering it because I miss being home. When you are a native of New York City, anywhere you live is just not enough. It's either too quiet, too slow, or the people are just too dumb. Plus, recent events have made me really consider getting away from Central New York all together. That place is just too small and there are very few women that I can meet that will not know who Raina is. That makes my dating life a mess, unless I strictly date white women.

"Well you know you can't live here." My dad chuckles again.

"Trust me, I know you're selling the house and getting out of here. I want to live on my own anyway. I'm too used to doing that as it is. No offense, but I wouldn't live here even if it was a possibility."

"None taken, son. I raised you to be independent so this makes me a great dad!"

"Well, I had a phone interview the other day with Columbia University."

"That's great news, how'd it go?"

"I think it went well but one never really knows how these things will end up. But, I'm confident."

"Well, I hope you get it before I leave. It would be nice to see you more often."

My dad finally serves dinner and that's when I get an

indication of how late it is. He serves the beef stew with egg noodles, which I love. I do everything within my power to not devour this meal quickly. It's about 7 pm when we start to eat and I once I'm done I'll have to shower and get ready to leave. The bad part of this side of the Bronx is that there is no train near by so I will either have to take a bus or cab to the Parkchester station or I will have to drive into Manhattan.

"You have plans tonight?" My dad asks

"Yeah I'm going out with some friends."

I haven't told my father much about Zenia. He knows that she exists in a "former lover" type of way, but I completely avoid bringing it up. With things being up in the air with her, I didn't want him to get a bad impression of her. If we end up being together somewhere down the road, I would rather he get a clean slate and not a whole history of messy situations he can judge her for.

"Where are you going?"

"Some place called 'The HK'. I never heard of it before."

"Oh, that's around 38th and 9th I think."

"39th and 9th, how did you know that?"

"You forget your dad was a firefighter. HK stands for Hell's Kitchen. Plus a buddy of mine had his retirement party there."

I laugh. "Here I'm thinking you just know the city like

you're swinging across buildings like Spider-Man."

"Not the point, I still knew where it was."

I take a nice long shower that feels epic. I shave the stubble from chin and jaw and I even straighten out and thin my mustache. I make sure that I have a fresh pair of contacts because I would hate it if they clouded up on me once I'm on the road. At some point I will need to get a new pair of glasses but I have finally found a pair of contacts that make my eyes feel good.

I take my time getting dressed and every so often I look at that the envelope and think about how far I've come from those days. I don't really wonder about Isabel much. In fact, I only think about her in a historical context. They say that you need to know your history so that you are not doomed to repeat it, but lately I feel that those mistakes could be inevitable.

Isabel doesn't live in Queens anymore. In fact, she doesn't live in New York City. Thanks to one of her old friends, I know that she lives somewhere in Texas. It turns out that she ended marrying some guy that she met off of the Internet. She has two kids and is happily married. I think I can be truly happy for her. I'm more affected by what she represents in my life rather than the person. I also find it quite hilarious that she's Facebook friends with all my college friends except for me.

I suppose I did act crazy when she broke up with me. The emotional outburst of "why can't you just love me" and the crying over her, I'm sure that went over real well. I think I was a borderline stalker at one point. It's embarrassing to admit that I was in a place that I wasn't proud of. But I can only imagine how she felt because years later I heard that the guy that she fucked in Colombia turned out to be bisexual. Apparently, he wanted to prove to his family that he can truly be a real man and maintain a relationship with a woman. After she broke up with me she went to visit him in Queens and walked in on him taking her brother balls deep in his mouth.

From what I heard she was devastated, but was too proud to tell me otherwise. So she just continued to be cold and distant. I was wrong for laughing at that story when I first heard it because, as someone who is now older, I can understand how that feels. Truth be told, I should never laugh at another person's pain because it is a pain that is all too familiar to me.

Oh well, I'm still going to burn these letters tonight. I made sure that my dad had some marshmallows. There is a grill in the back yard that I intend on lighting. Since I'm driving, I don't plan on drinking much tonight. Since I also don't know what to expect from tonight's festivities, I think being sober and not staying long will be best.

This thing is supposed to start at 11 and it's only 9:00 and I'm ready to go. That is the one thing that sucks about being me; I want to be on time to things like these even though no one will show up until like midnight or 12:30 am. Although, she did mention that cover at the door goes up another $20 after 11:30 pm, so perhaps being early isn't all that bad.

I almost forgot to text Ruben back.

Me: 9:32 pm Sorry I took so long. Yes, Janice will be there. Why do you care?

Ruben Morales: 9:35 pm I don't care all that much. I just want you to tell me if she is doing ok.

Sometimes this man confuses me. This was a bad break up. The one thing that I know about my cousin is that as aloof as he may come across he can be insanely jealous. I fixed these two up originally because at the time they were both single and lonely. I first met Janice at Zenia's undergraduate graduation. We got along pretty well and became fast friends. Ruben was single at the time too and I knew he wouldn't have minded dating someone, so I fixed them up.

For the first year they made me look like a master matchmaker. They did everything together and they were a little sickening about it. Then one night out of the blue she decided to check his phone. They were hanging out with some friends and-when he tells me this story he swore that he never gave Janice a reason to be suspicious-she came across some pictures of this girl named Nina. According to Ruben, none of the pictures were all that bad. They were mostly of her in a bikini, which he maintains was because she was showing him pictures of her trip to Cancun.

On this particular night there was also a lot of drinking. He claims that when she got back from her smoke break with her male friend, he saw him zip up his pants. He also noticed that her lipstick was gone. So in his mind he is trying to put two and two together and realizes that they had been flirting with each other all night. This made him think that Janice was paying him back for this alleged fling with Nina. Well, this entire combination was not good for him and he just explodes with accusations of blowjobs and all out fornication. At the end of the night, after way too many drinks and reckless accusations, their relationship was over.

It may have been the one of the strangest stories I have ever heard him tell. I can't say if I believe him or not, but what I do know is that Zenia wants to kickbox him. The way she tells it, Ruben was just out of his mind and perhaps was looking for any reason to break off their relationship. The break up devastated Janice and according to Zenia, she has never been able to trust a man since.

I respond to his text with: *Well ok, I will report my findings. Don't wait up honey.* I wait impatiently until its 10pm. Thank god for *Baseball Tonight* because when that was done I was out the door. I figured it would take about 30 minutes to get where I needed to go and then another 30 minutes to find parking. One good thing about New York at night is that you can park for free on the street after 7 pm.

Traffic was lighter than I thought and getting parking was even quicker than I expected so that makes me the idiot who is 20 minutes early. The question is how long should I wait? I text Zenia asking what time she was going to get there but I didn't get answer. My guess is that she's already in the subway. I'm also going to assume that she will want to get there before everyone else since its her party.

I just sit in the car with the windows open and the car off. It's a nice night so I'm enjoying it. I flip through my phone scrolling through Instagram and Twitter. Nothing really sticks out to me. I then decide to look at the pictures Lidia sent me. I can't help but stare at her body. The first two pictures are of her in that see-through nightie that she wore when she was at my place. She wanted to make sure that I got a good look from the front and back. These look like one of those classic self-portraits that you see on the Internet where you can see her room in background and her phone in her hand. The classic selfie pose and of course, she has a duck face too.

The third picture is very interesting. She is fully naked on her bed. Freshly shaven and her body posed with the perfect angle to show off her belly button ring. This is an incredible shot for a self-portrait indeed. I look closer, not because I want to soak in her nakedness but for the simple fact that I do not see a phone in her hand, was this taken by someone else? After a few minutes I'm convinced that this picture had to be taken by some other person. There's no way that a web cam could take this angle.

I'm not sure if this should shock me because it is completely possible that she could be seeing someone else. It seems like Frank is certainly having his fun. I try to convince myself that this isn't really my problem even though I'm getting nude body shots from Lidia sent to my phone. Then a message pops up on my phone: *We just walked in.*

Zenia and her sister are in the club, which is my cue to finally get out of this car. I roll up the window before I get out and lock the car with the remote. I parked about three blocks away from HK so it should take me a little under ten minutes to get there. I made sure that I did a self-assessment of how I looked before I left the car. I haven't been to a club in a long time so I will assume that black slacks and shoes are probably still important. I'm wearing a white *Guayabera* tonight and only now I'm thinking that I look like I'm in a Cuban band.

As expected, it does take me a few minutes to get there. There is a small line at the entrance that is being manned by a tall pale bald man in a suit. He's checking IDs at the door. With the number of events I seem to do at the university, I always do my best to make sure that I make the job of whomever is working the door easy. So in that respect, I have my ID out when I get to the door. He checks it and I walk right in.

The place is as loud as it seemed when I was outside. They are playing Spanish music, which I wasn't expecting. It's very dark and spacious. I see tables and furniture on the sides. The bar is at the back of the club. People are drinking and having a good time. It's not very packed in here but then again, this is still early. It doesn't take me long to find Zenia and Janice after I pay the cover. I guess this makes me the third person here.

I begin to walk up to them and I start to remember that this is the first time that I'm seeing her in months. Our last argument was based on the fact that she felt I was trying to force her to make a decision on what we are. It was Memorial Day weekend and she had just gotten back from a trip to Miami with her girls. It seemed like an all too familiar situation that I had been in before. She met a dude named Peter and she felt that in order to give him a real chance at dating her, I needed to not be in the picture.

This came at a time when we were exercising our rights to be friends with benefits. After the whole situation with Avery blew over, I thought we found ourselves in a better situation, but she didn't want anything deeper than just sex. So when this whole thing with Peter came up, I was surprised. Zenia was not my girlfriend and I knew that I had no right to be upset, but I was still disappointed because I knew she was right. No man was ever going to stand a chance given our history. It would not be fair to expect any man to accept me in her life. That is why I had to agree that we end our friendship. Zenia always saw this as a temporary thing, while I thought it was permanent. Maybe viewing things like that was foolish on my part, but it was best way I knew how to deal with it.

I spent those months believing that she and Peter were going to make a happy couple. I figured that he has to be interesting, even if I already didn't like him. When she finally called me a few weeks back she did make sure to tell me that she isn't dating anyone so I'm not entirely sure what happened between her and Peter. She never volunteered the information and I never asked.

Zenia looks at me as I walk up to them. She is every bit as beautiful as I recalled. She decided to put on some make up. While I feel that she is the type of woman that doesn't need make up, she does carry off the look very well. Her lips are a shade of a pale pink gloss that is stunning. Her purple eye shadow looks amazing as well. She has on this sleeveless black-striped eyelet dress that stops a little above her knees and it accentuates her curves. Finally her black open toe stiletto booties make the entire outfit come together. We hug and I kiss her on the check. I then hug Janice too. I know it's been awhile since I've seen her as well. She's not dressed so fabulously, in fact a part of me questions if she even wants to be here. She has a look of utter boredom and she just got here. She's wearing a short black jacket and I can tell that she has jeans on and flats. Her hair is pulled back in a pony tail. She's definitely sending out all the signals that she is not interested in male attention today. Zenia explains that her friends are probably going to be fashionably late so we shouldn't wait for them to order drinks. She already has a drink in her hand that I'll assume is her usual Jack & Ginger. I have no idea what Janice is drinking, but I need a beer. I have a feeling this is going to be a long night and beer might make this more manageable.

By the time I get back to where they were when I ordered the beer, some of her girls have arrived. I recognize two from the university. The music is pretty loud when we all exchange pleasantries. I drink my beer and see that Janice is next to me. Since Zenia is pretty involved with her friends at the moment I decide to a conversation with Janice.

"So how you been?" I ask

"Been good. You?" She responds.

"I've been ok. Just been working a lot these days."

"So how's the divorce?"

I almost spit out my beer. I begin to laugh and wipe my

mouth. "Well that was direct."

She laughs too. "Well, I just wanted to know. Besides, we are the only two here that are the same age so we might as well talk about something."

"The divorce was good. You know, the beginning sucked but the ending was wonderful."

Janice nods as we look at Zenia take pictures with her friends. "How's your daughter?" I ask.

"She's good. She's turning eleven in a few months." Zenia hands me her phone so I can take pictures of her and her friends. After a few pictures we all mingle and I ask if she needs another drink. She nods and I head over to the bar to order her a Jack and Ginger and a beer for me. As I wait I can't help but think about how awkward all this is. I really don't know what to expect from this but I have to keep in mind that this night is all about her. I'm also trying to ignore the possibility that perhaps I may see some people I don't want to see. Truly, the last person that I want to see here is Avery. I might be able to deal with anybody but him.

The drinks finally come and I tell the bartender to put it on my tab. I carefully navigate my way through the crowd that is forming at the bar because I don't want to spill these expensive drinks. As I turn to where Zenia and her party are, I see her getting a bear hug from this guy that picks her off of her feet and then he kisses her neck.

This is about to be a long night indeed.

SEVENTEEN

I've never met Peter or is it Pedro? I only recognize him for the brief time she posted photos of them on Facebook. Then again, it was more him tagging her in his photos. He's one of those guys that has five names on Facebook like, Peter "Pedro, the Fat Fuck" Aviles. I may be totally making that up but that is how I see it. I never really saw him all that much on her page. He is a lot taller than I thought he would be. Actually, he is a lot wider too. This is someone that I shouldn't probably pick a fight with. Besides, I think I am done with getting hit in the face.

She pulled away from his embrace. Maybe it was getting too much for her; she has never been one for public displays of affection. He's all smiles as he says happy birthday to her. I walked up behind her with her drinks and he must have said something funny because she bumps into me while laughing and spills some of the drink I was trying hard not to spill.

Zenia turns around, "Oh shit, I'm so sorry!"

I give her the drink as she looks at my wrists that are dripping from the spill. "I'm ok, here." One of her friends gives me a napkin and I dry my hands. Zenia says, "Louis, this is Peter."

He puts out his hand as I'm still drying mine. I then shake his and say "Nice to meet you."

He replies with a smile, "*Mucho gusto.*"

Peter has a noticeable accent. Not that this means I can tell which country he's from. He's dressed in a white long sleeved collared shirt that has thick blue stripes underneath a brown leather jacket with blue jeans and some nice black shoes. The rock hanging from his ear is very pronounced and of course, he has a Yankee hat on.

We all begin to mingle again and before you know it, I'm done with another beer. I'm not even close to feeling as good as I want to be and I have to be careful not too drink to much since I'm going to have to drive later. I suppose it was a good thing that I ate a lot before I left my dad's.

I sneak away to get another beer. I'm beginning to feel that my presence is not being missed anyway. There are only two guys in this group and it occurred to me that she has slept with the both of us. I guess she is feeling a certain way about this fact too but I certainly can't tell. The crowd at the bar is huge and I do my best to try to fight my way to the front. The club itself is getting busier but it doesn't seem as crowded as I thought it would be. I check the time at it is a little past midnight.

It takes me about 10 minutes to finally order a beer. I could never understand how a place like this can be so crowded and they only have two bartenders working. I feel my phone vibrate in my pocket and it is a message from Zenia: *Not sure where you are but we're going downstairs.*

This place has a basement? I suppose that would explain why it doesn't seem really packed. I get my beer and I start drinking it. I slowly find my way back out past the crowd. I need to think for a little bit before I head downstairs. I'm trying to figure out from a scale of one to ten just how jealous I really am right now. I said hello to Zenia when I got here. I gave her a hug and a small kiss on her cheek. I didn't do the nuzzling of the neck that fat boy did. Yeah, I'm going to go ahead and say that on my scale of jealousy I'm at least an eight. If I'm creating a name for him then it must be bad.

Another beer later and I'm still thinking. I take out my phone and send a text message to Ruben: *Janice seems to be doing fine.* I knew that he really didn't need this information right then and there but I just needed to keep busy doing something.

Ruben Morales: 12:33 am Word? How's it going?

Louis Ortiz: 12:33 am I'm not drunk enough yet.

Ruben Morales: 12:34 am That bad huh?

Louis Ortiz: 12:34 am It wasn't too bad until fat boy got here

Ruben Morales: 12:34 am Who is fat boy?

I see one of her friends emerge from the crowd at the bar. I remember her from the university. Nancy is her name I think. She's a lighter-skinned Puerto Rican girl with blond hair. She has a tight black dress on that has allowed her to get free drinks all night. She emerges from the crowd at the bar and is almost instantly pounced on by some guy who is trying to talk to her. I will give him credit; he takes being shot down extremely well. She notices me and walks over as asks, "What are you doing here? Why aren't you hanging with us?"

I really don't have a good answer for this. I'm sure that I look like a party pooper who may be feeling sorry for himself when in actuality, I'm just not getting drunk fast enough. I put my phone in my back pocket and say, "I was just talking to my cousin."

"Well, unless he's coming here I think you should join us downstairs."

I tell Nancy that she's right and follow her down the stairs. The basement level looks like a completely different club. The room is darker with flashing lights of various colors and there is a sea of people dancing to latest Drake song. We get to the bottom and I do my best to follow Nancy in this crowd. Before I know it I'm right in front of Zenia and the rest of her friends. I don't see fat boy or her sister.

I end up dancing because we're now in the middle of this crowd and I feel awkward enough as it is. It won't be much of a surprise if Nancy has already told her that she had to convince me to stop whatever thrilling conversation I was having with my cousin in order to come down here. In any case, I feel like the old man in the club that just sticks out like a sore thumb.

After about two songs I'm about ready for beer number five. The funny thing is that I'm not feeling all that inebriated. I tell Zenia that I'm going to get another beer and she gives me a look of concern. I swim across the sea of people to get to the stairs and before I make my way back up I notice there is bar down here too. That is when I see fat boy talking to Janice. They seem to be engrossed in some conversation. I find it hard to believe anyone could even talk with how loud this music is. I think I will just head over to this bar to see if I can hear what's going on, although I doubt that very much.

I get to the bar pretty fast by walking around the perimeter of the room. Janice is on the edge of the bar closest to me when I get there. Neither her nor fat boy are aware of my presence while I stand on her left waiting for a bartender. I turn my head to hear what is going on but it is no use, instead I hear another loud song from Beyoncé. I order my beer and I look at my watch, it is 1:14 am.

I ask the bartender to put in on my tab, but he tells me I don't have one. The bar upstairs and the one downstairs are not connected so I need to have some cash. I search my wallet for cash I know I don't have. Before I can tell him I don't have any money I hear, "I got this." Fat boy gives the bartender a twenty dollar bill and also asks for Jack and Coke.

"Thanks, my tab is upstairs so, I owe you a drink when we go back up." I say

"Don't worry about it, bro. It was my fault that she spilled drinks on you."

"Where did Janice go?" I look around. I can't believe she left me here with this dude.

"I think she went to the ladies room."

I take a swig of my beer. I feel a slight buzz now. Peter continues, "So how do you know Zenia?"

There's a loaded question. I'm not sure what exactly to tell him. Should I tell him that I'm the guy who has been fucking her on and off for the last four years or so? Maybe I should tell him that I'm the main reason why she was even remotely interested in him since we appear to be opposites. However, I finally decide to say this, "She's a former student of mine. I figured I would help her celebrate her birthday."

He seemed to accept my explanation and out of pure curiosity I had to ask him the same question. "So, how do you know the birthday girl?"

"We've been dating, actually were dating. We met in Miami." He stirs his drink before takes a sip.

Now it's time to play dumb, "Oh, that's the trip she and her friends took a few months ago."

"Yeah man, great times, South Beach was so live too." The music suddenly changes to old dancehall music. *Twice My Age* by Shabba Ranks is blaring through the speakers.

"Yeah it is." I take swig of my beer. I have no idea how I got here. I look over into the crowd and I can barely see where Zenia is. "If you don't mind me asking, how come you two aren't dating anymore?" I figured I would take shot at this question.

He takes another sip. "Well, I don't want to get too much into it but it just seemed that we were never on the same page. She told me that she didn't want anything serious."

At least she's consistent. I was almost afraid he was going to say something I didn't really want to hear. He looks over into the crowd and smiles a bit then looks at me and says "She is great girl though. The sex was awesome."

Thank God I was not drinking at that moment. I just say. "Ok…"

"My bad man, it must be the Jack talking." His apology seems sincere, but I would like to be done talking to him now. I feel my phone vibrate and pull it out of my pocket. It's Zenia. *Can you come here, please?* I feel like I can read her annoyance through text. I excuse myself and go into the crowd at her request. I finally reach her and she's not dancing. She is staring at me with this annoyed look.

"I need you to dance with me." She says

I look at her shocked, "What?"

"Either dance with me right now or you can go home with Peter."

Almost instantaneously, the song blends into *You Don't Love Me (No, No, No)* by Dawn Penn. I get really close to her and we start dancing slowly to the rhythm and then we begin to grind. We allow the music to move our bodies in a way that is not unfamiliar to either of us.

"Did you request this song?" I jokingly say in her ear.

"Shut up and dance," She responds.

Our past consisted of lust and heavy emotions that were always played out during sex. There never was a time when we danced out our frustrations. Our movements reminded me of how much I missed her naked body on mine and by the time the third song came on, I was exhausted.

I stop to catch my breath. "I need to go to men's room," I say in her ear.

She nods her head and leans over. "Are you coming back or will you start another conversation with him?"

I try not to smile because I know deep inside that she had been watching me.

"I will be back as soon as I can find a bathroom."

She points up. "It's upstairs."

Well that's wonderful. I can feel serious pressure in my bladder that I was ignoring up until this point. It probably wasn't the best idea to dance for so long but I also didn't want to give her the impression that I'm trying to get away from her.

I turn to where Peter was and I see that he's not there. I wonder if he witnessed the whole dancing routine. If he did, he must really be questioning who I am now.

I successfully fight my way up the stairs where it's less crowded. I walk past the bar to look for this bathroom that should be around here somewhere. The bar up here is less crowded than it was an hour ago, so I'm able to ask the bartender where the restrooms are without waiting 20 minutes to get her attention. She points me in the direction of where I just came from, past the stairs and over to the right.

I follow the instructions and I make the right into another corridor. The scenery of the place changes, I walk past a tall white dude and ask where the men's room is. He points to his left. I stop and look around for a moment only to wonder to myself if I'm in the same place. Unfortunately, my bladder is not willing to wait for me to figure that out so I go into the men's room. There is no line and go straight to nearest urinal and unzip my pants.

There are very few highs in life that can match the moment of emptying a full bladder, especially when you've had more than a few beers. I look straight up and I try not to moan. Five beers and I feel like this won't end. Just as I am about to let out a small grunt, I hear a low moan coming from one of the stalls to my right. Perhaps someone is as glad to release as much as I am because it is true what they say, you don't buy beer, you rent it.

It finally stops and I shake off as much as I can. I zip up my pants and head to the sink. I'm in a typical men's room where the counters are all wet and there are paper towels on the floor. I turn the water on and squirt soap in my hands from the dispenser when I hear another deep, long moan. Clearly this is not pissing and it certainly doesn't smell like it could be the alternative. Now I'm concerned and l look at the bottom of the stall from the mirror to confirm what I already know is happening.

I see two sets of legs. One of which is on their knees. I wash my hands as quick as I can. I have a bad feeling about this and I don't want to be here when that stall door opens. I turn the water off to and go to grab some towels when I hear in a low voice that's almost a whisper, "Holy shit your head game is amazing."

I dry my hands and head out quickly. I head toward the way I came and that tall white guy stops me. "I need to see your stamp." I just look at him.

"I never got a stamp."

The guy next to me says, "See? He didn't get a stamp either. I swear to you that I just came from that club." I look down at my hand to confirm that I never got stamp when I paid the cover. I look around again. I must be in the restaurant next door.

"Well, buddy without a stamp you are going to have to go back outside and pay for the cover."

This man is huge. I'm starting to think that clubs must breed these types of individuals. This situation is about to suck because I don't have cash and my bar tab open. "Look, I just asked you where the bathroom was not even five minutes ago." He looks at me and nods as I pass him by I look to my right and I see Fat Boy coming out of the bathroom.

Shit this is not good. I didn't see who was behind him but I pray to everything that's holy that it's not Janice. It just can't be, she would never do that to her sister. But, I have to find out. I race to the bar to order another beer and to close my tab. If this ends up being bad I will need this drink. I order my beer and wait for the receipt so I can sign. I see Fat Boy coming around the corner talking to someone shorter than him. He is all smiles again. I can't make out who he is next to.

Just as I lean over I hear, "Who are you looking for?" I look up and it is Janice with a puzzled look.

"Janice!" I say and I give her a hug.

"Um...ok, you can get off of me now."

I let go of her and she tells me that I must be drunk. She looks over my shoulder and sees Fat Boy with the chick that I thought was going to be her.

"Wait, did you think that was me?" She smiles in disbelief and then horror.

"Well, no, I was..."

"That is horrible. I would never do that to my sister. Wait. What did they do? Did you see something?" She tries to get a better look over my shoulder as they stand by the stairs.

"She was giving him head in the bathroom stall." I just say as a matter of fact now. I don't really care I just want to drink the rest of this and sign my tab.

She begins to type on her phone and says, "You know, I'm even more offended now. I'm not the type of person that would suck a dick in a bathroom stall."

I put down my beer and I just look at her because I know that's not the case. Then she looks up, "Ok, maybe I am the type to do that but not to anyone of my sister's ex-whatevers." The bartender finally gives me the tab and I sign for it.

"Listen, I didn't see you around and I didn't see him around. I go take a piss and the next thing I hear is him nutting in some chick's mouth. Trust me, I was hoping it wasn't you. Is he going downstairs?" I ask as I am signing my name.

"Not yet. He's just talking to this girl."

"Do you know who she is?" I take swig of my beer and for the first time all night, I feel that I'm in a better position. I can't be all that bad of person now, can I?

"I have never seen her before, but I can tell you that she looks tacky in that outfit." She says as she types on her phone. I turn my head slightly and I see them talking. The woman has a very slender build with short light brownish hair or maybe it is brown, it's hard to tell in this setting. She has on a dark blouse with an open back, a mini skirt, and the ugliest pair a boots I've ever seen.

"I don't think she looks that bad."

178

"Of course you don't, you're a man. Your cousin probably likes that shit too."

"Well…"

She looks up from her phone, "Don't even answer that." I just drink my beer without trying to laugh. I know how Janice can be when it comes to Ruben. It's always best to just shut up and let her talk about him, no matter how bad it gets.

We then notice that this girl gives him a kiss on the lips and she heads out the door and he goes down the stairs. We both watch her leave and then Janice says "Zenia thinks that may be the new girl he is seeing."

"What? Well that makes no sense, why come here then? Did she really pay the cover just to give head? There is something wrong there." I take another swig and continue, "Unless, he is packing. Maybe he has like a donkey dick or something." I amuse myself.

"He doesn't." Janice says very bluntly as she continues to text. I put my beer down and just stare at her in hopes that she may elaborate how she may know that. She looks up at me and says. "What? Zenia told me he is small. Don't be so surprised my sister and I tell each other everything." Well then, should I feel better about this or do I think about how Zenia came to this conclusion. I just had to make dick jokes. I shake my head.

"Men are stupid. He prolly convinced this little girl to come here just to make Zenia jealous and it may be ladies night too. I didn't pay to get in here." She says while still typing into her phone.

I don't even know how to take this. I'm starting to feel a really nice buzz and thinking about this may ruin this feeling that I've been trying to get all night. I put my debit card in my wallet and then put it in my pocket.

"Do you want to go downstairs and see what happens?" I ask.

"I'm not sure that's a good idea, besides I was on my way out."

"Leaving so soon?"

"Soon? It is after 2 o'clock."

I check my phone and she's right. It's 2:07am, amazing how times flies. "How are you getting home? You're not taking the train are you?"

Janice puts her phone in her bag. "No, I'm taking a cab. See ya." She turns around and walks out. I take one last gulp from my beer and my phone vibrates. I check it and it's another message from Zenia. I'm starting to feel like she talks to me more via text than in person.

Zenia Ocasio: 2:06am I'm coming up in a few minutes can you take me home?

Me: 2:06am Yes. I can do that.

Wow. Now I'm a little excited about this. Perhaps I can

spend some time alone with her.

Zenia Ocasio: 2:08am Can you give my friends a ride too?

Well, so much for that. I should've seen this coming. I was going to offer Janice a ride too. I think I need to sober up real quick. I ask the bartender for some water.

Me: 2:08am Sure, you want me to get the car now?

The bartender hands me a glass of water and a straw. I ignore the straw and gulp down the water. I guess I was thirstier than I thought. Now I have to piss again.

Zenia Ocasio: 2:09am Yes. Please.

I head to the bathroom to take another long and amazing piss. This time there is no one getting head in the stall. It's all business in here. In and out with the hands washed. I leave the building into the brisk late night air and walk towards the car. The air feels great and I'm trying to gauge how drunk I may be. I had six beers and I'm not too bad. At the very least, I can fake it enough for her to not be concerned about my driving.

The car is still where I left it. I'm always happy to see that my car is still parked because I've gotten towed too many times. That horrible feeling of walking to where you thought you parked only to find an empty space is all too real to me. So getting in the car and starting it up only reminds me that I was successful in not having to pay another NYC parking violation.

It takes me a few minutes to go around the block and avoid the traffic that is in front of Club HK. I find a good place to double park and put on my hazard lights. I send her a text to let her know I'm parked out front. I should consider myself lucky that I was able to get out before the rush of people. The bar tab wasn't that bad, just a little over $60. I try not to pay attention to the buzz that is going on in my head. I have to drive all the way to Washington Heights.

I begin to mentally plot the drive uptown when I see Zenia and her friends in my rear view mirror. Nancy and two others thank me in advance for the ride as they pile in the back seat, Zenia sits shotgun. It's always a funny thing having her in my car. She has been in this vehicle enough times to be familiar with it considering all the ways we have consummated our 'friendship' in it. Zenia sitting in the passenger seat next to me has always felt right.

Nancy is in the backseat with Elizabeth and her boyfriend Mike. I spoke to both of them briefly when we were in the bar, but the happy couple looked to be very much into each other. As Zenia fastened her seatbelt, they continued the conversation they were having on their way to the car.

Nancy starts, "So wait, was that his new girl?"

"She looked mad skinny yo," Mike says.

I check the rearview mirror and pull away. I decided to head toward the West Side Highway. That should take me to the Heights in about 20 minutes.

"What's her name again? Oblivion?" Elizabeth says. They all start to laugh and I have a very puzzled look on my face.

Zenia replies, "Her name is Olivia."

"Well she sure looks like a Dominican Olive Oil," Mike says barely keeping it together. We all begin to laugh.

"I just don't understand what she was doing there. Why would Peter even come to HK if he was going to invite his O-bitch," Nancy said. I try my best to keep my eyes on the road while turning my head every so often to see what Zenia's reaction to all of this was. She seemed fine from what I can tell but I just have this feeling that she is not. It makes me wonder if this is what it feels like to have a woman's intuition. In any case they talk about the two of them, Peter and Olivia.

When we hit a red light on 72nd and Riverside I decide to say something. "Personally, I think they are a perfect ten together." There was a hush in the car and I can almost see Zenia telling me to shut the hell up because no one asked me but I continued before anyone could interject, "She is the skinny one and he is the round zero." They all begin to laugh hysterically. I think I do my best jokes when people are drunk.

I drive into the northbound ramp and I can feel Zenia's hand on my knee as the laughter dies down a little. This is another game she plays with me giving me subtle hints that she may be interested in doing something later. I look over to Zenia and I ask her where am I dropping people off. She tells me that they all live in the Bronx but Nancy is the one that needs to be dropped off first because she is the drunkest. Elizabeth and Mike live in Riverdale so I can drop them off at 181st where they can either catch the 1 train or take a cab.

Nancy then says "Louis, so is it true what you saw? I have to know."

"I think we all want to know what you saw," Zenia says smiling.

I begin to chuckle, "I didn't see anything! I just heard some things that I cannot unhear."

I retell my story about my lovely trip the bathroom and how I made the mistake of thinking that it was Janice since I had seen them speaking earlier. Truth be told, I didn't know anything about his girlfriend. It seemed like an amusing story but I know Zenia was not all that amused about it. I suppose me telling a story like this about the person she used to date might be embarrassing to her. Again, I have a feeling I will be hearing about this later.

The ride always seems faster than it actually is. It barely takes me any time to merge into the George Washington bridge traffic and on to 178th street. I'm in Zenia's neighborhood but I know I'll have to make at least two stops before I drop her off. Nancy lives in the Mount Eden section of the Bronx which means I will have cross over the 181st bridge and then come back to drop off Zenia.

I park on 181st and St. Nicolas next to the entrance to the 1 train. They all get out of the car to say their goodbyes. I find myself yawning and I realize that it is indeed getting late. I look out and see the four of them talking about whatever and I just wait with the car running. Zenia gets in the car as her other friends wave. I ask, "What happened? I thought I was driving

Nancy home?"

"She changed her mind." Zenia says as she puts her seatbelt on.

"How is she getting home? There is no direct train to where she is."

"Relax. She is talking a cab to her boyfriend's crib"

"I could have taken her."

"I know."

There is a slight pause in conversation that makes this awkward. I break the silence by asking, "Are you ready to go?"

She looks at me and says, "Yeah, but I don't want to go home. Can you find somewhere to park?"

"Is everything ok?"

"Yes, we just need to talk."

EIGHTEEN

I finally park in the Bronx after a long process. My first thought was to go to Fort Tryon Park but when we got there the police were quickly on us to telling us that the park was closed. I thought about going to Van Cortlandt Park but for some reason that just did not seem like a great idea to me. So, I thought of only one place that would work.

There is a street off of White Plains Road that is behind Stevenson High School called Stickball Blvd. I know based on my childhood that it's pretty deserted at night. The city changed this street's name years ago to reflect to rich history that stickball had brought to the neighborhood. My dad introduced me to the game around 1985 when the New York Emperor's Stickball League was founded. There've been on going annual tournaments during Memorial Day weekends since that time and normal league play during the summers.

For the most part, no one parks here in the middle of the night. The only other cars that are here are cabs waiting to be called by their dispatchers. The reason why I know this would be such a good place for alone time is because this was our normal getaway spot. Sometimes motels can get expensive so having sex in a car in the middle of a deserted street saved me a good amount of money. It is about 3:15 am by the time I shut off the car and wake her up. Zenia wanted my full attention and while we made some small talk, she fell asleep by the time I left Fort Tryon. She looks around in her sleepy state. "Where are we?" she asks.

"We're in the Bronx. I couldn't find a better place than this to park." She pulls out her phone to look at the time. I have to admit that I was feeling a little bit impatient and anxious to figure out what she wanted to talk about. It could also be the fact that the beers are wearing off and so was my nonchalant attitude.

At first she was silent and then she began. "You know, when I asked you to come down for my birthday it was because I wanted to see you. I figured that would be a present within itself. I also figured that it would be a great way to have sex on my birthday. But what I don't understand is why you felt the need to talk to Peter. Were you checking up on me? Is that what that was?"

I recognize that I'm on a slippery slope. I suppose that I knew more about him than he did about me going into this night, if indeed he knew anything about me at all.

"That wasn't my intention. He bought me a drink since you spilled one on me. He said it was his fault."

"Is that all you had to talk about?"

"No." I replay that brief discussion in my head. I really didn't want to remember it but the only thing that keeps repeating in my head was *the sex was great.* Which I just can't figure out why he would even say that because didn't I mention to him that she is a former student of mine? I suppose in the moment and after a few drinks he felt the need to mention that as if I were just any other guy. Although I would never say that to someone I didn't know very well.

"Well? What else was said?" She insists.

I take a deep breath and say, "According to your boy, the sex was great."

Zenia looks startled. "He did not say that! Why would he say that?"

I shrug my shoulders because that is the best answer that I can give her.

"How did this even come up? I need to know."

"Well, he kinda asked me how I knew you and I told him you were a former student. Then I asked him the same…"

"Of course you did," she interrupts.

I pause and start again. "I asked him the same question and he told me that you and him dated for a bit, but that you and him were never on the same page. Apparently, you told him that you didn't want anything serious."

She seems uncomfortable hearing these details. "So then

he just blurted out that the sex was great?"

"Basically. He said you were a great girl and the sex was awesome."

"Wow..."

"Look, I didn't go the bar looking to talk to him."

"That is so incredibly awkward. Is there no sense of privacy?" She is upset and I can imagine why. "And he wonders why I stopped dating him. Of course, I wasn't looking for anything serious with him. He manages to tell you something like that and mind you he doesn't even know who you are."

There is a brief silence as I think about what she said, and then I ask, "So who am I?"

"What do you mean?"

"You said that he doesn't know who I am, so who am I exactly?"

I know that we had this conversation before back when Avery decided to join us for dinner but I need to push this a little further. I know how I feel about her and this situation, but I have no idea how she feels.

"What do you mean? We talked about this before our break."

"And yet here I am in a parked car with you."

"You are my…"

"Don't…" I interrupted her because I knew where she was going with this. "Do not say that we are just friends because that's bullshit."

"What do you want me to say? That you are my ex-boyfriend? We both know that's not true because maybe you forgot that you were married!"

"So because you can't define us that means that we are just friends? You falling in love with me means nothing then?"

"That is so not fair. You want me to tell people that I was your mistress? That you chose your wife over me when I knew for a fact you loved me more than her! No, you don't get to be defined to be anything more than just a friend because you know what? That is what we were before all this started. You were the person that I trusted the most in my life. So you don't get to have hurt feelings about title changes."

I have no idea what to say to that. This whole time I've made this situation about me. I just assumed that perhaps she still loved me without taking into consideration that too much time had passed. Yes, I chose obligation over love and I have been paying for that choice ever since. Maybe this is my karma or whatever that means, coming back to me.

I look at her and I realize in the darkness of the car that she is crying. Not in a sobbing kind of way, but there are tears running down her face. Now, I feel even worse. This is her birthday celebration and me, being the asshole that I am, made her cry. Real smooth Louis.

I turn to her. "I'm sorry for making you cry." I reach over to the glove compartment and pull out some napkins that I have in there.

"You're an asshole. How could you make me cry on my birthday?" Zenia says as she wipes her face.

"Yeah, I'm an asshole. I'm sorry for that."

"You made this about you."

She's right. Maybe this whole trip was about me. I have been so caught up in all the things that have been happening to me. But, I really wonder if they are really happening to me or am I somehow allowing them to occur.

"Do you want me to take you home?" I wouldn't blame her if she said yes.

"No. I just want you to hold me the way you used to."

This comes as a surprise to me. When we started seeing each other years ago, one of the few places we could spend alone time was in my car. When we first became intimate during the first year of her graduate assistantship there was a time when I drove her to Onondaga Park in Liverpool, NY. I parked along the lake and we watched the sunset. We would talk for hours about life, but as things got dark we would push the seats all the way down and she would climb on to the driver's side and lay on top of me. I would hold her until it was time to go.

The first time seemed awkward because these single car seats are not designed to have two people lay on them, but we made it work. She normally lays her head on my right shoulder and places her left arm around me. I have never felt closer to her than when we shared these moments.

"Ok." I tell her. I pull the lever on the left side of my seat and I recline all the way back. Zenia takes a minute and then unbuckles herself. She climbs over the gear stick and lies on top of me. We hold each other in the silence. I lay here wondering if I should move on from all of this. Maybe I've been holding on to all the wrong things. But it's hard to really feel this way when she is laying on me in what should be a romantic scene. I stroke her hair out of pure habit. I love her long black hair. I've missed the way it feels in between my fingers when I run my hand through it.

"Where does the love go?" Zenia voice almost startles me. We had been laying there for at least 10 minutes without saying a word to each other. "All this time I've been asking myself this question. What happens to the love when it's gone? Does it simply go away?"

"I don't know. Does it ever go away?" I reply.

She leans up on my chest. Her face is so close to mine that our lips can touch at any moment. "Did the love for your ex-wife go away?"

"That is hard to say. I guess it did. But I just have to wonder how deep that love was in the first place."

"But you did love her."

"I thought I did. I mean sure."

"What changed?"

"It was you. You came into my life and it made me rethink everything that I ever knew about love. I thought what I had with Raina was pretty real but I was only lying to myself. I mean what do you do when you are dating someone for a long time? The natural thing would be to move it along to the next step. I mean if you don't then what? You either get married or break up, right? I guess I was just cruising through life. I had my good job, I had a wife and I had a house. But even with all that, there just seemed like there was something missing. Zenia, you came into my world and changed it all around. You are my global warming."

Zenia smirks. "I'm your global warming? Really? So basically if I'm not dealt with I may end up destroying all life in your world."

I smile. "Well that is one way of looking at it."

"So I guess you still love me then."

"And that would be the other way to look at it. Yes I do."

Zenia puts her lips close to mine and we begin to kiss. This has been a long time coming. We haven't really kissed like this in a while. I can still taste the Jack Daniels on her lips and tongue. She pulls away and apologizes. "I'm sorry. I don't mean to confuse you." She puts her head back down on my shoulder and continues, "The truth is that I do just want to be friends and I know that friends don't hold each other like this. I'm still trying to figure myself out and I'm not sure that includes you and I being romantic."

I'm not shocked by what she said. I'm a little saddened by it, but I think that its time for me to start looking for closure. I have been going through this for a long time and perhaps this is for the best. While I'm not entirely sure how a true friendship with her is even possible, I owe it to her to at least try.

I tell her that I understand and that maybe its time for me to take her home since it is getting late. Zenia agrees and I take her back home. It is about 4:30 am by the time I get her back to her place in the Heights. I park the car by a fire hydrant in front of her building and leave on my hazards. I walk her to her building.

"I hope you had fun at least," I tell her.

"I did. I'm sorry if you didn't."

"I had fun. It was an interesting night indeed."

"When are you going back upstate?"

"Tomorrow afternoon. Hopefully I won't wake up too late, but knowing my dad, he won't let me sleep past eleven."

"Thank you for coming down. It was good to see you."

"It was good to see you too."

We both go in for final kiss. It was longer than the one in car and every bit a bittersweet gesture. We pull away and the she opens the door with her keys and before she walks in she says, "Text me when you get home so I know you made it there safely."

I walk back to the car and I drive away. I'm convinced that I finally got my answer from her. While I was not really asking a question, I think I was provided with the information I needed. The point is that I need to make a true effort to move on. I know that I'm a single man in his late thirties and I'm bound to find someone. I just need to get over my own shit and focus on me and my needs.

The only thing I need to do now is get rid of the things in my life that are stressing me the most. I need to burn those letters just for good measure and I need to get rid of Lidia.

PART TWO

NINETEEN

Monday mornings always seem the same. I get up later than I want because I'm worn out from the weekend, which leads to large coffee from Starbucks. Of course, I can't say large because it's actually a venti, but it's all the same to me. The walk to the office from the coffee shop is a short one. Campus is always quiet this early. There's always a student or two rushing to class. My office is just as quiet.

I say good morning to the work-study student up front and I open my door. There is a box on my desk. I put my coffee down and look at it. It's a medium-sized box that's taped up pretty well. I pick up the package and it's a little heavy. I read the return address and it's from someone in Syracuse.

"That came late Friday," Judy says as she walks in. She's wearing one of her tight dresses again. It is dark green and sleeveless with a round neck. She sits down and crosses her legs, as she normally does, to reveal her black-heeled shoes. She sips her coffee while she waits for me to open the box.

"Are you trying to break guy's necks today?" I say to her as I go back to inspecting the box. I really wasn't expecting any packages. As a matter of fact, I really don't get any real mail at work besides a magazine subscription to Diversity Magazine and random university memos.

"We have a reception today or did you forget that?"

I put the box down. "Shit, I did forget about that. That's at three right?"

"Four and mind you, I sent you an email about it on Friday too."

I open my desk and take out my scissors. "You know I don't read your emails." I smirk and shoot her a glance. I cut the tape down the middle and open it.

"Who's it from?" Judy asks.

I open the box and I see three hard cover books: *Story of O* by Pauline Réage, *Delta of Venus* by Anaïs Nin, and *Middlesex* by Jeffrey Eugenides. I look puzzled because I didn't order any books.

"I don't know who sent this." I say.

Judy gets up too see what's in the box. "I figured it was books. Check to see if there's a note." I take the books out and place them on my desk. Judy grabs *Middlesex*. "Clearly someone knows how much of a freak you are," she says as she turns the book over to read the back.

I look in the box and there's an envelope. I grab it and start to open it. Judy then says, "Are you gonna read all these? Can I borrow one?"

As I pull out the note I say, "You already have eyes on my stuff. It's like we're married with none of the benefits." It's a short hand written note from someone I haven't spoken to in years.

Dear Louis,

I saw these books and thought of you. I hope you're still writing.

Sincerely,
Abby

I give the note to Judy as I think about this. "Why am I not surprised that a woman sent you this? Who's Abby?" Judy chuckles.

I sit down and lean back in my chair. Judy takes that as her cue to sit down too. She still has that book in her hand and her coffee in the other. "Wow. I have not heard from Abby in a few years. Her name is Abigail and she lives out in Fulton. I met her at a poetry workshop at the community center before I got married."

"Obviously you fucked her," Judy said with a smirk.

"No, actually I didn't. We flirted for a bit though. She's a tall white lady with a very nice build. I wanted to, trust me."

"So why didn't you?"

"Well, I was seeing Raina back then. I didn't think cheating on her at that time was a good idea."

"It's not like you didn't cheat on her before. Why is Abby different? Was it because she was white?" Judy laughs.

"Ha, very funny, but not that's not the reason. As sexy as I found her to be, Abby is one of the reasons why I started writing again. I didn't want to ruin that by getting into a messy affair."

This is one time where I can say that this is absolutely true. When I moved up here I wanted to make sure that I didn't lose myself so I started attending writing and poetry workshops. I was already an English major and I loved to write, but I didn't want to lose my basic grasp for it. Abby was at several of the workshops and I got to know her somewhat well. She was telling me about this book that she was writing but had troubles with finishing it even though she had it all outlined.

We shared a lot of notes and I got some great insights from her. I shared some short stories that I wrote just to gauge how good they would be. She loved every story that she read and commented that she could really get a sense of my sexual prowess from my writings. We almost got hot and heavy at one point, I remember her telling me how much she loved black men. I used whatever good sense I had back then to not follow the curiosity my libido was feeling. Once I got married we lost touch.

The only time she contacted me since was when I started my blog years ago. She wrote a simple comment on one of my entries: *Keep up the writing.* I think she understood why I couldn't really keep in touch anymore and once my higher education career took an upward turn, I really didn't have much time to go to the writing workshops anymore.

"Very interesting. So she just decided to send you erotic books?" Judy asks

"I think she's trying to inspire me. I did write some short stories a few years ago..."

"Oh! I want to read!" Judy interrupts.

"No, you already know enough about me as it is." I chuckle, "Maybe if I publish any of them I will give you a signed copy."

"Well isn't that sweet of you. Are you going to give a signed copy to Zenia too?"

I shoot her a look. "You know I don't want to talk about her."

"Come on, it has been a week since you been to New York to see her and you told me nothing about it. Was it really that bad?"

"I told you, I got my answer. We're done. I don't think we really need to talk about this anymore."

It had been a very long week indeed. After her birthday weekend I needed time to think about everything. If she wants to be friends then that's exactly what she'll get from me.

Unfortunately for her, I don't really talk to my friends from New York City all that often, so we will talk when I get around to her. What makes this all the more difficult is listening to Frank pound Annette almost every damn day. Thank God, I got a reprieve this weekend. She got her period, which I'm sure that they are both very unhappy about it.

I'm still avoiding Lidia.

I never got a chance to burn those letters like I wanted to. I woke up late last Sunday, which made me rush. My dad wasn't happy with the fact that I left in a hurry and I definitely know my stepmother wasn't happy about it either. I barely saw her that weekend so I'm sure to get an earful about that later. I just brought the whole box up here with me so I can sort out what I really wanted. I've just been lazy and thinking way too much about what I want to do. I have a fireplace that I could toss those letters into, but the only problem with that is that I need to get a chimney sweep before I power that thing up. Imagine the irony of the house burning down because of those letters.

"Ok, I will stop pushing. But I just want to say that you don't look the same. I can tell that something's wrong and I know how much you try not to have your personal life affect your work life. I think you just need to turn it down a little."

Judy is right, I just don't want to hear it. "I'm just determined."

"I understand that Louis, I really do. But don't change who you are because life is not going your way." She gets up and before she leaves she says. "Oh, I'm borrowing this by the way," She smiles as she holds up *Middlesex*.

I hate the fact that she's right. Maybe I have been taking myself too seriously. I haven't written anything in over two weeks either. I think I need to go back to basics and start concentrating on what's going to make me happy. I look at the note again and then at the books. These books are brand new it seems. I feel bad for wishing I could have read these on my e-reader because I don't like to crack the spine of the books I read. I should contact Abby to at least thank her for the books. It would be nice to know what she's up to.

The rest of the workday is pretty uneventful. We spend much of the day preparing for the reception that our office is throwing in the student union. Today marks the end of Latino Heritage Month and we usually have an event to celebrate another month of great programming. Just minutes before the reception begins I find the time to email Abby, thanking her for the books and wishing her well.

I shut off my screen and walk out of my office. I'm the last one here so I close the suite and lock it. I take the elevator to the third floor and walk into the huge conference room where we are hosting the event. The room is pretty empty with the exception of a few students and some staff. The room is set up exactly the way I wanted it. It's an open space with a five high top tables spread out across the room. At the center of the room is where catering has set up the food we ordered on three round tables in a cloverleaf shape. This allows people to circle the room while they sample all the food. There is a podium on the north side of room in front of the huge bay window over looking the city of Syracuse. Judy and Frank are talking to Marvin in the far part of the room with some students. Ha, sucks to be them.

I head toward the podium to put my notes by the microphone. There is a bottle of water there like I asked. I look up to see some students walk in and I wave to them. I look for the iPod mini cable so I can pipe in some music from the office playlist. I check the floor to see that the RCA cables are connected to wall and trace it all the to the inside of the podium. I crouch down to pull the plug toward me. I take out the iPod mini from my back pocket and plug it in.

I made a particular playlist for this occasion that consists of all Latin jazz. I start with *Picadillo* by Cal Tjader and slowly raise the music volume to my liking. I stand up and right in front of the podium looking directly at me is Raina. I'm startled to see her there. I haven't seen her since…well I can't remember when. But the now infamous license plate incident is the last time we talked.

"Mr. Ortiz," she says.

"Ms. Bermudez."

This is our typical greeting to each other now. We do not say the usual *hello, how are you* type of greetings. It has become our way of not being endearing to each other. My only question right now is why is she here?

"I know you're surprised to see me here, but I need to inform you that one of my students will not be attending this reception due to a death in the family."

"Oh, I'm sorry to hear that," I look at my notes. "Which student is it?"

"Angelina Ramos."

"Aww…Angie? That sucks, it wasn't her dad was it?" I make notes on my sheet that she's not attending. She was supposed to get a Latina Leadership award today. I really do feel terrible. I know how much her dad meant to her.

"Yeah, her dad lost his battle with cancer."

"That's horrible. Thanks for letting me know. I will have to send something. Can I assume that you will be accepting the award on her behalf?"

"Yes. I will make sure that she gets it when she comes back from the city."

She says this and then she walks away toward the refreshments. Raina certainly came to this ceremony looking every bit as professional as the occasion called for. Her business suit must be new. I look over to Judy and Frank and they are looking at me with eyes wide open. I suppose they are wondering if her and I can be in the same room together. I shrug them off as sign to not worry about it.

Raina had been working for Academic Affairs as an academic counselor for the liberal arts school but was recently promoted to Assistant Director. She has been there for several years and has made a name for herself as a great counselor for young girls that are confused about the direction of their college careers. Needless to say that many of the women of color who attend this university either know her or know about her because of the work she's done. I respect the work she does, but our shattered personal relationship makes it hard for me to tolerate her presence.

When it came down to the end of our marriage I had no problem placing the blame squarely on me. While the divorce was mutual, New York State law (at the time) did not allow for no-fault divorces, which meant that there had to be a reason why we were breaking up our marriage. There were three options on the paperwork to choose: Abuse, Infidelity, or Abandonment. I suppose whomever came up with these choices must have thought these were as good as any other reasons to file for divorce.

Raina sought out infidelity first, but that is just too hard to prove in a court of law and you will need hard evidence to present. It also turns out that if she indeed had proven my adultery to the standards of the court, there would've been possible jail time if I got the wrong judge and really nobody wants that. Of course, with hindsight being 20/20, I'm sure she would have loved to see me behind bars. I know she thought about abuse being the reason considering that all this shit we were going through was causing harm to her mental well-being. I would argue that she verbally abused me every chance she got.

The final choice ended up being abandonment. I agreed with her wording on the paperwork that I was no longer in love with her and thus I abandoned our vows. Those were pretty harsh words, but I couldn't come up with anything better. Since then, there was a point where I felt that she was playing the victim role. The divorce was mutual because we both knew that the only ones to blame for this failed marriage was us. We both did things to each other that were not acceptable. But I suppose the people who supported her didn't see it that way. Raina was seen as a strong woman who persevered a long and hard marriage to a man who could not keep his dick in his pants.

The lines were drawn and sides were taken. I came to realize that certain friendships are based on marriages and when you get divorced those friends now become like everything else. There are friends that automatically choose sides and they are the friends that you divide amongst each other like the rest of your assets. Sure, I got to keep the friends I brought into the relationship like Frank and Brian, but I did lose others who happened to befriend us both.

I was fully prepared to be the bad guy and for a while, I was. She never really came outright and said that I fucked a student, but it was sort of implied depending on whom she spoke to. I remember getting dirty looks from a lot of women for about a year after the divorce. There were several rumors swirling around that there may be a hearing with Human Resources but nothing came of it. Frank would calm me down on many occasions saying that people are spreading false rumors in order to see me crack.

Now that I think about it, saying there's a rumor about anything is a bit of an exaggeration. There's a simple truth that there are very few people of color within the Division of

Student Affairs. At last count, there were about 15 of us across campus out of about 200 employees in the division. That isn't counting the other 30 or so persons of color on campus amongst hundreds of university employees. So, needless to say, any news that happens can spread around our sub-culture pretty quickly. That is the reason why I never attempted to date anyone else in division, much less the university in general. This can be a very small place and people love to talk.

Frank walks up to me. "Everything alright?"

I sort my paperwork, "Yeah, we're cool. You know Angie right?"

"Ramos? Yeah, I know her."

"Her dad died."

"Damn. That sucks."

"Yeah I know, that is why Raina came up to me."

"Interesting. So nothing else then?" Frank is holding a small plate of the food that we ordered.

"No. There doesn't seem to be."

"How was your discussion with Marvin?" I smile as I move towards the food.

"Man, that dude is killing me."

I walk past him to go get some food. I had a light lunch in

anticipation of the food we're getting now. I was very meticulous when I ordered this food because different people have different ideas of what a "Hispanic cuisine" might be. I'm also a bit of stickler when it comes to recognizing people's dietary needs so the menu goes like this: beef and chicken empanadas, yucca fries, a salad tray with avocado, *maduros*, and *rellenos de papas*.

I don't even know where to begin. I'm more proud and amazed that I was able to convince the catering manager to make the *rellenos*. Potato balls filled with meat was something that they had never heard of before, so I had to search for my copy of the *Puerto Rican Cookbook* to provide a recipe. Needless to say that it wasn't cheap and neither were the empanadas due to how labor intensive the preparation time is. Overall I was satisfied with the spread and I just take a little bit of everything.

More students walk in and enjoy the food, music and company. I nod my head as I hear *El Cuarto De Tula* by Buena Vista Social Club come through the speakers. I talk to several students that I mentor as I work the room from one side to the other. I finally stand by Judy and Frank, who managed to ditch Marvin some how without leaving this particular spot.

"Isn't the point of all this to mingle with students?" I ask.

"We are mingling, some students came up to us and we mingled," Judy says smiling.

I roll my eyes as I finally finish my plate. My supervisor walks in and she begins to mingle with the guests. She's an older black lady that has been with the university for almost two decades. She looks good for her age. You would never be able to tell she is about 55. As they say "black don't crack." We watch in amusement as she starts a conversation with Raina.

"Well that's gotta be awkward," Frank says.

"I wonder what they could possibly be talking about," Judy responds.

My supervisor Diane was never really a big fan of my ex-wife, although Raina has never known that. She would make comments to me that she felt that Raina was a little too ghetto in her attitude when it came to me. There were several times that my ex would make a scene or be generally loud during office hours. Of course, it always seemed that we were having an argument, because most of the time we were and that was all before Global Warming came into my life.

During a conference that I attended with Diane, she told me that she felt that we were never right for each other and perhaps Raina had no sense of sophistication. Back then I thought those were really harsh words, but when I reflect about recent events, I think she may have been right.

"Maybe she's commenting to her how funny the YouTube video was," I say.

"That is true. She did laugh the hardest out of any one of us." Frank says. Of course he would know because the man went from office to office showing this video to everyone. He had uploaded it to a flash drive and made a virtual killing that day. However, it wasn't so funny when it appeared on the internet. Had Lidia not taken it down when she did, he might have gotten fired for that.

"Didn't Raina try to get you fired?" Judy asks.

"Eh, that is debatable. I think she went to talk to Diane to inform her that her favorite employee was 'fucking the help.' Lucky for me it was already months after the fact and Diane had already spoken to me about it."

"Favorite employee though?" Frank says as he looks at me.

"Don't front big boy, I make this place turn," I say with a smile.

"Ok, before you two pull out the measuring tape, can I hear about what she said to you?" Judy says. This woman is a sucker for information. She always wants to know everything that's going on. Thank God she can keep a secret.

"I thought I told you this and by the way, don't think that I don't know that isn't part of your feeble plan to get me to tell you about Zenia and that weekend." When I say this to her she gives me this innocent look and puts both hands on her chest as if she is shocked that I could come up with such a conclusion.

Frank chuckles as she says, "Me? Why I would never do such a thing. I'm a good girl."

"Pffft, oh yeah, that's rich," I continue, "Anyway, after you know who graduated, Diane and I had a long talk and she told me that she had a feeling about what was going on and the only reason why she didn't fire me was because she couldn't really prove it. However, she did notice that I was a happier person when Global Warming was around. "

"Aww, that is so sweet." Judy replies.

"Give me a break. If that was me, they would have booted my ass," Frank says.

"Ha! They still might!" I exclaim. Judy and I both laugh as Frank gives me this eat shit look with his face. Then I continue, "Look man, you have to admit that the website with all its functionality still works. The only upgrades we've had to make since then are aesthetics. I guess my productivity went up. Just like yours is going up now."

We both just die again and as Frank is about to tell us to go fuck ourselves we hear, "What's so funny?" Diane walks up to Frank, "Are they making fun of you again?"

"Yes. Yes they are." He shoots this mean look at me. It's hard to take him seriously because I've known him for such a long time. Besides, this how we rib each other, the man is bound to get me back sooner or later.

"Well I feel sorry for Louis, because it's not like you can't throw him over your shoulder and toss him somewhere." Frank smiles while nods and Judy is laughing.

"Hey, let's not give the big angry black man any ideas! That is black on black crime. We are supposed to be role models." I say smiling.

"Role models? You're so full of shit." She says laughing and now they all starting laughing.

"It's ok Diane, I know where he sleeps." Frank responds.

"I see how quickly this can turn on me," I say. I put on the best pretend to be offended look I could muster.

"I think maybe we should get this program started," Diane says.

She is right. I'm the host of this reception and I need to get this thing started before all the food is gone and students start to leave. I walk to the podium and lower the volume on my iPod. I grab my notes from the shelf in the podium and I see a note from Raina. *We need to talk.*

I look up and she's talking to Marvin. I clear my throat and begin my speech.

TWENTY

I walk back to my office after the reception is over. I always make sure that I'm the last person to leave the room. This allows me to survey the space and make sure everyone leaves. The catering staff provided me with some take home boxes and since there is plenty of *maduros* left, I take enough for Frank and me. Of course he left halfway through my presentation to go see Annette, so it was up to me get the leftovers for the house.

I open my office and I'm glad to see that my phone is on my desk. I thought that I had lost it, but in my absent mindedness I left it right next to the keyboard. I put my stuff on top of the comfy chair that Judy loves to sit in and I finally sit down at my desk. I check my phone and I have some text messages, Facebook notifications and twitter alerts. I scroll through and I find nothing too important that needs to be addressed at the moment.

I have texts from Ruben, Lidia, and Brian that I will answer before I leave. I unlock my computer screen and address some work emails that I didn't get a chance to because of the preparation for the reception. It's getting late and I really should leave. I check my Gmail before I decide to pack up and I see that Abby responded to me:

Hey there handsome, I am glad you liked the books I sent you. I hope you get to read them. Maybe we can discuss one day. Keep in touch. xoxo

That's interesting since I haven't spoken to her in a while. It might be fun to start flirting with her again. The only thing is that I don't want to do this over email. So I write her a quick response:

The titles alone intrigue me. I would love to meet up and discuss. Is your number the same or did you change it? Let me know.

At this point I would rather just text her. Speaking of which, I need to answer these texts.

Brian Keegan: 3:50 pm Let me know if there are issues with the iPod connection. I should be in the auditorium until 8.

Ruben Morales: 5:15 pm What are we doing this weekend?

Lidia Pope: 6:09 pm I'm coming by

I look at the time and it's about 6:30. Shit, did she mean she was coming here or coming over the house? I'm almost done typing a text when I hear someone at the doorway. It's Lidia.

"Hi Papi." She says. She is wearing a gray jacket and tight

blue denim jeans that are tucked into her knee-high black boots. She walks in and sits down across from me. She puts her purse on the arm of the chair.

"Hello Lidia," I respond. I try my best to sound neutral about her appearance in my office. I continue, "So what may I owe this visit to?"

'Wow, so formal. I don't even get 'how are you?'"

"My bad. It's been a long day. How are you?"

"I'm ok, just wondering why, someone I've come to know too well over the last few weeks, is blowing me off."

Looks like the time for me avoiding Lidia is over. I didn't want to have this conversation right now but then again when was I going to get around to it? She looks very toned down today too, maybe she just came from her yoga class considering her somewhat casual look today. Her hair is pulled back in a ponytail but the only thing that is really standing out to me is her red lipstick. Did she just put that on for me?

"I've been busy. You know I do work and I was in New York City last week."

"Ah, New York City. You went to see that little girl. Did you get any?

"I'm not sure that is the point…"

"So, you didn't. Well, here is the thing about little girls in their twenties, they love to play games and be cock teases.

217

They pretend that they don't know what they're doing, but in reality, they just want you to chase them. And when the chase is over and they get bored with you, they move on to the next one."

"Is that coming from experience?"

"You know it. I've been around the block in my twenties. I'm sure she flirts with you and then tells you that she really doesn't want to be with you."

I have no response to this. I can't say that she is right or wrong, but I do know that she does play games too. I think Lidia doesn't like to lose and she is proving that to me right now.

"Ok, but what game are you playing though? You send me nude pictures that other men, I assume, have taken. You also have been flirting really hard when you know that Frank is a very good friend of mine. I'm not sure what you're getting out of this outside of playing a game."

"I'm not playing a game Louis. Yes, I'm a horny woman who hasn't gotten what she's wanted for a very long time. As I was saying before, I'm not sitting on the other side of this desk batting my eyes at you nor am I the type to make small talk on chat so I can lure you in with my cuteness. That is what little girls do. I'm a grown woman and I do recognize that I come on strong, but that's because I know what I want."

"Oh and that would be me?"

"Don't be so full of yourself. You think I'm that hung up

on you? Please nigga, they are almost lining up outside my yoga class. I just want a man who is going to satisfy me. Frank is nowhere near the freak that I would like him to be. I'm tired of just laying in the missionary position until he's done. God forbid a woman wants oral sex. God forbid I want to have sex anywhere but the bedroom."

"Wow. I'm really sorry that this is happening to you, but I'm not fucking stupid. I know that you can be with any man you want including the dope who took those pics."

She gives me a look. Perhaps she wasn't expecting a fight from me. But it's not a look of anger or submission. It's a look that perhaps she came here to start this fight.

"I love the spunk you have. If I didn't know better, I would say that you're jealous. You should really just take me on your desk right now."

"Lidia, I can't."

"I find that a little hard to believe. Shall I go over the last few weeks?"

"Listen to me, I'm telling you…"

"Because I remember someone being very happy to see me when he was sick. Do you remember that?"

"Lidia! I can't do this with you!" I say with a little more force.

"Really, why not? You're gonna tell me that you'd rather

be played by a little girl?"

"Frank is my friend and I won't do this to him"

She sits back and now she's not happy. "Really, so now you want to take the moral high ground? You didn't use Frank as an excuse when I was jerking you off."

"Well, I was drunk…"

"Ha! Your cock was so hard and you loved every minute of it. But, you know what? I knew you would be a pussy about this. I admit I was surprised you went so far with me, but you go ahead and you keep your friend and his little bitch too."

My eyes open wide. When did she know about this?

She continues. "That's right. I know about him and his little ratchet ass hoe. You guys think I'm fucking stupid? A woman always knows!" She gets up and grabs her bag and is about to walk out when she says "Let me just tell you something…" She walks up practically leaning over my desk pointing down at her crotch and continues, "This pussy is the shit and I would've made you forget all about that little girl in New York. I should've let Kevin kick your ass."

I'm completely puzzled right now. "What does he have anything to do with this?"

"I was the one who told him about the stupid YouTube video, asshole." She walks out of the office suite. Why would she tell Kevin? Wow, is she fucking him too? Is this why Raina wants to talk to me? I get up to go after her and I see Brian open the suite door. "Hey Lidia, how are…"

"Go fuck yourself." she says as she storms past him.

"Wow, what was that about?" Brian says as he watches her storm away.

I walk around the suite to make sure I was the only person here with her during this conversation. I don't need any witnesses of this exchange. "I think she is mad at Frank." I say.

"Well that's nothing new."

No one on the staff has any idea what's going on with Frank and Lidia, with the exception of Judy and me. I have no intention of telling Brian what's going because it's really not my story to tell. Brian was following up on his text about the A/V set up. I assured him that it everything went well. I can tell that he wanted to hang out for a bit, but I'm just ready to go home.

There was a time when Brian, Frank, and I would all hang out before the marriages. Looking back at it, the three of us got married in relative succession. I was the first to get married, then Brian tied the knot with his wife a year later, followed by Frank and Lidia the year after that. All three weddings were a blast and I think after Frank's wedding, our friends and co-workers had spent more than enough on each of us in terms of gifts. Those were some of the best times I had in my younger days with the university, back when I didn't know any better about how loves works.

Somewhere between the birth of Brian's son and the appearance of Global Warming in my life, things had somehow changed. We hung out less and became more serious about our work. I suppose it was maturity or at least the beginning of coming to grips with real responsibility. When you're a single man, you really don't have any real responsibilities outside of work. Sure, a man has to eat, pay bills, and clean himself up, but what comes after that? Marriage provided all of us with views that changed everything.

While I was the one who had the wandering eyes that would be a factor in my divorce, Brian seemed like a complete angel. Of course, despite his introverted demeanor, I knew better. I have always known that he had a thing for younger women that were above the age of 18. He never acted on it but I could always tell when he made a feeble attempt to flirt with a woman. Most women felt he was awkward in certain situations, but overall he is a great guy. Of course, it was those certain situations I thrived in.

Frank's teddy bear demeanor won him many women friends. They loved talking to him because they pegged him as harmless and for the most part he is. If anyone were to witness a conversation that Frank and I had with a woman that either one of us thought was cute, they would be in for a lesson on how to flirt without making it seem like you're flirting. Brian was always miffed about the whole thing and always commented on the fact that so many students, in general, liked us.

The reality of the situation was that Frank and I were never going to do anything with these girls, but we always loved to give Brian the impression that it was always possible. One time he came up and asked me how many white girls I've a slept with. My answer was plain, simple, and direct: *more than you have*. I never want to get into those discussions with him so I always made sure that my answers were short.

I watch Brian leave the suite and I can't help but feel bad. I really do owe him some favors. I run out of the suite before he gets too far. Maybe I can convince him to hang out this weekend.

TWENTY ONE

I set myself up with a glass of wine as I wait for my dinner to heat up in the microwave. With the free time I had this past weekend, I made a big pot of *Arroz con Pollo*. It may not last long with Frank around, but it's good to not have to spend money on buying dinner. I sit in my normal place on the couch with my portable table in front of the television. At this point, the T.V. is just background noise once I open my laptop. Abby's notes have me really thinking about the future of my writing. I have written several short stories as it is with really no hope of ever publishing any of them.

I search for the folder in my documents titled "stories" and I open to see word files that I have not looked at in some time. I hear the microwave beep and that means dinner is ready. I look up and I see the manila folder containing the letters that I said I was going to burn a few weeks ago. It's amazing that I can have the instant gratification of food, but I can procrastinate with everything else. I have made the excuse that I will have to get a chimney sweep in order for to burn them in the fireplace when in reality I have no intention of calling him. The truth is that I don't want to spend the money.

I grab my food and sit down to eat. I decide to open one of the stories that I wrote a while back called "Bottomless." I start eating as I begin to read:

Oscar wakes up slowly. There is a familiar scent in the air. Coffee. He smiles, not yet opening his eyes. He hesitates a little bit because something feels out of place. He tries to move his arms and legs. But something is stopping his movement. Oscar opens his eyes. He's tied to the bed! "What the fuck?" flies through air in a surprised and yet amused way. He smiles, knowing she did this to him.

Amy hears the words coming from the other room. Her "victim" has woken up. She stops herself mid-stir with a mug of coffee in hand. Is that what she calls him now? A victim? Well, it seems appropriate at the moment. Amy knows she has a complete asshole tied to the bed stark naked. She's willing to bet he's smiling right now. Last night was awesome, of course. He has the stamina of a racehorse and is almost hung like one too, but she wanted to use him for her own personal satisfaction. Why shouldn't she? She was tired of her ex-boyfriend taking advantage of her all the time and now she is going to take her past frustrations out on his friend, Oscar.

He wasn't going to fight his captor. How could he? Oscar was amazed how perfectly he was tied to the bed. Had she done this before? The thought was starting to arouse him. He continued to smile knowing that he may be in for just as long of a morning as he had the night before. He can hear her walking toward the door. Amy appears in the doorway sipping on a mug of what is probably coffee. She has her hair up in a ponytail and is dressed in nothing but a tank top that hugs her shape. Oscar's arousal only increases when he realizes she is bottomless. Her pubic hair is neatly shaved into a landing strip that makes her look much sexier than he remembered.

She can see his penis growing larger. Clearly he is aroused by this situation. He's such a willing participant that she'll enjoy breaking him. Amy sips her coffee realizing that he's staring at her navel. Is it the belly button ring? Perhaps it's the strip of hair she just had waxed a few days earlier. She's going to play this game and let him soak her all in. Amy turns around and places the mug on the dresser.

Oscar's eyes widen as she turns around giving him a view of her ass. This is the one part of her body that he fantasizes about the most. This almost perfectly round onion-shaped bottom makes him squirm and gets him as fully erect as he's going to be. She turns back around and asks if he likes what he sees and he barely gets out a "yes" from his lips. There's no question in his mind that this is the hottest conquest he has ever had. She is smart and completely gorgeous.

Amy gives him an evil grin. She knows what she's about to do. He's almost cute squirming there with his erection. She walks up to the bed and grabs it already wet with pre cum. "Well it looks like someone's happy to see me. I guess you couldn't get enough of me last night." She wants to laugh because she can feel his emotions in the palm of her hand. He is pulsating as he tries to say something intelligible. She learned this little trick that when a man is fully aroused, she rubs the tip of his penis with her thumb. This would make it almost impossible for him to speak in any type of coherent sentences.

He now knows that she's not playing fair by asking a question like that. The feeling of her fingers playing with his tip makes his feet shift in his binds. Why is he so turned on by this so much? Oscar watches as she sits on the bed. Her curly brown hair makes her look stunning. Amy brushes her hair back and engulfs his penis. Oscar fights hard to hold a grunt. He suddenly feels how truly helpless he is. He can't move his hands to stroke her hair or to even hide his obvious expression of pleasure. Oscar found out last night how good Amy's head game is, but now he cannot fight it at all.

Amy loves to give head. She doesn't like to admit that to just any one, but it is something that she loves to do. She could never explain why until this very moment. She is in complete control. The power not only to pleasure a man at will, but the fact that she has his entire manhood is in her grasp is exhilarating. He's like her puppet now. A flick of her tongue or a brush of her lips gets a reaction and when she puts his penis in the back of her throat, she feels his body tense up. She looks up at him to see how he is handling it.

Oscar looks down to see her looking at him. Her gaze almost hypnotizes him and it begins to dawn on him that she's in complete control. He's not used to this at all because after all, he's the player. Women love to flock to him and his good looks. He knows that he has a smile that makes all the girls melt and yet he finds himself in this position? Oscar can barely think straight because Amy is determined to make him scream. Every time he fights it, she does something different to get him to moan louder.

She knows that she has him right where she wants him. Amy now toys with him by changing her strokes. There is no denying that she's enjoying this. It's like something has awakened inside of her. This carnal lust overcomes her and she almost feels like she has to pull herself way. Amy may love his penis, but she certainly doesn't love him. He's an arrogant asshole and she will not lose control.

He watches her get up. Oscar was puzzled as to why she suddenly stopped. She was giving him the best head he has ever had. Amy looks at him and says, "I think you're having too much fun. Now it's my turn." He wasn't sure what that meant, but he was glad she stopped. Oscar was very close to ejaculation and he just wasn't ready for all this. The lack of control is a dynamic that he's not used to and right now she could do anything to him. Oscar didn't want to think about what that means, but for a moment he had a small measure of fear.

Amy had thought about this exact moment when she was stirring her coffee. Does she just sit on his face and literally rub his nose in the fact that she's in complete control or does she climb on top of him and treat him like the bottom he should be? She reminds herself that Oscar is indeed tied up and she can do both if she wanted to do, but what would be more effective? Amy decides she is going to give him the ride of his life.

I still don't know if I like this particular story. I think about the others I've written and why I wrote them. A few of them started out being a fantasy that I was acting out with various women I have met, sort of a "what if" scenario. But then something occurred during that thought process. I began writing more about the people and their tendencies and not just the physical act of sex. One of the critiques of this story from Abby was that it was clearly written by a man. I suppose there is no real way to make a blowjob seem any less pornographic unless you add some reasoning behind it.

That was the good thing about Abby, she was able to talk me through the thought process of characterization. She thought that I could be as graphic as I want to be as long as the character remains the focus of the book and not the act of sex. I struggled with this because I think that I was just letting my libido write the stories.

I start thinking about several ways to make this story better and perhaps more impactful. Should I add a horror element to it? The story is obviously about control and revenge. I could have her decapitate him. Yeah, that might be too much. I finish up my food when my computer beeps. It's a Facebook message.

Abigail Eastman: Hey there Handsome

Speak of the devil.

Louis Ortiz: Hey Abby! How goes it?

Abigail Eastman: It's going well. I'm glad you liked the books.

Louis Ortiz: It was indeed a surprise. We haven't spoken in a while.

Abigail Eastman: I know! You stopped showing up to the workshops once you got hitched. I didn't want to get you in trouble so I stopped calling. lol

Louis Ortiz: I'm sorry about that. I guess I was busy being married.

Abigail Eastman: And now look at you, a single man and you're still busy. I guess all those girls on campus must keep you that way.

Louis Ortiz: Well, I'm a busy man but it's all business with my students.

Abigail Eastman: I bet they want to still get into your pants though.

Louis Ortiz: Clearly, not much has changed with you over the years. lol

Abigail Eastman: Why would it?

Louis Ortiz: It's been a few years and you have a kid now and then there is the baby daddy...

Abigail Eastman: Please, that asshole gets on my damn nerves. He turned out to be only good for sex. But, the one thing I will give him is that he really loves his daughter.

Louis Ortiz: How old is she now?

Abigail Eastman: Jenny is 6.

I vaguely remember all of this. Abby had given birth about the time Global Warming and I began to start knowing each other. The only thing that I recall with any certainty was that her boyfriend at the time was black. Not that this bothered me, it's just wasn't a surprise. She reminded me of a Sarah Jay type of person when it came to Black men. Personally, I have always thought that that was one of the main reasons she took an interest in me.

Louis Oritz: Wow, it's been that long? So how are things with the father? Not so well?

Abigail Eastman: I'm no longer with Larry but I guess you wouldn't know it by the way he acts.

Louis Ortiz: What do you mean? Does he stalk you?

Abigail Eastman: Not really. But I rather not get into it.

Louis Ortiz: Why not?

Abigail Eastman: Because quite frankly he doesn't matter in my life anymore and I don't want to dissuade you into not seeing me. ☺

There is no secret that there was some chemistry between us during the workshop days. While she helped me write better, she also brought out a side of me she was dying to see. So when I wrote a story about how much the main character loved bottomless women, she ate it up and then some. She frequently would say, *all writing is biographical* meaning that no matter what I write, there will always be a piece of me that comes with it. Fiction is a sum of experiences that plays out in the imagination. To prove her point she would later show me a poem she wrote about her power of a clitoris. I often ask myself where in the world do I find these women?

Louis Ortiz: So you already have me coming over now?

Abigail Eastman: Of course. There's no way I'm letting you get away this time.

Those words linger in my head when I hear a knock the door. I look at the time on my computer and it is almost 9 pm. I'm not sure who is coming by, unless it's Annette again. That girl can't seem to get enough of Frank. Personally, I feel bad for her because it sounds like she's gonna lose her voice one of these days.

I open the door and there stands Raina. I guess she was serious about wanting to have this conversation, I just didn't think she would come by.

"Hi. I hope I'm not disturbing you." She says.

"No, I just finished eating. Come in." I respond. Raina walks in and I close the door behind her. I tell her that we can talk in the living room. She's still in her work attire, a grey suit that consists of a blazer and straight-legged pants. She has her flats on so I can only assume that she came here right after work. Must have been a long night.

She walks in the living room and looks around. I'm already rolling my eyes because I can see the judgment in her face. Raina hasn't been here since she moved out when we first separated. She has made a conscious effort to make sure that she doesn't even drive near the house. So I can only imagine what's running through her mind. When she left this room in particular, it was empty because she took all the furniture. It has taken me several months and multiple Ikea deliveries to finally have this room furnished.

"Nice furniture. You fixed it up nicely. Do you mind if I sit?"

"Please do."

As I sit on the couch I try not to smirk when she sits on the same chair where Vera rode me about a month ago. Of course it wouldn't be so funny if Vera is the reason why she was here.

"So you still cook. That's good." Raina comments. She was never that good with small talk.

"Yes, I do. But that's not the reason you're here."

"No. I'm here because I need your advice and help about something," She says as she looks into her hands. This must be one of the last things she wants to do.

I look at her very strangely. I can hear the Facebook chat alarms going off. "Excuse me a moment," I say and I pick up my laptop and type to Abby saying that I can't talk right now. I close the MacBook then continue, "So let me get this straight, after what you did you a few weeks ago, you want me to help you?"

"Yes, and in my defense, I've always had to push you in order to get something done."

"Even though we're no longer married you still want to push something that wasn't that big of a deal."

"It was the principle. I asked you to do something in January and as usual, it took you forever to get it done."

"And yet here is this theme, you're asking me for something."

There is a silence. I can tell that she wants to say something harsh but she fights and swallows whatever pride she may have left. "I didn't come here to fight with you, Louis.

I came here for your help because at one time we used to be friends. There was also a time when you used to love me."

After that statement I feel myself backing down. There really was a time when we got along great, but it's just hard to remember what that looked like. We started out as friends, which is what most people will say is the foundation to every good relationship. Out of that friendship, started a casual sexual relationship that lasted for several months. Then there came the precipice in which I had to make a choice of whether to date her or let her go.

Because we were friends with benefits there was the unwritten rule of not being exclusive. So at any point we could have chosen to see other people. I was the lazy one and didn't feel the need to date anyone because I was already having the sex I wanted without any of limitations of a relationship. I didn't have to check in, I could flirt, and I could do anything that normal boyfriends couldn't because we did not define each other as a couple. But that all changed when this guy, George, began to make moves on her. He took her on one date and I didn't like it. Soon after I had to step up and tell her that perhaps she should date me instead.

I take a deep breath and say, "Alright, I will let it go. What's going on?"

"It's Kevin. I think he's cheating on me."

She said it so quickly as if she needed it to get out immediately.

"What? How so? How do you know?"

"Please Louis, I learned very quickly how to tell when a man is lying." That was probably a jab at me and I cannot say that I don't deserve that.

"Do you have any evidence?"

"No. Its just a feeling that I get. Like, I know that he's up to something."

A woman's "spidey sense" will get men all the time. It's this feeling that has been the thorn in the side of every man who has had a wandering eye.

"But you don't really know. What's he doing that's got you so paranoid?"

"It's little things like closing his laptop when I come in the room or the late night text messages that he gets."

"Did you ask him who they're from?"

"I'm afraid to. I've already been there with you and look how that turned out. I'm tired of yelling and screaming and being the bitch all the time. I just want to trust someone. Am I that hard to love?"

This is not the conversation that I want to have. I'm not sure what the best course of action is here. Do I comfort her with the risk of her taking it the wrong way? There could always be a chance that she could try to slip in a final night of sex. If Kevin is indeed cheating on her then sleeping with me would be a pretty good way of getting revenge. It's not like she hasn't done something like this before. When she had her suspicions about Zenia and me, she decided to visit George and give him a blowjob he still probably remembers.

"Look, I know that I wasn't the best husband in the world and there will never be enough apologies I could give you but you can't look at this like the problem is with you. There is no real way of knowing that Kevin is cheating on you. Besides, you can't think that those actions mean anything without talking to him. I know I did those things too but Kevin and I aren't the same."

Great, now I find myself defending this guy.

"I guess you're right but I just don't know what to do. I don't want to follow him or check his texts. I've been down that road with you and I'm afraid of what I may find."

"Does he leave out his phone or laptop?"

"That's the thing, they are both password protected. I know have to talk to him. I just don't want to hear that he may not be in love with me anymore."

This may be another jab at me, although I think she may not have done that on purpose. I will never forget the week before she decided to finally move out. We had been fighting about something that I cannot even remember. All the fights leading up to this day all blurred together. However, she asked me if I even loved her any more. I couldn't bring myself to answer that question. Of course, no answer was the answer in and of itself.

What I remember most was her reaction. She burst into tears and ran into the guest room she had decided to move into a few weeks prior. Her loud sobs was something that I wasn't prepared for. I wanted to comfort her but that would not have mattered. I cried a little bit too because I knew, just as she did, that this eight year marriage was truly over. I had always hoped that perhaps those sobs were her body releasing all the pain and anger out of her system. Maybe there was a part of her that knew she didn't have to endure me anymore. It's something that still haunts me.

"What can I do to make you feel better? I'm not sure I can even help."

"Oh, but I think you can help."

"Ok, what is it?"

"I think I know who he's fucking."

"Who?"

"I think he's fucking Lidia."

Shit. Face-Palm.

TWENTY TWO

Raina is pretty convinced about this. What I didn't know is over the last several months Kevin and Lidia have become friends. While Raina is one to believe that men and women can be friends, she was always very cautious about these two. She never really cared for how flirty Lidia can be with him and to a certain extent, never cared about how she spoke to me when we were married. The point is she would not put it past Lidia to attempt to sleep with Kevin.

The problem is that Raina blames herself. Kevin moved to Syracuse from New York City because of her. The two of them met when she was she decided to take a week off to visit her family in the Bronx. Her family had a big cook out in Van Cortlandt Park and he just happened to know one of her cousins. After hitting it off, they slowly developed a long-distance relationship that apparently got real and he wanted to move up here to be with her. The issue is that he couldn't find a job. It's debatable to me how much he was really looking considering that Raina makes pretty good money and can support him for a little while if she wanted to. She introduced him to Frank and Lidia in hopes that he would make some new connections that may help him find a job.

Frank said that he would keep an eye out but it was Lidia who mentioned that she might know of a job opening at the gym where she teaches one of her yoga classes. This is how their friendship started and how he also started working at the gym. Since then they have been talking every day in some way, shape or form.

This explains how Lidia was able to tell Kevin about that YouTube video. Clearly they talk but what's bothering me is why Lidia didn't tell Kevin that she was the one that posted it online. I make the decision right away that I'm not going to tell Raina what's happening with Lidia. That would be a bad thing because it would ultimately get to Frank and besides, she still has no proof of any wrongdoing. Of course, it doesn't look good for him considering that I know that someone has been taking pictures of her.

"I'm sorry that you're going through this but my question is, again, what do you want me to do? You mentioned a favor?" I ask this but then I just get a bad feeling as to what she may actually want.

"I want you to talk to Frank, to see if he has any suspicions." She answers

"That's it? You just want me to talk to him? Why couldn't you just go and talk to him yourself?"

"Because you're his friend and you can probably get more

information than I could. I know they are separated but I just want to know if there is more to it."

"Well that's easy, I can tell you that Kevin is not the reason for their separation."

"Really? How do you know that for sure?"

"Because Frank told me. He mentioned nothing about any other man."

I could tell at this point that she had nothing to say. Raina holds her hands together and says, "Well, I don't know what to do then. He's fucking someone! I just know it." She may be even more upset if it isn't Lidia.

"Alright...alright, just calm down. I will see what I can find out. I still think that you should talk to him about this. Maybe not in the way you would have talked me about it, but perhaps in a non-threatening way."

"And how do you suppose I do that? It's taking everything in me to not go through his damn phone. I know that I have to trust him and maybe I'm wrong but how else am I going to find out?"

I can't even count how many times this woman used to go through my phone and my laptop. It got to the point where I could tell whether she had been snooping around. I learned very quickly that I needed to do things differently, like having an alternative email for all the stupid shit I was doing. Much of it didn't matter, even if I were to delete messages, she would still look through the itemized phone bill to see who I was calling and texting. Zenia's number would show up on pages upon pages of that damn telephone bill.

"Do you even trust him to begin with?" I asked.

Raina pauses for a minute and she nods. "I do. I'm just scared. I really care for this man."

"Well, then I think you need to go with that. You need to have a little faith in him and not let the little things bother you. I mean, I get that you have your feelings and that's very valid, but don't jump the gun or do anything rash that might jeopardize what you have with him. It may just turn out to be nothing."

I don't know much about this dude, but from the lovely conversation I had with him he does seem to care about her. A man doesn't just threaten another man's career for nothing. Unfortunately, this means I'm not done with Lidia yet. One thing that I have come to learn about her is that despite her plotting and scheming she will tell the truth if I just ask her directly.

"I should go." Raina says as she gets up. "Thank you for listening. Maybe it truly is nothing."

I walk her to the door, "I will let you know if I find anything out. Try not to worry." I open the door for her and she walks out.

Raina turns around and says. "Thank you again. I tend to forget that despite all the fighting that you really are a good guy. I wasn't the perfect wife either and I know that. Have a good night."

I watch Raina enter her silver Toyota Prius then back out of the driveway. I close the door with a lot on my mind. It takes me a few minutes to process everything that was just said. It has been a very long time since we have spoken to each other in a friendly way. But now I have to think about what I'm going to do. I have no real reason to speak to Lidia after our discussion today. I get that she's mad that I won't sleep with her but I think she's out of her mind to react like that. I do wonder if there is some kind of external force influencing her behavior, but over the top and a quick temper is just her M.O. Regardless, I'm going to have to confront her about this.

I go back to the couch and open my laptop. Abby has signed out but left a response. *That's ok handsome. We can talk later. If you consider coming over, just know that I'm freshly shaved. Everywhere. lol*

Dammit! Vera is still the last person I've had sex with. I have think about this now. It isn't too weird if I just drive to Fulton, which is a 45-minute ride, to fuck her brains out when I haven't spoken to her in years right? Now that I think about this, I haven't seen her in a few years so I check her Facebook page and scroll through some of her pictures. There is nothing here that is preventing me not to go. Of course, I do have to work tomorrow. I can go back and forth on this whole thing all night but the longer I take the more of a "no" it's going to be.

There is something that comes up in the back of my head. Her daughter is a 6-year old and I know she lives with her. I can almost hear my father's voice in the back of my head saying: *the last thing you want to do is get involved with a woman with a kid.* I remember him telling this to me years ago when we would talk about relationships. Not to mention that the baby daddy is still around in some way, so the last thing I want is to get into another fight. The last one did not go so well.

I think I have come to the decision that I will not go over there, at least not tonight. I have a very good feeling that I will be revisiting this same conversation with myself in the weeks to come. Its not that I don't want to have sex with her, but I feel that I've made some really poor decisions over the last several weeks and this one may end with a bad result. I should probably just focus on myself and let's face it, I have an unlimited amount of porn on my computer. I'm sure I will knock right out when I'm done and I don't have to worry about driving home.

It takes me about 40 minutes to clean up the dishes and the kitchen overall. It can be nice to have a roommate but not when he forgets to clean his shit up. Frank isn't an overall dirty person but he seems to forget to do the dishes. Since I'm the one who cooked I ended doing most of dishes in the sink anyway so I just finished what was left and then wiped off all the counters.

By the time I'm done I hear keys in the door. Frank walks in while in the middle of a conversation with Annette, of course. I hear another voice that is not so familiar, it sounds like another girl. Please tell me that this man is not going to have a threesome under my roof. This might make me go to Fulton right now.

Frank walks into the kitchen with some bags from Burger King. Annette walks in behind him with another girl. "Hey man what's up?"

"What's going on?" I ask

"Hi Louis," Annette says as she comes over and gives me a kiss on the cheek. "This is my line sister, Paula."

"Nice to meet you Paula," I shake her hand and she smiles in response. This must be the Paula that Frank told me about. She is shorter than Annette by at least 4 inches. She is wearing jeans and boots. Her black coat hides the rest of her body. She is cute, but young. I feel like her face is just telling me how young she is.

Frank puts the bags on the counter I just cleaned. "Did you eat? I got you a whopper with cheese and some fries." He says as he starts taking out the food.

"Well, I did eat but I'm not gonna turn down a whopper," I respond. I look over to the girls and they are texting away on their phones.

"Oh and I told Paula it was ok to stay in the other guest room tonight. Is that cool?" Frank says to me as he hands me the burger and fries.

"Sure why not?" I say as the two girls grab their food from Frank.

"Thank you so much. I appreciate it," Paula says.

They both walk into the living room. I place my fries on the kitchen island on the far wall so I can unwrap my burger. Frank has already torn into his and has taken a couple of bites. "So, guest room huh?" I say to him with a smug smile.

"What does that mean?" he asks with a full mouth.

Then I hear from the living room, "Louis, you mind if we change the channel? We really need to see the Kardashians tonight," Annette asks.

"Sure!" I say then I take a big ass bite as if I didn't already eat tonight.

"Her line sister is here from Binghamton and she just needs a place to crash tonight," Frank explains.

"Hey you don't have to explain anything to me. I'm quite ok if you decide to have a threesome. I promise to not tell a soul," I smile and give a thumbs up.

"Nice. We all can't be like you," Frank smiles back.

Clearly he is referring to a time when I just happened to have gotten lucky a long time ago. Sometimes you just need to be at the right place at the right time. That place just happened to be in the Bronx and I was bold enough to ask the woman I was seeing if she would ever have a threesome. Her response was something like "only if I was drunk." So I took it upon myself to try to set up the variables. I just happened to have somebody in mind that was a friend of hers that I had my eye on. I had a discussion with both of them and they both agreed to it only if we had plenty of drinks available. A week later we got together at the old apartment with plenty of Jack Daniels and it was a done deal.

"You could live that life too man. Shit you are practically living it now. Unless you think you're too old."

Frank gives me a very sarcastic look. "Ha ha, fuck you. Maybe I'm too much of a gentleman."

"A gentleman? You kill this chick every night. I'm surprised she doesn't have PSD."

"PSD? What?"

"Pussy Stress Disorder," We both laugh.

"You're such a fucking asshole," He says in mid laugh.

I take the last bite of my burger and dig into my fries. "I'm going upstairs to take a shower and knock the fuck out. I will put some new sheets on that bed for her."

"Aight man." Frank says as he pulls out another burger. I wonder if he smoked tonight. I can't really tell from his eyes, but the dude is munching hard. I go to the living room to fetch my laptop and I see both girls glued to the television. I excuse myself while I grab the MacBook and cord. I'm about to grab my phone that's on the coffee table but my hands are too full. I will have to come back for it later before I go to bed.

Before I leave, I say to Paula, "I will put some sheets and towels in the guest room so you don't have to go looking for them."

Paula looks up really quickly, "Thank you." Then she faces the TV again.

I head upstairs to my room. I put the laptop on my bed and I open it up. I turn the small television on and head back outside to the hallway. The linen closet is right outside my door. I get a nice set of sheets for the twin-sized bed, a fresh towel, and a washcloth. The guest room is adjacent to my room so it's just a matter of flipping the switch on and placing the linens on the bed. Before I go, I realize that I haven't been in this room in a few weeks. I look around to make sure there are no spiders around. This was the same room that Raina moved into when both knew our marriage was over.

What I do find on the other side of the dresser is a paper shredder. I totally forgot I had this. Raina bought this one year to shred the massive amounts of junk mail that we got every day. This was just another task I would procrastinate on. However, I think I have a very good use for it. I pick it up, turn off the lights and carry it to my room. I think the best idea is to take those damn letters from Isabel and run them through this shredder. I think I will do that tomorrow as I begin to yawn. Clearly this is my body telling me how tired I am so I get undressed, put on a robe and head for the bathroom.

I'm not one for long showers. I clean what I need to and get out. I brush my teeth for good measure and I head back to my room with every intention on falling right to sleep. This has been a very long day and this is going to feel great. Before I close my laptop I do notice that there is a flashing message from someone called Zenia. I kindly ignore it and close my laptop. I place it on the chair next to my bed and shut off the television I wasn't watching. I finally go under the covers then shut off the light and close my eyes.

Bang Bang

What the hell is going on? Can't a brother get any sleep? I look around in the dark for my robe on the bed but I cannot find it. I get up to search the floor.

Bang Bang

"Hold on! I'm coming!" I can't find this stupid robe. Where did I put it? I hate this feeling when I'm startled awake and nothing makes sense.

Bang Bang

Ok, now I'm pissed. Whoever is knocking on that door is about to get full-frontal. I open the door and no one is there. The hallway light is still on. I'm so puzzled right now. I thought for sure that someone was knocking on the door. Am I that tired?

Bang Bang

Shit, maybe it's the *front door*. I head downstairs slowly and I can hear the television on. I'm quite impressed with my ninja skills right now because these normally creaking stairs are quiet. I can't make out what is playing because the volume is low but I can still see the bluish light coming from the living room. The lights down here are off. I peak into the living room and see Annette's head bobbing up and down between a pair of legs that we're just going to assume are Frank's. I back away slowly.

Is that porn they're watching? I double check by peaking slowly again and it looks like they are on the television too. Oh God. I close my eyes with the realization they've made a sex tape. Jesus be a fence.

Bang Bang

I jump and try not to make noise as I cover my mouth. I'm right by the front door. I open it slowly and there is Zenia. Her hair runs straight down her back. She has a deep blue shade of eye shadow with the blackest lipstick I've ever seen. She's only wearing a long black raincoat with pumps. I think I'm getting turned on.

"Hello lover." She says "How could you forget about me so quickly?"

I struggle to say any words. I look down I see she is tugging on me.

"Can't speak can you? It appears I have you by the balls." She smiles. I can hear the moans coming from the TV in the living room. I wish I could turn around but I'm totally fixated in this moment.

Bang Bang

I look up and I see two people coming from a car that I didn't see in the shadows of night. Lidia and Raina come into view. Lidia's hair is in pigtails. She wearing a white shirt with red overall shorts, knee high socks and sneakers. She has a face that is telling me that she would rather be the one tugging on me. Raina is wearing a French Maid outfit with high heels and a whip in her hand. She, however, doesn't look happy at all.

Raina looks over to Lidia and asks, "Why are we even here? You think I want to be in *her* presence?"

Lidia says, "Well she is about to let go at any minute, then he becomes mine."

"Good Luck with that." Raina says

Zenia is still looking at me and says, "Bitches and birds, you should know, just like he does, that all of this is mine and it has been for years." She begins to squeeze. "Isn't that right, honey?"

My mouth opens as pain shoots up my abdomen. I want to scream but nothing comes out. I can see all three women smile.

Bang Bang

I fall to my knees as she let's go. I yell out, *what do you want from me!?!* I can still feel them looking at me.

"It's not about what we want. It's about what you want." I hear a voice that is not quite familiar, a voice that I haven't heard in a very long time and along with that I hear footsteps. I look up and I see the three ladies move slightly out the way when I see Isabel walking up to me. Her dark brown hair is pulled back and she has a pair of Ray-Bans on. Her brown trench coat hides whatever she's wearing, but it's her deep red lipstick that distracts me. It's almost like she stepped out of a scene from *The Matrix*.

"Just look at you. All of this, everything you see here in front of you, is your creation. Your fucked up, misogynistic, creation of what you want us to be. You put us on a pedestal secretly thinking you're the best man in world despite your faults. Your mind dresses us up in these outfits that turn you on because in some sick twisted way, you rank us. And in the end, you want to believe that you can just forget about us. I got news for darling, you can't."

"Yes, I can forget all about you! I just need time to let the pain go away," I say while I'm hunched over still clutching my balls.

"Aww, isn't he cute ladies?" Isabel says as they all giggle.

She puts the tip of her black leather boot on my forehead and kicks me back. I land on my back and as I try to get up she places the heel of her boot on my chest. I watch her slowly pull out a revolver and point it to my face. She takes off her sunglasses with her free hand so I can see her brown eyes as she says, "The thing is, sweetie, we define you. Say goodnight."

Bang Bang

TWENTY THREE

I startle myself awake! I think I make a noise that is kind of like a scream but came out more like a giant gasp. Holy shit what a dream! I put my hands on my chest and then my head to feel around because I swear to God those bullets felt real. I reach over to my iPhone and realize it's not there. Maybe I left it downstairs. Then I search for my glasses on the nightstand as well. Once I find them, I fumble them around in my hands and put them on. The cable box says its 2:26 am and I hold my head in my hands. This is the last time I eat any fast food at a late hour.

Bang Bang. What the fuck is it? I jump out bed and rush to the door. I listen very closely. The banging is actually very consistent with...Frank fucking. Jesus this dude doesn't give it a rest. How is this even possible? I thought she had her period, unless it's over? Has it been a week already? I grab my robe from the bed and put it on. I find my slippers in the dark and walk out of my room. Now the sound is just loud. I can hear her moaning.

I walk in to the bathroom and take a piss. I'm just annoyed for so many reasons. I won't even think about the jackrabbits in the other room. That dream has got to be the weirdest dream I've ever had. I get that dreams are messages from your subconscious, but what kind of message am I sending to myself?

I flush and wash my hands. I just look at myself in the mirror. Why am I driving myself crazy over this? I should be able to get over Zenia. I should be able to get past all the women in my life that had any meaning at all. For some reason I start thinking about my mother and our unresolved issues. I can't recall the last time I spoke to her.

I take a deep breath. One of my oldest friends, Naomi, once told me that she thought that I may have serious trouble finding happiness with another woman if I cannot resolve issues with the one woman who should be the center of my life. The truth is that my last falling out with her had to do with Raina and the fact that I married her. Now it's been about a year and a half since my divorce has been finalized and I still haven't spoken to my mother.

I'm not sure that I can sleep now with all the fucking going on around here and from the way things sound, I would not be surprised if he was indeed having a threesome. I turn the hall light on before I head downstairs. I think I will just have some chocolate milk or something. The stairs can creek loudly unless you go down slow but since I give zero fucks right now, I go down as loud as I can without making it seem as if it was intentional. Clearly I want to be passive aggressive about this situation.

All the lights are out down here and it just gives me a creepy feeling that my nightmare is about to come true right now. I walk into the kitchen and turn on the lights. I'm very pleased to see there are no dishes in the sink. I grab some soymilk out of the fridge and grab a glass from the cupboard. I pour the milk and I just pause and relive everything that happened in that dream again. I have never dreamt about all four of these women at the same time. In fact, I can't remember the last time I dreamt about Isabel. Maybe I'm over thinking everything that's going on in my life.

I turn around to get the chocolate syrup when I see Paula. I almost jump out of my skin! Her eyes widen and she apologies immediately, "I'm so sorry, I didn't mean to scare you." Second time tonight I have been startled.

"Its ok." I responded. "I was just having some trouble sleeping." Evidently, Frank is not having a threesome at the moment.

"So am I," She says. She's a pretty thin girl wearing a black tank top that shows a pretty decent amount of cleavage with faded blue boy shorts. I can just tell she had been tossing and turning, but I didn't hear her come down the stairs.

"Did you want some milk?"

"No thank you. I don't like soy milk."

"There is regular milk in the fridge."

"Ok."

I grab her a glass after I put away the soymilk and take out the regular milk that Frank drinks. I think he owes this to our guest since she's lacking in sleep presumably because of him and his new girlfriend. I pour her a glass and ask, "I was going to have chocolate milk myself. Would you like some?" Paula declines my offer and I hand her the glass. I then grab the syrup and pour myself a nice sized serving.

"So the noise is keeping you up too, huh?" Paula asks.

I stir the milk and say, "I guess you can say that." I take the spoon out and take a sip then continue, "It doesn't help that I had a nightmare." I put the spoon in the sink then tighten my robe. It is not lost on me that I'm commando right now.

"That sucks," She replies.

"I didn't hear you come down the stairs."

"Oh yeah, I tried sleeping in the room but I couldn't so I just took the pillows and went to the couch."

"Have they been going at it long?"

"Long enough, you know. I didn't believe her about these marathon sessions she brags about. I guess I was wrong."

"Pfft, at least you don't live here. I'm almost better off putting on some porn and leaving it on mute."

She laughs a little bit. We both drink from our glasses and the silence is filled with the noise of a bed creaking. Annette's moans are pretty consistent. I figured I should try to distract us from the obvious fact that sex is going on in the floor above us.

"So you're Annette's line sister. When did you cross?"

Her eyes light up a little. Perhaps she didn't expect me to know anything about Greek life. "We crossed this past spring".

"Oh, really? Still a neo then."

She smiles again. "Yeah, I am. Sadly that ends in a few weeks when the new girls cross. Plus I graduate in December so at least I experienced it all before going into the real world. Are you Greek?"

I shake my head. "Nope"

"Really? I would have sworn you were a Lambda."

"Nah, I thought about it in college but Greek life wasn't for me."

"Well I love it. I'm so glad that I went through the process."

"Of course you are, you are a neo. Most kids I work with that are neos are in this euphoric stage where they get as much ass as possible," I chuckle.

"Yeah, most guys I know certainly celebrate in that way but it's more than that to me."

"That's cool. When I was in school there was a Black frat and Latino frat that seemed to have interest me. I wasn't sure which way to go but in the end I decided to do neither."

"Was there a reason?"

"Hazing. I didn't want to be a part of that culture. Of course, I wasn't as articulate about it then as I am now, but I wasn't willing to take an ass whipping from someone and then call him my brother later. I suppose that means I have no heart."

"I dunno, you seemed to have plenty of heart to me," She says as she drinks her milk.

I already know I need to be careful. I can already feel her starting to flirt with me and being commando under this robe doesn't help. I'm also a little bit self-conscious since I'm not sure if she has caught me staring at her chest. Over the years I have learned to have blinders on around young girls dressed with their goods hanging out. I would have little to no reaction. But after Global Warming, my views began to change. Once Zenia graduated and we went our separate ways, I've found myself looking at all girls.

"I would like to think I do. Are you finished with that?"

She hands me her empty glass and I place it in the sink along with mine.

"Thank you," she says. I turn on the sink so I can at least put water in them. I turn off the water and that's when we both notice it. There is silence.

"Wow. I guess they're done," Paula says.

"Maybe, for all we know they are changing positions, taking a break or let's be honest, maybe she put it in her mouth."

Paula covers her mouth in shock and then starts laughing. "Wow, you went in!"

"I apologize. It's late and as much as I would like to go back to bed, I know that they will continue, excuse me."

I walk by her and into the living room. I turn on the light so I can find what I'm looking for. I noticed that I left my phone on the coffee table next to the envelope. I totally forgot to come back down for it. Maybe the nightmare was a good thing because I would have been late to work without my phone's alarm.

She follows me, "I dunno, they have been going at it pretty hard. I mean he is older than her."

I stop what I'm doing and look at her. "Are you serious? Is that the story you're going with?"

Paula smiles, "My bad, I wasn't really talking about you. I don't even how old you are."

I grab the envelope with the letters and my phone.

"I'm the same age as Frank. I'm 38."

"Sorry."

"It's ok. I know you think being in your thirties is ancient, but it isn't. You see, being in your twenties means you think you know what you're doing until you get to your thirties. Then you realize everything you thought was wrong. Thirty is when you become aware of yourself and everyone around you."

"What happens when you reach forty?"

"Hopefully success and more money. Anyway, I think I'm gonna to head to bed before they catch their second or third wind. Can you make sure you shut off the light in the kitchen for me."

"Sure I…"

Bang. Bang. Bang. Bang.

I put my head in my hand and say, "Jesus be a fence."

I walk over to the loveseat and just sit down. Paula sits on the couch where she did her best to transform it into a makeshift bed. I'm pretty sure that I can sleep through this if I wanted to. I would put the pillow over my head and hopefully just drift off. But it's more the dream than the actual act of falling asleep. As long as I can hear that banging I will be afraid to have that nightmare again tonight.

"So Paula, have you known Annette for a while or did you meet during the process?"

"We went to high school together. I met her when I was junior and she was a freshman, so I've known her for a few years. We really didn't plan on being in the same sorority but it just happened. We lost touch after I graduated high school but we reconnected when she started going to SU."

"Wait. I thought she went to the community college?"

"Well now she does. She completed one year at SU but she couldn't afford tuition for her sophomore year and was forced to transfer."

That would explain why Annette seems to know her way around campus. "Well that's great. I've known Frank for a long time, since college actually. We lived with each other for about a year. Now we work for the same university we used to attend."

"Really? What year did you graduate?"

I squint my eyes at her. "After that whole old joke, you really think I should tell you?"

She laughs, "Wait that's just a joke. I mean you look young, so it can't be that bad right? You're 38, so it has to be somewhere in the nineties."

"Class of 1998," I say with some pride, but also with the expectation that she may say something snide.

"Wow. I was born in 1991." She says as she smiles.

She is 22, which makes her older than Annette. I can only imagine what Ruben is going to say when I tell him that I'm practically naked with only my robe on, in my living room with a 22-year-old girl sitting on my couch. Not at all mentioning what's happening upstairs, which is very hard to ignore.

"Well that's pretty young."

"Yeah, I'm young, but old enough as you can tell from my friend."

I laugh. "Well, she must be into older men."

"...or perhaps your old roommate is really into younger women"

"I'm not sure I can argue with that. You do have a point."

"Well, so do you. Annette loves to feel wanted and I think that Frank really does his best to show that."

"He really does though."

"I'm just afraid for her."

"What do you mean?"

"Not that I should be telling you any of this, but you just make it real easy for me to talk to you." She takes a deep breath before she speaks again. "I'm afraid that she's going to get hurt again. I mean, I'm sure Frank is a great guy but how long until he gets back with his wife?"

There is a silence between us that is only interrupted by the noise upstairs. I certainly don't know what to say to her. She does make a very good point even if I find it hard to believe that Lidia and him may get back together anytime soon.

"Annette went through a really bad break up after we crossed last semester. Her boyfriend was less understanding about Greek life than most. He felt that she would be a groupie and suck mad niggas dicks and so forth. They had been going out since high school, so that's the only man she's really been with. It turns out that he had been sleeping with another chick from Cornell that's in our sorority. When we were on line, he was banging this bitch on the side. Annette was devastated on so many levels. This was our sorority sister, that we barely knew of course, but you know, birds come in all shapes and sizes."

This doesn't sound good right now. I hope Frank is aware of this. "Did she tell Frank about this?"

"She said she did but who really knows? Frank has a huge dick and she enjoys it. She showed me a picture of it." Paula makes a gesture with her hands showing roughly how big she thinks it is. I hold up my hand hoping she would stop.

"I get it. I believe you."

"Anyway, as you know, she has been seeing a lot of him and I'm just hoping that she doesn't fall in love with him."

"Why are you telling me this?"

"Well, you know him the best. I just figured you should know in case something happens. Besides, you're here in your robe, 'all commando', so I figured it would be polite to share information," She smiles.

I get up. Thinking that perhaps she can see it and she starts to laugh. There is no way she could tell. I had my legs closed. I still hear her laughing.

"Well, aren't you funny?"

"I was only kidding. It was a guess."

I sit back down. "So what's your story Paula? Why are you here? Frank tells me you need a place to stay but don't you have sisters who live on campus?"

"I do have sisters living on campus. But, since it's late and this is not my chapter, I really shouldn't be around the girls that much during this point of their process."

"But, didn't you come here to see them? I'm sure you pledged them when you had the chance."

"Actually, I came to see Annette for the weekend since she was hosting a workshop at the community college. Seeing the line was something she wanted to do after. We weren't there long at all. She called her 'dial-a-dick' and we got some food and thus, I'm here." She smiles and continues, "So what's your story? Do you normally walk around in just your robe when your roommate is having sex?"

Her sarcasm is almost appealing. "No. Most times I'm fast asleep. I've gotten used it. Although, I wasn't expecting this when he moved in."

"How do you deal with it though?" She asks very inquisitively.

"What do you mean?"

"I mean how do you deal with all the sex. It has to make you wonder if she's being this loud on purpose. I don't know you very well but come on, a few good tugs and when it's all over you are fast asleep right?"

I see where this is going. She is a very clever girl. "One would think that for sure, but as you can clearly see this does not have an effect on me. But you, on the other hand, are welcome to what you gotta do when I head to bed. Of course, as you are aware I hardly know you either, I will assume that since you brought it up, self-love is not beyond you."

"To be honest, I have too much respect for myself to do that on someone's couch. Besides, I still have my clothes on."

"You are not going to let that go, huh?"

"Nope," She smiles again. I can tell that she's enjoying this conversation that went from semi-serious to just flirting. I can't say that I'm not enjoying this, but it does make me wonder how far this is going to go. Before I can say anything else Paula asks, "What's in the envelope?"

I look down at the envelope. It has been sitting on my lap this entire time. "Just some personal items that I need to shred."

"At this hour?"

"Maybe, its not like either one of us is getting any sleep."

"It must be very important for you to shred so late."

"Yeah, they are important enough for me to want to shred them now. But, there are too many papers in here. There is no way I would get it done tonight and hope to get any semblance of sleep." I look at the time on the cable box. "Speaking of which, I need to go to work tomorrow." I get up with the folder in one hand and my phone in the other.

"Wait, you never told me your story."

"There's not much to tell. I'm a divorced man who lives with this former college roommate that seems to get too involved in other people's shit before I can really take care of my own. I'm just trying to live, taking each day as they come."

"Wow. How long were you married?"

"Eight long years."

"That doesn't seem that long."

"Trust me. It was long enough."

There is a bit of an awkward silence between us and then I say, "You have a goodnight. It was really nice talking to you."

"You have a goodnight too."

I walk toward the stairs.

"Hey." She says. "Thanks again for letting me stay here."

"No problem. I hope you are able to get some rest."

"I hope so too." She lies back on the couch.

I walk into the kitchen. I pause for a moment to think about what could've happened. I could have been spent the night in Oswego or I could have offered to take Paula upstairs. None of that matters at this point. I'm wide awake and now I'm about to shred some letters.

I shut off the lights and head upstairs. I can still hear banging coming from Frank's room but this time I'm not bothered by it so much. I shut the hallway light as I get to the top of the stairs and in the darkness I find my way to my bedroom. I turn on the light and place the envelope on the bed. I debate if I should even put the television on. I'm not sure I want to watch more reruns of whatever is in syndication right now.

I plug in the shredder and then grab the envelope. I sure did wait a long time to do this. Apparently my subconscious thinks that perhaps I'm not trying hard enough to get past these women in my life. I also know that the one person that I'm avoiding is the one person that I think about the most. I certainly don't want her to know that.

I open the envelope and pour its contents on the bed. It's hard to believe that Isabel wrote me so many letters. I spent years after the break up hating her and thinking that all women were cold and heartless. I forced myself to forget that I even had these. I grab the first letter that she wrote. The pink parchment paper that just felt weird when I touched it. I don't even read it. I'm not interested. The shredder is set to automatic so when I slip the page in the gears turn on instantly.

I watch as the paper goes down slowly but then it stops. The gears are still going but the paper is not moving. What the fuck? I pull the paper up and it rips at the base. The texture of the paper is making it hard for the machine to cut at it causing a paper jam of sorts. I roll my eyes because I can't even do this right. I switch the machine in reverse and some of the torn up bits come up.

It looks like I will have to rip up the remaining parts of this letter. Thank God the other letters are on loose leaf. I rip into the sheet as best I can. I feel my anger of this whole situation bubbling up. I tear up the page as best I could and just throw them on the floor. This is bullshit. I can't even get rid of these memories the way I want to. I start taking the other pages, three and four at a time, and start putting them into the shredder. It produces one continuous sound.

Then someone knocks on the door. I want to just scream out *who is it*, but I notice the time on my phone. I wonder if I'm keeping Paula up. Maybe there was some substance to her flirting. I open the door and it's Frank in his basketball shorts. I walk away from the door and continue to feed the letters into their final doom.

"Shouldn't you have a shirt on? We have a guest," I say.

"Um, I'm sure she will be fine seeing my belly. Whatcha doing?" Frank asks as he closes the door.

"Doing something I should have done a long time ago."

"I see, it's...uh, kinda late to be doing that. Don't you have to work in the morning?"

I put my head down wanting to laugh and I just continue to add more paper. "Well, let's just say that I couldn't sleep. Isn't it past your bed time or are you taking another break?"

I see Frank smiling from the corner of my eye. I always knew that he enjoyed the fruits his of lusting. "Nah, I think I'm good for the night. I'm sorry if we kept you up."

"No you're not. You're making your statement to the world. I'm just the only tree in the forest that hears you knocking 'em down."

"Aren't you the poet."

"I am a writer." There is a bit of awkward silence as I continue to shred. I'm almost done at this point. "What do you want Frank?"

"I don't want anything, I'm just wondering what you're shredding with such importance."

"Isabel's letters."

"Isabel? Are you serious? I thought you got rid of those years ago?"

"Well, I did. But apparently my dad kept them in a box with the rest of my other shit. So I thought I would bring them back here and burn them."

"Um, why don't you just use a match?"

I stop feeding the shredder and I just look at him. "I changed my mind. This is much more cathartic."

"You seem angry, I hope you don't still think about her like that."

One of the letters stops midway down the shredder, which most likely means the bucket underneath is full. I pull the bucket out slightly and mash the shredded paper as far down as I can and then put the bucket back. "I'm not angry. I just had a dream that made me realize that I hold on too much to the past. I need to move on past her, past all of them," I continue the shredding.

"This isn't about Isabel is it?" He asks

"You're a genius."

"This is about Zenia."

"I thought we weren't going to talk about her..."

"Well, that's a lie, because eventually you will have to talk about her. I know that much about you. You can try to replace her with someone in hopes that you can magically fall out of love with her. But you can't."

"But you can Frank?"

He just looks at me. "I'm not trying to replace anyone."

"You sure about that? Because it sounds like you pound this girl with a vengeance as if you want Lidia to hear her from blocks away."

"I don't know what you're talking about. I'm finally having the sex that I didn't have when I was married. I would expect you to understand that."

"I do understand that. But I also know you're avoiding each other."

"...and you're not avoiding Zenia?"

"Avoiding? She doesn't want me. So I'm giving her space."

"Did she ask for that?"

"No. She wants to be friends and I'm being such a great friend by giving her the luxury of not having to deal with my issues." I fit in the last piece of paper in the machine. I get up and place the paper shredder against the wall then continue, "You have anything else enlightening to say?"

"I think you need to read between the lines. If Zenia wanted out of your life she wouldn't be trying to start a conversation with you over the last few weeks and I definitely think that you wouldn't have had that little hug in your car."

"Again, you're a genius."

"You know, Annette was hoping that you might hit it off

with Paula tonight. She saw your picture and thought you were cute."

"That's nice."

"Of course, I told her that the possibility of you actually seeing another woman would be next to impossible."

"You're on a roll. It's like you stayed at a Holiday Inn Express last night." It's amazing to me that Frank just rolls with my sarcasm. This is a sign that he knows me all too well.

"How can you not be interested in Paula at all? She's cute."

"Actually, she's gorgeous and I'm sure that in some parallel universe we dated, but you know me. I have to get over my own issues before I can really take someone like her seriously. Besides, she's kinda young," I smile as I say it.

"Really? So ten years younger than you is where you draw the line?"

"Uh, yeah. Currently your magic number is nineteen so I think I'm good at where I am."

"Dude, I'm loving this. You know that."

"Right, until you have to realize that she was still diapers when Biggie died."

Frank pauses and gives me a look saying that he totally had not thought about that.

"Well, I'm going to let you get some rest now." He says as he almost chuckles.

"Thanks! Glad to know you're still in shape."

Frank leaves and closes the door. I close my eyes. I really do need to calm down.

TWENTY FOUR

A few days go by and I'm sitting in a booth across from Ruben who is looking at me blankly. "You talk so much shit you know that, right?" I just told him all about my night and my meeting Paula and his reaction is nothing out of the ordinary. It has been a couple of weeks since I last saw him and he was just dying to meet up so we can hang out. I felt lunch would be appropriate. We decided to go to this place called Tully's on Erie Blvd. This place is quite loud, so any outburst would be fine.

"What are you talking about?" I ask as I take a drink of water.

"You put on this act like you can't get pussy and nobody is out there for you and yet here you are letting a perfect chance to get some ass go...some college ass too!"

Ruben found his way back to Syracuse on business. He travels here frequently which makes it easier to stay in touch with him.

"It's not like that. I barely know her."

"Did you at least get her number?"

"No."

"What the fuck. Look at you, I think this Zenia shit is going to your head."

"How is that possible? We haven't had a real conversation in a while."

"But you still speak to her?"

"Well…"

"Dude, I commend you on your actions with this Paula chick. I get it, you want to be a gentleman, but is there no wonder why you are having nightmares about these women. You're letting them haunt you because you're too busy being the nice guy. Cut those bitches off."

I look at him as he gives me this smug look. He's never really angry when he talks, although he may sound like it because he's not entirely serious about 70% of the crap that comes out of his mouth. I love him because he is family, we grew up together and I have always known that he has my best interest at heart. But quite frankly, there are times where I feel that joking or not, he is an asshole.

"Cut those bitches off? How did that work out with Janice?"

He leans back on his chair. "Wow. You went there. You know that's different."

"How's that different? Did you not break up with her for reasons that are questionable?"

"What is questionable about it? I just didn't want to be with her anymore."

I sit back on my chair. "So you think she really cheated on you?"

"The evidence was there. This dude zipped up his pants as they were walking into the room. What was I supposed to do?"

"What if his fly was open and he just wanted to close it? Do you think anyone would be that bold as to do that in front of her boyfriend?"

Ruben takes a drink from his beer. "Look, I totally understand that my reaction may have been based on some sort of fear or irrationality, but I just couldn't shake that feeling that something was out of place." He pauses for a moment, maybe to really think about it clearer. I certainly don't know what to say. "I just didn't like the way that made me feel. I don't want to constantly think about the possibility of any woman cheating on me. It's just not a good thing and I think in the long run we would have broken up anyway because of that feeling."

"Cutting her off has not let you resolve that situation."

"Oh, I disagree with that. Sure, like any break up, it was

hard to deal with at first but life became routine for me."

"I see, so I guess it was just routine for you to ask me to report in about Janice when I was in New York a few weeks ago."

"I was curious bro, I'm not completely heartless."

"Sometimes I'm not so sure about that," I say a little under my breath.

"What are you trying to say though?"

"I just find it interesting that you don't want to think about the possibility of a woman cheating on you when Nina was a factor in all this"

"I didn't sleep with her though, not while I was with Janice."

"That may be the case but you still had her pictures on your phone."

"She wasn't naked though."

"Dude, that's not the point. Maybe you should consider that, like me and my own bullshit with Raina, that you may have been the cause of all this to begin with." Ruben stays silent for a moment to contemplate what I just said. I feel compelled to ask him another question, "Did you ever cut off Nina?"

He smiles, "Not totally. We still talk every now and then."

I fold my arms and reply with "Uh huh."

Ruben chuckles, "It's not the same thing though. She never broke my heart. I was never in love with her. I can still date other women without the threat of some 'Global Warming' situation." He made sure to finger quote that.

"But, when was the last time you spoke to her?"

"Today actually..."

"Oh that's good."

"See, what had happened was, she posted this picture on Instagram and I just wanted to have a copy for myself."

I shake my head. I know the history. They are very on again and off again. She has a boyfriend when they met and he bided his time as her friend. When they broke up she took solace in him and before you know it, they are out on a date followed by multiple nights of debauchery. All this happened weeks after that infamous night with Janice. They have remained friends over the years and I just wonder how long that will last.

Ruben's phone vibrates on the table. He picks up his phone and looks at it. "Hold on, I have to take this." Ruben gets up and walks towards the door. He doesn't make a great case for cutting Zenia off. Granted, we may not be in a good place right now but I suppose being friends is better than nothing. We have a lot of history that I'm not willing to throw away just yet. Of course I still can't get rid of the images from that dream and I do have some unresolved business with Lidia that I plan on handling today.

I look down at my phone and I have some work emails to answer. I text Judy that I have an errand to run so I will miss our regularly scheduled bullshit chat. Then I scroll over to Zenia's text when Ruben walks back to the table.

"Yeah, I gotta run. We'll have to continue this later." He says as he takes out his wallet and sits down, "I have this client up my ass about appraisals."

I look around for the waitress and I give her the signal for the check. "How long are you here for?" I ask as I look down at my phone again. I have a few thoughts in the back of my mind as too what I want to say to her.

"I will be around for the next few days. I'm staying at the Sheraton."

The waitress comes to the table with the check and she asks if there's anything else she can do. We both say no and I continue to look at my phone wondering what's taking me so long to write something. Ruben looks at the check and digs into his wallet where he pulls out some cash. "Here, that should be enough to cover my end plus tip. Are you ok?"

"Yeah, I'm good. Just have a lot on my mind. I'm going to run over to Lidia's and confront her about all of this."

Ruben shakes his head slowly as he gets up. "Wow, well I don't envy you right now." He puts on his jacket. "Let me know what happens." We bump fists and he leaves. After a few minutes of pondering I finally decide to take out my debit card and place in the billfold that the check came in. I would rather keep the cash for practical use. The waitress comes to take the payment and I finally decide on what I'm going to say to Zenia.

I can't be too cryptic because it's not like we stopped talking all together. I just haven't been paying much attention to her, which is a very hard thing for me to do. It is very intentional that I don't hit her up first. If she texts me or hits me up on chat on any given day I would happily have a conversation with her. I just make sure that I keep my adulation to a minimum. The best way to do this was just to have short conversations.

Now I'm about to break my own rule and initiate a conversation. I know that the timing is probably not the best considering that I'm about go see Lidia. I put the phone down and I look up. Maybe I shouldn't text her. Who knows how long this conversation will be. Fuck it. I send her a message, *Hey there. How are you today?*

I'm already disgusted with myself the moment I hit send. I made a pact with myself to not go the extra mile with her. It's almost like the times I told myself to leave Isabel alone after the break up. I was just so desperate to figure out what happened that I know I was a consistent pest and a borderline stalker. While the situations are completely different, I can't help but try my best to not give a fuck.

The waitress comes back with my card and receipt. After I sign it, I put on my jacket and leave. Lidia lives about three blocks away so it takes me about five minutes to get there. I thought about calling to let her know that I was dropping by but considering how our last conversation ended, I think I will just be a dick and show up. Of course, it would be my luck if it turns out that she is not home, but I know that her yoga classes normally begin around 4 pm and that's about three hours from now.

I check my phone when I get out of the car and nothing. This is another reason why I shouldn't have sent Zenia a text message. I know myself and I will be checking my phone every ten minutes to see whether I get a notification or not. I put my phone back in my pocket and just hope that I can do my best to not look at it until I'm done here. I knock on the door and I wait for a response. I'm not in a real rush so she can take her time to answer the door. Judging by the car in the driveway, I assume she's home.

The door opens and Kevin appears. He seems to be just as shocked to see me as I am to see him. I have no idea what to do right now because the whole purpose of this meeting was to try to find out if Lidia is fucking him and now I'm just about convinced they are. I also forget how tall this man is. He has got to be about 6'4" and towers over me since I'm about 5'8". He is wearing his normal athletic gear of sweatpants, a tight black dri-fit shirt and some Air Jordan's.

"Seems like it's a party now." Kevin says with a smirk on his face.

Having no idea what he means I just simply ask if Lidia is there. He opens the door further inviting me in. I walk in and I hear people talking over in the living room. I walk over to the left and I see Raina, Lidia and Frank sitting around the coffee table. I'm in a bit of a shock as I try to make sense of what it is I'm seeing here. They look at me in a bit of a shock as well. Kevin walks by and says, "Are we expecting anyone else?"

There is a silent pause. I have such a bad feeling about this. Who knows what the hell they've been talking about? All I know is that Raina thinks Kevin is fucking Lidia, Frank and Lidia are separated which has led to them to sleeping with other people, Lidia has been trying to fuck me and Kevin doesn't give a shit about me. None of this explains why they are all together right now having lunch. The coffee table has this assortment of foods. It seems like someone ordered a platter of cold cuts and some rolls of Italian bread. I can only assume the food was good considering most of it is gone.

Kevin sits down next to Raina as Lidia asks, "Louis, what are you doing here?"

I hesitate a little while looking at Raina and then at Frank.

"I actually came here because..."

"Because he wanted to see if you and Kevin were fucking." Raina interrupts.

I stop and just stare at her not even knowing what I may have gotten myself into. Lidia and Kevin just laugh. I notice that Frank is smiling but he seems confused as well.

"Why would you think that?" Kevin asks.

"Were you jealous of our relationship or maybe jealous of

their relationship?" Lidia says smiling pointing at Kevin and Raina.

I give a sarcastic smile. "No."

"It's ok. I asked him a few days ago to have a conversation with you about Kevin..."

"Really?" Frank says

"Yes, really." Raina turns to Kevin and continues, "I know how close both of you became since you started working together. I wasn't sure what to think. But, of course, after the conversation we just had, I realize I was wrong."

"Well that's comforting," I say with all the sarcasm I can muster up. Clearly they all seem to have an understanding of sorts about something. Now that I think about it and seeing how the three of them are setting across from Frank, it seems like I may have interrupted an intervention of sorts.

"Sorry, I was gonna call you right after but you obviously came here first." Raina says.

"Do you want to sit down and join us?" Lidia asks.

I shake my head. "No, I'm good. I have to go back to work and I'm not trying to interrupt whatever intervention shit you got going on over here."

Frank immediately gets up and says, "You know what? Lou is right. I have to go to work too."

Lidia then gets up and says to Frank. "What? We're not done."

"We've been here for like an hour and a half, talking in circles about all of this," Frank says.

"Yo, I can't believe you thought I was fucking Lidia," Kevin says to Raina.

Raina replies, "Well, I've learned from my ex-husband that I can't trust anyone."

Voices begin to get loud as two separate arguments erupt. I start to back away slowly. Frank is trying to leave as he keeps making his point that he will think about getting back together and Lidia is talking about how they put too many years in this marriage for him to wimp out. Meanwhile Kevin and Raina are arguing about the lack of trust that has seemed to creep into their relationship and points out that she went to her ex-husband for advice. I see that I may have stirred the pot a little bit after being in this room for less than two minutes. With a few more steps I will be out of the door laughing about all of this.

I manage to slip out of the front door amidst all the arguing. I start to laugh a little bit because I felt like I may have walked into a potential trap and now it's just a damn frenzy in there. I get into my car and I start it up. I check my phone and still no message from Zenia. I look up and Frank is coming down the stairs and he's trying to get my attention. I watch him walk to the passenger side and I lower the window.

He pops his head in the car. "Yo, I need a ride back to work."

"Hop in."

He gets in the car and I see Lidia coming out. "Just pull away," Frank says.

I put the car in gear and just peel out. We zoom by and I feel Lidia scowling at us.

Frank smiles, "You just had to peel out."

"I think it was an appropriate effect considering that I just rescued you. Technically you're in the getaway car," I say with a smile.

There is silence for a block or so. Frank is just looking out the window. When I get to a stoplight I look over and ask, "Are you ok? What was that all about?"

Frank looks down and shakes his head. "Dude, it really was like an intervention. My wife asks me to come by so that we can just talk. I originally was going to say no but I remembered our conversation from the other night so I figured I'd give it a shot. So I get there and Raina and Kevin are there too. Now, I know that the four of us have hung out before and we've been chums, but how did this become a forum?"

I nod my head as I continue to drive. I feel my phone vibrate in my pocket, I know it's a text message and it's taking everything in me to not pull it out at this moment.

"So it starts off all nice with the little sandwiches and shit and I thought maybe this won't be so bad. All the while I'm thinking, 'don't we have to talk', you know? Small talk ensues and then Lidia starts talking about the reason the four of us are there. She feels that I've been very irrational and even though we are both doing our things, I don't seem to want to work on our marriage."

I pause for a moment so that I can process what he just said. Then I reply, "But didn't she kick you out the house?"

"That's exactly my fucking point and I know she's been fucking. I'm not stupid enough to believe that I'm the only one who has been getting their rocks off. I just don't want to know who she's been dating or doing shit with. I just don't want to know."

I'm beginning to feel a measure of guilt here. There is no way I want to tell him all the shit that Lidia has tried. I know that I also have a measure of fault in this, but I think at the very least I should be somewhat proud of the fact that I never slept with her. Lord knows how hard it was to fight that temptation off.

"Anyway, so she starts out by saying how she wants to work on what we have and that my friends are worried about me and my drug abuse."

"Drug abuse?" I say. I shake my head as I chuckle, "Son, you been hitting the weed that much?"

"That's the thing. I really have slowed down. Annette has

been taking up a lot of my time these days…"

"…Don't I know it," I interrupt.

Frank stops and looks at me with a smile. "Really?"

"What? I'm agreeing with you, bro!" I say smiling.

I pull into the front of the parking garage and take out my key card to press against the pad before being let in by the automated arm that goes up. Frank continues, "For the most part I let her talk. Raina and Kevin chime in about how they think we would be happier if we just simply started working on our issues instead of being separated."

"I'm not one to talk about how to fix a marriage but maybe they have a point."

"Maybe they do, but there is just a whole lot of hypocritical shit going on for me to take all of this seriously."

"What are you going to do then?" I say as I finally find a parking spot. I pull in to one of the spots on the fourth level.

"Honestly, I don't know. I know this is something I really need to think about. The problem is that I like Annette and I like my life as it is right now. All I would be doing is going back to a regimented schedule of arguments, emotions and obligated sex."

"Well then, I think you just described how most people feel about marriage but if you've always been this unhappy why did it take you until now to figure that out?"

"I guess I really didn't know I was unhappy. I was always so busy going to work, coming home, doing errands, going to bed then getting back up to go back to work. I got lost in the cycle. This doesn't mean that I don't love Lidia, but maybe we want different things now. Although I just don't know if giving up on our vows is the right thing to do."

We get out the car and as we walk toward the entrance I pull out my phone. I have two text messages that pop up on my screen:

Zenia Ocasio: 1:43 pm Hello. I'm well. How you are you?

Lidia Pope: 1:57 pm Your such an asshole. You just let him walk out like that? Why don't you let him be a man and take responsibilities for his actions?

Lately, Lidia just finds the right words to piss me off. She has always flown off the handle so damn quickly. I've heard her defend herself by saying that she is a hot-blooded Puerto Rican and that is how they roll. Well our *boriquen* ways must be different because while I may have a quick temper, I don't have the sense of irrationality that she has.

We continue to walk to toward the exit. We are both on our phones. I can assume that Lidia might have texted him as well. My first reaction is to message Zenia back, but I really feel the need to piss off Lidia. I simply type *you're then I press send. I flip back to Zenia and begin typing my response to her. Frank starts talking about how Lidia just texted him saying how he shouldn't walk out on her like that because he has a marriage to think about. He begins to read the texts word for word. I would care about what she said but at the moment I'm concentrating too much on my response to Zenia: *I know that it's been a while since we really spoke. I've gotten caught up with a few things that have been going on around here. Maybe we can chat later about it?*

"Did you even hear what I said?" Frank asks.

I look up at him. "I'm sorry man. What did I miss?"

"Maybe Lidia is right. I should try to make this work."

"Wait. How did you come to this conclusion?"

Frank takes a deep breath and says, "What I was saying is that in the long run, I need to think about my future. I mean, I may owe it to myself to try to work this out at least one more time right? Isn't that what you did with Raina?"

"Yeah," I say with the acknowledgment that Frank does have a point. Years ago, I chose Raina over Zenia out of sheer obligation. Marriage is something that shouldn't be taken lightly and while I've admitted to myself that perhaps I was too young to get married, I made that critical choice because I thought it was the right thing to do. You can see couples that are together for 40 years because they choose to live with the good and the bad, so what's the difference now? The only problem is that I ended up making the wrong choice. I chose my unhappy marriage over a chance to be happier than I ever have been. I'm not sure I can stop Frank from making that same mistake.

"So, I think if we try again and it doesn't work then I

know we were never meant to be."

"Are you sure about this? I mean, it's not like I haven't enjoyed your stay, but what about Annette?"

Frank does stop for a moment. "You know, she is a great girl and I like her a lot." He pauses.

"But...?" I interject because I want him to get to his point. Sure, I think that him going back to Lidia is a huge mistake but that is his wife no matter what.

Frank continues, "But, it would be totally unfair to her if I dragged this out any farther because I will always have the thought in the back of mind that maybe I should have tried harder with Lidia."

We continue to walk up the block in silence. His words are still hanging in the air. I break the silence as we're about to enter student union. "So that's it then? When will you talk to Annette about this?"

"I will have to end it tonight."

TWENTY FIVE

The last few days have been crazy. Frank really did break up with Annette. At first I thought she was going to take it well but there were a lot of tears. I think she may have fallen hard for him. I haven't seen her since Frank moved out. Yup, that's right, homeboy moved right the fuck out. It took him less time to move out than it did to move in. Then again he didn't have that much stuff, it kinda makes you wonder how long this whole separation was going to be anyway.

I have no idea what she said to him. I remember having a conversation about it but I wasn't paying attention to what he was telling me at first. Then, all of a sudden he's talking about giving his marriage one more shot. The one thing I do know is that he was feeling a little guilty about everything. I think he found himself in a position he never was in before and when he took a step back he wasn't sure he liked what he saw.

But, I can sure tell you what Lidia saw. I think she saw that Frank was slipping away from her. For all the pandering and whoring around she was doing, she was probably never happy with herself. Frank just seems different so she did what she had to do to get him back. Of course, the first thing she made him do was get an HIV test. Jury is still out on that. I wonder if she in turn got one too. I mean, how does that even work? Do you go down to the health clinic as a couple and ask for his and her HIV tests? Perhaps this is the new wave of the future in marriage counseling. I dunno.

Yes, you're right, he did say he was happy with Annette. But was he really? Who am I to tell him how happy he really is? I figured at some point he would go back to Lidia but after all those days of seeing Annette I wasn't sure anymore about what would happen. I was just glad to share the house expenses with someone even if it was for only about a month and a half. Frank being there made me realize how great it would be to have roommates even though his extracurricular activities kept me awake a lot of the times.

No. I have no idea what I'm going to do now. I suppose I could start looking for people to live with. Craigslist is a good place to start right? I dunno, I had roommates in college and that was always a crapshoot. Most times they didn't work out but I suppose that I'm just used to the illusion of Frank being around. He was either working or spending time with Annette which, if you think about it, was not that bad because I would still feel alone without actually being alone.

I haven't spoken to Lidia since the intervention either. I think she's going to go about her business as if nothing ever happened. There are things that I suppose will go unanswered like why she told Kevin about that YouTube video. It makes no sense to me. At this point it doesn't really matter. We don't really get along much anyway.

Why don't we get along? Damn, well that's a long story and I'm not sure we should really talk about that. Yes, I know we're friends but very few people know about this situation and I just don't feel comfortable telling you at the moment. Of course I trust you.

Yes, I agree. You're right. We are good friends and despite it all I should feel comfortable telling you everything. The fact of the matter is that Lidia had been trying to sleep with me ever since she kicked Frank out. I considered it, but in the end I just know that I could never look at Frank in the face knowing that I slept with her.

What did she do? Well she threw herself at me several times. She flirted with me at a club and practically stripped naked in front of me on another occasion. But despite all of that I feel very proud of myself. I'm glad I was able to say no to her.

Hello? Are you ok? What's wrong?

"...and that is when she hung up on me," I say to Judy who is sitting in her usual spot in my office. She had been listening to me tell the story of how Zenia and I got into a huge argument just when we were finally able to get into each other's good graces.

"Honestly, I cannot believe you told her. I think you're an idiot for doing that," Judy says. This is one for the few times that I have seen her annoyed with me about something I did in regards to Zenia.

"Ok, granted that I haven't made the best decisions over that last few months but she wanted to be friends. Why can't I tell her what I tell you?"

"Because she loves you! Don't you understand that? The girl is still in love with you."

"Judy that makes no sense to me. She told me when I was in New York that she didn't want to be with me. How am I supposed to think that she is still in love with me?"

"Because she's scared. It's very obvious to me. In any case, even if you don't know that, you can't be telling her shit like this because of your history and because of how you two are always on again and off again. Quite frankly, it's rude and insensitive."

"Ok, but why are you getting upset by this?"

"It's not that I'm upset at you, but I just don't understand how guys don't get it. Are women over sensitive about things? Sure, but the lack of rational thought from men can be overwhelming so I can totally understand why she was and still is upset with you. It's like you lack basic empathy."

Sometimes I forget about the bad relationships that Judy has been in. I often joke with her that she needs to date a black man because all of her dating experiences have been with these trashy white guys that only seem to be interested in her because she looks exotic. She had never heard the term "rice chaser" until I introduced it to her. A former colleague who left the university a few years ago familiarized me with the term and she explained that these are men who simply have a fetish for Asian women. Judy always seemed to be caught up in these situations where she wanted more from the men she was dating, but they only seemed to care when it was convenient for them.

I take a deep breath and say, "If this is going to upset you, we can talk about something else."

"No, you know that I'm curious about all of this, just continue the story."

I sit back in my chair and I retell the story from this point:

I'm standing in the freezer section of the supermarket looking at my phone because I can't believe that Zenia hung up on me. We had been talking pretty much non-stop for the last few days since I texted her outside of Lidia's house. It took her three days to get pissed off at me and I'm trying to figure out what I said wrong. Did I say too much? Or should I have not told her about Lidia at all? I should call her back on the off chance that maybe we got disconnected. She has always complained that my iPhone has crappy reception. The phone rings a few times and she answers with an abrupt, "What?"

Now I'm a bit nervous because I really don't want to fight with her plus, I'm also in the middle of a very busy supermarket. I only came here to grab a few things. I hate to be one of those people you walk by that are yelling into their phones.

"I assume you hung up on me. Why?"

"Because I can't deal with you right now." Zenia says which usually means that she is more upset than I thought she would be.

"Ok...is it because of Lidia?"

"Yes, of course Louis, why else wouldn't it be?"

"But, I didn't sleep with her. So what's the problem?"

"The problem is that you considered it. I mean, what is wrong with you? Frank is one of your closest friends and you actually considered fucking that bitch? That's his wife, there is nothing to consider. You just simply say no."

"Wait, so you are pissed that I considered it, that I actually thought about it? That is crazy. I think about everything in my life but that doesn't mean that I should be condemned for thinking about it."

"Really, so if my sister wanted to suck your dick how long would it take you to consider that? How am I supposed to feel if you tell me that you would never ever fuck Janice but for this one tiny second you would consider it?"

"That's totally not fair."

"Oh like it's fair for me to hear that you would consider betraying your friends? You try so hard to be friends with me, how can I even trust you with this?"

"Whoa! Hold on one fucking second. How is this suddenly about you? This has nothing to do with you."

"It has everything to do with me and how you treat women."

"Ok fine, but you can't tell me that thoughts both good or bad don't run through your head. The thing is they are just thoughts."

"Oh, so if I tell you that I would never let Frank fuck me, but guess what, I've considered it."

Time almost stops when she says this to me because there is a certain way that I feel about all this. Zenia may have a point here, but as much as I had to suffer through Avery and Peter I can hardly take the notion that she could possibly be with anyone except for me. There was an almost forgotten incident in our history that involves Frank that I really don't like to think about.

Frank knew that I was into Zenia almost before I did. He could always tell that I would have a little more of a spark in my eyes than usual. The first summer that she worked for me was very much an intense time, so by the time our annual Latino Fiesta dinner came around, her and I had known each other extremely well. This is a formal type of event with round table seating and a dance floor in the middle. We had a live salsa band play for most of the night. This is the type of event that I created to really allow our Latino students to enjoy their culture in a predominantly white institution.

Of course I was with Raina at the time and I never really danced with anyone else, at least not seriously. I will never forget what Zenia wore to that event. She wore a blue low-cut blouse with a very elegant pair of black pants and these black pumps that made her just a little bit taller than me. There was only one thing I wanted to do that night and that was to dance with her. I would sit at my table and watch her most of the night laughing with her friends and dancing with some other guys that I didn't know. But then I saw her dance with Frank and my heart sunk so low that when it rose again in my chest, it was filled with a silent rage.

It was palpable. I could feel my face getting hot and the

only way to hide that from Raina was just go to the men's room and cool the fuck off. I was very upset but I could not show that. I thought for that very brief, yet intense moment that she might have considered sleeping with Frank. She was incredibly shocked when I told her this story, which is why she just had to bring up this point about Frank in this argument.

I grit my teeth and say, "So you are basically saying that we should be held accountable for our thoughts?"

"No. What I'm saying is that you need to think twice before you tell me something like this! I'm not some bird you fucked and then dropped. I was practically your woman until you opted out. I think I deserve some kind of consideration."

"Why? Aren't we friends? Isn't that what we agreed to?"

"Yes, but that's not the point!"

"Please tell me what the point it?"

"The point is how am I supposed to be with you if this is the way you think and act!"

Pause.

Judy is interrupting me because she cannot believe that Zenia just said that.

"Wait, she said that?" Judy asks emphatically.

I smile because I almost know what she is about to say the second I answer this question. She will say something like, *I told you so.* "Yes that's what she said."

"See I told you! She does love you! Please invite me to your wedding!"

"Jesus, you are so predictable. We are not together. I find it hard to believe that someone you claim to be so in love with me would rather stay single rather than try to work things out."

"And I think you are blind. You really don't know women at all do you?"

"Does any man?"

I continue the story.

So, there I was in the freezer section of the supermarket. This argument seemed to last for an hour when in reality it was more like ten minutes. The weight of her last statement was just looming over me. Did she really say *how am I supposed to be with you?* I'm confused because I think this may mean something, but every other time I thought something she said meant something more, I would get shot down.

"What do you mean *be with me?* Just last month you told me that you this wasn't a possibility."

"I never said it wasn't ever possible. Things can't always be black and white. My point is that you go hard for that possibility of the both of us being together and then this happens. How do I know you won't try to sleep with any of my friends like you did with.... whatever that bitch's name is."

Vera. Another clear example of how I just need to be very mindful of what I tell Zenia. I just assumed that when we took on this idea of a friendship that all the rules that come with that type of relationship would apply.

"Despite what you may think of me at the moment, I would never consider having sex with your sister or any of your friends for that matter. I have never thought about them that way. Look, this entire year has not been easy for me, especially since you and I stopped talking to each other. Sure, there may have been some women but overall, none of them came close to what I had with you. So, yeah if some woman throws herself at me, I may consider it because I'm a single man with a single purpose and that is to get over you."

There was silence on her end. I look around to make sure that no one was really staring at me. I was so into this conversation that I thought I may have caused a little scene, but from the looks of it, I didn't.

"I need to go. You caught me off guard with this whole conversation. I need to catch the train and head home. We can talk about this tonight if you want."

We say our farewells and I finally finish shopping.

That is where the story ends. Judy sits there and looks at me blankly.

"What does all this mean for you the both of you?"

"I don't know. It took a few days for her to stop being upset. I did call her back that night to try to smooth things over. I suppose it worked, but she is not happy about the whole Lidia situation."

"I can imagine. I bet she still thinks that she has a bit of ownership of you. I mean, this could be just plain ole' jealousy, but I still think this is really your fault for believing that telling her was a good idea."

I do realize that now. Telling her was the wrong move but I still feel that at some point she should know, which may just mean that my timing was wrong. However, is there ever a good time to tell someone that you have been involved with intimately a story such as that?

"I still don't see the ownership argument but I'm going to give this a rest for now. Besides, I think we both should do some work now."

I have an 11 am appointment with one of my students. I just happened to glance at the clock on my desktop. Judy agrees and she gets up from her favorite seat. Before she leaves she asks, "So what are your plans for her then?"

"Well, we will remain friends, you know, once she cools down. Besides, I have a date tonight."

Judy now looks shocked. She wants to yell but ends up whispering. "A date?? With who?"

I smile. "You know that I have a meeting in like three minutes."

Judy crosses her arms. "I don't care. My next meeting isn't

for another half hour. Let me, at least, take a guess."

I sit back. "Ok, shoot. I'm sure you know who it is."

"That lady who sent you the books last week."

"I knew you were going to guess correctly. Yes, I'm meeting Abby tonight for dinner."

"Did you read any of those books? I'm sure she is going to want to talk about it. Maybe she will want to reenact some of those scenes," she chuckles.

I shake my head. "No, I did not read any of those books yet. Besides, its just dinner."

"Yeah ok, I'm also sure that she wouldn't mind you rounding the bases a bit. Which reminds me..." Judy leaves my doorway to get something at her desk. She comes back with a book in her hands. "I finished *Middlesex*. Can I borrow one of the other books since I know they are still in the box?"

I nod my head and point to her where the box is. I left it on the top of my bookcase. I wasn't sure it was appropriate to add it to my library. I have quite the collection of books from authors like Junot Diaz and Pierre Thomas, in addition to the numerous books about Latino success in college. I'm not sure if Abby's selections would fit. Judy finds the books and pulls out *Story of O*. She puts the other book back in the box and then she looks at me and asks, "Did you tell Zenia about your date?"

"No and I don't plan to."

TWENTY SIX

Being that I'm from New York City, I've always found dating to be very difficult in Syracuse. The city is a lot smaller and the places to go on a good date are not what I've come to expect. I tend to stray away from the chain restaurants or the sports bars, which leaves fewer establishments to choose from. I also stray away from the ethnic establishments because those places tend to be way too small. Sure, it is nice to have the ambiance and some *bistec encebollado* but I'm not trying to rub elbows with people while on a date.

I finally decided on a place south of the university that is expensive, but I know the food is quality. Saratoga Steaks was the perfect place because it's right off of Route 481 and while she may work in Syracuse she does live in Fulton. This way, she as a direct route to go home if she chooses to.

The plan was to meet her here at about 7 pm, but I arrived fifteen minutes early. I figure I'm just about late to everything else, so I should at least be on time for a date. This place is always nice so I don't mind waiting at the bar until she arrives.

It's raining outside, so it will not be surprising if she ends up being a little late. The weather could be a lot worse today. Normally this time of year it would've started snowing by now, but I guess the real global warming allows it to be about sixty degrees on the first day of November.

Abigail shows up about five minutes later, she must be on the same wavelength I am. She is wearing a nice leather jacket that is covering a long black dress that falls slightly past her knees. She shakes off her umbrella and the first thing I notice when she takes of her jacket is her cleavage. If memory serves correctly, she is about a 42DD. I do my best not to stare so I just look at her shoes. She has wedges on with straps around her ankles. Her shoes make her even taller than she already is. She has to be about 6'1.

What sticks out more than her chest and her shoes is how blond she is. I was always under the impression she was a brunette. Maybe she dyed her hair over the last several years, but who knows. I have never really been in to blondes either. I've always preferred dark-haired women.

The one thing that I know about Abby is that she's older than me by a few years, which anyone can say is a change for me. Raina is about a year older than I am and, of course, I've got ten years on Zenia. Anyway, I consider Abby to be a real milf and that's because she has the type of ass that you rarely see on a white woman. It reminds me of one of the crushes I had back in college. One of my R.A's had such an incredible ass for a white girl that she was immediately popular with all the men of color on campus.

Our eyes meet when she looks around for me. I walk up to her and we hug each other for a few seconds because it has been such a long time since we've been in each other's presence. Facebook chatting doesn't really count. After confirming our reservation, they sit us down by a window.

Dinner was awesome and the conversation was great. It's a strange to talk to someone in public considering the things that we talk about online. Much of our online chats are X-rated in nature, so having a normal conversation was interesting. She did grill me about the books, but in my defense she sent them last week. There was no way that I was going to be able to read all of those books by this time. She laughed at that because she knew that I have the propensity to get caught up in my own life.

We talked about what's going on in our lives. Abby talked, in length, about her daughter and all the challenges that come with being a parent. She considers herself a single parent even though, according to her, the baby daddy is always around. I reciprocate by giving her a brief synopsis of everything that has gone on in my life since the divorce. I avoid getting into deep explanations for the simple fact that giving away too much information on the first date may be reason to not have a second one. So when she asked me the reason for the divorce, I simply told her that I was too young to get married.

For the most part, this is a good date. Nothing out of the ordinary has taken place thus far, although every so often she would check her phone. I'm not sure if it's phone calls or text messages that keep distracting her, but in either case she never responds. The phone itself never makes any noise so I guess she has it on vibrate.

We talk about the workshop days and the writing we should be doing. I enjoy this conversation because I don't talk to many people about this need that I have to create in written form. The funny thing is that when I ask her what she is writing, it turns out that she is still working on the same book that she was working all those years ago. Her excuse was that she cannot hurry inspiration.

"So when are you going to start this book?," Abby asks to get off the subject of her writing.

"I wish I knew. I don't think the story I want to tell is complete yet," I reply as I look at the dessert menu.

"What do you mean?"

"Well, I do have a story in mind but I'm not ready to tell it. I guess you can say that in some ways I'm living that story right now. I'm just waiting to see how this whole thing ends."

"That is fascinating. You can't just make up the ending you want?"

"I could but then I'll feel that's a bit disingenuous. If I'm going to be true to anything in this world, it needs to be my writing."

"The good thing is that it sounds like you really have something to write about."

"I do, but I'm not ready to do it yet."

"Do you at least have an outline?"

"Inside my head I do," I chuckle a bit as I say that.

As she gets more interested in what I have to say, the more I feel the need to look around and see if people were staring at us considering our difference in skin tone. This is something I've had in the back of my head since she walked in. Personally, if I was one of them, I would be staring but that is only because she is just taller than me. I should be glad that I don't have issues with taller women because it might be awkward otherwise. Let's face it, we're all the same size in bed.

"Well tell me, what would this story be about?" She asks as she drinks some water.

"It's a story about a man and his journey from one relationship to another and that includes the tragedies and the successes."

"Clearly you are basing this from your own experiences. I think that sounds interesting. I would love to read it, if you ever write it."

The waiter comes by asking if we would be interested in dessert this evening. I pass because I'm way too full from having the surf and turf. Annette agrees that her prime rib was a bit filling. "I can take this whenever you're ready." He places the check in front of me and then walks away.

"I will write the story but I don't think I'm at the point in my life where I can."

"That's fair. I just assume that with the amount of blogs you have written that it would take you no time to write a book."

"Yeah, that would be a good assumption. We'll see what happens."

She grabs her phone again and this time she apologizes. "I'm so sorry, I know this has been happening most of the night, can you excuse me while I take this?"

I nod my head and when she leaves I take the opportunity to look at my phone as well. I fought off the urge to check my phone all night. I wanted to check mine as much as she checked hers, but I was afraid I was going to read a text or a tweet that I didn't want read. I'm reminded of a previous encounter I had with this chick I was "seeing" a few months back. I was on my way to meet up with her when I got a call from Zenia asking me for a favor. She had no way of knowing what I was up to but it just seemed that her timing was impeccable because it totally wrecked my mojo. Ironically, the very next week we stopped talking to each other.

I'm pleased to see zero notifications, but I do have two missed calls from an unknown number. There are no messages either. I don't know the number but sometimes, it's a student who's number I haven't saved but generally they leave a message. I see Abby outside the window talking to someone on her phone while being very animated. Lucky for her the rain died down. The waiter comes by and grabs the credit card for the bill while I wait. I hope everything is all right with her daughter.

After a few minutes she comes back in looking a little flustered. She sits down and says, "Again, I'm very sorry about that. That was my ex and as you know he can be needy at times."

Yes, I do know. She has told me quite a few stories about this dude and how he always seems to interject his way into her life. The problem is that he's her daughter's father and of course, she adores him. He takes her to school every morning and drops her off everyday. Abby points out that he's a better father now than he ever was when they were a couple.

He's also a master cock blocker. I knew this going into this date and I really didn't have any high hopes of getting laid on the first date anyway. Regardless, I'm very leery about this dude. Abby has also told me stories about how he has managed to scare off any possible suitors. I'm not sure that I would consider myself as such, but I suppose anything is possible.

She insists that he hasn't gotten physical with anyone but I still reserve judgment. I know first hand what jealousy can make anyone do. I had a fit of rage once where I wanted to fight a guy who I thought was being disrespectful to me after the break up with Isabel. If it wasn't for Frank, I think I would have gotten the shit kicked out of me by this dude and his fraternity brothers.

"Is everything ok?" I ask.

"Yeah, he's just being an asshole. Every time I'm out he wants to text me every ten minutes asking dumb ass questions about Jenny and her homework or her friends. It's quite ridiculous. So I had to take this call and tell him that he needs to figure some things out by himself."

"I take it he is at your place looking after Jenny."

"Yeah, he is. The good thing about working so far from Fulton is that I can at least go out on a date with a nice handsome guy like yourself," She smiles at me. Abby did a great job of turning that subject around.

The waiter comes back with the receipt as I ask her, "Do you have to go home?"

"I probably should before he tries to do something dumb like over cook the leftovers I left for Jenny to eat. I'm sorry, I hope I didn't disappoint you."

I sign the receipt. "No, not at all. I think we had a lovely time here. It had to end at some point right?"

We both get up and put on our jackets. Then she says, "I tell you what, I promise to make it up to you."

"Oh yeah and how do you plan on doing that?"

We both walk out of the restaurant and then she answers, "Well, I will have to come over one day and wear that black lace bodysuit that you love so much."

I have seen pictures of this. In fact, I have whole emails with her in this outfit that leaves so little to the imagination.

"I think that sounds like a fabulous idea," I smile.

I walk her to her car, a red Mitsubishi Eclipse. We talk about the possibility of having another date since this one was going so well or perhaps at the very least, me going to the next writing workshop this weekend. She puts her purse in the car and turns around to give me a hug that turns into a long kiss.

We pull away and she says, "Wow, we must do this again. You take care of yourself and try starting that book sometime."

I reply, "I'll see what I can do. Be careful getting home. Text me when you get there."

I walk to my car and watch her drive by. We both wave and then I go into my car and start it. After such a good date, I feel like listening to some music so I connect my iPhone to the auxiliary plug underneath the radio. I scroll through albums until I get to *Illmatic* by Nas. I turn up the volume to *N.Y. State Of Mind* and I drive off. When I get to the first stoplight, I start to bob my head to the beat. I love this song so much, in fact, I love this album so much. It's just so appropriate right now.

Then I hear the volume on the song go down and it's replaced by the ringtone of my phone. I look at the screen and again, I think it's that number that called me earlier. I've trained myself to not answer any calls that I don't recognize. Again, if it was of any importance, they will leave a massage. I press the top button on my phone to ignore the call and the music returns. In this case, there is no message so I'm think it must not be a big deal but I does make me wonder if I should pick up if they call again.

I try not to think too much on the way home, but that's always a difficult task for me. Abigail is a nice woman but I really have to ask myself if I see any future with her. I already know that whatever this is that we're doing, will not result in a positive relationship and a lot of that has to do with Zenia still being in the picture. There is no way I will be able to take anyone seriously while she's around, so I'm going to need to be more self-aware and truthful to myself. I've spent too many years lying to myself for the sake of obligation. So, as long as I can admit to myself that I went into this date knowing that there is no future with Abby, then perhaps I can just relax and be myself.

There is also the thought in the back of my head about me moving back to New York City. I think my time in Central New York is coming to an end. After spending the last ten years here I think it is time for a change of scenery. Truth be told, there is no upward mobility for me so I will need to start thinking about my career, which is why I'm so interested in hearing back from Columbia University about that phone interview I had a few weeks ago. I emailed the search committee chair but she told me that they are still interviewing candidates. Based on my experience this probably means that I didn't make it past the phone interview stage.

Of course, if I did move that will put me in close proximity with Zenia. Frank believes this will be the tipping point and she will have to shit or get off the pot. I guess we will see what happens because without hearing a positive response from Columbia, the most important thing for me to do right now is to find roommates.

I pull up to my driveway and as I turn off the car, I notice again that the same number that called me earlier is calling me again. It's a 315 area code but I know it can't be Abby because this is not her number. It isn't Raina because even though I deleted her contact information from my phone, I still know her number by heart. This time I choose not to ignore this. I hope it isn't one of my students trying to reach me. I answer the phone and there is nothing but silence. I say hello a few times with no response. I end the call.

I get the mail from the mailbox before walking into the empty house. Although Frank moved out days ago, it still takes me a few minutes to get used to the silence. I do the usual routine when I come home. I go to my room and get undressed then turn on the laptop and the television. I log into my email and load up Firefox and iTunes.

My phone rings again. The same number and this time I'm annoyed. I answer the phone and again, silence. I don't even hear any breathing. I say hello again with no response. I want to give this person the benefit of the doubt, perhaps there's a bad reception on the other end but I decide to hang up anyway. This cannot be a coincidence now and perhaps someone is fucking with me.

I decide to call back the number to see if anyone answers. No answer after four rings and the automatic voice message comes up. I've always disliked people that do not have a personal voice mail greeting. Now, I won't be able to figure out who has been calling me. I end the call and put my phone down. I'm almost tempted to go on one of those websites where I find out who owns that phone number, but I'm not trying to pay for that.

I will have to put this out of my mind for the moment. I need focus on finding a roommate. I go to Craigslist and search for listings on "roommates" in order to get an indication of how to write an ad. I look at various listings and I notice that most people have included pictures and described their place of residency in detail. This is something I know I can do, so I begin to draft an ad.

I'm going to have to take some pictures of the bedrooms, kitchen, living room and the exterior. I can't do this right now because it is too dark outside and I want to highlight the natural light that fills the rooms. Sigh, that is going to be a lot of work. I get up to turn the PS3 on. I think I will watch a movie. I scan through my list of DVDs and I settle on *Transformers: The Movie*. I always loved that cartoon.

The phone rings again as I put the disc in the Playstation. This time it's Abby. I answer the phone. She did get home on time and had to deal with her ex again. Larry wanted to know why she was home so late and they had argument about boundaries and how things like this are none of his business. She ended their fight by kicking him out for the hundredth time.

"How is your night hun?" Abby asks.

"Not bad. Just watching a movie and dealing with some hang up calls."

"Really? When did those start?"

"Well, I just started the movie." I chuckle

"No, silly, the phone calls"

"Hmm, I think they started during dinner."

"They started today? That's strange. All they do is hang up?"

"Yeah, I didn't even answer the first couple of calls since I don't know the number. The last time I answered no one was on the line, maybe they had it on mute. I dunno, but it's very annoying."

"What's the number, is it a local call?"

"Yeah, it's a 315 area code, hold on."

I press the recent calls button on my iPhone and I tell her the number.

"Jesus Christ. That is Larry's number."

TWENTY SEVEN

I spend the next morning cleaning up the rooms in the house that I'm willing to rent out and so that I can take pictures of them. I actually got up before 10 am to do this because I want to get ready to see the game today. Unfortunately it is a typical grey Saturday morning and it's not giving me any additional motivation to get this done. Thank God that most of the rooms were generally empty anyway. Cleaning out the clutter from each room is helping with the fact that I'm still annoyed from what I found out last night.

There is no one else to blame for this annoyance more than myself. I knew what I was getting into. I knew that Abby's ex-boyfriend Larry was a nut job, but no I decided to ignore all those warning signs because I would rather get into her pants. Now, I'm not so sure if I want to go through with any of this. I totally get it now. I understand why guys are "scared" off by this dude. I originally thought there was an intimidation factor with all this, but now I see this guy is nuts.

The sad thing is that I have been through this before when

I was in grad school. It was months after Isabel broke up with me and I was dating this black girl named Serene. I remember her ex somehow finding my number and calling me. We almost had a fistfight but I called his bluff and he didn't bother me anymore. Not that any of it mattered, that girl and I stopped seeing each other shortly after.

Abby had no idea how Larry got my number. She apologized several times and told me that she would speak to him. Any confidence I may have had in anything with her is pretty much out the window. I have enough drama as it is, I don't need any more. I think I need to focus more on myself.

I go outside to put the trash I collected into the garbage cans. It's a pretty brisk day and I hear it's gonna rain again today at some point. I made sure to wear my fleece sweater outside since I would rather not have a repeat performance of the cold I had last month. I keep forgetting that I need to rake these damn leaves. There's something about this particular chore that I hate more than anything else. Maybe it's because it never seems to be done, especially since I have a huge tree in the front yard. I also hate to rake these leaves after it rains. The water and the mud just make this task more difficult. I can almost hear my ex-wife's voice in my head nagging me about how I should've had this done already.

Just as I cover the garbage can lid, I see Lidia's car pull up in the driveway. Frank gets out the car. It's hard to not notice his Buffalo Bills jacket, too bad they suck. "What's up dude?" Frank says

"Just cleaning up," I reply.

"Clearly not cleaning up the leaves."

Franks smiles when I give him the finger. "I'm cleaning up for the roommate search. I had to take some photos for the listing I'm about to post."

"You miss me that much?"

"You wish. I miss your rent money that much."

"Good point. I came by to drop off these keys, since I won't be needing them."

He tries to hand me the keys and I just look at his hand. "I think you should keep them," I reply.

"You think so? Why?" Frank puts his arm down.

"You never know if you may need those again."

"So, you think I made the wrong decision?"

Clearly, I'm not going to tell him no. Even if I feel that way, which I do, Frank needs to find his own way. I don't want him resenting me in anyway. Bottom line, I think that he was happier with Annette but I get why he would want to stay with Lidia. For better or worse that is his wife, they took vows together and who am I tell them anything about his marriage?

"I'm not saying all that. But who knows what issues I'm going to encounter with these roommates. I may end up needing your help for something."

"Alright. I can deal with that." He puts the keys in his pocket.

"So have you heard from Annette?" I ask.

Franks smiles an awkward smile. "Yeah, I had to block her number."

"Wow, really? Was she calling you that much?"

"In order to really give my marriage a chance I had to cut off all ties with her."

"In other words, Lidia said get rid of her or we're done forever."

"Basically. But yeah, Annette called and texted me quite a few times and I had to put a stop to it."

"What about your test results? Did you get them back yet?"

"No, not yet, I think I get them back on Monday."

Frank explains that things are going really well with Lidia. They are seeing a marriage counselor through the EAP benefits that the university provides. They're also thinking about moving to East Syracuse and buying a house. All of this seems to be really fast as if nothing happened, but there's nothing I'll say about it. I do wonder how they will pay for such a thing.

"So what about your weed habit? Are you returning the

keys to that too?" I ask.

Franks smiles, "The funny thing about that is that Lidia told me that she doesn't want to change me. So, if I want to smoke I can, but I should be mindful of the amount."

"Really, how does that make you feel?"

"I think I'm just gonna chill for while."

"Wow, well that's a good thing right?"

"Yes it is, I get to waste my money on other shit," he smiles.

"You mean on things like that horrible Bills coat you got on," I reply.

He spreads his arms out, "You don't like it?"

"I'm trying really hard not to judge you right now."

Frank puts down his arms, "This is coming from a Mets fan?"

I smile, "Touché my friend."

It's amazing what a few days can do. I'm not going to judge Frank and his new and improved life. If he wants to move to a new place and give up his weed then I think he's welcome to it. I just hope they're not trying to brush all their issues under the rug. I know that seeing a counselor will be good for them, I just don't think it will solve everything. I really couldn't stand the counselor that Raina and I saw before the ending of our marriage. According to her everything was my fault and I just needed to change, but that was my interpretation of things. I'm sure that our marriage counselor did wonders for my ex-wife.

"The most important thing is that you're happy," I say.

"I am happy. I think it was a mistake for Lidia and I to split and I'm willing to do what I need to make my marriage work," Franks replies. I have been there. I have said the same things. Sometimes we say these things to make ourselves feel better. I just hope that he means it.

We say our goodbyes and before Frank pulls away he says, "All these leaves are not a good look for the photos, you might want to rake them."

I give him the finger again and say, "Funny, my old roommate told me he would take care of this. Besides, I can crop it out the picture. Asshole."

I go back into the house ready to post my ad on Craigslist with pictures. I log into the account and edit the rest of the ad. I add about five pictures of the different rooms and then finally submit the listing:

$300 Looking for Roommate in Private House

Hello! I have a large, sunny bedroom available in a spacious 4 bedroom, 1.5-bathroom house (which also features a separate full kitchen, dining room complete with dining table). The room features 1 closet, 3 large windows and will fit a full-sized bed and work desk with plenty of extra room for drawers and additional furniture.

Laundry facilities are conveniently located in the basement and are free to use. We are steps away from the Lemoyne College and 10-15 minutes from Syracuse University. We are also close to Erie Blvd and Shopping Town Mall.

You would be sharing the house with me. I am looking for a very positive roommate to share this house with. I prefer a graduate or medical student, if not someone who is reliable and clean.

The room is available now and rent is $300 plus $40 to cover Wi-Fi/Cable internet and shared household supplies like sponges, kitchen soap and garbage bags for a total of $340 per month. A security deposit as well as 1st month is required upon move-in ($600).

About me: I am a 30s professional. I generally keep to myself but definitely friendly and up for fun, intelligent conversation.

The images below show the outside of the house and three room views. It's difficult to show the full size of the room in pictures - it is spacious! The pictures also do not capture the warmness of the room. Come by and see it for yourself.

I just stare at the page. I'm really looking for two roommates and with the rooms being so similar, I'm hoping to get more than one response. I think this is a new step for me. I don't really try to think about my financial issues but they are prevalent in my life. Having to pay the mortgage on this house alone has been difficult even though I have found ways to make it work. But now I have to hope that I'll be able to pay off long overdue bills. Normally when people talk about getting a divorce they focus on the cost of the divorce itself. No one ever mentions the lack of financial stability afterward. I'm very fortunate that I have been able to maintain my head above water for so long, but I almost forgot what it's like to actually save money.

It just occurs to me that I'm mainly asking for a certain type of college student. That's going to be hard to find considering that this is the first Saturday in November and the semester is just about halfway over. Maybe I can get lucky with some graduate student that hasn't found a place and is slumming it at a friend's place. I would hate to wait until January when the second semester starts, but it may be a real possibility when I think about students who are abroad now that will need a place and any potential transfer students as well. The only thing I can really do is hope for the best.

I decide to make myself some brunch from whatever I have in the fridge. The outcome is a two-egg French omelet with American cheese and bacon. It sounds fancy if one were to say that out loud, but I have always been determined to make the best French omelet I can. I took a cooking class in college and I ended up with a B because I failed one meal. I was supposed to make this particular omelet for class and what

I ended up with was crappy eggs that I could not fold in the pan. Ever since that day, I have made perfect French omelets just as a reminder to myself that one mistake shouldn't mean everything.

I sit back in the living room with my food ready and a big glass of orange juice. I turn on the television and of course there is nothing but college football pre-game shows on at this point. The game that I want to see comes on in about an hour. Syracuse is playing Wake Forest at 12:30 pm. I guess I could rake the lawn before the game begins.

After inhaling half of my food I look over to my laptop and I notice that both Zenia and Abby are online. Normally I would play this game of waiting to see who hits me up first, but I'm not in that type of mood. It has taken Zenia longer than I would like to get past what I told her. She's very much the type to hold grudges and she has more than enough on me to last her a while. Abby has not yet gotten back to me on how Larry got my number. The only positive is that he has not called me back.

I open the window on G-chat for Zenia and say *Hello*. If I don't get a response within the next ten minutes it may mean she is still not happy with me. I begin to eat the rest of brunch as the minutes pass. Finally she responds to me.

Zenia: Hi

Me: How are you doing?

Zenia: I'm ok, you?

Me: I'm chillin' having brunch what are you up to?

She takes about a minute to respond which makes me guess that perhaps she is busy.

Zenia: I'm getting ready to go out with my sister.

Me: That's cool. Where you girls headed?

Zenia: Just shopping.

She's being short today as she has been for the last several days, which basically means that she's having none of my shit today. In a normal conversation, we can talk for hours about nothing, but if she is feeling particularly chatty then it is mostly about Lady Gaga.

Me: I guess you're still not happy with me.

She makes me wait again. I doubt she's doing that on purpose but sometimes you can never tell when you are talking to someone over the Internet.

Zenia: I'm fine. I just don't care to think about it, you're still not my favorite person in the world, I'm not mad at you.

Me: Well that is good to know.

Zenia: I do have to go though. Janice is waiting for me downstairs. I will call you later.

Zenia is offline. Messages you send will be delivered when Zenia comes online.

I suppose I can't ask for much else than that. Maybe she will get over it, but I can never tell for sure. Although I can imagine what Judy or Frank would say at this moment. They would probably tell me that I'm bugging out and that if Zenia wanted to be done with me she would have been already.

I get up to put my dirty plate in the sink. I guess I should really rake these leaves. I really don't want to, but if I want to attract potential roommates I guess I should. I open the door to the garage, which is located on the other side of the kitchen. I do my best to avoid the mess that I have left in here from previous projects never finished so I can get to the rake. It would be a novel idea to clean this up and put my car in if it wasn't for the fact that the garage door is broken.

Christ, this is what I get for being a homeowner. People will always tell you that the best thing you can do is own a home. What they don't tell you is how much of a pain in the ass it is to do everything yourself, especially when you don't have the time or the money. Sure, it can be better than renting an apartment, but when the pipes start leaking then it is all up to you to either fix it or find someone who can in the hopes they do not leave you with a hole in your wallet.

Of course, the damn rake has to be in the corner. It takes me a few minutes to shimmy my way in and the same amount of time to shimmy my way out. I place the rake by the front door. I hear my computer chiming. Someone on Facebook is sending me a message.

Abigail Eastman: I'm so sorry about yesterday with Larry. He can be such an annoying asshole. I feel that I need to tell you that he got your number from my phone bill. I confronted him about it and he told me the whole thing.

I sit down after reading her message. I can tell that she is still typing. As much as I want to say something it might best to let her continue.

Abigail Eastman: He heard us on the phone the other day and he didn't like the fact that you made me laugh so much. So when we went on our date he took that chance to look through my phone bill to see who I'd been talking to for the last few weeks. He took it upon himself to call you. I'm so sorry I let this happen. I hope you will still consider a second date.

Before I type something like: *Woman, you are bugging the fuck out, there is no way I'm taking you on date number two.* I have to think about what she just wrote. There is something that's bothering me about the whole thing. She sent me the books a few weeks ago and I started really talking to her last week. So how in the world is he going to find me on a phone bill? I have an idea and I just want to see if she's going to confirm it for me.

Louis Ortiz: I will have to think about this, but I need to ask you a question. How is it possible that he looks through your phone bill when we have been talking on the phone for less than two weeks?

Abigail Eastman: He logged on to the AT&T account.

Louis Ortiz: Really? So he has the password to your account.

Abigail Eastman: No. I'm actually on his account.

Louis Ortiz: Wait. You both share an account? How is that acceptable? No wonder he found out my number.

Abigail Eastman: I know. We're on a family plan so that just makes it easier to pay the bill.

Louis Ortiz: A family plan. Wow. It sounds to me that there's more going on here than what you told me.

Abigail Eastman: No! That's not it at all. We're not a couple, but he's in my life for the sake of my daughter.

Louis Ortiz: Who pays for the bill though?

Abigail Eastman: Why does that matter? I just told you that we are on the same plan.

Louis Oritz: It matters a lot actually. Who pays for the bill?

Abby is taking her time to answer this question. This is a make or break question although I think I already know the answer. This all stinks to high heaven. This is not to say that she's still with him or that they even have sex, but my point is that she is using him as a crutch. Maybe there's the feeling that she can fly away from the nest just long enough to have fun. Then when things do not go the way she wants, she has her safety net with Larry.

I'm quite sure that he's not stupid. He's protecting his interests. Of course he's going to scare possible suitors away. She allows that kind of thing and I'm betting that when everything is said and done they have that angry sex you see on cable shows.

Abigail Eastman: He pays for the phone bill.

Louis Ortiz: Of course he does. Next thing you'll be telling me is that he pays for just about everything else or at the very least contributes.

Abigail Eastman: Jenny is his daughter so he likes to pay for things around the house.

Louis Ortiz: You mean like child support? Is that court mandated?

Abigail Eastman: No, it's not.

I want to kick myself. I should have asked these questions before. I was so caught up in the possibility of getting into bed with her that I made a major mistake by not asking the simple questions that I needed to ask. Besides, that is her daughter's father! There is no way I'm going to try to mess with that dynamic now. I'm not going to be other black man her daughter sees every few days. I've been through hell as a kid watching my parents break up, so I can only imagine what this little girl would go through. Even though they are not married, there is no way in hell that I will be the reason they split. That little girl would always remember me as the one who did it.

I don't even know what to say. There are really no more questions to ask.

Abigail Eastman: Are you there?

Louis Ortiz: Yeah

Abigail Eastman: So… what do you want to do?

Louis Ortiz: I dunno Abby. This changes a lot of things.

Abigail Eastman: I figured it would. I was really hoping to have some fun with you. I was hoping that he wouldn't scare you off.

Louis Ortiz: This is not about him scaring me off. This is about you leading me to believe that your baby daddy shit wasn't that big of a deal. You're on a family plan. Do you even know how that sounds right now?

Abigail Eastman: I know it sounds crazy but he's so good to my daughter. Him and I are really not right for each other.

Louis Ortiz: Yeah, you mentioned that before. Maybe you should try telling HIM that.

My phone begins to ring. It's always hard to stop an Internet argument. I look for my phone and I see its Brian calling. Thank God, I'm not sure how I would have reacted if it were Larry.

Abigail Eastman: I have told him that.

Louis Ortiz: Apparently he doesn't believe you.

I answer the phone. "What's up, white boy?"

"Hey homeboy! You wanna go to the football game? My brother bailed out on me," Brian asks. Well this is a nice turn of events for my day. Brian always has tickets to the SU games.

Him and his brother have had season tickets for as long as I have known him. His brother, Steve, has been known to flake every now and then. I'm the first person he usually calls.

"You know I don't turn down free games, Brian. But damn, you're cutting it close, kickoff is less than an hour from now."

"Fucking Steve and his girlfriend. Let's just say *'bitches be trippin'*."

I die every time Brian hears something remotely black or Latino and then repeats it in a conversation we share. The laughter coming from my gut is real. From the corner of my eye, I notice that Abby continues to write whatever is she is writing. I really don't care for it, so I close my laptop.

"Oh my God, Brian. I needed that. When will you be here?"

"I will pick you up in twenty minutes."

"Cool, I will see you then."

I end the call and I look at the rake. Looks like I will not be cleaning up the leaves today after all.

TWENTY EIGHT

I'm drunk and it's raining again. I try not showing it as Brian pulls away but it's really challenging to get the key in the door. I'm not a fall down drunk, but we can just say I'm tipsy. I had way too many beers at the football game and few others after. All in all it was a great game! We won! We beat Wake Forest 13-0! I need to get used to this new ACC conference because I didn't even know Wake Forest had a football team, I just knew they had Tim Duncan and he's a great NBA player. We were also sitting next to this really hot girl. I should've gotten her number, but I think women in general are just done with me so I didn't even bother.

There, I finally get the door open. It's really dark in here! I go to turn on the lights and I trip on that damn rake! Somehow I manage to not hurt myself as I hit the floor hard. I stand up gracefully and then start laughing to myself. I turn on the lights and close the door.

What time is it? I dig into my pocket for my phone and when I take it out I realize it's dead. Shit. I totally forgot that

by half time my phone was at like 3%. That's what I get for live
tweeting the game. Oh well, I clearly didn't miss it and I doubt
anyone missed me. Well, I'm sure my dad does and now I can't
remember the last time I spoke to him. I guess I should call
him, but not tonight. I normally don't talk to my dad when I'm
inebriated so I think I'll just walk right over to the couch and
plop my ass down.

I've absolutely no plans tonight. I think I will just watch
some cable. Hopefully there is something good on if not I will
have to check the DVR. I know I have some episodes of *The
Walking Dead* that I wouldn't mind seeing again. I also think I
may need to rub one out too. I shake my head because I know
I could have gotten some from Abby, but then I have to
contend with this guy Larry. I certainly don't want a repeat of
the fight outside the club. I was lucky on that day because
Corey is rail thin. With my luck, Larry will be built like Deebo
from *Friday*.

I was better off having the jumpoffs I dealt with when
Zenia first started her hiatus from me. I met two white girls on
this site called *Tagged* a few months ago. This one lady, Peggy,
came by here a few times. She's a nurse that works for St.
Joseph's that was unhappy with her relationship but instead of
breaking up with her man, she decided to have some fun. I
think about how dangerous that is these days but I'm glad all
my tests have come up clean.

I need to charge my phone. I also need the remote. I move
my head around to see if I can see the chord or the cable
remote. Of course, my iPhone cable is still connected to my
laptop that I left on the couch and the remote is on the coffee

table. I can't decide what to do. Fuck it, I just turn on my computer and plug in the phone. I don't want to get up to get the remote but it is awfully quiet in here. I finally reach for the remote and start channel surfing. My eyes are heavy and according to the clock on the cable box, it's almost 7 pm. I certainly don't want to sleep yet. The night is young!

I wake up an hour later from the best nap of my life. I'm still in the same position I started in, sitting down with the remote on my leg. I stretch a little and look at my computer and then at my phone. It's now charged to 77%. It looks like I had several missed phone calls. My dad called me, which is not a surprise. I guess we are on the same wavelength. Abby called me, several times actually. I have four voicemails, two from her alone. I also see two numbers I don't recognize but this time one is from a 347 area code. That's New York City right?

I scroll through my text messages first:

Abigail Eastman: 2:19 pm Why are you not answering me?

Abigail Eastman: 2:19 pm Are you that upset that you're not answering your phone either?

Abigail Eastman: 2:21 pm I thought we were friends.

Abigail Eastman: 2:12 pm You can't let Larry's nonsense ruin this.

I totally forgot that I left her hanging before the game. Shit, she was typing something when I closed my laptop. I barely cared at that moment. There are ten more texts messages just like this. Interestingly, the last text message was when I was napping. All it says is "I'm really sorry for everything." I think I will just let her stew in the mess she's created. I'm not sure I even want another friendship. This is something I can just live without.

There is one text from that number that that I did not recognize. I notice right away there is nothing from Zenia. I suppose shopping with her sister went well.

3475553244: 4:46pm Hi Louis, this is Paula. I got your number from Annette. I was wondering if we can talk for a moment? I called you earlier but it went straight to voice mail.

This is a total surprise to me. What would she need to talk to me about? I can almost hear Ruben in the back of my head telling me that she wants to ride the hobbyhorse. I send her a message telling her that I'm home and she can call me when she gets the chance. I don't even know what to think at this point, but I'm sure it has to do with Annette.

I listen to my voicemails. One is from my dad saying that he is just checking up on me and I should call him back when I'm not so busy. I think I have done a good job of explaining to him how busy work can be. The thing about Student Affairs is that it's a thankless job where you can easily put in sixty hours plus a week. The 9 to 5 workday is just a suggestion. The point is that he doesn't really know when I'm working so he just considers me busy all the time. I'll have to call him tomorrow.

The other voice mail is of course, from Abby. I can tell that this one was before the texts. But it's pretty much in line with everything else she was saying. Whatever, I delete that voicemail. I just look at the TV as it plays yet another college football game. As much as I love Syracuse football, I just can't take too much of college football all together. It just does nothing for me. College basketball is a completely different story. I do wish baseball was on, but the damn Red Sox had to win the World Series on Halloween.

I click on the third voicemail and I hear noises in the background. I use the remote to lower the television. Then all I hear is a flapping sounds almost like skin on skin. What am I listening to? Then it happens. I hear a moan. I cover my mouth asking God *please tell me this is not Zenia. Please tell me that this is not a butt dial situation!* I look at the phone number at it's a 315 area code. Then the reality hits me. This is Larry's number.

Is he really leaving a message like this on my phone? Then I hear him talking. "Yeah, that's right. This is my ass." Normally I would laugh at stuff like this because it's just dumb, but I'm pretty disgusted that this man has the nerve to leave me a message of him laying out some chick. Before I pull the phone way to end the message I hear him say, "Who's pussy is this Abby?"

I put the iPhone down on the table and put in on speaker just so I can hear this:

Flap Flap Flap

"Come on, Abby. Say it louder. Who's pussy is this?" Larry asks.

"Oh my God, Larry it's yours," Abby says.

Flap Flap Flap

Larry then laughs. "That's right. Let your boy know."

"What…what are you doing?" She asks in surprise.

"Turn your head back around."

Flap Flap Flap

"Are you on the phone?"

"Hell yeah, girl!"

Flap Flap Flap

"Wait, stop, who are you on the phone with?"

There is some rustling and the flapping has stopped.

"No one important."

"Give me the phone!"

"No, I'm just leaving a message…"

"Oh my God, Larry. Give me the…"

More rustling.

"Damn girl, see for yourself. It's your boy."

"You motherfucker! Why would you do that???"

The phone hangs up.

I'm in shock. I want to be angry but all I can do is just laugh. I thought nothing would ever top the footage of Raina and Kevin trying to pull off my license plate. I was so wrong and the thing is I don't even care anymore. I shouldn't be surprised at the lengths guys will go through to claim women as their property. I mean, I get Corey and Kevin because they are protecting what they feel is theirs. But this dude, he has gone past anything I've ever seen before. I have no real reason to be angry because Abby has the right to sleep with whomever she wants. While I will make no excuses for her, she is not my girlfriend by any means.

I'll just let him believe that he has bested me. Abby will have to deal with him and come to terms with the fact that she feeds into his desire to scare away other guys. Maybe she just wants the attention she gets from making him jealous. I think the better question is, can we be friends now? Oddly enough, I have to think about that.

My phone vibrates. It's another text from Paula: *Actually, do you mind if I come over? I'm right across the way at Lemoyne.* You know, my life is never dull is it? Lucky for me I did some cleaning up today so I shouldn't be too worried about how the house looks. The leaves, of course, are going to have to wait until another day. I was hoping to have them done by Halloween but I felt watching the World Series was a better option.

I text her back that she's welcome to come by and as much as I want to get up to check a few things, I just sit in front of the television switching channels. I debate to myself if I should delete these voicemails but I think about how much Ruben would appreciate hearing this. I finally land on a channel that is showing *Friends*. I haven't seen all of the episodes over the years but I have seen most. This is the episode when Ross and Rachel break up. I put the remote down and watch intently. I remember this episode very well because it aired as a repeat a few weeks after Isabel and I broke up so it was still a fresh wound when I saw it. I remember being upset because they aired this particular episode a few days before Valentine's day! I blame the Winter Olympics for being so damn prominent that year. I should have bitter memories of this episode, but the show is just too funny to really care.

Just as Ross and Rachel start their argument, I hear a faint knock on the door. I open the door and there is Paula and Annette both dressed up in coats. They are sharing one umbrella. I invite them in and a chilly breeze comes in with them. They wipe their boots on the welcome mat. I close the door take their umbrella as they sit on the couch in the living room. I offer them both a beverage and they decline. The room is silent except for the television blaring. The mood of the room shifts. Something is wrong and I can see it in their faces. This must be serious.

I get the remote and shut off the television. "Ok. What's wrong?" I say as I sit down on the love seat. They remain quiet. I notice that Paula is looking at Annette. Her eyes are puffy which suggests that perhaps she's been crying.

Then Annette looks at me and speaks, "Sorry for coming over like this on such short notice but I was literally out of ideas on what to do. Frank, he has..."

"Frank doesn't return any of her calls and he changed his cell phone number," Paula interrupts. I can hear the anger in her voice.

Annette responds, "All I want to do is talk to him. But ever since he went back to...to her, he pretends I don't exist." Her voice breaks as she speaks. I can tell she's trying very hard not to break down.

"I'm sorry to hear that but what's this all about?" I ask.

Another silent pause then Paula says to Annette, "Do you want me to tell him?"

"No, I will tell him. Just give me a minute." Annette is wiping her tears with her hands.

"Please, take off your coats. Let me get some tissues," I say as I get up and head to the bathroom. I should have a box in there. This whole thing seems really bad. What if she has an STD? I wouldn't be surprised if they didn't use any protection and the more I think about it the scarier it seems. She's not going to walk in here to tell me she has crabs or gonorrhea? Is this something more serious? What if she's HIV positive? I can almost imagine Lidia's response to all this.

I grab the box of tissues from the bathroom and I give it to Annette. She takes a few and dries her eyes. I place the box in front of her on the coffee table and then I sit back down on the love seat.

"I'm pregnant." Annette says

My eyes widen and I cover my mouth. "Are you serious?" I ask in disbelief. I thought this was impossible. Frank had always felt a bit inadequate because he was sterile or at least that's what he thought. This was pretty much the main catalyst for everything going on with him and Lidia.

"Yes, she's serious. What the hell kinda response is that?" Paula replies giving me a look that signifies her willingness to fight.

I get up and start pacing. "I don't how this could have happened."

"I know, we should have used condoms," Annette says.

"No. That's not it at all. Frank told me he's sterile."

Paula looks at me in disbelief. Annette puts her head down.

"Are you kidding me?" Paula says and looks at Annette. "Did you know about this?"

"Yes. He told me that he was."

"What the fuck, L.S.?"

"I swear to you that he was the only guy I was sleeping with. There's no way that this isn't his child."

"This is fucked up," I say.

Paula looks at me and says, "Look, we came here because we both know that you're good friends with Frank. Maybe you can call him over so he can find this out for himself."

"Really? And what is he supposed to tell his wife about where he's going on a Saturday night?"

"That's really not my problem. I could give a shit about his wife. It's very clear to me that he got Annie here pregnant and now he wants to be Mr. High Ground and go back to his crazy wife? Fuck him and his feelings," Paula says as she gives more tissues to Annette.

"I can't exactly make him come here."

"Yes you can," Paula says. "You may remember that Annie was here the night you were sick. She told me how you were on this couch and his lovely wife was naked on top of you."

My jaw drops. "How did you...?"

"I heard everything. I know you were trying to stall her so that I could hide out at least until Frank got here. But just how did you think that she knew someone was here or that later on she knew about me?" Annette says.

"She saw you?" I respond.

"My light was on and she saw my shadow."

341

"You don't know that."

Paula interrupts, "Hmm. The bitch tracked her down after her and Frank got back together. They had a little chat about how she wants Annie to stay away from him."

Damn it! That sounds exactly like something Lidia would do. But what would be the point in that? She already got Frank back, why make that situation worse? There is only one question now. "Why didn't you tell her what you just told me?" I ask Annette.

"I did tell her. She laughed and said that Frank would never believe it. She said that she would deny it and blame me for just wanting to break them up."

"I see. So if she is not worried that you know about this, then why should I? I never fucked her."

"No, but she did send you some pictures," Paula says

"And how would you know this?"

"You left your phone down here the night of our discussion. You stored her pics on your phone next to the dick pics you have. Which, I have to say that I've seen bigger," Paula says with no change in her facial expression. She has the same cold look she has had since she walked in, which is such a stark difference from when we first met.

"So you came here to pretty much blackmail me."

"Basically," Paula says. I'm not happy right now. A few

months ago the university pushed an update to my phone via the email interface that would force my phone to have password protection since it's possible for someone to get sensitive information about students with an employee's email. This was a way to safeguard information in case our phones were stolen. I hated this and thought this was a breach of my privacy and my personal property since I paid for my own phone. So, I decided to take the university email off my phone and thus I never kept the password protect feature. Now I wish I had.

Annette interrupts while looking at Paula, "No, please it's really is not like that." She continues as she looks at me, "I'm just desperate. I know both of you are good friends and you took him in when he needed a place to stay. I would never want to break your friendship but it's just that I love him." Annette stops mid-sentence and I'm now feeling terrible for not helping her. I just don't care to be in the middle, but if that really is his child he'd want to know. She then continues, "I just think he should know. If he doesn't want anything to do with me or the baby then I will deal with that. But he has to know!"

"Ok. Ok, I will call him," I say. I pick up my phone, which is by Paula. I look at her and she smiles shamelessly.

Before I press the button to send the call I ask, "Do you always look through other people's phones?"

"I do actually. Especially if they are dumb enough not to lock the screen."

She smiles. I roll my eyes as I call Frank. "You know, he could be working right now. You both should have just gone to the student union."

"He's not there," Annette says.

There are times when I call Frank and he doesn't answer. You can never tell if he's ignoring you or if he left his phone somewhere. Nine times out of ten it is always the latter, but he does it enough times that you begin to wonder. Right now is one of those times. Homeboy is not picking up and it goes to voicemail. I leave a message:

Dude. You need to call me back right away. Something has...come up that you might want to hear.

I end the call. "Hopefully, he will call back soon."

"Do you mind if we stay and wait then?" Annette asks.

"I guess not. I don't know how long he's gonna be though."

This man needs to call me back soon. This whole situation got real uncomfortable very quickly and I'm definitely in no mood to entertain. I sit down on the love seat and Paula asks if she can use the bathroom. I tell her to make herself at home. It's almost 9 pm and I have no idea what is going to happen tonight. I think about texting Frank because I really want to alert him to this situation, but considering that Lidia just might check his phone, it's not such a great idea. As much as it may sound nice, I wouldn't want a girl fight in my house.

344

Then there is a knock on the door. Annette looks at me. "Could that be him already?"

"It can't be. That would be way too fast," I say as I get up and walk to the door. I suppose it could be possible that it's him. Maybe he didn't answer his phone because he was driving. I open the door and I was right it's not Frank.

Abby looks at me as she stands under her umbrella. She cracks a small smile and says, "I think we need to talk. Did I catch you at a bad time?"

She has no idea right now.

TWENTY NINE

In the future, when I look back on this night, I know that I will have the benefit of 20/20 vision. In fact, I'm willing to bet that this moment won't be thought about as much as the outcome of the situation going on inside my home. I look at Abby and instantly become annoyed about everything. Why can't things be simple? I hear stories about people who live easy lives that involve love and great times. I just get this impression that maybe I'm doing something wrong here.

Falling in love with another woman while being married is bad enough. That whole situation was just doomed from the start, but does that mean that everything following that has to be so difficult? Maybe this is just karma coming back to me since I hurt Raina. Perhaps fate is just laughing at me as I sort through the shit I put myself in.

"Actually, this is a bad time," I say to her.

"Can you just give me five minutes?" Abby asks.

I look at her then roll my eyes. "Stay here. Let me get my coat." I close the door and I grab my jacket that I had left in the living room. Both girls look at me as I put it on. "What? No, it's not him. If he calls me I will let you know. I'll be outside, this won't take long."

I head back outside and close the door behind me. It's drizzling a little bit so I'm ok without an umbrella.

"Is everything ok? You have a visitor?"

"Yes, I do. But that's really none of your business. You have five minutes," I say very coldly to her. If there's one thing that I have learned from my ex-wife, it's the subtle art of being cold. The key is to have a stone face that never smiles.

Abby shifts a little as if she is uncomfortable in her boots. "I feel very embarrassed." She starts off speaking slowly as if she wants to make sure that she says the correct things. She continues, "I know you think that I'm probably a liar and maybe a whore. But, I'm not. I've known Larry for such a long time and he has always been there for me when I needed a shoulder cry on or when I needed a man to help me around the house."

A gust of wind blows and I can hear the leaves in my yard rustling. Some leaves blow by our legs and she looks down. My gaze is fixated on her. She says, "Yes, I still have sex with him. I didn't expect him to call and leave that message. It's shameful."

I hope she wasn't looking for me to agree with her but I

do ask her, "Abby, why are you here?" She looks up at me. Maybe trying to figure our how to answer that question. I ask another, "Is he watching over your daughter right now while you come see me? Is that what you freaks are into?"

"I came to say I'm sorry."

"You texted me that already. What makes you think I want to hear it again?"

"I dunno. I guess I was hoping we could still be friends."

"I'm not sure that's possible. I think I'm done giving away my 'all access friend passes.' You knew I was having a rough time when it came to relationships and you still chose to take me down this road. But you know what? I blame myself for allowing this to happen."

There's an awkward silence between us that makes me think that her five minutes is about up. "I wish I could take this back. You're a good man. I just let myself get caught up. I felt lonely." Abby says as she wipes her face. "Again, I just wanted you to know that I'm sorry. Sometimes a text just doesn't say enough."

She begins to walk back to her car and I just watch her close her umbrella and fumble her keys. "You know…" I say and she begins to turn around, "…I was starting to really like you."

She opens her door and smiles at me and says, "Me too."

Abby backs her car out of the driveway and heads down

the street. It begins to rain hard and I walk back inside the house. The girls are watching TV, which is a good sign that perhaps the mood has lightened a little bit. Of course, they are watching some reality show I don't recognize. I take of my jacket and put in on the banister.

I walk into the living room and ask, "Shouldn't you be watching Glee or something?"

The both of them are still sitting next to each other glued to their phones. If they were watching this show, I certainly couldn't tell. Paula responds without looking up, "Glee comes on Wednesdays."

"Pardon me," I say sarcastically as I sit down again. I take out my phone to see if perhaps Frank called while I was outside. Surprisingly there are no notifications. I really hope he doesn't have us waiting all night. That would suck because I had an eventful night of nothing to do all by myself.

My phone vibrates in my hand just as I was about to go on Facebook. Frank is calling. I answer it right away.

"Dude, you home?"

Paula grabs the remote and mutes the television.

"Yeah. What's up?" Frank asks.

"You need to come over."

"Why? Is everything ok?"

"Um. Annette is here." I look at her. He is silent for a moment.

"Why?"

"Can you talk?"

"Not really. How important is this?"

"Important enough for me to call you and tell you to get your ass over here."

"Look, I'm really not sure about this. Lidia and I are really trying to make all of this work. Tell Annette to go home."

I'm looking at Annette and shaking my head. She is looking very concerned and I can see the swelling in her eyes. "Frank, I think you really need to hear what she has to say."

"Lou, I think I heard enough as it is already. She has been blowing up my phone when I clearly told her it was over. Please, you are my friend and I just need you to understand I need to work on my marriage."

"Ok, man." How can I argue with him? I have to respect that this is what he wants. I end the call and put my head down.

"What happened?" Annette asks softly.

"He's not coming."

Annette looks around. There is silence in the room that

makes this situation a lot more eerie than it needs to be. Paula sits next to Annette and begins to comfort her. Then Paula asks what Frank said and I tell both of them the very brief conversation I had with him.

"What a fucking asshole." Paula continues. "We should go over there right now and bang on his damn door until he comes out. Fuck him and his stupid wife."

"I'm not sure that's going to solve anything. I mean it's getting late and there may be a better time to tell him," I say.

"Like when? I can't continue like this hoping he will just pick up the phone. Maybe I should just forget about the whole thing. I don't need him." Annette says as she holds back tears. Paula gives her a hug. At this moment I just feel very small. All the bullshit that has been going on in my life is really nothing compared to what is going on here. There were always moments when I was having that affair with Global Warming where I thought I would completely ruin her life in some way, that I would hurt her in the way Annette is hurting right now. I can't even imagine what life would be like right now if I had gotten her pregnant.

There are no words I could say that would comfort her. I find myself going to the kitchen to grab some water. She has been crying enough and perhaps water might help her in case she is feeling dehydrated. It has been a very interesting day and I as I pull out the pitcher of filtered water I realize that I'm totally sober right now. I pour the water into the glass when I feel my phone vibrate. It's a text message. Paula walks in to the kitchen. "I thought you should know that we're leaving."

"Oh, are you both headed back to Lemoyne?" I ask.

"No, I don't think so. I think was are going to head back to main campus. One of our sisters is meeting us in the student union. Listen, thank you for trying."

"How is she?"

"I think she will be ok. She's a strong girl."

"Do you need a ride? I can drive you down there. It's the least I can do."

"Sure, I don't think we can turn down a free ride."

"Ok, we'll leave in a few minutes. Can you give this to her?" I hand her the glass of water and then she walks out of the kitchen. I check my phone and it's a text message from Frank.

How soon can you and Annette be at the Student Union?

Looks like he's had a change of heart. Maybe that whole speech on the phone was an act to convince Lidia that he's a changed man. I respond that we will be there in about fifteen minutes. I walk into the living room as the girls are putting on their coats. "Ok girls, change of plan. Looks like Frank changed his mind."

"Really?" Paula asks.

"He's coming here?" Annette asks.

"No," I answer, "He just texted me, he wants to meet us at the student union."

It takes us a few minutes to actually leave. I had to get my coat and find my keys. Paula and Annette take their time but still end up waiting for me. Some times finding my keys is a chore within itself. Where did I leave them? Are they in the kitchen or the dining room? Perhaps I left them upstairs. Since I didn't drive today, I have to backtrack my thoughts and that leads to me the slacks I wore yesterday. Despite my personal key drama, the movement around the house is very silent. "OK! I finally found my keys, so let's go!" I say to break the silence after coming down the stairs.

No one says a word even when we enter the car. The only thing I can hear are the light raindrops hitting the windshield and the roof until I start the ignition. I turn on the headlights and the wipers. I put on my seat belt and check the mirrors. The ride from my house to the university is roughly nine minutes depending on traffic. At this time of night the roads should be pretty empty. I plug my iPod into the auxiliary plug and select the *Girl on Fire* album by Alicia Keys that I have been listening to non-stop for the last few weeks. I back out of the driveway and head to campus. The girls are not saying much. Maybe it was a good thing that I put on the iPod, otherwise it might be a somewhat depressing ride.

I make a slight right on to Genesee Street. This street is pretty much empty as I predicted. I look down briefly to see what time it is and then I see a white flash that makes me look up. I hear a scream coming from Annette who's in the passenger seat as we both see headlights directly in front of us.

Instinctually, I swerve the car left as a sound comes out of my mouth that sounds like NO!

The car heads straight for a tree. Everything moves in slow motion as I slam on the breaks. The music stops and I brace for impact.

There is a loud bang as the car grazes the tree on the passenger side and flips over. I feel my body tumble in slow motion. I can hear the breaking and twisting of metal. The sound of the car's engine is frightening. I feel the full impact of the airbag as the car's side windows burst. The car lands on the roof and then comes to a dead stop.

There is complete silence. I can feel the tires still spinning.

I'm hanging upside down.

As I sit in this car in complete silence, I close my eyes and wonder how I got here. I'm just hanging here wondering what has become of my life. I can feel the blood rushing to my head. My luck has been so bad over last few weeks that I'm almost surprised to still be alive. The only thing holding me in place is this seat belt.

My head is resting on the roof of the car.

I keep my eyes closed because I'm afraid of what I might see. I say a small prayer thanking God that I can feel all my limbs. I apologize for all the things that I've done wrong. I've been so selfish and I could have died without any type of penance.

My nose hurts a lot. I open my eyes.

Oh My God, I've been in a car accident! I look over to Annette and she's not moving. Her air bag did deploy and she's just hanging there like I am, but her body is limp. I can finally tell she's breathing. I look in the back seat and see Paula clutching her arm. "Are you ok?" I ask.

"M-my arm. I think it's broken" She responds. I can see her holding it in obvious pain. Thank God she has her seat belt on. I unclip my seat belt with my right hand while holding my left to the roof of the car. I manage to crawl out slowly. I feel the rain hitting the back of my neck as I look around. There are pieces of broken glass everywhere and I do my best not to cut myself on the way out. I hear voices coming closer. My head is beginning to swim a little bit. I get up and head back over to my car to try and get Paula out. I can hear her screaming in pain.

I kick some of the glass away and then I get to my knees to see if I can pull her out. "Give me your other hand," I say as I reach for her.

"Annette, she's not moving! Is she dead?" Paula says as she's crying. I can tell that she's terrified. This whole time I thought she was crying out in pain when in reality she's panicking.

"No. She's breathing. I can see her from here. Can you unbuckle your seat belt?" I ask calmly.

"I can't!" Paula says without really trying, but I cannot

blame her. I want to be terrified too but I can't. I refuse to lose my shit right now. I get up to go to the other side of the car. I must've gotten up too fast because I feel dizzy. I see a woman coming toward me as I try to maintain my balance. She must have left her umbrella at home because her dark hair is getting soaked.

"Oh my God! Are you ok? What happened?"

"This guy came out of nowhere and ran us off..." I point to where the other car was and I see that it crashed head on into a telephone pole. Before I can finish the sentence, a man runs up and asking the same questions, *is everyone is all right?*

Everything is moving in slow motion.

A few more people show up and it almost becomes chaotic. Cars drive by slowly with people trying to figure out what happened. A small crowd begins to form around both cars. I can't help but watch as some people try to get Paula and Annette out of the car. Finally the flashing lights of a cop car show up. The cops get out yelling and motioning to everyone to clear the area and to stop trying to remove either girl from the car. One cop has radioed EMS, while the other one begins to divert traffic.

Another police car arrives and as far as I can tell they are heading to the car that ran us off. Too many faces seem to keep coming up asking me what happened or if I'm ok, but the one face I remember is the cop telling me to sit down on the curb until the ambulance gets here. I don't even remember him asking me my name. I put my hand on my head because I feel a massive headache coming on.

I'm not feeling well.

I feel like all the heat is leaving my body. The only person I can think of right now is Zenia and she's probably not even thinking about me right now. I know that she went shopping with her sister hours ago and mentioned she would call me. My phone is still in my pocket I wonder if she had called. I can see flashing lights. I pull out my phone only to see no notifications. I suddenly feel this huge pressure building up and I hurl on the sidewalk.

I feel cold.

I wipe the tears from my eyes after I cough for what seems to be forever. If I die tonight, Zenia needs to know that I've never loved anyone the way I love her. I find her name on my phone and press send. I put the phone to my ear. I want to tell her how much of an asshole I've been. I'm sorry for hurting her and putting her through everything. I never had the courage to leave my wife until it was too late. I want to tell her that I'm such a foolish man and that no other woman matters in my life. Vera, Lidia, Abby and the other chicks were all feeble attempts to distract myself from the fact that I wasn't with her.

I can see the ambulances but my eyes become blurry. I rub my eyes and I realize that I'm crying without assistance from the vomiting. This is what my life has come to right now. The last few months have been horrible. All the wrong decisions come bubbling up. I have no idea what I'm going to do with my life. I feel like I'm a human check box labeled *divorce*, which is just another way of saying I will never truly be single again.

Why am I crying?

All I can see and hear are people standing around looking at the car wreckages. The phone is ringing. EMS is pulling a body out of the other car. Another cop shows up telling me that my seatbelt saved my life. Annette is still knocked out as the paramedics finally get her out of the car and attend to her. The phone is still ringing. Paula is standing a few feet from me holding her broken arm. She wants to be closer to Annette but they tell her to stand back. I see my iPod in the middle of the street. I want to reach out for it but an ambulance just backed over it.

The ringing stops and it goes to voicemail. *Hi, this is Zenia, leave a message and I will get back to you as soon as I can. Have a great day.*

I end the call as I see a paramedic walk up to me saying something. "I'm so sorry," I say. I feel light headed and I feel my head hit the grass behind me.

My eyes get heavy. I see the paramedics rush over to me shining a light in my eyes.

She is pretty.

The other one picks up the phone.

I close my eyes.

THIRTY

Darkness slowly becomes light.

A face slowly emerges and it's Ruben. I look around. I'm in a hospital bed with an I.V. in my arm. Before I panic, I make sure I can feel all my fingers and toes. I still have a headache. I squint my eyes because the lights are very bright.

"Hey man. How you feeling?" I hear Ruben say softly. All my fingers and toes are accounted for. I think I have my own room but I can't tell since there's a curtain around me. I swallow and say, "It only hurts when I laugh. How long have I been out?"

"You've been out for a few hours. The doctor said you had a concussion."

"Great, what time is it?"

Ruben looks at his cell phone and says, "It's 2:15 in the morning."

"Wow, and you're up here on a Sunday morning? It is Sunday right?"

He looks at me with concern and says, "Yeah, It's Sunday."

"Why are you looking at me like that? I'm not dead."

"I'm sorry, it's just that I never thought about seeing you in a hospital bed."

I look around for my stuff. Ruben asks me what I'm looking for and I tell him that I'm looking for my cell phone. He hands it to me from the food tray that has a small cup of water on it.

"So, are you ok? What happened?" Ruben asks me as he gives me my iPhone. I look at the phone and I'm surprised that it survived this whole ordeal without a scratch. The phone case was worth the fifty dollars I spent on it.

I look up at Ruben and say, "It all happened so fast. This guy was driving on the wrong side of the road. I barely got out of the way in time. Then I hit a tree and the car flipped. Oh my god..." Then I realized that I never saw Annette awake and she's pregnant. This is going to be so bad.

"What is it?"

"The other two girls. What happened to them?"

"I'm not sure. I think one of them was admitted."

"Damn it, I was on my way to meet Frank."

"I know. He was here earlier. He went to check on some chick named Annette. Apparently, she's not doing so well."

That doesn't sound good. She was out cold the last time I saw her. I will feel terrible if anything happened to her and the baby. "Do you know if he's still here?" I ask Ruben. He shrugs and says he doesn't know.

The nurse opens the curtain and walks up to the bed. She speaks in a low voice. "Nice to see you're awake. My name is Carla and I'm the nurse on duty. The doctor on call will be here in a few minutes to explain some things to you. Is there anything I can get you?" I shake my head and she continues, " Alright, I will be back in a few minutes to check your blood pressure. In the meantime, if you need anything just press the button on the remote right next you." She closes the curtain and then I hear her leave the room.

I ask Ruben how did he know I was here and he explained something that I totally forgot about. He is my emergency contact. Once the divorce was final, I had to take Raina's name off of everything including beneficiary and emergency contacts. Naturally, they looked up my information and immediately called him.

"I guess you're kinda lucky since I happened to be in Syracuse today. I wasn't going to come up this weekend, but I had a few things to take care of."

"Did you call my dad?"

361

"Yeah, he was the first person I called. I told him I would let him know if he has to take a plane up here. But the doctor told me that you will be fine."

"I can't believe I totaled the car. You have no idea what its like to walk away from something like that." Ruben is silent. I'm sure he has nothing to say so I just continue, "Nothing really prepares you for being in a car that flips over. There is no ride at Six Flags that comes close to this horror. I can still hear the sound of my car rolling."

Ruben takes my hand. "I'm glad you're ok."

I do my best to not be emotional. I'm just glad that I have someone here for me. Ruben and I have been through a lot over the years but our family bond is strong. The doctor on call opens the curtain and asks me to sit up while he checks my heart rate and breathing with a stethoscope. His name is Dr. Robertson and when he's done he asks me how I'm feeling before explaining that I had a minor concussion. My preliminary results are positive, but they want to do a CAT scan in the morning to make sure there are no internal injuries to the brain. They plan to keep me overnight for observation but they are hopeful that I can be released by the afternoon. He also mentions how lucky I was to have worn a seat belt because according to the accident report, it was probably the only thing that kept me alive.

I have always made it a point to wear a seat belt. I have been in a few car accidents in the past, but nothing to this extreme.

"Dr. Robertson, can I ask you a question?" I ask.

"Sure thing," he says as writes something on my chart.

"Can you tell me what happened to the other passengers in the car?"

"Well the young woman that I believe was sitting in the rear suffered a small hairline fracture below the elbow. She will be fine. The young woman in the passenger seat, however, she's in surgery right now. She had a bit of head trauma." I just sit there in silence taking in the news. The doctor then says, "I should inform you that the police will be by in the morning to get your statement."

I'm taken back by this information. "Head trauma? But she had her seat belt on." I say.

"I know. But sometimes these things can occur in car wrecks and particularly in cars that flip over. It could have been the whiplash effect, but most likely it was the impact itself."

I just shake my head. This is not good. One moment I'm driving these girls to the student union and the next moment I'm in the university hospital. I knew something was wrong with Annette the moment I looked over at her. Sure, she was breathing but now that I think about it, the sight was horrifying because she looked lifeless.

Dr. Robertson interrupts my self-loathing thoughts by saying, "Do you have any other questions?" I shake my head and he continues, "Alright, get some rest. I'm sure you'll be out of here tomorrow." He walks out as Ruben returns to my bedside. He looks exhausted.

"Dude, you look like you got no sleep today," I say.

"Yeah, well, it has been one of those days."

"It really has. Why don't you go get some rest?"

"It's ok, I'm fine here."

"No, seriously. Take my house keys. I'm sure they're around here somewhere and just knock out on my bed. Besides, I need you to bring me back my phone charger and my glasses," I say as I smile.

"Oh, so that is why you want me to back your house? You just need to have your phone so you can update your status and check into Foursquare to say that you're in the hospital."

I make a weak laugh. "Truth be told, I just need to think about my life and how I got here. I need you to be well-rested when you drive me home tomorrow." Ruben agrees and after about twenty minutes he leaves with my house keys.

I lie awake in my bed with as much silence any hospital can have. The machines in my room are rhythmically beeping and I can hear the nurses talking at the nurse's station. They are trying to be quiet but I'm just so wide-awake at the moment. I replay the accident over and over in my head.

Tumbling.

The blinding white light. Annette's scream. The tree.

Tumbling.

The mental image of the car rolling over and my world spinning in slow motion.

Tumbling.

I can still hear the scream that came from my lungs as if it were coming from somewhere else.

Tumbling.

I look straight up at the ceiling.

There was a time in my life when I prayed everyday. I was a child then and I was taught all the different prayers I could ever learn in the twelve years of catholic school I attended. As I got older, I began to question the ways of the Catholic Church. Call it being educated, but when I read the history of slavery and other subjugated people across the world, all in the name of God, one tends to wonder what religion is for.

Despite how I feel about the church and all the rules and all the preaching about how gay marriage will destroy the sanctity of marriage, I maintained my own personal beliefs in God. I came to understand, as I got older, that I could no longer pray for the things I wish for. I began to realize that I was the key to my own happiness as long as I stayed true to my heart.

Somewhere along the way I must've gotten lost. I wanted

365

to believe that I was living a good life but every decision I've made has just led me where I am now, alone and childless.

Tumbling.

The only thing that separated me from death was a thin strap across my chest. I was that close to not being here anymore.

Tumbling.

I need to rethink a lot of things about my life. I think it's time to let it all go and just find a different way to be happy. I take a deep breath and begin my discussion with God.

I pray to you now Lord. I don't want anything material. I just ask for strength. I need the strength to hold it together. I need to be able to not freak out about the fact that I totaled my car. I pray for the health of Annette and hope that she and her child can pull through. I never intended for this to happen.

I pray that you give strength to my father. I can only imagine how worried he is about me. No matter how independent I try to be, he will always remind me that I am his son. I just want him to remain calm so that his blood pressure does not spike while I lay in this hospital.

I pray for Zenia. I love her so much that I realize now that I'm just not the one for her. I've done too much. I've pushed the envelope too far and now she can barely talk to me. I truly want her to be happy with someone even if that someone isn't me. I've been so worried about us getting together that I've turned into a selfish man. As much as I want pray for us to be together, I simply can't. I need to let her go.

I pray for that type of strength. The strength to move on past everything I've done, all the transgressions, all the cheating, all the lying. I want to move past my divorce. I want move past Isabel. I want to move past...my mother.

Lord, I pray for the strength to speak to my mother again. I know that it has been too long since we've spoken. I've treated our estranged relationship as some sort of twisted badge of honor. I would say that her not liking Raina was the only reason for us becoming estranged but that is simply not true. The truth behind this is that I'm a child of divorce that found myself in the middle of such a horrible custody battle that I never forgave her for abandoning me. Of course, that was twenty years ago and I'm slowly starting to realize that it was never about me getting past Isabel that would lead to some solution to my issues with women, it's forgiving my mother for everything I blame her for. Yet, I know that every passing day turns into weeks and then to months with the knowledge that she is not getting any younger.

I pray to you Lord that maybe one day I can love someone again.

I never know how to end a prayer properly. I do the sign of the cross as my eyes tear up. This the first time I feel completely alone. Most people my age have at least had one child. It just never happened when I was married. It wasn't for lack of trying. I guess my boys didn't take. That's why I had to try to convince Frank to see Annette last night. I knew that his feelings on have kids were strong.

One of the first things most people say upon hearing about my divorce is, *well at least you didn't have kids it would have been harder.* I've always taken that statement to mean that my life is some how easier with no children in it. I totally disagree with that. I wanted to be the kind of parent that my parents never were. Alas, I really try not to think about it. I try not to look at babies in strollers or baby photos on Facebook. I'm not sure it matters any more, forty will be around the corner soon and unless I make it a habit of dating girls ten years younger than me, the possibility of having kids is just another thing I'm going to have to let go. I should've prayed for strength enough to let that go too.

The fact is that I spent so much time thinking about myself. I spend so much effort trying to find the right person only to realize that things have a way of ending in the blink of an eye. Why did I spend so much time trying to fend off Lidia or trying to get into bed with Vera? Why did I waste all those years with Raina only to divorce her because I was in love with Zenia.

I look at my phone. It's at 45% battery. It's almost 3:00 am and I wish I had the courage to call her at this time. My headache has gone down a bit and I think it might be that time to shut my eyes for the night. This should stop them from tearing up, at least, for the moment. I just need to let it all go and just rest.

THIRTY ONE

I open my eyes and the room seems brighter. I blink a few times so that I can take way the blurriness of my contacts. I've had them on too long. The curtains are drawn and I can see the movement of the nurse coming and going as she checks the other patients in the room. I think there are four of us in this space. She opens the blinds as well so we can all see the daylight. The sun is out. It must have finally stopped raining. I guess all this commotion is what woke me up. I didn't realize I even feel asleep.

I keep hearing a strange buzzing coming from somewhere near me. It must be my phone. I look around for it and I see that someone placed breakfast on my tray. Its covered so who knows what's under there. Right next to it is my buzzing phone. I take it from the tray and look at it.

Zenia is calling me.

I answer the phone and hear a frantic voice on the other line:

"Oh my God. I heard what happened, please tell me you're ok!"

"Yeah. I'm fine. Just a flesh wound," I try to giggle while still sound groggy.

"Please don't try be funny right now. I need to know that you're ok."

Zenia's voice begins to break as she speaks. I'm still somewhat out of it. It's almost like my body is still trying to figure if I should be in pain or not. I decide to sit up so I can give her my full attention. "Zenia, I'm ok. I'm in the hospital. They should be letting me go after the results of the CAT scan come in," I answer.

I hear silence over the phone. Then I realize what's happening. She's crying. There are a very few amount of times that I've heard or even seen her cry. Zenia once told me that she would never allow me to see her cry, at least, not when it came to me. The last time I saw her cry was two nights after Raina told her to stay away from me. We met in the loading dock of the student union and we took a ride to Thornden Park to have our final discussion. She wanted to hear from my lips that I truly wanted this over.

"Zen, I'm ok. No broken bones, just a concussion. I crawled out of the car…"

"Oh Jeez…," she interrupts, "The car flipped? That must've been so terrible." Now I can really tell she is crying. Her voice quivers when she speaks. "I thought I lost you. I

370

thought we had more time and when I found out you were in the hospital, my heart just sank. If you had died last night, I don't know what I would've done. You were almost taken away from me and all I want to tell you is that I still love you. I never stopped loving you."

Damn it! I can feel the tears streaming slowly down my face. I just don't know what I'm crying about, but for some reason I'm thinking about my mother. Maybe all this time I've thought Zenia abandoned me in my time of need. Maybe that is why I felt the need to call her because I just wanted her to be there for me.

"I love you so much, but I'm broken Zenia," I say, as she stays quiet. "I've always been this flawed and broken little man that has pretended to be in control when I'm really not. I'm sorry that I dragged you into this mess that I call my life."

"There's no reason to apologize," She says softly. "I should apologize to you for being so cold."

"But there is a reason I need to apologize. I always knew that my marriage with Raina was going to fail. I would be in the shower thinking about my life and I would always mentally refer to her as my first wife. This was even before you. Why would I do that? I fooled myself into thinking that I could be in love with two women at the same time and I fought my feelings in order to maintain some vows that I clearly didn't value. Then when you were finally a part of my life, I drove you away because I wanted to work it out? What is that? That was so dumb of me."

"I can't fault you for trying to work things out with your wife..."

"Ex-wife," I interrupt.

I hear her laugh a bit. There were times in the past where she would still call Raina my wife even after the divorce was final as a way to mess with me. "Yes, Ex-wife. If it wasn't me in that situation with you then I would've thought what you did was noble. Unfortunately, I knew you made the wrong decision even before you did. I just wasn't willing to wait for you to realize it."

"So then why are you still here? You should be out right now dating somebody like Avery or Peter. I don't get after all these years why you even decided to remain here in my life."

"Avery and Peter are idiots. There is a very good reason why I'm not with them anymore."

"Oh this should be stunning."

"They are not you. They could never BE you. I did everything I could to get past you and with Avery I almost did it too. But then something happened, besides the fact that you would never seem to leave me alone. He could never make me smile, laugh or make me feel as special as the way you made me feel. This is why I was always so angry with you. I knew you loved me more than you have ever loved her and yet I settled for being number two."

"I'm..."

"But, now you're divorced and that's something I can't ignore anymore. I never really thought you would actually do it. I always had this feeling that she would never let you go and you would keep on feeling obligated. It just took me this long to understand how single you were when you actually considered fucking that bitch."

"Does this mean you forgive me?"

"Yes, I guess it does mean that. But, it also means that I don't forget things very easily. Most of our relationship is based on you lying to another woman. That is just hard for any two people to sustain."

"We can always try to rebuild."

"Yes, I know. But you can't be flipping your car anymore!"

That entire situation seems light years away now. This is the first time we've had a real conversation since our argument. I didn't expect to hear from her this early. I look around to see what time it is. The clock on wall show a little passed 9:30 am. I'm in a much better mood now and I can feel my stomach rumbling. Did I have dinner last night? I'm getting hungry but I don't want to end this conversation just yet.

"How did you even know I was in a car accident?"

"Frank texted me."

"Really? When?"

"He texted me late last night explaining what happened

and how you were in the hospital. I didn't really check my phone until I got up this morning."

"Wow I totally didn't see that coming."

"I know, I was frantic because he didn't give me much information so I took a chance and called you."

"Why are you up so early this morning? I would figure that if you were out late with your sister that you would still be asleep."

"I know, I really do love to sleep but I wanted to run the bridge this morning" I totally forgot that she likes to run across the George Washington Bridge. Her apartment is right on Cabrini Boulevard so she can run from her apartment door across the bridge to the toll station in New Jersey and back. I have done this with her before. It's not as much fun as I was led to believe.

"Wow, you still run that bridge huh?"

"Of course. I think you need another crack at it." I can tell she is smiling. The nurse comes to check my blood pressure and I take that as a cue to get off the phone. I'm not sure when my CAT scan will be so I should at least eat and use the bathroom.

"Listen, the nurse is here to take my blood pressure so I should go."

I hear her take a big sigh. "I feel like I need to take the next bus up there."

"What about work tomorrow?" I switch the phone from my right hand to my left so that the nurse can wrap up my arm.

"I could call in sick tomorrow. I just feel bad that you don't have anyone up there to take care of you."

"I will be fine, Ruben is here. Besides, I really don't want you to miss work because of me. I will be out of here by tonight. I will call you to let you know when I get home."

"Are you sure?"

"Yes. I'm feeling better already."

We say our goodbyes and the nurse finishes with the blood pressure. She tells me it looks normal and that I should eat. I ask her if she knows when I will get my scan done and she tells me that she is not sure but will check with the doctor on duty.

I put down the phone and open the covered plates on my tray. Eggs and sausage with the smallest orange juice I've ever seen. I feel this may be the best breakfast I have ever had. For some reason I feel like I just got a second chance at life. I'm not sure what is going to happen at this point, but I am ready. Maybe God answered my prayers. I guess it takes a near death experience to understand that life is fragile. In either case, I went from hopeless last night to being hopeful this morning.

I take my fork and I dig into my food.

THIRTY TWO

The problem with having the highlight of your day happen early in the morning is that it can only go downhill from there. Being that it's a Sunday, getting the actual CAT scan done seems to be the hardest part of the day. So I spend most of my day being entertained by the TV and endless amounts of football coverage, which bores me endlessly since this is one of my least favorite sports. Ruben came by to give me my phone charger and my glasses. Thank God because I really needed to peel these contacts off my eye balls. I'm a little annoyed with myself. I should've asked him to bring my laptop as well so I could make some roster changes to my fantasy football team before the games start. I guess I will have to use my phone. This is the only thing that makes football bearable.

The phone calls started coming just a little before 10:30 am. My dad was the first to call me, which makes sense since he does seem to get up around this time nowadays. This phone call was not nearly as emotional as the call with Zenia. He wanted to make sure I was ok. Ruben had reassured him immensely about my health last night. I manage to convince him not to come up because I will be fine. Although he did leave one question in my mind, what am I going to do about a car? I'll have to think about that.

Judy called me about ten minutes after that. Frank had also sent her a text telling her about what happened. She called asking for full details of course. I already know that I'll be re-telling this story about a million times before all of this over. She's upset because she thought I might have been hurt. There has always been a running joke around the office on how prepared we are if something bad happened to one of us like me getting hit by a bus. Needless to say the joke is no longer funny and after the story we had a little moment where we agreed on the impact we've had on each other's professional career and that has lead us to being great friends.

Brian called me during my moment with Judy. I ended the call with her to talk to him. This is one of the few times that I hear concern in his voice. It's different from the work stress that we're used to. Apparently, Frank must have texted everyone. It's almost like the license plate video all over again. What Brian was concerned about was not just the fact that I was ok, but that I wasn't driving while intoxicated. He knew I was drunk when he dropped me off, but I assured him I wasn't drunk when I was in the car.

It seems quiet now after Brian's call. Ruben has been a trooper sitting in the chair next to the bed. I've been on the phone non-stop since I spoke to Zenia so I know he has to be bored. It's only been a few hours and I'm already tired. I do feel my eyes getting heavy, so a nap will work right about now. I think I will go take a leak first. "I'm gonna take a piss," I say to Ruben who had been staring at his phone.

"You need any help?" He chuckles.

"I think I got it. Go back to your porn."

"Actually, I'm going to get something from the vending machines. You want anything?"

I shake my head in response. Ruben watches me get up from the bed. I guess he is making sure I don't hurt myself. I feel like an old man getting up from a hospital bed while dragging my I.V. on a pole around with me. I do my business and when I'm done I decide to wash my face.

I look in the mirror after I'm done drying and ask myself "How the hell did you get yourself into this?" This is one of those times where I wish I had the right answers for myself. I leave the bathroom and I see two police officers standing next to the bed.

"Are you Mr. Louis Ortiz?" asks one of the officers.

"Yes I am."

So, the police finally show up to get my statement before the 1:00 pm games start. They are both very tall white men, one is slender and the other is kind of buff. Both seem to have an aura of command about them and their freshly pressed uniforms are just a further indication that they do not play games.

"Hi, Mr. Ortiz. I'm Officer Cruz and this is my partner

Officer Byrne. We just have a few questions about the car accident last night."

"Sure, no problem," I say. I try to be nice to the police whenever I can because the truth is they make me nervous. Historically speaking, police officers seem to be less than kind to people of color. I've been pulled over enough times to have a certain feeling of mistrust. While they can't stop me right now for a DWB, I will just tread water very carefully.

The first question is a no brainer. Officer Cruz wants me to recap last night. I explain everything I remember from when I got into the car with Annette and Paula, up until I ended up here at the hospital. Cruz takes down notes sporadically while looking interested in the story that I'm telling. His partner, however, looks like he could give two shits about even being in the room. Officer Byrne is the taller one and far more menacing of the two.

Officer Cruz finishes writing in his pad and after a brief pause, he asks, "Did you have anything to drink last night before you got into the car?"

I can feel the blood rushing to my face. Am I in trouble here? I panic for a brief moment but I will just tell the truth. "I was at the football game earlier and I drank there. I went home afterward and took a nap."

"What time would you say you got home?"

I have to think about this. I'm reliving the memory of staggering through the door and tripping on the rake. Fuck, I can't really remember the right time because my phone was dead when I got home. I will just have to make a general guess. "I think it was sometime before 7 pm when my buddy dropped me home. I can give you his number if you want to ask him."

"That won't be necessary."

"Am I in some sort of trouble?"

"Not unless you think you should be."

"What does that even mean?"

Then like a loud bang in the dead of night, Officer Byrne speaks, "Your blood alcohol content was higher then we expected it to be." Now I want to freak out. I was sure that I was sober enough to drive. I took a nap for about an hour and at best we left around 9:30 pm. That is at least two to three hours of not drinking. I couldn't have been that drunk.

"I don't understand what's happening here. Am I under arrest or something?" I nervously ask.

"No. You were under the legal limit. We just wanted to make sure we had all the facts together for the report," Cruz responds. I guess I know who is the good cop/bad cop. Clearly they wanted to scare the shit out of me.

"So basically you asked a question you knew the answer to."

"We wanted to make sure that you were aware of how bad this could have gotten for you."

"Consider it a warning." Byrne chimes in with his arms folded. I wonder if he enjoys intimidating people. I just glare at the both of them. Then right before either of us says anything, one of the nurses comes into the room asking for assistance with something that is going in the waiting room.

"I'll take care of it," Byrne says. The bad cop leaves to see what's going on.

Officer Cruz hands me a card. "This is the report number that you will need to give to your insurance company. It also has my information on there in case they need to follow up with any questions."

I look at the card and say, "I actually do have a question. What happened to the other driver that ran me off the road?"

"He died on impact. Not only was he not wearing a seat belt, but he was also driving drunk. Thank God that there were no other passengers in his vehicle otherwise it would have been worse. The best thing you could've done was swerve away when you did."

I can't even imagine what that may have been like. Those headlights were closing in so fast that I seriously doubt I even had time to blink. "Yeah, I was extremely lucky."

Officer Cruz seemed satisfied with my story and wished me a speedy recovery before leaving. I was finally alone with my thoughts. That whole conversation just unnerved me. I need to calm down a little and make myself comfortable. I lie back on my bed and draw the sheets over me. When I look up at the television I realize that I'm now stuck watching the Bills game since that is considered local coverage around here. This makes me wonder about Frank. I haven't seen him since I've been conscious. Ruben said he was here last night when I was out, but still I wonder what's going on.

Looks like a promising game since Buffalo scored first but I doubt this will last. Before I know it the first quarter is over. I drift in about out of sleep as if this bed is the most comfortable thing I've ever laid on. I guess I will just continue to do this until someone comes to get me. I look up for a moment to see the score of the game when I see Ruben walk into the room. He pulls up a chair and sits right next to me. He doesn't look happy.

He says this next sentence in a very somber voice.

"Listen, that girl who was riding with you? She just died."

"Annette? Are you serious?" I ask. Ruben nods his head. "How did you find this out?" I ask as I cover my face with my hands.

"I was there when Frank found out."

"I don't understand how this happened."

I cannot believe that Annette is dead. Even with her seatbelt on, she sustained life-ending injuries. It was her side of the car that hit the tree before we flipped over. Ruben explains how the doctor talked about an intracranial hematoma caused by the caving on the roof. She never stood a chance and when I stared at her while I was upside down, I almost knew that she was not going to make it.

We sit in silence then I ask, "How did Frank take it?"

"Not well. Lidia didn't take it well either.... actually it was quite a bit of a shit show down there."

Ruben begins to tell me this story:

So I went down to grab some food while the police interrogated you. Yeah, I passed them by when I was leaving. I figured you would be fine. So I hit up the vending machines and after I was done with that I ran into Frank and Lidia on the way back. On all accounts, Frank looked worried and Lidia seemed to fake it pretty well considering who else was in this hospital. They were actually coming up to see you when I told them you had some visitors.

As we're talking about how fucked up things are, I saw that other girl who was in the car with you. Paula right? Well I see her walking out of the patient's area into the waiting room and she was talking to some of her sorority sisters. She was about to sit down when she saw Frank and Lidia. She shakes her head and rushes over to us as she yells at Frank, "You fucking punk! You couldn't accept one fucking call from her? Not one? Did you ever think that maybe there was something important she had to tell you?"

I had to hold her back. Yup, broken arm in a sling and everything until her sisters started forming behind her then I had to let go. There was like six of them all wearing letters. Frank is like, "What the hell are you talking about?" Then Lidia responds in her typical "you better get outta my man's face" or something to that effect. Frank stands in front of her telling her to chill out because this is not the place to make a scene. I need to say that this Paula chick is stronger than she looks because she was struggling hard telling her sisters to let go of her. I asked her what the problem was. Then she says, "The problem is that last night and this morning is one big fucking fail because this asshole right here didn't have the balls to realize that his girlfriend was trying to tell him she was pregnant!"

Yo, that shit was like a shot heard around the world! Frank stopped dead in his tracks. I'm not sure he believed it at first, although Lidia refused to believe any of it and called Paula a liar. She tried to lunge for her in order to beat her ass but Frank was able to hold her back. Then that big white cop that was in your room, he comes out of nowhere and starts warning people to calm down. A big argument ensued and the cop basically told everyone to shut the fuck up. That dude was fucking scary. We all just kinda walked away.

I think that's when his buddy was done with you because the other cop comes out and they both leave after a few minutes. I was about leave this mess myself but then Frank walks up to Paula and her friends and asks if she was serious. Paula, now with tears of anger nods her head and says "And now, she's in there. They operated on her hours ago! They said she could have brain damage. She is laying there in the ICU. What if she loses the baby? What if she dies?"

Then, of course, Lidia rushes over shouting how Paula's entire story is bullshit and how Annette was nothing but a whore that Frank fucked to get his cheating ways out of his system. "You need to take that bullshit story back if you know what is good for you," she says. Frank now spins her away from Paula while telling her to calm down. I had to get in the middle of this shit again, dude. All those girls looked like they were going to pounce on her ass. It was crazy!

"Lidia please, you need to chill!" Frank yelled at her.

"I will not chill the fuck out while this little bitch tells a lie when I know for a fact that you can't have kids."

"Maybe I can," Frank says.

Lidia asks him, "What is that supposed to mean? It was you who got the tests back from Dr. Jacobs that said you were sterile so what the fuck are you talking about negro?"

"The test said that I have low sperm count. I just assumed the worst."

The room became silent as Lidia began to contemplate what she just learned. Her face turned angry. I swear she was gonna turn green, "You assumed the worse? You stupid motherfucker! You spend all that time smoking weed and fucking this cunt instead of having sex with your wife!" This woman rambled on in two languages about how she sacrificed her life to make him happy. I couldn't keep it all straight.

I really was at the point where I was just gonna let these girls tear her apart. The girls were upset and angry, Frank was pissed and arguing with her and then the doctor comes out looking for Paula. She got up and said some words to her. Then she sank to her knees and started bawling. Her sorors all start crying.

I went up to the doctor before she left and she told me she was sorry that there was nothing that could be done to save her.

THIRTY THREE

The last few days seem to fly by not to mention that funerals have a way of reminding us how fast life goes. The mood is very somber which is why I wanted to sit in the back of the church. As the driver of that car, I really didn't want draw too much attention to myself. While there was some reconciliation within the last few days with her parents, I still feel responsible in some small way for the death of their daughter. Annette grew up in the Bronx and there seemed to be like a thousand people in attendance at the Church of Saint Raymond. Her casket hasn't arrived yet, but the front of the altar is draped with flowers. All the flowers that we saw at the wake the previous days made its way to the church, along with numerous pictures of her through the years.

Yesterday's wake was the saddest thing I've ever been to. Both days were packed with friends from her high school and college. At times there were too many people for the funeral home to hold which is why they tried to have the viewing over two days. Frank was taking this all very hard. I can see from the look in his eyes that he may never be the same. It started to make me wonder the true validity of their relationship. This wasn't just a fling that he got into to get over Lidia. He really cared about her. Also, losing a potential a child is life altering. At least, that is my opinion on things. I guess Annette was his Global Warming.

I recognized quite a few students from the university. Many of them would see me and give me a hug but very few words are spoken in general. There were many tears shed for a girl that died way too young. I can tell Frank is still a mess and Paula remains pissed off at him for everything that's happened. I still feel guilty for just being in the same car with her. Sure it's not my fault, but I just feel that I'm partly responsible for her death.

Her parents, however, were very cordial to the both of us. I personally apologized to them for everything that happened when I met them in Syracuse. They arrived at the hospital on Sunday evening after I was discharged. I asked Paula to text me when they came in so I can personally meet them and express my condolences. I saw them on Monday morning at the hospital and it did not go well for me. I was a bumbling idiot that felt the weight of being a student affairs administrator. Annette was not a current student at the university but she was one of ours nonetheless. It was her mother that consoled me; meanwhile her dad was just a mess. He couldn't really look at me, yet they did place blame solely on the drunk driver. The SPD did explain that I was cleared of any wrongdoing.

Annette's sorority sisters showed up in large numbers to the wake and because of this it seemed like so many girls spoke fondly about her over those two days. They spoke about how she was a friend, a sister, a mentor, and a truly inspiring young woman. What made this entire experience heartbreaking to me is when Frank got up to speak last night at the wake. He was one of the last people to speak for the night. We were sitting down and he got up and walked to the center of the room. He looked at her lying there in the open casket.

He was so nervous that he placed both of his hands over his mouth and pulled them down slowly. Frank began to speak slowly. "I met Annette when she was on one of her trips to Syracuse. I was introduced to her by one of my student employees, Maya. I knew from that moment when I saw her that she was the most beautiful woman I have ever met." Frank pauses and from where I'm sitting, even I can tell that his eyes are watering. He was fidgeting with his hands as if his wedding ring was getting too heavy.

"I soon came to realize shortly after getting to know her that she was beautiful both inside and out. Her greatest gift to me was her love and her constant smile. I will never forget her need to always see the good in everyone and I will never forget the positive light she put on everything."

Frank cleared his throat and took a deep breath. He was starting to get choked up and began to battle for his own manhood as he continued, "Annette. Dear Annette taught me how to live again and I have no way to repay her generosity." A tear rolled down his face and he turned towards her open casket. "I will always love you. May you rest in eternal peace."

I'm not sure what he did with his wedding ring. It's not until right now, in this church, that I realize that he is not wearing it. I can't say that I'm surprised because when I finally got home Sunday evening, I found him sitting on the stoop in front of my house. There were no words exchanged except for me thanking Ruben for dropping me off. I walked up to Frank and just placed my hand on his shoulder. I couldn't imagine what he might be going through. I opened my door and Frank walked in minutes later with the same bag he had months ago. I just assumed that this move was now a permanent one.

Everything after that point seemed to happen so fast. I spent most of Sunday night on the phone with Zenia, although it seemed like everyone I knew gave me a call. Even my supervisor called to check on me and to tell me to take the week off which was a relief. It's very telling that she had to tell me not to be a hero and come in because she knows that I'm dedicated to my work. It all worked out for the best because it was Paula that kept in touch with me about the funeral arrangements. We all knew it wasn't a question of if we were going.

The only real question was who was going to drive the rental car. I wasn't so ready to get behind the wheel again and Frank was in a daze that may take him a few weeks to get out of. By the time the paper work was signed, I decided to just get over it and drive because he doesn't know how to drive in the city like I do. Thankfully, we ended up staying with my dad.

The church continues to fill up. We decided to get here early because we knew how packed this place was going to get. It's a huge church and judging from the wake, I wanted to make sure Frank got a good seat. I'm still not used to him being this quiet. From time to time on this trip he would make subtle jokes, but that four hour ride coming down here was not particularly fun. I was trying to tell him that there was some good news in all of this, Columbia University did end up calling me on Monday morning to schedule an in person interview for Friday. I really wanted to be excited about that in front of him but I just couldn't bring myself to tell him. Just like I can't flaunt the fact that I've seen Zenia for the past two nights. I guess I can call it a date or two, but quite frankly I can never seem to know with her and there's a good possibility that I may see her tonight and again tomorrow.

The family starts walking into the church and down that long center aisle heading toward the first few pews. All that can be heard is light sobbing as the casket is finally carried in by the pallbearers and placed in front of the altar. Everyone goes to their places and the mass begins.

I feel incredibly bad that I'm not focused enough to pay attention. I can't help but think about the same thing I have been thinking about all week. I've been granted a second chance at life and it's making me a little antsy. I can't help but try to maintain a somber demeanor in all this. If the car hit that tree a few inches to the left it could've very well been me in a coffin. I just can't ignore that. I can't ignore that all of a sudden I get a call for a job interview or that all of a sudden Zenia and I are having sex like nothing happened.

I'm not even sure I can even call it sex. I think this may have been the first time we really made love. I almost cringe when I think about that because I can hear Ruben telling me to return my man card to the nearest Blockbuster. Yet, I think it was this lusty love kind of thing we were doing, as if all the pent up frustrations of our past came out in series of bursts. The truth in all this was that I didn't meet up with her the other day with the sole purpose of sleeping with her. I just wanted to see her. This was the first time since her birthday party that I got a chance to just sit down and talk. One thing led to another and I ended up staying over her place. Twice.

The eulogies begin and Annette's older brother begins to speak at the microphone. A good-looking young gentleman in his mid-twenties begins to talk about how talented she was at poetry. The resemblance to her is striking. I can tell that all their looks came from her mother. He holds back tears as he begins to read a poem that she had written in high school about her hopes and dreams.

Frank leans over and whispers, "She wrote me a poem once. It was this long poem that she ended up performing for me one day. I never understood her fascination with words until now." All I can do is just listen to Frank and the poem. Once her brother is done, another person goes up and begins to speak about her time at Onondaga Community College. Yeah, I may have to wait until next week to tell him about what's going on.

The entire ceremony was a series of people talking about how great this young woman was. It makes me feel sad all over again knowing that I only really got to know one side of her. I knew Annette as the girl who had a great set of lungs and yet everyone else keeps talking about how deep she was into community service, her studies, and her sorority. It does make me question the merits of my own decision to not pledge a fraternity. There is no denying the network one can create with a plethora of members at their disposal. The show of support for Annette is indeed in incredible. Frank was a lucky man even if it was for a short time.

This just makes me think about my own luck. I need to be really honest with myself. I feel altered in someway. I know that I haven't been the best man or even the best person. At best, my morality is grey. Does that make me a bad person? For all the good work that I do with students and trying to get them through college and through life, does it even make a difference in the end? I know that I've said many times over that I have to change and make better decisions. When I said those things to my ex-wife I knew those were false promises laced with crocodile tears.

But things are different now. As I watch them carry the coffin out of the church and see even more tears from people leaving, I realize that I need to make a change for myself. Everything that has happened in the last few months should be an indication that I need to change things in my life. All this drama is not normal. It just can't be normal. I need to knock this interview out the park. I need to get this job and move back here to the city and start over.

"Yo, I'm not sure I'm ready to put her in the ground," Frank says to me as we begin to file out.

"I think you need to man up." I respond to him in a low voice and say it as direct as possible with no sarcasm.

"This has all been too much for me."

"Why? Because you haven't been dulling your senses with weed? Look at all these people. They are hurting too, but you better believe they will be at the gravesite and so will you. It's time to man up. Life is too short to let fear dictate your actions."

Annette Reyes was buried at Saint Raymond's cemetery on a cloudy Thursday morning in November.

THIRTY FOUR

It's almost 12:30 pm and I'm sitting in a restaurant in Morningside Heights called Havana Central. Ruben said he wanted to meet me here for lunch after my interview. I haven't seen him since Sunday when he dropped me home from the hospital. I asked him to stay in Syracuse for a few days if he could to conduct some of the roommate interviews that I wanted to line up. I had gotten quite a few emails regarding the ad I put up.

I could say he's late but I think I'm earlier than I thought. I'm still thinking about the interview and I'm not sure I did well at all. The only thing I have going for me was the fact that a few of the people who conducted the interview were at the conference I hosted in September. I texted Zenia when I left campus to tell her that I think I bombed it. I'm quite annoyed with myself.

Ruben, in all his glory, walks in with a pair of sunglasses and a brown leather jacket. He talks and smiles at the girl working in the front. He looks over and finds my booth.

"Wow, look at you," he says, "Is that your funeral suit or your interview suit?"

What a funny guy. I wore my charcoal gray suit with a white shirt and a red power tie. "After today, I should've just worn the black one I wore yesterday," I respond.

"The interview went that bad?" Ruben takes off his jacket and sits down. He is rocking a beige V-neck sweater and I may have to ask him where he got it. Ruben picks up the menu and begins to scan it.

"The interview sucked. I feel like I didn't do well at all. Dammit, I tried to focus but in the end I think I just failed."

"Wow. Really? Did you prepare?"

"Hell yeah I did. I researched the position, the department, the people who worked there and I even studied the map of the campus. Maybe it wasn't meant to be."

"Maybe you're exaggerating. You know you can be your own worst critic."

"This is true, but I'm trying to be honest with myself these days."

After the waiter comes over to take our order, Ruben tells me that he broke it off with that older chick he was seeing. Things were getting too real for him. She wanted a kid within the next year and he was not willing to comply. Ruben explained that he is at the point at his life where he is simply not ready to settle and isn't willing to hurt someone else because he doesn't know what he wants. He essentially is taking himself off the market.

"So you're taking a pussy break?" I ask.

"Whoa, don't get ahead of yourself there. Ok? No one is saying that I need to stop fornicating. There is always Nina," he says smiling.

"Of course, there is Nina. God forbid you cleanse though," I say.

"Are you suggesting that I'm some kind of whore? My magic number is lower than you would think."

"I'm sure that it's higher than mine."

"That's not the point. Although, I personally think that you tanked your chances a few years ago."

"When I got married?"

"Oh please, your number went up after you got married. I'm talking before then, when you went on that epic drought the moment you started dating Isabel. Three years? You could have done some damage in those years."

"Yeah, well I'm content with my sexual life at the moment."

"Oh really? Seeing Zenia again huh?"

I smile. "Yeah. I am. It's crazy how things can change in a

week."

"Does that mean you two are finally a couple?"

"That is a good question. But, I think we'll take it slow."

"I can understand that. We're both not getting any younger and I know eventually I will have to settle down. I just need to do it under my terms."

I think Ruben may be finally serious about his love life. I think this whole death thing has gotten to all of us. Maybe he will just concentrate on work. Although there is this thought in my head that maybe I should hook him up with Judy. I know how much she has been dying for the perfect opportunity to jump his bones.

That thought quickly fades because I'm not trying to make that mistake again. I don't want to put myself into another situation where I set two people up and it results in something completely horrible…again. Judy will kill me if she knew that I could have at least provided her with this chance, but I will deal with it. I think I will just enjoy my time here in the city since I need to go back to work on Monday.

THIRTY FIVE

The view from The Cloisters is heavenly, especially from the side where New Jersey is the view. The sunset from here is stunning. I would never live in New Jersey, but the sight of all the different colored leaves at this time of year makes it perfect for me to take a picture and post it on Instagram. This is exactly what I needed, a chance to just look around and "smell the roses"

"You done sight seeing?" Zenia says as she smiles.

"It's beautiful up here," I say.

"I know. I told you that my neighborhood is really nice."

Zenia is sitting on the bench in a small area over looking both the Henry Hudson Parkway and the river. When I turn around I can see much of Washington Heights, Inwood and the Bronx. It's one of those fall days that make me want to stay in the city. There's a light breeze that makes the leaves fall off the trees. I love this weather. It's about 60 degrees and sunny.

I sit down next to her and we just enjoy the view. I spent the night with her again. Her apartment is right off of Fort Washington near the A train. I think it's by 187ᵗʰ Street. We walked here holding hands. I would be lying if I said I wasn't confused about this situation, but I have been keeping quiet about it since I'm reaping the benefits of this "relationship."

However, in my heart I know that I cannot leave to Syracuse tonight without knowing what's going on between us. This past week has been a mixed bag of emotions with the funeral, the botched interview and seeing her. I know my dad had felt a certain way about me leaving Frank in the house because he just sits there in the room, so I asked Ruben to take him to *Sue's Rendezvous*.

As we sit there I look over to her and say, "I need to know something before I leave. It's been on my mind for the last few days but I just need to get it out."

"So get it out. What do you want to ask?" Her tone is so peaceful that is almost makes me afraid to rock the boat. But, I have to stick to the advice I gave Frank. I cannot let fear dictate my actions.

"What are we doing? I'm just confused as to what we have here. Are we just friends or are we more than that? I need to know because no matter what it is, I just need it to be clear with no more bullshit."

"I know. I'm sorry that this has been so confusing. This week has gone by so fast. How is it Saturday already?" She pauses for what seems like forever. I thought about answering since the silence lasted more than a minute. Then she continues, "This has never been simple. This thing between you and me has gone on for years. There's a lot of anger that is still there and yet for one reason or another I think I'm ready to let it all go. Maybe it was the thought of you dying or maybe it was seeing you just about every day this week or maybe it was both. In either case, I think I'm ready."

"Ready for what?" I know I play dumb sometimes and ask what seems to be an obvious question, but when I'm looking for a solid answer playing dumb is the only option I have.

"I'm saying that I want you to date me."

"Are you sure about this? You once said you wanted to just be friends and not be romantic."

"I also said that I'm still figuring myself out."

"But, why the change? And please don't take this as me telling you no. I guess I almost expected you to tell me that we are better off as friends."

"That is fair. Do you recall the first time you told me you loved me? Not the time it slipped out in your office. When we were in Armory Square?"

"Yes. I remember."

This story takes me back a few years. Raina was on one of her trips to see her mother and like the bad husband I was I took the opportunity to go out with Zenia. In all the years that she studied at the university she never really got to see what the city of Syracuse had to offer. Armory Square was one of my favorite places to hang out. Aside from the bars, there were these little shops on Walton Street that kind of reminded me of home. We walked down Walton past the sushi place and we crossed this small bridge that goes over the Onondaga Creek. The view is not the best but with her right next to me, it was one of the most beautiful creeks I'd ever seen. It was there that I looked her in the eyes and told her I loved her.

"I know I told you this before but I always knew you loved me even before you gathered up all your courage to tell me. I also knew that you loved me more than you would ever love your wife."

"Ex-wife," I interrupt.

"Right. My point is, that I knew it was only a matter of time before you had to make a decision that I never forced on you. When we talked about what would happen if you two ever split up, I said that I would I never date you right a way. That I would have to give you the space you needed in order for you figure out what you really wanted."

This was true. A conversation that I vaguely recall, but I know it happened. I guess I figured that there were just too many things that we had gone through for us to end up together. I was very sure that once she came back from her trip to Miami, I would just fade away just like I did when Isabel returned from Colombia.

"Yeah. I remember. But I also remember the many things that have happened since then. I just assumed you changed your mind about all of this at some point, especially when you said to me that we would never be together."

Zenia chuckles a bit and she raises her hand to caress my face. "I'm sorry that I put you through all that. I just felt that I needed to get away from you for a while and try to get my head straight. Sometimes, when a woman says never, we never really mean never." She brings her face up to mine and we kiss. "Besides, it's not like you really gave up." She smiles again. We kiss for a moment.

"Are you sure you ready for this? We are talking about a long distance relationship," I say.

"Yes, I know. I think I can manage that. I just have one request. Cut the fat."

"What do you mean by that?"

"I mean that any women you have on the side or any birds that are lingering around need to be cut loose."

Well there it is, the final declaration that she is now posting her flag up. I want to respond by saying "what women?", but that will not go over well. The past transgressions from my previous life suggest that there is always a chance for side chicks. But she is right. I need to need to cut any fat that is left.

"That will not be a problem."

THIRTY SIX

Raina sips her coffee and says, "Guess who finally got married?"

I look down at her finger, which has no ring. "Who?"

"Vera and Corey."

"No shit. Really? After all this time."

We decided to meet in the cafeteria at the student union. It was my choice to meet here. It's a public place and now that I've been dating Zenia for a few weeks, I don't want to give any false impressions as to the nature of what we would be talking about.

"Yeah, we went to the wedding. It was beautiful. She looks happy."

"Good for them."

Raina and I were always good at small talk. Unfortunately,

we still have some obligations that need to be taken care of as per the divorce decree.

"So were you able to find some roommates to help you with the mortgage?"

"No. This is actually more difficult than I thought it would be, but Frank helps me with the mortgage," I reply.

The deal that I had with her was that I would sell the house when I had the means but it never worked out the way I wanted. There is still tons of work to be done that are beyond my abilities. This news will not make her happy considering that her name is still on the mortgage. I'm sure that she has contemplated taking me to court to get half of the house, but the problem is that neither of us have the funds to retain a lawyer for long periods of time.

"Well I think you need to sell it. I'm tired of my name being attached to the property. I don't even understand why you can't take my name off of it in the first place."

"Let me ask you a question, where exactly is Frank going to live? Let's not even mention the fact that if I do sell the house right now, there will be no way we can get full market value for it and I will also point out that taking your name off of a mortgage is not that easy. I can't just erase it. Besides, if I default, they still go after you."

"Hmph. Well, you are a resourceful guy and you seem to bounce back from anything. I mean look at your car accident, because of the insurance claim you will be getting a new car soon and I'm quite sure that your boy can find a place. Besides, I think you should sell the place to Lidia."

"What? Why would I do that?"

"Because after everything that happened she needs a reboot and let's be honest, the sooner you sell the house the sooner I'm out of your life."

I'm not one to judge but I'm pretty sure that Lidia doesn't deserve a reboot. I get it, she is hurting and it sucks. Frank and her are getting a divorce, but really? Plus, selling the house to her only means that I have to deal with her again and I've had quite enough of her. I also know that Zenia would absolutely hate this idea. Although, I would totally sell the house to Frank if I had to but he is broke and the divorce he is about to go through is only going to make his life worse, which gets me thinking.

"I get all of that, but how can she afford this house alone while she is going through a divorce? Not to mention where am I going to live?"

"You must think that I don't read your blog or your tweets. You have been making it very obvious after the car accident that you want to get out of here. Especially since you now have a girlfriend in New York City."

This would be a good time to say that I don't have a girlfriend, but that's not entirely true. We are in fact dating so that's a start, but I do know for a fact that Zenia is of the belief that unless it's on Facebook, it isn't official. In any case, Raina is right, I do have this need to leave Syracuse. It goes far beyond just Zenia, my family is down there and I think that is something that I'm sorely missing.

"I just began my job search a few months ago and that kind of move will take time. It has taken months, sometimes years, for people around here to land a job somewhere in this soft economy."

"Maybe, but I know you. I'm sure you will find something faster than you think."

She stops almost as if she wanted to continue her thought. I didn't notice it at first since I was finishing up my turkey wrap. But then she just went quiet.

"What is it?" I ask.

"I guess it all just hit me. You're really going to leave here. I guess I'm a little envious."

"I don't understand why you would be."

Raina takes a deep breath. "We spent so many years being married and I don't ever recall you knowing what you want as much as you do right now. I mean, you always agreed with me when it came to getting the house or buying something major, but I just get this sense from you that you really know what you're doing. I guess I didn't do it for you."

I finish chewing and respond, "I don't think you should really think about it that way. You know that I deal with students everyday. They come into my office with the daily tragedy about this person or that person. Some relationship always seems to be failing and it's the worst thing in the world to them. My best advice to them is the same as I give to you now. Everyone in our lives is there for a reason, regardless of the length of time. No matter if they love us or hate us, no matter if they break our hearts or simply hold open the door. I really believe things happen for a reason. I can't say I believe in fate, but rather I believe that we all play a role in each other's lives. It's up to us to decide what that role is."

She looks at me and smiles, "I forgot how good you are at giving advice. These students will miss you."

EPILOGUE

It's hot. I never thought that I could sweat this much but that's the case every time I run this route. It's one of those typically humid days in July that I hate to run in but I can't let that stop me. I have been training for this 5k that's happening in a few weeks and it's crucial that I push myself.

It helps that I'm blasting Daft Punk's "Get Lucky" on my iPod because racing up this last hill is always difficult. We picked this route because it provides the best cardio workout. I always run about two laps so that I can get used to the outdoor running I never did in Syracuse. I was a treadmill person that has grown to slowly loathe the simplicity of it.

I finally get to the top of the hill where I do my best not to die on the spot. I check my running app to make sure that my speed and time have been recorded. I'm currently two minutes faster than I was two days ago. My back aches and I guzzle down some water in the plastic bottle I carry. I take a few steps onto the sidewalk and look around.

I still can't believe that I finally live in New York City

again. I find myself still staring at landmarks and signs as if they were still new. I have been running in Fort Tryon Park for the last several months and it all still seems so very new to me. I never thought that things would have worked out the way they did. Tomorrow will mark six months since I started working for Columbia University. I feel like a new man with a new purpose. Apparently, I didn't do as bad as I thought. Two more interviews and they offered me the job.

I check my phone as I continue to try to catch my breath. I scroll through texts that I gotten today. Judy finally found a man that may make an honest woman of her. She keeps telling me that things are not the same since I left, but she's happy with her boyfriend. She professed to me that she might just be in love. I'm just glad she finally listened to me and started dating a black man.

Frank also hit me up the today. I still worry about him considering that Lidia is going in on him during this divorce process. He isn't fighting back much because he just wants it to be over. I'm glad I decided on not selling the house to her. Instead, I decided to rent it to Frank and the two roommates we found weeks before I moved here. It only made sense. Although, one thing I never saw coming in a million years is that he's been dating Paula for a few months. She graduated from Binghamton in December and found a job working in Syracuse. I really hope I don't hear about noise complaints from his roommates.

I also don't hear much from my ex-wife. Every so often I would check her Facebook page to see what she's up to. We're not friends so it's a little annoying to type her name in the search engine every time, but I don't do it often enough to care. Turns out that she's single again. While that might sound like something she would be sad about, she has decided to travel during her vacation. Last time I checked she was in South Korea.

Of course for good measure, Brian also reached out to me. He was thinking about meeting me at Comic Con this year. Tickets went on sale in late June and we were lucky enough to score four day passes. It's funny how true friends still manage to stay in touch no matter the distance.

I decide to sit on the bench and wait when it just hits me that I have to see Ruben tonight. He wants to meet up for drinks at this place around my neighborhood called Apt 78. He is bringing his new girlfriend that we will meet for the first time. I think deep down he thinks this is the one for him. We will see.

I look over to my right and I finally see her make it up the hill. Zenia is almost out of breath but she manages to slow down and drink some water. Sometimes I forget how beautiful she is when she's just being herself. She sees me and walks over. I stand up and take one of the buds out of my ear. Zenia looks at her phone app and comments that she thinks this is the fastest she's ever run. We walk around to the entrance of the park, which is a circle that connects the streets of Fort Washington and Cabrini Boulevard, until we get to the A train subway entrance.

Zenia stops and asks, "What are we doing tonight again?"

I reply, "We are meeting up with Ruben and his new girl."

She rolls her eyes. "I thought you were going over to your mom's today?"

"No, that's tomorrow. Remember they are having a little picnic over in New Rochelle."

She nods in acknowledgment. We hold hands as we walk down Fort Washington Ave. I would have never thought a year ago I would be living in Washington Heights. Things truly fell into place even when it came to finding an apartment. We both thought it would be a good idea to just move in together. We spent so many years apart and there was no reason to continue being that way.

"You know, I think I finally came up with the name of my book," I say.

"Really? What would that be?"

"The Book of Isabel."

ABOUT THE AUTHOR

Anthony Otero is a writer/blogger with a BA in English from Syracuse University. In addition to his blog called Volume 2, he has written for the Huffington Post.